Where Loyalties 1

Praise for

Where Loyalti

The world he created felt exactly like a world populated by pirates should feel; fun and vulgar and more than a little dangerous. – **Booknest.eu**

I strongly recommend Where Loyalties Lie and consider the duology to be Hayes' best work and up there with Mark Lawrence as well as Joe Abercrombie. – **C.T. Phipps**

With Pirates, sea battles, & magical dieties, this is epic nautical fantasy at its finest. – **Fantasy Book Critic**

This really was one of those rare books that has everything you could want. Witty and strong male characters. Sarcastic and possibly even stronger females. Swashbuckling hijinks and devastating losses. Dark Pirate Captains and even darker monsters. - **The Blogin' Hobgoblin**

Rob J. Hayes

Copyright ©2017 by Rob J. Hayes
(http://www.robjhayes.co.uk)
Cover image ©2016 by Alex Raspad
Cover design by Shawn King
Edited by Toby Selwyn
All rights reserved.

Where Loyalties Lie
(Book 1 of Best Laid Plans)
by
Rob J. Hayes

Rob J. Hayes

*For always heeding the call to Suit Up,
I would like to thank my Alpha Team:
Mihir, Rhian, Vicki, and Charles*

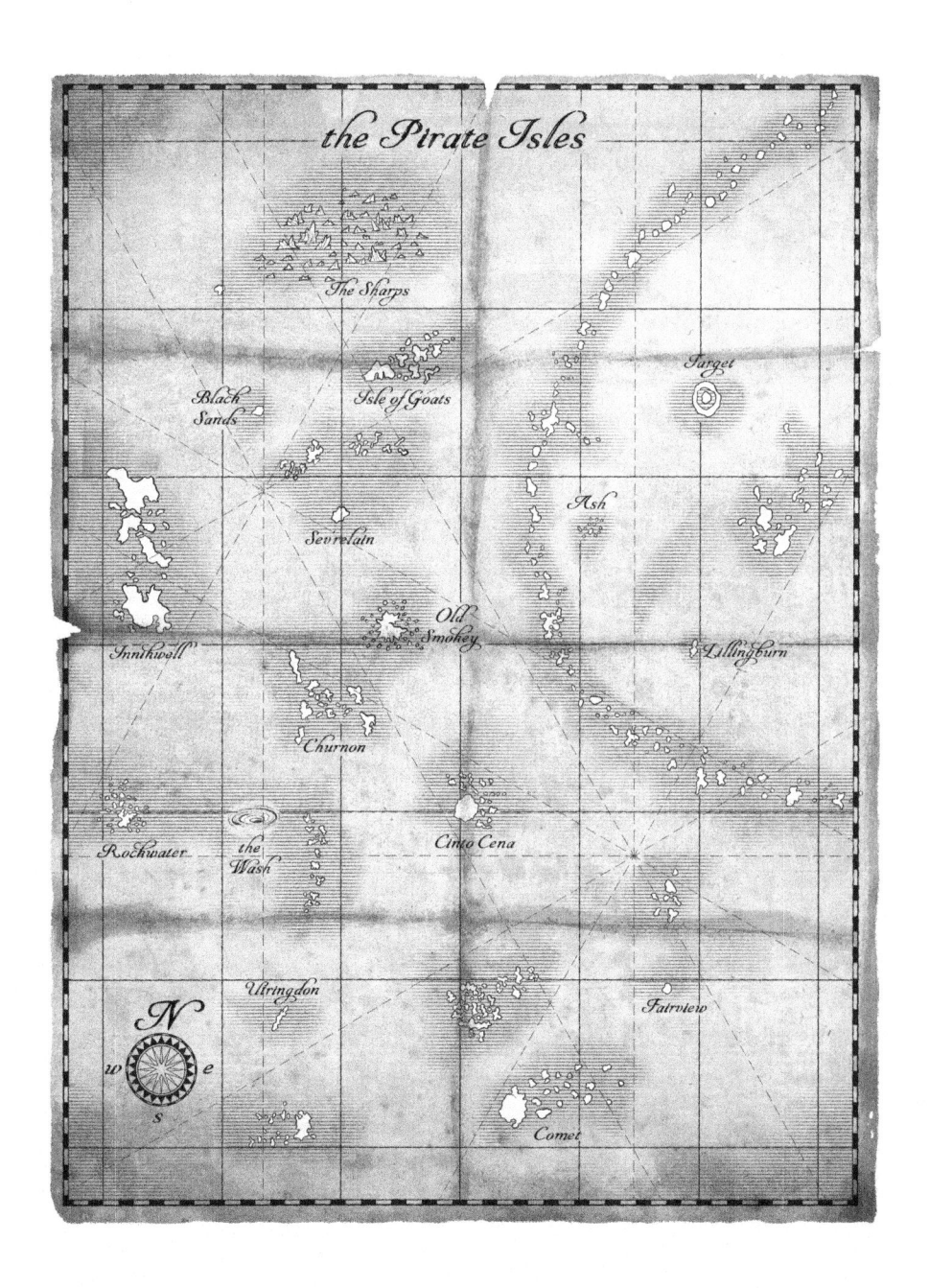

Where Loyalties Lie

Fortune

Black Sands burned and the fire danced in Drake's eyes. It wasn't the first town he'd seen disappear in the way of smoke and ash, and by the time his plan was complete it sure as all the Hells wouldn't be the last.

The flames eagerly consumed everything they touched, racing from the dark, sandy beach to the nearby encroaching jungle. Great plumes of black smoke billowed up into the sky, where they blotted out the twinkling stars.

It was a grim day for the pirates of the isles, but a glorious night for Captain Drake Morrass. The rest of his crew were witnessing the deaths of hundreds and the extermination of one of the few safe havens left for scoundrels like themselves. Drake was witnessing the birth of an empire. His empire.

A single dinghy crewed by eleven men rowed back to the *Fortune*. Ashore, the Werry Meather, Black Sands' largest building and only tavern, collapsed in upon itself. Even from out in the bay, all of the crew heard the crack as the final supporting beam gave way. There was a long moment's silence from the crew; every one of them had been drunk and worse than drunk in that tavern. Drake would miss the place and no mistake, but there were plenty of places to buy grog and he wasn't about to shed a tear over the loss of one. Besides, it was taking every ounce of control he had not to grin at his good fortune.

The dinghy bumped against the hull of the *Fortune* and the silence was broken as pirates leapt to their work, knowing better than to slack. Ropes were lowered and secured, men scrabbled on board, and in a short time the dinghy was no longer in the water but on its way to the deck of Drake's ship.

A single man approached the foredeck, where Drake stood in a bubble of isolation. Weather-beaten skin, long lank hair, and a gaunt complexion made plain the pirate's long experience on the sea. He was, if anything, slightly older than Drake, and looked every year of it.

"What's the news ashore, Princess?" Drake said.

"Town's on fire," his first mate replied casually.

"No, you don't say." Drake let slip a brief grin, but quickly removed it lest any of his crew noticed. "Any survivors?"

"Not a single one. Seems those bastards wanted ta be, what ya call it, thorough."

"Did you happen to witness who committed this terrible tragedy?"

Princess nodded; a loose clump of hair flapped in front of his face, and he tucked the errant strands back behind his ears. "Jus' so happens I took a few of the boys to check on the other side of the island, Cap'n. Would you believe it, there was one of them nice new Sarth navy ships jus' setting course away from the deed."

"Good. Make sure the whole crew know about that, Princess. Wouldn't want anyone missing out on such a vital piece of the puzzle. We'll set course for Port Sev'relain come first light, and I want the whole crew talking about nothing else."

"Right y'are, Cap'n." Princess turned and walked away, leaving Drake alone once again on the foredeck.

He stood there for a while, watching the town burn. "Break out one of the barrels of rum, boys. I want everyone to have a drink for Black Sands. Then I want everyone to have a drink to never letting those bastards do it again."

His crew cheered, their sombre mood replaced with a rowdier, more vicious temperament better suited to pirates. But his crew were the easy marks. The real test would come in recruiting the other captains.

Part 1 - Before the Storm

*Stillwater said the Oracle
You're fucking joking said Drake
I'm not said the Oracle
Shit said Drake*

The Phoenix

"She doesn't look like much," Keelin Stillwater said, peering through the monoscope. It was the only artefact of his old life he still kept; all the rest had been lost to either fire, the sea, or the debt collectors.

Next to Keelin, his first mate, Yanic Bo'larn, peered out across the open ocean. "She looks to be riding low."

"How could you possibly tell from here?" Keelin said. Without the use of the monoscope the ship on the horizon was barely more than a speck.

"Good eyes," Yanic said, with a nod that made his hangdog expression seem utterly serious. "My ma always fed me plenty o' greens. Gave me the eyes of a hawk."

Keelin lowered the monoscope from his eye and glared at his first mate with such severity that any other member of the crew would likely have fled; Yanic, however, just smiled. "Last week you told me you were orphaned at the age of four and never knew your parents."

"Boggles the mind some, don't it," Yanic said seriously.

Keelin laughed and returned his attention to the ship in question. "You're not wrong though. She is sailing low."

"Full hold, I reckons."

"Full of what though?" Keelin mused. "She doesn't look like a slaver."

"Could be gold."

"Could be stone."

"Stone sells."

"Not for much."

"We'd get more for stone than we will for nothin'. Hold's looking a little empty, Cap'n."

"And who would we sell this stone to?"

"Stonemason?"

"You know any?"

"No," Yanic admitted solemnly before his face broke into a grin. "But I reckon Quartermain does."

Keelin considered the situation carefully for a few more minutes. He'd already made the decision, but it did his crew good to wait on the captain's pleasure. Yanic looked just about on the verge of mutiny when Keelin finally gave voice to his decision.

"Aye, let's do it. Pile on sail and change course to intercept. Wake all hands and chase Lumpy into my cabin. We don't want the mangy cur attempting to jump ship again. Oh, and fly the colours…"

"So soon, Cap'n?" Yanic sounded sceptical.

"Might as well make some sport out of it." Keelin grinned wide, showing plenty of teeth, and Yanic returned the grin for just a moment before turning and bellowing the captain's orders to the rest of the crew.

The Phoenix couldn't claim to be the fastest ship on the seas, but she flew through the water with even the barest breath of wind, and they had more than that as they chased down the heavily laden fluyt. Keelin watched through his monoscope with a smile as their quarry attempted to increase its speed by piling on more sail. They bought themselves a little longer, though nothing more. Before long *The Phoenix* was alongside the other vessel, and Keelin could see its small complement of crew spread out along the railing with all manner of weaponry, from swords to axes, to crude knives clearly fashioned out of whatever happened to be lying around.

"Ho there," Keelin shouted to the other ship, pitching his voice to carry across the water between them. "Quite a force you have arrayed against us, mate."

Some foolish soul on the fluyt loosed an arrow in Keelin's direction. The shaft flew high and wide and completed its flight somewhere in the depths of the ocean. Some of the crew of *The Phoenix* bristled, but most just laughed away the impotent attempt at defence.

"Now now," Keelin shouted. "No need to get all violent. You boys start shooting arrows, then my boys start shooting arrows, and before long we'll have plenty of folk hurt or dead, and out here the one's often very much the same as the other. So how's about you lot do the clever thing and settle down, drop those nasty sharp objects into the blue, and let me and mine come aboard. We'll see what you got worth taking and let you be on your way in just a spell. No violence, no blood, no dying. Good?"

One of the crew aboard the fluyt pushed his way past another man and raised his voice. "You promise you won't kill any of us?"

Keelin let out a loud laugh and many of his crew joined in. "No," he said with a wide grin. "But it may be you're missing the point behind pirating. We're looking to take what ain't ours and what can be sold for a profit. Ain't no profit in taking lives, far as I can see. They don't tend to be worth much after the taking."

The captain of the fluyt looked on the verge of resisting; his crew did not.

In Keelin's experience most pirating could be accomplished with minimal to no bloodshed. Most sailors wanted no part in a fight and knew full well they couldn't win against a determined pirate force. They were, after all, there to sail and get paid, not to fight. Captains were often a different matter; losing a cargo could ruin them, and many were willing to fight, even to the death, to avoid that. Of course, not all pirates agreed with Keelin over the matter; there were many who relished the fight and would board a ship and slaughter the crew even after the ship's surrender.

The captain of the fluyt drew an old sabre from his belt and dropped it over the side of his ship, and within moments his crew were following suit. "OK," the captain shouted. "Come aboard then."

It took only a couple of hours to loot the surrendered vessel. They took a selection of the cargo that Morley, the quartermaster, determined could be sold for a profit, but Keelin was wary not to laden *The Phoenix* too much in case another opportunity for piracy presented itself. They also took a good portion of the fluyt's remaining food and all the remaining rum. If Keelin had learned one thing in his decade of pirating, it was to keep the crew happy with the occasional, but generous, portion of rum.

"Good doing business with you," Keelin shouted as the fluyt got under way, significantly lighter for her brief stop. "Do stop by again."

The other captain shot Keelin a baleful glare over the widening stretch of water. Keelin smiled back.

"Where to, Cap'n?" Yanic asked from Keelin's side.

"Port Sev'relain is closest."

Yanic sucked at his teeth and spat over the side of the boat.

"Out with it, mate."

"Quartermain will give us a better price on the spices."

"I'd really rather not run into Tanner," Keelin said with a heavy sigh.

"You and me both, Cap'n. Reckon the entire crew is behind ya on that one. Still, better price."

Keelin was silent for a while, weighing up the risk of running into Tanner Black versus the reward of cold hard coin. Greed won out. "Set course for Fango."

Fortune

"No wonder the bastards are attacking us," Princess said loudly to the group of pirates who had gathered near him. "Ya ever seen so many bloody pirates?"

"How many ships is that, Princess?" asked Kerry.

"Eight in all. Five flying colours, and three look ta be merchants. Reckon they'd be Loke's ships."

Loke owned near most of Port Sev'relain, and he was the only reason the little town had grown as large as it had. He was a middle man, a merchant who purchased from the local pirates of the isles and then transported those goods on to cities that could use them better. By all accounts Loke made more than his fair share of profit from the illegal endeavour.

Port Sev'relain had grown from a couple of warehouses with a single jetty to a thriving little town complete with moorings for ten large vessels. It now sported no fewer than three taverns and two brothels, and housed a stable population in the hundreds. That population swelled whenever pirate vessels were in the area, and these days there were always a few.

"See anyone we know?" Drake asked, stalking up to the railing to stand next to his first mate. Some of the crew, those with jobs they ought to be doing, took the opportunity to slink away, but just as many stood proud beside their infamous captain.

"Looks like the *Mary's Virtue* over there, Cap'n," said Princess with a grin. "Reckon we might have to put up with Poole."

Drake laughed. "Fucking wonderful. I look forward to hearing once again how he's the only born and bred pirate left in these waters. Anyone else?"

Princess shook his head. "All look a bit new, truth be told, Cap'n."

A couple of skiffs were being rowed towards the *Fortune* from the shore. They would tow the bigger ship into port. Drake started towards the aft deck, leaving Princess no choice but to hurry after him.

"Any issues?" Drake leapt down the five feet from the aft deck to the main deck.

"Well, there's the repairs," Princess said hesitantly. "Looked over it my own self and reckon we'll need a week in port with the shipwrights to get her squared away good and proper."

"A whole week? We haven't got time to be sitting on our arses for a week, Princess. Besides, the crew will pickle themselves with that much free time. Buy whoever you need and get it done in three days."

"Can't be done, Cap'n."

Drake rounded on his first mate just before they reached the ladder to the aft deck. He didn't look angry so much as really displeased. Princess would have preferred anger. Anger was predictable, displeasure could go either way, and it was the uncertainty Princess hated most.

"Might be able to push for five days, but a couple of those ships at port look to be taking repairs already. We'll have to…"

"Do it! Any of the other captains make waves, I'll deal with them my fucking self. Five days, Princess. Anything else?"

Drake turned again and started up the ladder. Princess scratched at the back of his neck before continuing. "We got rats."

"There ain't a ship built don't have rats."

"Yeah, well ours are as big as my foot and they've been getting into the food, making a mess of things. Need to do something about it or next time we set out might be we got sickness to deal with as well as those navy ships. Problem is, ever since Zothus took the *Bride* for his own ship and Rhi went with him… well, there ain't anything hunting the bloody rats no more, Cap'n. We need a cat."

"No," Drake stated firmly as he shooed Joelin away from the wheel and took hold of it himself. There wasn't really much steering to do at the moment, but Princess had to admit the captain cut a right striking figure doing it, and that was maybe the point. "Might be this has escaped your notice, Princess, but I am Drake Morrass and this ship is the *Fortune*. Now the last little predator we had on board was a big fucking spider, struck fear into the hearts of men and all that. I can't go back and just have a cat on board. Get me something – I don't know – more monstrous."

"More monstrous than a cat?"

"More monstruous than a giant spider."

Princess knew his mouth was hanging open, but at that moment he was finding it more than a little difficult to remember how to close it. A stern glare from Drake soon fixed that malady, and Princess nodded his affirmation before scuttling off to lament ever being made first mate.

No sooner had Drake's recently polished and gloriously buckled boots touched the ground than all sorts of people wanted a piece of him. Some folks shouted offers for any wares the *Fortune* might be carrying while others offered services either to him, the ship, or the crew, and some just stood around watching, no doubt hoping to get a glimpse of a legend. Drake was more than willing to accommodate that last desire.

"Ladies and gentlemen," Drake started in a loud voice that instantly quieted all the others. "For matters of booty procurement all requests shall be dealt with, as always, by Byron. You can't miss him; he's the tall fella up on deck with an extraordinarily small head." Byron was one half simpleton, one half genius, with an intimidating manner that was matched by his intimidating size. He was certainly not the brightest of folk, but he knew the inner workings of numbers like no one else alive and also happened to be even more loyal than the average dog, so Drake let the man manage the books.

"For any matters of employment or payment for rendering of services I direct you to my first mate, Princess." Princess looked less than pleased to be given yet another responsibility, but Drake couldn't really find it in himself to care – and what was the point of a first mate if not the delegation of the more boring aspects of the job of captain.

"Now it may be some of you have already heard some of the rumours regarding Black Sands…"

"Where do I go for matters of retribution?" said a dishevelled young man with fuzz on his chin and none on his head. He wore an old, faded tan jacket and sailor's leggings, and a cutlass dangled at his hip. Drake also couldn't help but notice that the man's boots were, if anything, even more polished than his own.

Drake smiled at him. "Reckon ya might be looking in the wrong place, boy."

"You killed my father!"

"Probably."

The man began to draw his cutlass, and five of Drake's pirates surged forwards, carried him to the ground, and proceeded to give him what Drake assumed was the worst and last beating of his life.

Stepping around the group murder taking place on the pier, Drake continued his way into Port Sev'relain proper. Some of those who had accosted him on the pier stopped to watch the young man die, and others followed in Drake's footsteps.

"As I was saying," Drake said, "some of you may have heard of Black Sands, some maybe not. Any that want to know can join me over at the Piper's Flock, and I'll treat you all to my very own retelling."

The Piper's Flock was about as fancy as a tavern got in a town founded by a crook and populated by pirates. The floor was clean, for the most part, and the tables were new and sturdy. Unfortunately, no matter how sturdily the tables were constructed, they tended not to last long in a place that saw more blood than the average battlefield. The ale wasn't exactly what anyone could call safe for consumption, but it had one thing going for it over what was served in the other taverns in Port Sev'relain, and that was that it had never given Drake the shits.

Drake took a seat at the centremost table in the common room and took his hat from his head, laying it on the table next to a gold bit. The barman and owner, a portly man by the name of Arst, didn't take long in slithering over to the table to stare at the coin, a greedy glint in his eyes.

Drake gestured to the entire room. "This round is on me." Without a word Arst snatched up the gold bit and scurried away.

Now Drake found himself the real centre of attention, and he counted a good thirty-three people in the tavern, including two burly bruisers by the front door, and every single one had quietened to hear what he had to say.

As Arst began bringing drinks around, starting with Drake, one of the visiting pirates lost patience. "Ya said ya had rumours about Black Sands?"

"Do I know you?" Drake said.

"Sienen Zhou. Captain of *Freedom*, out in the port."

The man had distinctive tattoos around his left eye and cheek. "Slave?" Drake asked.

"Use ta be, 'til the Black Thorn set us free."

Drake almost laughed, but he settled for a grin. "Well, you don't know me yet, Captain Zhou, so I'll tell you this for free. Drake Morrass doesn't deal in rumours. Everything I'm about to tell ya is cold, hard fact, and you'd all do well to listen with the utmost concentration. First things first…" Drake paused to take a large gulp of foul-tasting ale. "Black Sands ain't there no more."

The reaction was much as Drake expected: a mixture of shocked silence, outspoken denial, and fervent disbelief. He rocked his chair back onto two legs and basked in the whirlpool of attention.

"What do you mean, it ain't there no more, Morrass?" came a voice that Drake could only describe as big. He looked around for the owner and found it belonged to a tall, broad man with olive skin and a stark white tattoo of a skull painted on his face, which gave him the appearance of a walking, talking, glowering skeleton.

"It's been a long time, Captain Burn. Didn't see your little boat out there. Could it be you've gone and got her sunk, Deun?"

"I never bring *Rheel Toa* into port," Captain Deun Burn said around a mouth of teeth all sharpened to points. "Answer my question, Morrass."

Drake shrugged and dismissed the threat implied in the Riverlander's voice by turning away. "Black Sands is gone, wiped off the charts if ever she was on any, burned to the ground. Saw her turn to ash with my own two eyes."

Captain Burn pushed his way through the gathered crowd and leaned on the other side of the table. The man's visage was beyond ghastly and more than a little off-putting, yet Drake stared right on back.

"And how much of a part did you play in its end?" Burn asked, his voice gravelly.

For just a moment Drake considered drawing steel and attempting to run the man through. Unfortunately he wasn't as confidant of his ability to do so as his own legend would suggest. He also hated to admit it, but he needed Deun Burn. He needed all the captains on his side. Then something caught his eye for a moment, a small figure wearing a flat-brimmed hat that obscured her face. She drew a weapon and manoeuvred herself to stand behind the skull-faced captain. If Drake couldn't kill the man himself, he sure as all the Hells couldn't allow someone else to do it for him.

Drake rocked his chair back onto all four legs and stood, placing his hands on the table in a mirror of the Riverlands captain and keeping eye contact all the while.

"Just this once, Deun, I'm gonna pretend you did not just insinuate that I may have had something to do with the death of over two hundred of our brethren."

"Dead?" asked another man. "Are you sure?"

"Aye. All of them dead. Sent a boat ashore to check. No survivors." Drake could see the woman with the flat-brimmed hat now, and she had at least six pistols strapped to her leather jerkin and another one in her hand. Drake couldn't see the woman's face, obscured as it was by her hat, but he could tell by the way she stood that she was ready for a fight. Right then he'd have paid good money to know her identity, yet he had the more pressing matter of his audience to attend to.

"Who did it?" someone asked.

"Why?" asked another.

Drake sucked at his golden tooth. "Can't say as to the why, but the who – my boys spotted a ship sailing away from the other side of the island. Warship flying the colours of Sarth."

That set the whole tavern to shouting, and even Deun Burn had the good sense to look worried. Any navy vessels braving the waters of the Pirate Isles were bad for business; that they were willing to raid a pirate town and slaughter all the inhabitants was almost unheard of outside of a purge.

"Is that it?" asked an old sailor with fewer teeth than fingers and only one hand. "They stoppin' with Black Sands? Or are they comin' for us?"

The whole tavern went deathly silent again as the patrons waited for Drake to answer the old sailor. This was exactly where he needed them, scared shitless and looking to him for answers. He briefly considered sitting back down, but decided it would look more commanding if he remained on his feet.

"Doesn't seem likely to me they'd stop. If Sarth is willing to burn one of our little towns, don't reckon they'll be stopping there." He paused and looked around the room. "I reckon Black Sands is just the beginning."

Again the tavern burst into sound and activity. A few pirates bolted out the front door, while Arst set to frantically wiping down a nearby table. The old sailor with only one hand collapsed back into a seat, and a woman nearby wearing the trappings of a merchant made a sign in the air to ward off evil sea spirits. Drake almost mentioned to the woman that making such signs on land was a good way to draw the attention of said spirits, but he decided to leave the foolish in their ignorance.

"What do we do?" The voice broke through the general din, and Drake recognised it as belonging to one of his own crew, playing their part perfectly.

"For now all ya can do is warn folk," Drake said loudly. "Make sure everyone knows the danger and keep an eye out for unfamiliar ships on the horizon and such. Be ready, aye." He turned his attention to Deun Burn. "Leave the rest to me and my fellow captains. Together we'll see all of ya through."

Some of the crowd began to disperse, folk taking Drake's advice and running to tell their fellows about the massacre at Black Sands and the potential threat to Port Sev'relain. Captain Deun Burn remained, staring at Drake through his ghastly tattooed mask.

Drake had never credited any of the Riverfolk with having an abundance of intelligence. They had some strange magics, that couldn't be denied, but they also had some strange beliefs and practices that involved regular human sacrifices and the subsequent cannibalism of the victims. Cannibalism didn't sit particularly well with Drake, and he was thankful it was one of the few things he'd never been accused of. Despite his general dislike, distaste, and poor opinion of the Riverfolk in general, Drake needed the support of this particular one. So instead of following his first instinct and having the man drowned in a puddle of his own blood, he waited while the Riverlander made up his own mind.

"Is this real?" Deun Burn asked eventually, once they were all but alone.

"Said it, didn't I? I'm many things, Deun, but I ain't a liar," Drake lied.

Captain Burn stood up to his full height, a good inch shorter than Drake's, and nodded gravely. With that the man walked slowly from the tavern, leaving Drake none the wiser as to whether he'd just gained his very first ally.

The woman with the pistols was still standing by the bar; her hat was tilted, so Drake couldn't see her eyes, but he fancied she was watching him. He had no idea who she was nor what her intentions might be, but long ago Drake's mother had told him that fortune favoured the bold, and Drake would never allow anyone to call him otherwise.

As Drake approached, the woman tilted back her hat, giving him a view of her face. He treated her to one of his most charming smiles, the same one he'd practised in front of a mirror hundreds of times long ago. She had fine, strong features, golden hair, and blue eyes the colour of the sea. The fact that she had six small pistols strapped to her chest, and another hanging from her belt, was a little disconcerting, but then Drake had never been one to stay away from a woman on account of danger.

"Who are you?" he said as he stepped within stabbing distance of the woman.

"Straight to the point." The woman's voice was sweeter than honey and twice as dangerous as the bees that made it.

"Well, you had me covered back there, and I reckon I've never met you before, so that puts me thoroughly in the thinking of who the fuck are you and what do you want with me?"

The woman shot Drake a thoroughly unimpressed look. "I am Arbiter Beck."

Surprise wasn't good for Drake's reputation, but right now he was well and truly shocked. After taking a moment to compose himself, he let out a chuckle and scratched at one of the tattoos underneath his shirt. "Don't all you witch hunters have one of those fancy coats?"

"That wouldn't be very discreet," Arbiter Beck whispered. "And it would have made it much harder to get so close to you."

Drake inched his hand towards the sabre sheathed at his hip. Beck's eyes flicked to the movement and then back again.

"I wouldn't advise it, Captain Morrass," she said. "I'm faster than you, and at this range, I promise you I wouldn't miss."

"Aye? Where would you be aiming?"

"Unfortunately, not at your heart."

Drake raised an eyebrow. "There's worse places you could be aiming for."

Arbiter Beck smiled. "Then I'd aim for one of those."

"Right." Drake pushed away from the bar. "Lovely banter, Lady Beck. Reckon I'll be on my way now. Feel free to bugger off."

"I'm going wherever you go," the Arbiter said with a sigh.

"What's that now?"

"From now on, *Captain*," she said, spitting the title as if it were distasteful on her tongue, "I am your new shadow and a marked improvement on your old one. Much prettier, you see."

Drake let out a groan. He saw his brother's hand in this. He couldn't see any other reason for a witch hunter of the Inquisition to be stalking him; they had far more important things to do, such as burning folk alive and generally putting the fear of their god into anyone and everyone they met.

"I have been ordered by an Inquisitor to protect you, Captain Morrass," Beck said, confirming his suspicion.

"Aye. He happen to tell you why?"

Beck narrowed her eyes. "No. I presume it must be because a heretic is trying to kill you. I can't see any other reason. You strike me as just another common thief."

"I prefer pirate." Drake grinned.

"I don't care what you prefer. My orders are to follow and protect you until further notice, and that is exactly what I intend to do. Feel free to refuse my protection and sail away without me. I will happily return to the Inquisition with the knowledge that I tried."

Drake was fast forming a dislike for this woman. Unfortunately, if Hironous had sent her then it was for Drake's own good. His brother had the sight, the ability to see into a person's future, and Drake had long ago learned to both trust and rely on his brother's advice.

"Fine. When you're on my ship you follow my rules and do as you're told."

The Arbiter snorted. "Not likely. I will require my own cabin, which will be completely private. Anyone caught snooping around will be killed on sight."

Drake sucked at his golden tooth as he glared at the woman. "You can have my first mate's cabin. Don't go killing folk just for walking past though. Good?"

"I will also require use of the ship's galley. I will prepare my own food."

Drake waved away the demand. "You can take that up with Curden, he's the cook."

"You will also inform your crew that I am not fair game. If any of them so much as attempts to touch me, I will kill them."

Drake laughed. "Rule on ship, you want folk to leave you alone then you tell them yourselves. Violence is acceptable…"

"No," Beck said in her honeyed voice. "You will tell them, and make it an order. If any of your crew so much as touches me, I will kill them and ten more. Unless you can afford to be captaining a ghost ship, Captain Morrass, you will acquiesce to this."

Drake didn't just want to lay a hand on her; he wanted to lay a fist on her, and more than one at that. But there were some things Captain Drake Morrass wasn't allowed to show, and frustration was one of them, so he let out a jovial laugh and decided he'd make his brother pay for sending Arbiter Beck to him.

"I can see why Inquisitor Vance sent you." Drake started towards the tavern exit, not waiting to see if she would follow.

"How do you know which Inquisitor sent me?" Beck asked from behind, and Drake felt her compulsion, her magic, attempt to lock on to his will and force the truth from his lips. To be fair to Beck, her will was strong and would have easily dominated most men, but Drake was not so ignorant to the tricks of Arbiters as most men. The tattoo branded onto his skin countered her magic, allowing his will to slip away from her grip, and her compulsion failed.

As Drake reached the door he gave the woman a withering look over his shoulder and relished in her confusion. "Not quite so common as you might think, Arbiter."

The Phoenix

Yanic didn't like the situation one bit. "I don't like this situation one bit, Cap'n."

Captain Stillwater turned an incredulous gaze on his first mate. "It was your bloody suggestion to come here. Quartermain giving the best prices and all that."

"That was before I saw *Starry Dawn* sat at dock, Cap'n." Yanic had been with Keelin on *The Black Death*, and he'd seen the two of them together. Nothing good ever came from their close proximity. "I was there on *The Black Death* with ya, Cap'n. Seen you two together…"

"I'm well aware how much of a shit storm that was, Yanic."

"Beggin' ya captain's pardon, but ya really ain't."

Keelin turned a dangerous glare on his first mate, and Yanic decided to shut up and take a real interest in a gull that had landed on the *The Phoenix*'s figurehead, a beautiful carving of a bird emerging from an egg surrounded by fire.

The sea around the Isle of Goats, a descriptive rather than artful name, was stained a permanent brown-green colour that was off-putting to look at and stuck to the hull of a ship long after she'd left its waters. The Isle of Goats was one of the larger habitable land masses in the Pirate Isles and was vaguely crescent shaped. There were three ports to speak of on the island, but only one town, Fango.

Legend had it that long ago, the old Captain Black, the most notorious and bloodthirsty pirate ever to have lived among the realms of men, had pirated his way across the seas for decades before his death. Captain Black had amassed a fortune, a sum to rival even the wealth of the merchants of Acanthia. The old, dead Captain Black had reportedly hidden his riches on the Isle of Goats. In more recent memory the new Captain Black, a man equally as bloodthirsty but lacking in fortune, had settled the island as his own personal haven, and, as was like to happen around powerful men, folk had followed him. Before long the town of Fango had arisen, and it soon became one of the most populous of all the pirate towns. Unfortunately Fango still had very real ties to the new

Captain Black and that put Yanic, Captain Stillwater, and the whole crew of *The Phoenix* in more than a little jeopardy every time they visited the town.

Dense forest occupied much of the island, along with a small range of mountains and an inland lake that never seemed to run dry. Rumour had it the lake had no bottom, and if the waters were ever to run clear one would be able to see all the way into the realm of the dead, and might even catch a glimpse of lost loved ones staring right back.

It took a full three days to sail around the Isle of Goats, even if the wind was with a ship, and if its captain didn't know the coast too well, there were very real risks of the vessel being gutting on the jagged rocks hidden just below the surface of the murky waters. Luckily for *The Phoenix* and her crew, she not only had a captain who knew the local waters intimately, but also a first mate who had indeed drawn the charts of those same waters.

"Is it too late to turn tail and run?" asked Yanic. "Port Sev'relain is barely a week away and Black Sands ain't out of distance neither."

"We're here now, Yanic," Captain Stillwater said with grim determination.

"More's the pity."

"It could be worse."

Yanic cocked an eyebrow at his captain. "How?"

Keelin Stillwater drew in a deep breath and let it out as a ragged sigh. "You could be me."

Yanic could find no argument with the statement so decided to keep quiet. "Ain't nothing ya didn't bring on yaself," he then said in direct opposition to his decision.

The captain glared at Yanic, then shrugged. With a sigh he moved to the wheel and took it from Freman.

"We'll head around to south port and dock there. I want to be in and out in two days."

Yanic drifted away from the railing and stood behind his captain. "Two days is a long time, and the island ain't that big. She'll soon find out about ya, Cap'n."

Fortune

"This here is Lady Beck. She'll be taking your cabin so long as she's aboard," Drake said to Princess as he stormed up the gangplank onto his ship.

Princess spared a long-suffering glance towards the woman and sighed. "Aye."

That there, Drake decided, was why he would never give Princess a ship of his own. The man was an excellent first mate, able to shout orders and knock heads with the best of them. He was competent with a sword and no coward in battle either. He was as loyal to Drake as folk came, but the man had no conviction; Zothus would never have given away his cabin so easily. Unfortunately Zothus was true captain material, and Drake needed as many friendly captains as he could find, so he'd been near forced to give the man a ship of his own. In one unfortunate but necessary decision Drake had given away the best first mate he'd ever known and the most terrifying ship-board pest-hunter any pirate had ever heard of. Drake would never admit it, but he actually missed Zothus' giant spider at times.

"Beck, this is Princess." Drake paused, waiting for the comment about the man's name. The Arbiter kept her mind to herself. "You need anything, I reckon you should just go see him."

"If I need anything I'll bring it straight to your personal attention, Drake," Arbiter Beck said. There was cold iron as well as honey in the woman's voice, and ordinarily Drake would have found that appealing, and more than a little so, but she was on his ship now – and nobody gave Drake Morrass orders on his own ship. He rounded on the woman, grabbed hold of the collar of her tunic with one hand, and, with more effort than he liked to admit, sent her stumbling down the deck. She collided with the main mast shoulder first, yelping in what was either surprise or pain. Drake sincerely hoped it was both.

Beck pulled a pistol from its place on her jerkin, pointing it at Drake. Her hat had fallen from her head, and for the first time Drake saw something other than disapproval in her eyes: he saw fear. To the

Arbiter's credit, her aim was steady in spite of it. Drake stopped just in front of Beck, her pistol barrel poking him in the chest.

"Now, might be you think ya safe on account of the Oracle sending you to me. You ain't. Or maybe you reckon those little pistols'll protect you. Thing is, I counted 'em and you got seven. One word from me and my crew'll descend on you like particularly hungry laughing dogs, and there's a few more than seven of 'em. So no matter how safe or protected you think you are – you ain't.

"Captain's word is law on board a ship and I just happen to be captain on this one, so you live and die by my leave." Drake leaned in closer and stared directly into the Arbiter's icy blue eyes. "You wanna fuck off, be my guest. Something tells me you'll be staying though. You follow my orders to the fucking letter, or I swear to your god and mine that I will put one of those little pistol bullets of yours through your chest and throw you overboard for whatever fucking denizen of the deep'll have ya."

Drake didn't bother waiting to see if the woman agreed; he turned away and raised his voice so all his gathered crew could hear. "This here is Arbiter Beck. Our friendly Oracle sent her to look after me." That earned a chuckle from the pirates. "She's off-fucking-limits. Good?"

There was hurried assent from the crew in general. "Good," Drake continued. "Now get the fuck back to work before I decide to make an example out of one of ya."

Drake turned back to Princess and Arbiter Beck with a smile. "Pirates – sometimes they just need a good threatening to keep 'em in line." As the Arbiter lowered her pistol, Drake laughed and shook his head. "How are we looking with the repairs, Princess?"

Princess took a step backwards and winced, his long hair falling in front of his face, and that face looking like it really wanted to be elsewhere. "About that, Cap'n. We need to beach the ship."

There was far too much at stake and far too much to do, and Drake was not about to lose weeks to beaching the ship. "No," he said in a voice that brooked no argument.

"Aye, Cap'n. Only thing is..." Princess sighed and pointed at an unassuming bucket sitting by the mast. It appeared to be filled with murky water.

"Shit," said Drake, staring into the bucket and seeing that it wasn't water, but rubbery, grey flesh.

"Ying noticed it on the starboard bow, Cap'n," Princess continued. "Got it off pretty quick, but there's at least one plank that's gonna need some repair if not replacing."

"Any more of them on my ship?"

"Won't know for sure 'til we get her beached. Get a good look at her belly."

"What is it?" Arbiter Beck asked quietly from beside Drake. He felt her compulsion tug at his mind, but as before his will slipped away from her magic.

"A gipple," Princess answered immediately. "Fuck me, that felt odd." No doubt it was his first encounter with an Arbiter's compulsion.

"A pain in my arse," Drake said testily. "One part seal and one part demon."

"Demon?"

"Maybe. Attach themselves to the hull and… here." Drake reached into the bucket and grabbed hold of the creature's oily skin, turning it around in the bucket to reveal its head. "See the mouth? That circle of teeth there moves back and forth in a rasping motion. Fucking things chew right through the hull all slow like. Can take weeks, but once they do – well, ships don't do so well when they're full of holes."

He turned to Princess. "Get her beached. We're gonna need to slap another coat of lime tar on her as well. Can't afford to have these little bastards putting holes in my ship."

"Aye, Cap'n," said Princess as he moved away to begin preparations.

"You found me a replacement for the spider yet?" Drake called after him.

"Depends, Cap'n. You still dead set against a cat?"

"Aye."

"I'll keep looking."

Drake looked at Arbiter Beck; the woman seemed to have backed down a little after his earlier threats, but she was in no way cowed.

"Might not wanna move aboard just yet, Arbiter. Reckon we might be here a while."

The Phoenix

Only one ship occupied the berth at south port, a sloop by the name of *North Wind*. Keelin had never seen the little ship before and, more importantly, had no idea who captained the vessel. What Keelin did know for certain was that it wasn't *The Black Death*, and it was therefore not captained by Tanner Black.

No sooner had Keelin set his boots onto the decking of the jetty than the harbour master – a truly superficial title as he was master of nothing, but more accurately a caretaker of the jetties – was beside him, bowing and offering "sincere" opportunities for monetary advancement. The man obviously didn't remember Keelin, but Keelin remembered him, and not fondly. Even ten years ago the harbour master had seemed ancient, with thin greying hair hanging lank about his face, a mouth dotted with decaying brown teeth, and breath that could kill a shark at fifty paces. Keelin was ashamed to admit he'd been young and naive, and the man had swindled him out of nearly a month's pay. These days he was neither.

"Good fortunes an' fair weather, Captain." The man's voice had an annoying habit of whistling through his teeth when he spoke certain sounds – it did very little to endear him to Keelin. "S'nice ship ya got there. Very nice. Plenty o' ruffians round these parts though, real bad eggs, some would say. Might be they see ya nice ship there as a bit o' fun. Of course, I could look out fer it for ya, make sure those ruffians don't touch it, nor none o' yer men either. Keep it safe. Fer a small fee…" The man's voice rose annoyingly high at the end of the offer, and a greedy glint lit his eyes.

In a fit of what could only be described as compassion, Keelin didn't run the man through, but instead gave him a shove that sent the old fool careening off the jetty into the murky waters of south port. He spent a moment flailing about before paddling to shore, all the while attempting to both keep his head above water and shout insults Keelin's way – all of which seemed to revolve around his mother's profession and how she most certainly went about it on her back.

Keelin stopped, turned back to his ship, and shouted up to one of his crew. "Anyone ain't one of our boys comes anywhere near the *The Phoenix*, Olly, and you show them a real warm greeting."

Olly laughed and gave a mock salute from his perch on the railing. He was a small lad, ever jovial and never without a quip or a story, but never had Keelin met someone so eager to get to the stabbing when there was stabbing to be done.

South port barely deserved the name, Keelin decided, and not for the first time, as he set foot on dry land. It was little more than a collection of rotting wooden huts held together by rusting nails and the tenacity of their inhabitants. North port was big, loud, heavily populated, and bordered on being considered a town in its own right. South port was small, run down, populated only by the dregs of humanity, and left discarded and forgotten by all those with better sense. Or, Keelin decided, all those who weren't trying to hide from their past.

An old dirt road led out of south port into the looming forest, which Keelin knew from past experience was hot, close, and insect ridden, filled with dangers both mundane and beyond explanation. He also knew that the old dirt road led to Fango.

Yanic coughed, and Keelin noticed his first mate was standing beside him with a knowing smile on his face. "Boys are unloading the loot. All is left is ta haggle with Quartermain, Cap'n."

"Suppose we best go see the old bastard then," Keelin said. "Watch my back, Yan. Hostile waters and all that."

With a last glance back towards his ship and one last glare at the harbour master, who was still preoccupied with insulting, threatening, and cursing Keelin all at once, they walked into the jungle.

Fango was by no means a normal town even by a pirate's definition, and Keelin well knew piratical definitions were broad, meandering, and colourful at the best of times. The jungle on the Isle of Goats seemed to resist almost all efforts at deforestation with something approaching intelligent aggression. The more trees the residents cut down, the more sprang up from seemingly nowhere. An old sailor might fell a tree and build a house in its spot, and within a few months hundreds of new saplings would tear through the building, slowly turning it into an uninhabitable wreckage. The inhabitants of the town had, therefore, after many years of war with the jungle, learned to live with their giant wooden neighbours. Buildings were constructed around trees, some of which were the only reason said buildings were still standing. Keelin knew all too well that the town's brothel had a giant of a redwood standing tall and straight in the main common area, and the owner had actually built cushioned seats onto the trunk upon which to display his wares.

Many industrious residents of Fango had even taken to building their houses halfway up the trees, so that a ladder was needed to reach their homes. Just how they'd managed to accomplish such a feat was a mystery to Keelin, but he suspected it took time, effort, and a lack of acrophobia. The result was clear though; the inhabitants had not only compensated for a lack of space by building upwards as well as outwards, but had learned to live with and even take advantage of an aggressive forest that resisted most normal attempts at habitation. Unfortunately, the entire town was under the sway of Tanner Black, and that cast a dirty shadow on what should have been world-renowned innovation.

"Place has grown some since we were here last, Cap'n," said Yanic, staring in wonder at a building that was constructed around five separate tree trunks. It was at least three storeys high, and judging by the sign hanging outside it was a new tavern that had sprung up in their years of absence. "Prospered, ya might say."

Keelin caught himself nodding along absently. "Let's just go see Quartermain and get this over with."

Their arrival went anything but unnoticed, and more than a few sets of eyes followed Keelin and his first mate as they entered Fango. One child, wearing dirty rags for clothing and no shoes, spotted them and ran off, scaling a tree without the use of the ladder set into its trunk and disappearing into a building at least thirty feet from the ground. A moment later an older face, female and wizened, leaned out of a window and watched them pass.

One giant of a man – Keelin guessed he stood at over seven feet –

made no attempt to hide his interest in the newcomers. He watched them with a smile and pointed them out to his companions. Keelin noticed all three were armed, and all three looked as though they knew how to use those arms. He found himself thankful for the comforting presence of his twin cutlasses hanging from his belt, but wished he'd possessed the sense to instruct Yanic to come similarly prepared.

"Do folk seem a little... hostile ta you, Cap'n?" Yanic said as they approached the area of Fango that Quartermain called his own.

"Wary, I think is more appropriate, Yanic." Keelin felt a distinct lack of confidence in his own words. "You would be too if you lived under Tanner's rule."

Yanic cleared his throat. "I did live under Tanner's rule, and I was not wary – I was hostile."

Keelin stopped outside a door he remembered well, a door with a sign nailed to it that read "Quartermain's". He looked at his first mate. "You were very hostile." With that he pounded on the door three times and waited for a reply.

It wasn't long before a muffled "Come in" drifted back, and Keelin pushed open the door to find the place much as he remembered. A burly oaf of a man, shorter than Keelin but with arms as thick as the trees that sprouted through the building, stood to the side to allow the pirates to pass. He nodded his thanks to Quartermain Junior and stepped through the doorway.

Quartermain Senior was standing behind a wooden counter, frowning down at one of numerous scrolls haphazardly sprawling its surface. "Sorry about the mess. Busy time and all that." he said, indicating the immaculately kept front of his business. He looked up, squinting. "That you, Stillwater?"

Keelin grinned at the reaction; it had been many years since he'd last been back to Fango, and it was good to know those in charge still remembered his face. "Aye, 'tis me, Quartermain. How is..."

"Very sorry about this," Quartermain interrupted just as the door slammed shut behind Keelin.

Keelin spun around, both hands going to the hilts of his cutlasses and both cutlasses unhooking smoothly from his belt. The first thing he noticed was Yanic looking anything but comfortable with a knife to his throat and a Quartermain attached to its hilt. The second thing he noticed was the person rated second highest on his "never wanting to see again" list.

"Stillwater," Elaina Black said in a voice that fair dripped with smug satisfaction.

"Elaina," Keelin replied in a voice that left no one in the room under any illusion that he didn't regret making the decision to come to Fango.

Yanic cleared his throat. He looked panicked.

"Yanic," Elaina said by way of greeting.

"Long time no see, Elaina. Ya mind telling this fool to drop his knife?" Yanic said, his voice rising with every word.

"Of course, Yanic, just as soon as your captain drops his, eh. So how about it, Stillwater?"

Keelin considered his options and decided they were camping on the bleak side of hope. He had no doubt that in a fair fight he could take both Elaina and Quartermain Junior, but he also had no doubt that Elaina never fought fair – and the first proof of that was the knife currently pressed to his first mate's throat. With a heavy sigh he dropped both cutlasses to the floor and took a step backwards.

"Excellent," Elaina said with a smile that made her plain features seem both vicious and beautiful at the same time. "Now, I had to run all the way here to beat you after seeing ya ship sail right on past north port, an' I'm feeling a little bit sticky, so what say me an' you continue this after a bath, eh?"

Keelin made a show of considering the offer.

"Don't keep me waiting, Stillwater."

"Fine," he said. "But you're undressing first this time. I want to make sure you ain't hiding any weapons – anywhere."

"Ya really think I'd use that trick twice?" Elaina grinned, already opening the door.

More water sloshed over the side of the brass bath as Elaina rhythmically moved her hips back and forth and Keelin struggled against the rising tide of pleasure. He gripped hard at her buttocks, hard enough to bruise, but Elaina didn't cry out and she didn't stop, just stared down into his face as she ground her groin against his. Unable to hold back any longer, Keelin grunted, gasped, and released with a contented moan, all to the braying laughter of Elaina Black from atop him. More water sloshed over the side of the bath.

"Looks like I win again," Elaina said with a wiggle and a devilish grin.

Keelin nodded his assent. "You always win the first round, bitch."

"Rematch already?"

Keelin laughed. "I might need a quick rest first. Besides, we should talk business."

Elaina cocked an eyebrow at him. "We have business?"

"Aye, of a sort. First things first. Where's your father?"

Elaina grinned and squeezed Keelin with her thighs; it wasn't comfortable, and she was easily strong enough to hurt him. Elaina was tall and plain-faced, toned from years of hard life and hard toil aboard ships. She had more experience on board pirate ships than any sailor Keelin could name, despite her youth, and could be as cruel as her father or as kind as her mother in equal measure.

"Are you really asking where Tanner is while you're still inside his daughter?" Elaina said. "What happens if he's here? What happens if he walks through that door right now?" She pointed at the door just to make her point.

"I reckon he'd slit my throat on principal and beat you half to death for not doing it first."

Elaina grinned and opened her mouth to reply just as a hurried banging on the door startled them both into rigid inaction.

"Is he here?" Keelin whispered. He could feel his heart racing.

"I fuckin' hope not," Elaina whispered back. He could feel her heart racing.

"Cap'n," Yanic's shout came through the door. "Got news, seems urgent."

Elaina relaxed a little atop Keelin; he couldn't help but notice she had yet to dismount. "Come in, Yanic," she shouted back.

The door opened. Yanic froze mid-step, his mouth hanging open. Elaina took the cue to arch her back and stretch her arms, giving Yanic full view of her breasts. The poor man seemed lost and unable to look away. Keelin couldn't exactly blame his first mate; it was taking all of his own willpower not to follow the man's lead, and he could feel that willpower slipping away even now.

Keelin attempted to move Elaina, but she only tightened her grip with her thighs. "You ain't going nowhere, Stillwater. I'm not done with you yet."

"What is it, Yanic?" Keelin said.

"I, uh, there's… um… damnit! Elaina, could ya put some clothes on or something?" Yanic still seemed unable to tear his eyes away from the naked pirate.

"Why? Am I distracting you?" Elaina said, and her own eyes flicked down for a moment. "Ya definitely look distracted."

Keelin attempted to move again, but Elaina's thighs squeezed him tighter still and she shot him a dangerous look that threatened real physical harm should he attempt to force the issue. Content that he was much safer off in the woman's good books, Keelin relaxed back with a sigh. "Just… What is it, Yanic?"

"Aye. Um… news, Cap'n." Yanic's eyes seemed locked on Elaina's chest. "Boat in from Black Sands. Town's gone."

"Gone?" Keelin and Elaina said in unison.

"Burned," Yanic clarified. "Couple of lads… um… from the *Nipples*… um… no, not that."

Elaina laughed. "I think ya need to order ya first mate to the brothel, Stillwater. I'm starting to think he's never seen a pair before."

"The *Narrow Escape*," Yanic continued quickly. "A, uh, couple of lads went ashore. Said the place was burned to the ground and… um… folk had wounds and such from swords, I guess."

"And this couldn't have waited?" Keelin said. "We're busy, Yanic."

Yanic's face somehow managed to find an even brighter shade of red. "Seemed… um… important, I think. Oh – Drake!"

Keelin frowned. "Morrass?"

Elaina let out a noise worryingly close to a growl, and her grip on

Keelin's midsection tightened even more. He was beginning to find it hard to breathe. "Elaina," he wheezed, "this hurts."

The woman sneered at him but released some of the pressure. "Don't go soft on me, Stillwater. What about Morrass?"

Yanic startled back into life. "They said... um... that is, the boys from the *Narrow Escape* said they saw the *Fortune* sailing away – from Black Sands."

"He did it?" Keelin shifted his weight slightly in the cooling tub of water, and quickly held up placating hands to Elaina as she sent a glare his way.

"They reckon so."

"That it, Yanic?" Elaina asked coldly.

"Aye."

"Good. Fuck off."

"Aye," Yanic said, backing towards the door, bumping into the door frame, and then backing out into the waiting hallway. His eyes never left Elaina's body even as he was shutting the door.

Keelin decided it was his turn to stare at the naked pirate. He found Elaina watching him curiously. She leaned in towards him, far enough down that her breasts dipped into the tepid water and her face was just inches from his own.

"Do you know him?" she whispered.

"Drake?"

"Aye."

Keelin stared into Elaina's bright blue eyes. "I've met him once or twice. Why? Do you know him?"

She smiled then, and it made her pretty, if not beautiful. Keelin felt the urge to kiss her, but he resisted; Elaina wasn't the type for such affection. "Everybody knows Drake."

Keelin felt blood rush to his face. There was something in the way Elaina said it that made him unreasonably jealous, and he didn't like it. "What's that mean?"

Elaina leaned backwards until she was upright and shrugged. Keelin felt the urge to grab hold of her, and this time it wouldn't be gentle. He surged out of the water, picking Elaina up and turning her around before bending her over the side of the tub.

Elaina laughed as Keelin manhandled her, but she spread her legs and braced against the tub. "It's about fucking time, Stillwater. You promised me round two."

Fortune

The waves lapped up the stretch of sandy shore, the wind breezed through the nearby jungle, the gulls cawed high up above in the blue sky, and the *Fortune* sat still and silent, keeled over to her port side.

Drake hated seeing his ship like this. On the water the *Fortune* was sleek and fast and indomitable: a truly unique design. Drake had made certain of that by murdering the genius who had built her. She was the fastest ship he'd ever had the fortune of knowing, and her reputation was as dark as his own. The *Fortune* had haunted the seas from Sarth to the Five Kingdoms to the Dragon Empire to the Wilds; all knew her name, and all knew to fear her. There was no sense in running from a ship that could outrun the wind itself. But that was out on the water. Here, on land, she was nothing but silent, dead wood. Drake hated seeing his ship like this, and he also knew she hated being seen like this.

"She's lookin' pretty banged up, Cap'n Morrass," said one of the shipwrights. He was a squat, balding man with one eye and a jawline the likes of which a stone Adonis would have been proud to own.

"Aye," Drake said, morose. "Been a long while since we last put her in for real repairs. Couple of leaks here and there, but nothing we ain't been able to handle or patch until now." He missed the sound of her creaking under his feet and the spray as she cut through waves. Strange that he could go months at a stretch on land and away from his ship, yet the moment she was beached he couldn't stand to be apart from her.

"What about the gipples?" asked another of the shipwrights, as different from the first as day from night. This one was tall, thin, and chinless, with skin as dark as onyx and eyes as bright as the bits Drake was offering to pay him to fix the ship.

"Dead." Drake pointed to a stretch of beach where dark shapes were splayed out in stark contrast against the yellow sand. "Found four of them in all, and all had damn near chewed through the hull. Plenty of wood needing replacing. My boys could patch it, but I want her fit as a fiddle and tarred up to stop this happening again."

"How else is she lookin'? Any other damage?" The third

shipwright was a young man who barely looked as though he was off his mother's tit, but he was the son of an old man Drake knew well. While Drake couldn't say he trusted the fellow – he wasn't given to trusting any living soul apart from his brother – he would happily claim to respect the ancient ship builder.

"Bugger me, lad," Drake said with a snort. "She's been out on the waters for about three years since anybody last had a good look at her. What do you think?" The older shipwrights laughed, as if the boy's question had been so obvious he needn't have asked. "Minor damage for the most part. Some railing replacement and the like. Might as well give her a new mast while we're at it, I suppose. That one's been set fire to once or twice."

"I suppose you'll be wanting the good wood for replacements?" said the squat shipwright. By way of response Drake only stared at the man. "Of course. Well, I reckon I could do it for seven hundred and fifty bits. Three weeks' work at most."

The chinless shipwright chimed in next, while Drake looked at all three of them, thoroughly unimpressed. "Seven hundred bits and two weeks." He grinned at his fellows as though he'd just secured the deal.

"My da'll do it fer five hundred just to have the opportunity to work on the *Fortune*," said the child with a smug grin. "Still take two weeks though. Can't rush good work, he always says."

"Five hundred?" said the stout shipwright in a voice so high most singers would have been envious. "You can't do it for that, won't even cover the costs."

The young lad grinned at them both, and within moments all three shipwrights were arguing as though who Drake chose to fix his ship was up to them. With a sigh he turned away and went back to staring at his poor, beached ship. Nearby he could see Princess and the Arbiter arguing about something. The woman was becoming a constant pain in the poor man's arse with all of her demands, but Drake wasn't about to turn her away. An Arbiter was a powerful ally, and Hironous had, for some reason, ordered her to protect Drake.

He thought about what his brother had said the last time he'd seen him. Not only was Hironous Vance the youngest Inquisitor the

Inquisition had ever seen, but he also had the sight. The sight manifested in women as the power to look into a person's past through their own eyes, but in men it manifested as the power to look into a person's future – and for that reason Hironous Vance was also known as the Oracle, though not to many outside of Drake's crew.

"I don't have time for this," Drake said quietly. "I gotta find that bloody pretend pirate, Stillwater."

"Did you say something, Captain Morrass?" said the chinless shipwright.

Drake looked over his shoulder at the arguing fools. "Reckon ya might have mistaken the point of me bringing you here," he said with a charming grin. "I ain't asking you what price one of ya can do it for. I'm telling all three of ya to get to work and fix my damned ship. And I'm giving ya one week to do it."

"I already have a client."

"One week?"

"They couldn't fix it in a month!"

Drake spat into the sand. It was a small gesture, but enough to silence all three shipwrights. "I don't care about your other clients and I don't care about your issues with each other. Ya each get one thousand bits, all nice and shiny, and if the *Fortune* ain't back on the water in a week, I'll cut ya noses off and sew them to your arseholes. Good?"

The three men looked at each other quickly and, as one, nodded their assent. "What should I do about Captain Barklow?" the stout one said.

"Who?" Drake had never heard of Captain Barklow, which put the man well and truly in the realm of inconsequential. Captains came and went all the time out in the isles, and unless they'd proven they had a name worth knowing, Drake didn't bother taking the time to know it.

"The Captain of the *Hearth Fire*," the shipwright said, nervously scratching at his chiselled chin. "My workers are currently fixing his ship."

Drake considered the situation for a moment, then grinned as opportunity once again presented itself. "Pull the workers and get them to fixing the *Fortune*. I reckon I'll go have myself a chat with this Captain

Barklow."

Drake looked over at his first mate. "Princess," he shouted. "I want you and Byron with me. We're going to town. Beck, might be you want to tag along as well. Maybe you'll get to see what us pirates are really like." He turned back to find the three shipwrights watching him intently. "And you boys might want to get to work. You've got a week to fix my bloody ship."

Port Sev'relain was fair buzzing with activity and noise. Drake wagered he'd never seen so many folk out and about in the town at once. Pirates walked about in groups, some enjoying snatched days of shore leave while others hauled loot and supplies to and from their respective ships. Horses and carts may be the accepted method of transporting goods in most civilised places, but the Pirate Isles were far from civilised and the people that lived there even less so.

Pirates were many things, Drake knew, but work– shy wasn't one of them. They were men and women who eschewed rigidly lawful societies in a bid to make something for themselves, and there was no better way to make something for oneself than by taking it from someone else. It was a work ethic Drake could agree with. The pirates of the isles were his people, and he'd make sure they all knew that soon enough.

Their entrance into the town proper, from the beach upon which the *Fortune* sat sad and silent, didn't go unnoticed. Drake had been the one to bring the dire news of Black Sands, the first major pirate town to be destroyed since the days of the old Captain Black and the Great Purge. Deun Burn had already cast doubt on Drake's legitimacy simply by suggesting that he may have had a hand in that destruction. Whether that accusation was true or not, the Riverlander would need to be turned or buried before he began speaking out against Drake. But the Oracle had been clear and crystal on the matter: Stillwater had to be recruited, and soon, before he joined the other side.

Drake felt himself growing warm and sticky under his clothing, but it would take more than hot weather and a lack of a breeze to remove him from his jacket and hat. Instead, he decided somewhere with a more indoors locale was in order, and preferably somewhere that served something wet and alcoholic. With those thoughts in mind he made for the Piper's Flock.

"Run off down to the docks, Princess. Find the *Hearth Fire* and let me know when you discover where its captain might be hiding."

Princess didn't change direction. "What if he's already having a drink?" the first mate said, pointing at the tavern.

"Then I reckon we'll be seeing you real soon." Drake dismissed the man with a wave towards the docks and continued on.

With a groan Princess turned and trudged off through the heat and dust towards the harbour. Drake spared the man a quick glance, but he couldn't be seen to care too much for a single disgruntled crewman, even if he did count Princess as a friend and ally.

"The more loyal the dog, the more it hurts when kicked," Arbiter Beck said smugly just as Drake reached the door to the tavern.

Taking his hand from the door, Drake turned to find Arbiter Beck taking off her hat and shaking out her golden blond hair, which reached down past her shoulders and made her skin glow in the bright light of the sun. Drake decided right then that there wasn't much he wouldn't pay to see Arbiter Beck naked, but that was a matter for another day.

"Cover your ears, Byron," Drake said to the giant, who looked either pleasantly uninterested, bemused, or possibly constipated; it was hard to tell, as the man's head seemed too small for his body and his features too large for his head. Despite his inscrutable expression, the big man took two meaty hands to his ears and covered them obediently, which made for a strange sight and no mistake.

"You might wanna be careful who ya go calling a dog, Arbiter," Drake said. "Some folk around here don't take too kind to such insults. Even folk as placid as my first mate can be a real terror when ireful. And you don't reward loyalty with laxity. Now, just what were you and he arguing about earlier, down on the beach? Looked fair intense."

"You said I should take all issues to Princess," Arbiter Beck said with a cold stare. "You were quite adamant on the matter, as I recall."

"Aye."

"Well, I've taken an issue to Princess, and if he knows what's good for him he'll soon start handling it."

Curiosity nagged at Drake, but he had enough matters to worry about and he trusted that Princess would acquiesce to the Arbiter's demands without giving away the ship. With a shrug he tapped the hulking Byron on his arm, and the giant uncovered his ears.

"Fancy a drink, Byron?" Drake said slowly.

Byron seemed to think about that for a moment, then looked up at the tavern. "Piper's Flock. One copper bit for an ale," he said quietly. "Two copper bits for rum. For five copper bits ya get a room an' a woman." The giant's mouth twitched up into what Drake could only assume was a smile. "Carol always calls me sweetie and pats my arm."

Drake winced. "Carol ain't here no more, Byron. Not since you… It's why you don't get to go anywhere on your own no more."

Something close to a frown pulled Byron's features into a strange mimic of the expression. "I like Carol."

"I know," Drake said. "Come on, let's get us a drink, eh? Just one for you though." With a friendly wink Drake took hold of the giant's arm and led him through the door.

Inside, the tavern was busy but not bursting. Pirates and residents of Sev'relain occupied the tables in equal numbers, and Drake spotted a few of his own crew wisely spending their shore leave in the company of alcoholic substances, some drunk, some spilled. Why folk felt the need to waste good drink by spilling it was something Drake would never understand. The mood of the tavern seemed merry despite the recent ominous news, and an energetic musician with a trio of pipes was quite loudly making his presence known. A cheer went up from Drake's boys when they spotted him, and the owner saw him only a moment later.

"He ain't allowed in here!" the tavern keep stated very firmly, hurrying over towards Drake and his strange procession.

"Aye, he is," Drake stated even more firmly. "He'll be quiet as a breeze. You won't even know he's here."

"I don't give half a shit how quiet he is. He…"

"Listen," Drake said cheerfully as he put one hand on the owner's shoulder and the other in front of his face. "We're all staying, Byron included. Now, here's one for the privilege." With a flick of his fingers a silver bit appeared in Drake's hand. "And two for the drinks." Another flick, another bit. The man's eyes went wide with greed.

"Quiet as a breeze?" he said as he reached for the coins.

"A particularly calm one at that," Drake cooed as he handed over the two silver bits. "Grog for me and all my crew, eh."

As the owner scuttled off, Drake waved over to the table where his crew were seated. "Pip, look after Byron. One drink and then you take him back to the ship."

If Pip harboured any ill will about being made sitter for the giant, he showed none of it but instead leapt up and swaggered over to take charge of Byron, leading him back to the table.

Drake selected a table of his own and sat down. Waiting patiently for his drink, he leaned backwards and placed his boots upon the table. Beck, thankfully not wearing her Arbiter's coat, sat down opposite Drake and shot him a curious look.

"You didn't bring him along to intimidate?" she said over the general din of the tavern, and Drake shrugged off the nagging feeling of her compulsion attempting to lock onto his will.

"Oh, Byron may be intimidating, but he's less than useless in any sort of altercation. No, I brought him 'cos if I don't get him off the ship from time to time he'll never leave. He ain't much one for social situations unless someone drags him. He enjoys himself a drink when he's out though. And the crew shine on him some."

Two mugs arrived and Drake took a deep swallow. He tasted rum heavily watered down by ale. It wasn't fine drinking, but it was close to the best Sev'relain had to offer, at least this side of town. Opposite him, Beck picked up her drink cautiously, sniffed at it, and with a shrug followed Drake's lead.

"What happened to Carol?" Beck said eventually, much to Drake's satisfaction. He'd wondered how long she'd be able to last before asking. The thing about people accustomed to hearing the truth from folk is that they're curious by nature. "Why didn't that man want Byron in here?"

"Ain't really his fault. Byron simply isn't all there." Drake tapped his head. "Never met anyone quite so good with numbers and what not, but..." Drake drummed the fingers of his right hand on the table. "Ain't really my place to say."

"Quit the false modesty, Morrass," Beck said with a snort that was out of place with her delicate features. "I'd bet you know everything that happens with your crew, and you consider it all your business as much as theirs. My guess is you just enjoy being able to withhold information from an Arbiter."

"I reckon it does more to darken your mood than it does to lighten mine," Drake said after another pull on the rum. "Byron doesn't fight. He keeps the books, watches the money, and stays below when there's trouble or piracy to be done. Far as I'm aware he's never picked up a weapon, nor swung a fist in anger.

"About a year back we were merrily docked here at Sev'relain. Couple of the boys took Byron for a few drinks under my orders. Carol was always nice to him but… well, Byron went outside for a piss and a few ticks later someone heard him scream. Folk rushed outside to find Carol's head a mite thinner than it used to be and Byron with the red of the crime all over his hands, shouting about the darkness having tried to take them both. No one could make any sense of it, and the townsfolk didn't take too kind to what was clearly murder."

"Pirates up in arms over a murder?" Beck asked with a grin that made her look cruel and callous.

"This ain't the lawless Wilds, Arbiter. We've got rules here. Laws, you might say if you were so inclined. A good old-fashioned beating is one thing, but murder…" Drake grimaced as he remembered the night. "They had the lad strung up by the time I arrived, crying, and without a clue as to what was happening or why. A lot of folk wanted him dead, folk that live here and pirates that don't, though I wager many of those just wanted to see a spectacle and didn't much care where it came from."

Beck shot Drake a disgusted look.

"Said we've got laws, didn't say we were civilised. Besides, you lot are known for burning folk alive – hanging ain't a touch on that for barbaric."

"There's a cleansing power in fire," Beck said defensively.

"Aye, no doubt. Bet it still hurts though, eh."

"You stopped them from hanging him?"

Drake grinned. "Either that or I brought him back from the dead."

"You care about your crew."

Drake's grin vanished. "Loyalty deserves loyalty, Arbiter."

The door to the tavern burst open and the music stopped. All eyes turned to see Princess standing there, casting about the place. He spotted Drake and started forwards, his mouth open to speak, just as the door burst open again.

The figure in the doorway now was shorter than Princess, but stockier, scruffily dressed with a round hat on his head and a shaggy main of straw-coloured hair. His eyes settled on Drake, and he started making his way towards him, pushing past Princess. From the corner of his eye Drake saw Beck's hand inch towards one of the pistols strapped to her jerkin; he held a placating hand to the Arbiter and stood to meet the man in the bowl-shaped hat.

"Drake," said the man.

"Poole," said Drake.

"Call me Daimen."

"No."

"Probably for the best – only me ma calls me Daimen. Bless her." Poole cracked a grin, showing a gap where one tooth was missing and the others were stained a dirty brown from the regular smoking of casher weed. He extended an open hand to Drake. "Good ta see ya again, mate. Who's the little lady?"

Drake took the man's hand and gave it a shake. "Newest member of my crew and steadfast protector of my back. Got enough folk thinking to put a knife there these days. What is it, Princess?" His first mate had been desperately attempting to get Drake's attention as the two captains greeted each other.

"Captain Barklow…" Princess started, stepping forward to stand next to Poole.

"You been stealin' work crews now, mate?" Poole interrupted.

Princess sent a quick glare at Poole before continuing. "Barklow is over at Herence's shipwrights right now, threatening to gut the man for pulling his crew from repairs on the *Hearth Fire*. Herence is throwing your name around everywhere, Cap'n, but it ain't coolin' Barklow down one drop."

"Bollocks," Drake spat and started for the door. "Lead the way, Princess. You coming, Poole?"

"Aye, mate. Wouldn't miss this one fer all the wet in all the seas."

Outside, Drake let Princess take the lead. He knew his way around Sev'relain for the most part, but the town was big for a pirate settlement, full of twisting alleyways, and new hovels could spring up or disappear overnight. It was a town with a constantly changing layout around a more permanent core, and it would be the seat of Drake's empire one day.

Despite the criminal nature of the Pirate Isles, thievery was uncommon. Honour among thieves was a good way to describe it. Folk didn't steal from folk who were likely to steal right back. It was a tense peace, but one observed almost everywhere. Instead, merchants, or those pretending to be, attempted to fleece drunken pirates out of their hard-earned bits by selling useless trinkets at extortionate prices or useful trinkets at even more extortionate prices.

"Might be I can offer a fair suggestion, Drake," said Poole as they followed Princess through the maze of roads and alleyways, "that could lead t'a better resolution o' your upcoming confrontation."

Treating the offer with the rightful scepticism it no doubt deserved, Drake nodded to his fellow captain to continue.

"Well, I know ya usual course would be ta go in there all scary and throw about ya big, fancy name and ya dark reputation an' all that, but I don't think that'll win ya any allies here and now."

"What makes you think I need or want allies?" Drake asked with a sideways glance.

"I ain't a fool, Drake. I can see which way the wind's blowing, an' I know well as any it's better ta let it take ya where it will rather than break ya ta its will."

Drake stopped. They were on their way through a narrow alley with high stone walls on either side. It was about as private a place as any they were likely to find in Sev'relain. "This your way of siding with me, Poole?"

Poole grinned. "*Mary's Virtue*'s been sided with ya for longer than you realise, Drake. Better the devil ya know than Tanner Black. I've been ta Sarth an' I've been ta Land's End; folk don't build that many ships 'less they plan ta use 'em."

"The Five Kingdoms are building a fleet?" Drake said quickly. "I thought it was just Sarth."

Poole shook his head. "Way I see it, they're either goin' ta war with each other, or us. Bad times are comin', mate, an' I don't much fancy Tanner as leadin' us through 'em. So if you're thinking o' stepping up, an' I reckon I know ya well enough ta see that ya are, I'm right here with ya."

Drake needed time to think and time to plan, and for that he needed privacy. He'd expected Sarth to come after them, but if the Five Kingdoms joined them in a purge of the Pirate Isles… There was simply no way the isles could stand up to that magnitude of pressure. Despite the whirlpool of thoughts and possible plots spinning through his head, Drake kept himself calm and decided to deal with the matter at hand first.

"Keep on, Princess," he said, effecting his usual self-satisfied grin. "Let's stop this Barklow from killing our shipwright, eh?"

The situation wasn't hard to find once they got closer. The shouting was drawing people in from all over Sev'relain, and by the looks of things some blood had already been spilled. Drake approached the edge of the crowd with his hand on his sabre and Poole, Beck, and Princess in tow. Despite the mounting threat of violence he was determined to fix the situation with diplomacy rather than his usual tactic of a healthy dose of threatening behaviour followed by sharp pointy objects inserted into the offending party.

There was the unmistakeable sound of fist hitting flesh, followed by a cry of pain. As Drake pushed through the last of the gathered crowd, the shipwright with the impossibly square jaw and one eye hit the dirt and rolled to a stop at his feet. The man's empty socket had swollen shut and his mouth was bloody. He clutched at his face as he stumbled to his feet and noticed Drake standing in front of him.

"Help," the shipwright slurred through a bloody mouth and broken teeth.

Facing Drake and his growing entourage were six men ranging from large to larger in stature, and one man dressed in what appeared to be the last remnants of some sort of naval uniform. His jacket was unbuttoned and faded and his pantaloons were stained from years of hard wear. He wore an impossibly large hat which bordered on the ridiculous, and at his side hung a sturdy-looking and well-used sabre. The other six were also wearing what looked to be the old, tattered remains of naval uniforms. They would no doubt jump to their captain's commands without hesitation.

"Give us the fool shipwright and crawl back to whatever tavern you stumbled out of, friend," said the biggest of the six sailors, a man with scruffy brown hair, a thin moustache, a shirt bulging with muscles, and the unmistakeable accent of the Five Kingdoms. He also had bloody knuckles, and most of it undoubtedly belonged to the shipwright who was even now cowering behind Drake.

"Hold there, Jerem," said the man with the giant hat as he stepped forward and put a hand on his companion's meaty arm. "I believe this may be the offending party. Fits the description. Are you Captain Drake Morrass?"

Drake tipped the front of his hat. "And you must be Captain Barklow. I'm afraid I haven't managed to catch your first name."

"Merridan. Merridan Barklow. And this is my bosun, Jerem Fields." If any of the other men under Barklow's command were put out by their lack of introduction they didn't show it. Drake did, however, notice that all of them were armed with a variety of threatening weaponry.

"Well, this here is my first mate, Princess, and it's possible you might already know Captain Poole," Drake said, purposefully not introducing Beck. "Now by the looks of things you appear to be having some form of disagreement with my friend... um..."

"Herence," said Princess.

"Herence." Drake spared the bleeding shipwright a glance. "How's about we talk that over somewhere a little more private?"

Captain Barklow laughed. "Lure us away so the rest of your crew can work us over until we submit? Not fucking likely, Morrass. I know the way you operate. *Everyone* here knows the way you operate. Only I'm not about to roll over and let you have everything your way. There's one captain here in Sev'relain with the stones to stand up to you yet."

A couple of folk nearby, passersby from the town most likely, gave a small cheer at Captain Barklow's words. Drake couldn't allow dissent among the people; he needed their support as much as the other captains'. They all needed to see him as their hero, not a villain.

"Actually, I was just going to suggest getting out of this damned heat, but if you like we can do this here. Why are you beating on my shipwright?"

Barklow glared at the assembled crowd before letting his gaze fall on Drake. "We paid for his time, paid for his service to fix the *Hearth Fire*, and he took our money, agreed to do the job. So what do I find earlier today but his men packing up and leaving my ship half fixed, the job half finished. I asked why, and what did this bilge water say but Drake fucking Morrass has acquired all the shipwrights in town to fix his ship first.

"So I asked him, politely of course, to tell this Drake Morrass to go bugger himself, because those men rightfully belong fixing my ship. The man says he can't do that. So I took it upon myself to educate him in proper etiquette."

Drake pulled an affronted expression. "I reckon there might have been some mistake, Captain. It appears he pulled his boys away from your fine ship before I had a chance to approach you myself. I have in fact been trying to find you since this morning to discuss just this matter." It was only half a lie.

"You have?"

"Aye. See, the *Fortune* has had a bit of bad luck of late..."

"Not so fortunate," said the giant bosun with a snigger. It was perhaps telling that no one else joined in, and so Drake ignored the interruption.

"In need of a few repairs here and there..."

"That doesn't mean you get to jump the line, Morrass," said Captain Barklow. "We were here first."

"Usually I'd agree, Captain, but these are exceptional circumstances. You might have heard about the fate of Black Sands." Many in the crowd started talking, or making protective signs in the air.

"Well, you see, the boat that did that – Five Kingdoms navy, I might add…" Another lie well worth telling.

"We left their ranks long ago," said Captain Barklow defensively.

"Deserters, is it?" Drake said with a grin. "And who could blame you? Ain't a more noble profession on the seas than piracy. But this ship, I believe it to still be in our waters, making ready to destroy another one of our towns. Well, my crew and I don't hold to that, and as soon as the *Fortune* is shipshape again we're gonna hunt the bastards down and make them pay for what they did and who they killed." It sounded heroic enough, even if Drake had no idea how to go about it.

A cheer ran through the crowd. Barklow narrowed his eyes at Drake.

"Now that being said, if you think your *Hearth Fire* is better equipped for the job then we'll hand over the task to yourselves."

"I, uh…"

"There's also the matter of compensation," Drake continued.

"What?"

"I'm well aware that pulling the men from work on your ship will delay your departure from Sev'relain, and that could well cost you some income."

"That's right," Captain Barklow said quickly.

"Which is why I was looking for you, Captain – to discuss compensation for that delay. Monetary compensation." Drake knew there was little that bought allies quite like the glint of gold.

"Uh, Captain…" Princess started, but Drake held up a hand to silence him.

"Well, I suppose that does sound fair," Barklow said slowly. "Assuming we can agree on an amount."

"Good. Then we're agreed. So how about we go find that place out of the sun, preferably somewhere with some liquid refreshment, and discuss what we both consider to be an agreeable figure."

The Phoenix

Keelin studied the chart, Yanic made a sour face, and Morley, the quartermaster, sucked in a whistling breath through his teeth. They were crowded around a barrel of salted beef in Quartermain's office, looking at what was claimed to be a chart of the seas around the Forgotten Empire. Quartermain stood nearby, attempting but failing to show little interest in the crew of *The Phoenix*.

Keelin scratched at the stubble on his chin, gestured at the chart, opened his mouth to speak, then shut it again and scratched at the stubble on his chin.

"Is that an island or an old stain?" Yanic asked of no one in particular, and received no particular answer.

"What about tis whole area here?" said Morley, pointing to a fairly obvious and significant hole in the parchment.

Keelin plucked a dagger from the corner of the parchment it was pinning down and thrust it through the centre of the chart.

"Hey!" shouted Quartermain. "You damage it, you pay for it."

Keelin turned a dark glare on the man. "You can take it out of the debt you owe me for setting me up with Elaina."

Yanic snorted. "Aye, Cap'n. Looked like ya hated every moment of that."

"That woman has ne'er been owt but trouble fer you, Captan," said Morley, his bright eyes flashing in his dark face. "Even before you were Captan."

"Hey." Keelin suddenly felt very defensive of both himself and, foolishly, Elaina. "She and me may have had some problems in the past but… that ain't even the issue right now. This chart is shit."

"You aren't gonna find a good chart of that region." Quartermain moved over to stand by his thick-headed son. "Problem is, only one fool is brave enough to go anywhere near that forsaken bit of land, and he ain't about to give up his charts."

"Who?" demanded Keelin.

"You know who." Keelin did know who, but he didn't want to

admit it. "That there is the best you're gonna get. Take it or leave it. Ten silver bits either way, due to your damaging of the merchandise."

"You were using it as scrap," Yanic said.

"Was not."

"There's an old shopping list on the back."

Quartermain coughed into his hand. "Surely just suggested supplies for any expedition to those lands, as recommended by the original cartographer."

"And tis little drawing?" Morley said, pointing to a section of the chart.

Quartermain walked forwards with his head held high and glanced at the chart. "Sea serpent. Clearly the cartographer's ship encountered one of the giant beasts and thought it best to note down the location as a way of warning for future perusers of the map just such as yourselves. No doubt you would want to avoid that particular location in case there might be a nest of the creatures."

Morley looked down at the chart again, then back up at Quartermain. "It is a crude drawing of a penis."

"Sea serpent."

"Penis."

"Enough," Keelin said in his best captain's voice. "We'll not be paying a bit for this chart, Quartermain, and I take it as an insult that you would attempt to sell it to us as legitimate."

"Suit yourself. I'll just take the ten bits out of your payment for the cargo I purchased from you."

Keelin advanced on the smaller man with violence a clear intention, but Quartermain stood his ground, wiping his sweaty forehead with his sleeve. Behind him, his son stepped forward with a thick wooden truncheon in one hand and a bell in the other. It would only take a moment for him to ring that bell, and then the odds would quickly fall in Quartermain's favour as workers from the back would rush to their employer's aid.

"I won't forget this, Quartermain," Keelin promised.

"I should hope you will not; it will prevent future misunderstandings. Now then, shall we settle accounts?"

Two hours later – along with enough bits to keep the crew in booze and pussy for a few days – and Keelin could honestly say he'd had more than enough of Fango and the whole damned Isle of Goats. He wasn't about to say his time with Elaina hadn't been enjoyable – though he was feeling more than a little sore in more than one area – but given the grief he was receiving from both Yanic and Morley and the undebatable trouble that always seemed to follow Elaina Black about, it was fair to say he was regretting having run into her at all.

After once again making his way through the jungle without being molested by the unnatural spirits that Keelin knew from personal experience dwelled there, they emerged into south port and were greeted by the unmistakeable stench of burnt octopus. A small group of sailors were cooking the unfortunate creature over a fire and periodically spitting alcohol onto its carcass, sending up plumes of flame. Quite what the creature had done to them to deserve such treatment was beyond Keelin, and the meat was long charred past edible, but he knew better than to get involved in the affairs of four foolish, drunken pirates.

The Phoenix was out in the bay, floating languidly in her anchorage, and she wasn't alone. Keelin counted a small sloop and two longboats, one making the trip from the sloop, and the other returning to shore from his own ship.

The harbour master was nearby, talking to a giant of a man whom Keelin recognised as the one who had paid him particular attention the day before, when they entered Fango. The big man wore sandals, loose-fitting shorts, and nothing but a strap across his chest, upon which a sword was fixed across his back. Keelin guessed him at easily seven feet tall, and his girth was equally impressive. A round belly did little to hide the man's obvious strength, and he sported arms as wide as most men's thighs. A black bandana tied his long, dark hair in place, and his beard was just as long and just as braided. Keelin would have put good money on the man being from north of the Five Kingdoms – no doubt a member of one of the ruthless, bloodthirsty tribes that haunted the mountains of that region. He decided to give the man, his two companions, and the harbour master a wide berth. Unfortunately it was at that moment that the harbour master turned, spotted Keelin, and pointed his way.

"Stillwater," shouted the giant in an accent that confirmed Keelin's suspicions about his origins.

"Aye?" Keelin shouted back in an accent that hid his similar origins. Keelin had, years ago, gone to great lengths to hide his natural accent. The fewer people that knew he came from the Five Kingdoms, the better.

The giant pushed away from a flimsy railing and started walking towards Keelin with both his companions in tow. The harbour master remained behind, watching eagerly through cruel eyes.

"Captain?" Yanic whispered from behind.

"Let's just see what he wants," Keelin replied quietly.

"What if he just takes a swing at ya?"

Keelin reassessed the size of the man swaggering towards him. "Then you get to be captain, Yan."

The giant stopped at a good ten paces and crossed his arms, giving Keelin the stare of a lifetime. There was a peculiar smell about him: sweat and, unless Keelin was very much mistaken, black powder. To have such a pungent stench of the stuff about the man, it was possible he bathed in it.

"Keelin Stillwater," the giant boomed in a deep voice, "captain of *The Phoenix*?"

"Aye," Keelin said hesitantly. "And you?"

"T'ruck Khan, captain of *North Wind*."

Keelin looked out into the bay and the only two ships occupying it. "The sloop?"

"Yes," said Captain Khan with a definite note of defiance in his voice.

"She looks like a fine little ship," Keelin said with a friendly smile.

"Little?"

Keelin coughed. "Well… yes."

A noise resembling a growl escaped from Captain Khan's lips and he narrowed his dark eyes. "They say you are the best, Captain Stillwater. The best fighter the Pirate Isles has to offer. I wish to challenge you."

Keelin laughed before realising the other captain was obviously not joking. He then realised his own hands were resting, as they often did, on the hilts of his twin cutlasses, and that seemed a dangerous place for them right then. He quickly held up his hands in what he hoped was a placating manner.

"Why? For calling your ship small?"

"To see which of us is the better."

"You can be better."

"Captan," Morley said with a tug on Keelin's arm.

"Look, friend," Keelin said, ignoring his quartermaster. "My life is plenty dangerous enough, what with pirating and knowing a great number of unsavoury folk. Last thing I want, or need, is to add duelling with giants to that list. If it makes you feel better, you can tell people we fought and you won."

"Captan!"

"What is it, Morley?"

"The boat. Coming from *The Phoenix*."

Keelin tore his eyes away from the giant wishing to cut him in half and focused on the longboat Morley was pointing at. The very same boat that had, until recently, been docked at his ship. What he saw made his blood both freeze and boil.

"Nice to meet you, Captain Khan," Keelin said in a voice like steel without even looking at the man. "Perhaps another time." With that he stormed off towards the longboat that was even now being secured to one of the smaller piers.

"What in the Hells were you doing aboard my ship?" Keelin shouted as Elaina Black gracefully leapt from longboat to pier.

"Your ship?" Elaina asked with a smile. "Interesting."

She was wearing clothing all as black as her name. Leather boots that ran up to her knees with silver buckles that had been polished to a shine. Tight trousers that did nothing to hide her hips and a low-cut top that did nothing to hide her cleavage, and a dark coat that was completely at odds with the heat of the time of year. Keelin had to admit that, while she did look enticing, she also looked every bit her father's daughter.

"Yes, Elaina, my ship…"

"Stolen fair and square, was she?"

Keelin resisted the urge to throw the woman into the water. Humiliating her like that would likely only make matters worse, though it would undoubtedly make him feel a lot better.

"Answer my damned question."

"Just sayin' hello to a few old friends while they were around, Stillwater. Ya may have… civilised the folk you stole along with the ship, at least to some degree, but many of 'em still remember the good ol' days."

"You stay the fuck away from my ship, and my crew, Elaina."

"Boundaries, is it, Stillwater?" she said, staring into his grey eyes with her sparkling blues. "And what if your crew don't stay away from me?"

Keelin opened his mouth to reply, despite having no idea what he would say, but was interrupted by a bird somewhere above letting out a screech that sent painful shivers down his spine.

A black-winged monstrosity swooped down behind Elaina and came to a perfect landing on her right shoulder. Keelin noticed her wince, though only for a moment, as the raven's talons gripped. The bird was larger than any other raven Keelin had ever seen. It had one black eye and one milky white one with a scar that ran through it and down the length of its razor-sharp beak. Again the creature let out a loud screech and focused it malicious gaze on Keelin.

Elaina let out a mocking laugh as Keelin turned and started towards his own longboat. "Better run, Stillwater," she shouted after him. "Looks like my da is home."

"Yanic, get back to Fango. Find any of the crew on shore leave and bring them back to the ship."

"They ain't gonna be happy 'bout that, Cap'n."

"I don't give a fuck if they're spitting fire. Anyone not aboard in two hours gets left, and they can take up their displeasure with Tanner."

"All aboard in two hours. Aye, Cap'n." Yanic ran off in the direction of the jungle.

"Morley," Keelin continued, "soon as we're under way I want to know who Elaina spoke to and what the fuck she said. Bloody woman is likely trying to steal the ship out from under me."

"Can't steal what's already hers, Captan," Morley said quietly.

Keelin glanced back at his quartermaster and shot him a dark look. "Not the time, Morley."

The Phoenix

Two days out from the isle of goats and neither Keelin nor any of his crew had spotted so much as a sail, let alone the distinctive dark-wood hull of *The Black Death*. Keelin had managed to escape his brief return to Fango without running into Tanner Black and with only minor injuries at the hands of the pirate's daughter, who had been relatively gentle considering their long estrangement.

The seas were calm, the wind was gusting, and the sky had barely a cloud in sight. It was perfect pirating weather if only they could find themselves some quarry, but as Keelin had ordered them not to stray into any shipping lanes, they were unlikely to find any.

For the first time in a long while Keelin found himself without a course. He was drifting, letting the wind and the sea take him where it would. He didn't like it. The charts Quartermain had sold him under duress were worthless – any sailor worth a pinch of salt could see that. Worse, the merchant had been truthful when he'd said only one man would have accurate charts of the waters around the Forgotten Empire, and that man was Drake Morrass.

Keelin had no problem with Drake for the most part, but he knew the man wouldn't give up the charts for nothing. Everybody knew Drake Morrass never did anything that wasn't in the best interests of Drake Morrass. That left Keelin with two options.

He could attempt to take the charts by force. Given that *The Phoenix* was no match for the *Fortune*, either in speed or crew compliment, that course seemed unwise. He could also try to trade for them, though he was fairly certain Drake would demand nothing less than Keelin's soul for the transaction. His only other option was to forget the whole affair and give up on the Forgotten Empire. Of course, the moment the crew heard about that decision would be the moment he'd have a mutiny on his hands. He'd promised his crew treasure, and they would demand nothing less.

From behind the spokes of the wheel, Keelin spotted Morley approaching. It felt good to take personal command of his ship for a period.

"Captan," Morley greeted him. "A word, if ya please."

Keelin passed control of the wheel back to his navigator and waved for Morley to follow as he went to his cabin. Some discussions were best held in private, and there were very few places truly private aboard a pirate ship.

The captain's cabin wasn't just his home; it was also Keelin's sanctuary to escape and distance himself from his crew. It was just one room, but he had sectioned it off into two areas. The first was his living quarters, containing a small cot for sleeping, a single low table with two cushioned chairs, and a large wardrobe. Regular washing in anything but salt water may be a luxury never afforded aboard his ship, but he'd be damned if he wasn't able to change into a clean set of clothing at will. The second area was for ship business, and it contained a small desk upon which he could look over charts, a secure cabinet in which he could keep those charts, and an entire wall dedicated to paraphernalia he'd collected over the years of his captaincy. Front and centre was the ship's original flag; she'd long ago been an Acanthian navy vessel flying a strip of green fields and a red sun.

"Drink?" Keelin said as he opened a drawer in his desk and pulled out a mostly empty bottle of rum and two clay cups. Many captains preferred to deck out their cabins with all sorts of finery, including glasses to serve their guests, but Keelin was generous with his crew's share of the loot and most of his spare bits went on clothing to fill his wardrobe.

Morley took the cup and threw back the rum, wincing at the taste. "One day, Captan, I will improve your taste in rum."

Keelin looked at the unlabelled bottle and shrugged. He didn't really have a taste for rum – one tended to taste the same as any other – but it was cheap and fiery and sometimes that was just what was needed.

"The crew?" Keelin said.

"Ain't happy, Captan," Morley said with a knowing nod of his dreadlocked head.

"Any in particular, or just as a whole?"

Morley shrugged. "Smithe is the ringleader, but he ain't alone,

Captan. Tempers be sizzling."

"What has them riled up?"

"Ain't just the one issue, Captan. Things been mounting for a while now."

"If you're being purposefully vague, Morley, please feel free to stop."

"Where to start, Captan? Not much of a shore leave for many or any this time round."

"Pressing need to be gone from Fango is at fault. I'll set a course right away and the men can drink and fuck themselves blind as soon as we reach land."

"Some of the crew take exception to the lack of *real* pirating. Your... predilection towards taking ships without bloodshed."

"The men want a fight?" Keelin interrupted.

Morley sucked at his bottom lip. "Some men never feel more alive than when they're taking another's."

"With every fight comes the risk of death. Peaceful encounters are safer."

Again Morley sucked on his bottom lip. "Some men never feel more alive than when they're risking theirs."

Keelin considered the man's suggestion for a moment before banging the table with his fist. "I am not Tanner Black. I will not slaughter innocent sailors who are willing to surrender. Any crew member not good with that can jump ship at the next port."

"Don't reckon it'll come to that, Captan."

"Good."

"Much more likely to come to mutiny."

Keelin paused with his clay cup in hand. "That isn't funny, Morley."

"Not entirely joking, Captan." Morley quickly glanced at the rum bottle, then away. "Men ain't much pleased what with you not delivering on the treasure."

"They get more of a share of the loot we take than the crew of any other ship out there."

"Aye, and that's good enough for the most, but not for the all. You promised them riches, Captan, and you ain't yet delivered."

"Not like I haven't been fucking trying. From the moment we heard about that bloody treasure I've been looking for a way to navigate the waters around the Forgotten Empire."

"I know, Captan."

"Problem is, there aren't any charts."

"I know, Captan."

"Everyone who goes anywhere near those shores never returns."

"I know, Captan."

"And the only damned ship, crew, and captain who could possibly help us getting to that treasure…"

"I know, Captan."

Keelin realised he was squeezing his little clay cup almost hard enough to break it, and forced himself to relax and put the vessel down. Morley was watching him with something approaching sympathy.

"He was last spotted at Black Sands as it burned back to the sand," Keelin said through a clenched jaw.

"Only one place he's like to be," Morley agreed with a solemn nod.

"You'd best make sure the crew feel bloody grateful for this, Morley." Keelin drew in a deep breath and let it out as sigh. "I'll plot a course for Sev'relain."

"Might be worth you talking to the men as well, Captan. Personal touch, ya might say."

Keelin glared at his troublesome quartermaster. "Fine. Gather them on deck. I'll be out soon."

By the time Keelin appeared from his cabin Morley had assembled the majority of the crew, and first and foremost in the crowd, making his displeasure obvious, was Smithe. The man was six feet of bronzed muscle, with a temperament like a forest fire and a mean streak most alley cats would envy. Keelin couldn't help but notice the man had a dagger thrust into his belt. Weapons were generally forbidden on deck unless there was a good reason.

"Finally he graces us with his presence," Smithe said with a smirk. "Only takes a visit from her who actually owns the ship, eh?" A couple of other pirates laughed their agreement. Keelin would have rid himself of the man long ago, but Smithe was well liked among the crew.

Keelin turned, climbed up onto the aft deck, and looked down upon his assembled crew. "Smithe," he said with a cold stare. "If you wouldn't mind. What is the nature of pirating?"

"Takin' stuff that ain't ours," the man said instantly.

"I'll let you think about that for a moment."

Resting his hands on his twin cutlasses and sweeping his gaze across all the crew, Keelin raised his voice. "So you had a visit from Captain Black, the pretty one, and then what? You decided your current captain ain't up to the task no more?" There were a couple of coughs, but even Smithe remained silent at the accusation, so Keelin continued. "Times are hard. Prey is scarce. But we're still pulling in the loot, aren't we? And if any man here can name another sailor on another boat taking as big a cut… well, I'll happily call them a liar."

"You promised us the haul of a lifetime," Smithe shouted. "Riches beyond imagine and…"

"Aye, I did," Keelin shouted back, interrupting the surly troublemaker. "And I almost have what I need to make good on that promise. But if you would prefer to sail into the waters of the Forgotten Empire without the guide of a chart, I think you might be on your own there, mate." Some of the crew laughed, and Smithe's expression grew darker.

"I ask for just a little more time," Keelin continued. "To make you all very rich men. For now we head to Port Sev'relain." There was a cheer from the crew. "But if anyone should spot a juicy prize on the way…" Keelin grinned and let the possibility hang in the air.

Fortune

"Beautiful," Drake said with a grin.

"There is a... grace about her that the other ships don't have," Beck agreed.

The one-eyed, square-jawed, badly bruised shipwright grunted his own agreement. "Ain't never seen another like her. Who designed her?"

Drake gave the shipwright a dangerous grin. "No one standing on this side of humanity."

"Eh?"

"Long ago I found myself shipless and very much needing of one," Drake said, stealing a glance at Arbiter Beck out of the corner of his eye. "Lucky for me there are things greater and more powerful than men in this world, and it just so happens I know how to find a few of them. Ever heard of the Kraken's Maw?"

"No," Beck said with a shake of her head that set her tail of blond hair stirring underneath her hat.

"It's a maelstrom," the shipwright said. "The biggest and strongest any man has ever seen." At a glare from Beck, he cleared his throat and added, "Or woman. Opens up once every ten years or so and always right underneath a ship. Takes it down into the depths. It ain't natural though – folk say that when it opens up you can see teeth down at the bottom of it. Some folk say it's caused by the biggest beasty the sea has to offer: a kraken so big it can eat other krakens whole."

Drake laughed. "Superstition for the most part, I assure you. The Kraken's Maw is something far more dangerous. It's the one and only gateway to the court of Rin."

The shipwright gasped and struggled from his chair. "Are you mad? You say *her* name standing on dry land?" The man pulled a bronze bit out of his pocket, spat upon it, and threw it as hard as he could into the ocean. "Quick," he urged. "An offering for her peace!"

Drake loved it when people played their parts, and right now the superstitious shipwright was playing his as well as any man could have. "Oh aye," he cooed. "For most folk you'd be right – saying *her* name with your feet planted on dry land would be to invite disaster. Why, she's been known to wipe entire islands off the charts. But me, see, I'm not most men. I'm one of her beloved. One of her chosen. The sea goddess, she smiles upon me. Said so herself when I met her."

Drake glanced at Beck. The Arbiter looked anything but impressed.

"Pirates believing in a capricious sea goddess. How quaint."

"You got yourself a walking, talking, living god, and you think to mock our beliefs?" Drake shook his head. "Might be you should put more stock in powers greater than yourself. There's things in this world, Arbiter, that would find great pleasure in corrupting and destroying one of Volmar's faithful. Might be our quaint beliefs are all that's keeping you safe."

Beck narrowed her eyes but didn't reply.

"You really met *her*?" the shipwright said.

"Aye."

"But nobody ever called to her court returns."

Drake shrugged. "There's at least one that has. Though can't say I was all the same when I came back."

The shipwright sagged back into his chair, a look one part astonishment to three parts awe on his face. "How?"

"Well, I found myself all sorts of stranded on an island, you see, needing of that ship I mentioned. So I built a raft, nothing but logs lashed together with coconut hair really, and I set out to summon the Maw. Made all the right offerings and said all the right words, and it opened up right beneath my little raft – just as you said, only without the teeth, I reckon. Waves taller than the tallest building man has ever built and waters rushing in every direction faster than a bird can fly, and down I went on my little raft into the depths." Drake paused and took a deep breath. "And that there is where I died."

"You died?" Beck said, her eyes narrowing.

Drake felt her compulsion brush against his will. "Aye," he said with a grin. "Can't exactly get to Rin's court without drowning. Waters closed in over my head and filled my lungs and the light went out. Next thing I know, my eyes are opening and there's the goddess herself, breathing air back into my lungs. Must've wretched up half the ocean before I found myself speaking again."

"What was she like?" said the shipwright, leaning eagerly forwards in his chair.

Drake gazed off into the ocean and smiled. "She was ever changing. One moment her skin would be driftwood and her hair seaweed, then she might seem to clear, like she was made of water itself. Or she would appear to be part of the coral throne she sat upon." He took a deep breath and let it out as a ragged sigh. "Only thing I can say for sure is she was beautiful no matter what form she took. Not human beauty though. Beautiful like the sea, eh.

"Turns out not many men seek her court willingly, so she was a drop curious as to why a man like myself might throw his self upon her mercy. So I told her. Said I needed a ship, one like no other. But deals aren't lightly struck with gods now, are they? I agreed to give her something no other man could." He paused and glanced at Beck; the woman was making a good show of feigning disinterest, but Drake could see she was listening intently. "Something no other person in this whole world of ours could give. And in return she gave me the *Fortune*. Fastest ship ever to call the seas its home."

"What did you give her?" the shipwright asked right on cue.

Drake smiled out at the ocean, well aware that both the shipwright and the Arbiter were watching him, waiting for him to answer. Eventually he turned and walked away, heading towards the town. After a few moments Arbiter Beck began to follow.

"How much of that story you just told is truth?" she called.

"How do you know any of it is?"

"The best lies are half truths," she said, struggling to keep up with Drake's longer stride in the sand. "Makes the shit easier to swallow. Folk of my profession learn to spot them pretty quick."

Drake nodded along. "I can honestly say, Arbiter, that there is more truth than not in that tale. I can also say that we suffer under a different set of gods out here on the sea, and you would do well to be more careful. Volmar won't be able to save you out there in the blue, but our quaint gods might just."

"Where are you going this time?" the Arbiter demanded as she quickened her pace to catch up with Drake.

"Why are you following me?" Drake shot back.

"Because I have to protect you."

"And what if I'm just going for a piss again? Didn't get a good enough look last time, eh? I know my cock is fairly impressive an' all, but a woman of your age and passing good looks, I reckon you've seen better and bigger. Just how old are you, anyways? I know you Arbiters tend to live a bit longer than us mere mortals."

"Old enough to know the difference between a man with purpose in his stride and one just wandering off for a piss. So where are you going?"

Drake stopped and grinned at the woman. "I do like it when you get all commanding." Beck didn't show a hint of a blush, and that just made Drake want her more. "Might be you happened to miss that ship on the horizon over there." He pointed and the Arbiter turned to look. Drake pounced on the opportunity to walk away, but she quickly turned and caught up with him again. "Reckon I might just go wait for their arrival."

The Phoenix

Port Sev'relain was exactly the sort of place Keelin liked. It wasn't one of those trading towns that claimed to be a free city, but neither did it belong to any sort of empire. It was a small town, though large in comparison to most pirate settlements, full of hard-working honest folk just trying to get by. Here people raised children, enjoyed their lives, and weren't subject to taxes or the rule of another person. That wasn't to say there weren't rules, but they were the rules of the people and any justice that needed handing out was also handed out by the people.

The buildings were small, ugly things mostly made from the trees that crowded the island. It seemed every island of any sort of habitable size in the Pirate Isles was swamped by tall green trees that threatened to label themselves as a jungle. It made clearing an area for a new settlement hard work, but it also had the benefit of providing handy building materials for both houses and ships. Not that many ships out on the water were built by the pirates that infested the isles – just stolen by them.

A one-legged man wielding a wooden crutch began hobbling along the pier towards *The Phoenix*'s dinghy as it was rowed into position and Morley leapt up to secure it to its berth. The one-legged man made good speed despite his affliction, and the small boy behind him carrying a large tome moved just as fast.

Keelin climbed out of the boat and signalled for the rest of his crew to wait. He'd brought just eight men ashore.

"Come on," said the one-legged harbour master. "Let's hear ya voice. My eyesight ain't no good no more, but unless you're another new one I reckon I'll know you by your voice."

Keelin smiled and briefly considered using a fake accent. "I'll pay you an extra copper bit for the berth if you get it right," he said.

The old harbour master snorted. "I'll accept no bribes from you or anyone else, Stillwater. Still *The Phoenix*, is it?"

"No other ship for me, old man."

"Old man? I have the good manners to remember your name," the harbour master snapped. "Damned least you can do is repay the favour."

"Uh…"

The harbour master spat into the bay. "Ask around. Loading or unloading?"

"Unloading," Keelin said, feeling a little embarrassed. "Just a little."

"Little or a lot, you all pay the same. How long a stay?"

"A few days."

The old man sighed. "Few is not a fucking number, lad. I thought captains had to know how to count."

Keelin heard a few of his crew laugh from the boat, and he turned and shot them a glare. "We'll say four days then."

"One gold bit," said the harbour master. "That's ten silver bits, in case you're still finding the counting hard. Some people use their fingers as aids."

Keelin decided the best course was to smile through the humiliation. "It was only eight silver bits last I was here. That's a two-silver markup."

"More pirates these days," the old man said, and he wasn't wrong. Keelin counted more ships than he'd seen in one place in the Pirate Isles for a long time. "Space is at a premium. And I'm charging you an extra bit for your attitude."

The old man waited, and the boy behind him carrying the tome watched Keelin. Clearly most captains would attempt to haggle. Keelin knew better than to waste his time. "Sounds reasonable," he lied as he pulled his purse from his belt and began counting bits.

The boy with the tome stepped forward and expertly opened the large book to a half-filled page. Keelin couldn't help but notice that his name and that of his ship were already scribbled on the bottom of the page with only the particulars, and the cost of his stay, left blank. He spilled ten silver bits onto the book, which promptly snapped shut. The boy took a hasty step backwards.

"I wonder, um, harbour master," Keelin said quickly as the man turned to walk away. "Has anyone from Sev'relain seen the *Fortune* recently."

The boy stepped forward again, and again opened the book. Keelin noticed the ten silver he'd previously deposited had already vanished. He dropped another bit onto the book, which again snapped shut.

"The *Fortune* is currently undergoing repairs on a beach just a short walk that way," the harbour master said with the briefest of nods as to the direction before turning away again.

Keelin considered asking after Drake Morrass specifically, but decided his purse had suffered more than enough for one day.

"Two boats, Morley," Keelin ordered without turning to look at his quartermaster. "Prioritise men that didn't get ashore at Fango."

"The cargo?"

"Can wait. I've got crew with bits burning holes in their pockets. Let the men have some fun first. Business can come later for once." His declaration was greeted by a cheer from the men that had accompanied him.

"And you, Captan?"

Keelin gave his quartermaster a brief grin. "I've got things to do."

She wasn't beautiful – Keelin knew – but there was something about her that drew him in like a fish on a line. He'd always been that way, and couldn't explain why. Things caught his attention, things most people would dismiss in an instant, but with Keelin he couldn't help but think about them.

Once, long ago, Keelin's brother, Derran, had noticed that their father's old cutlass had caught him in just such a way. Keelin was only six at the time, and Derran nine and much bigger, already allowed to train with swords. Together they broke into their father's armoury and Derran had taught Keelin the basics of fighting with a sword. They both caught the beating of a lifetime when their father found out. Beatings had been a staple of Keelin's childhood.

This woman wasn't the first to catch Keelin's attention. Long ago Elaina Black had been the object of his obsession. That particular infatuation had died the moment the cursed woman had revealed herself to be very much her father's daughter. Keelin suppressed a shudder as he remembered Elaina covered in red as if she'd bathed in blood, her eyes wide and a manic grin on her face.

A man with ruddy cheeks, from both drink and the obvious exertion of simply staying upright under such intoxication, bumped into Keelin's table. The man and his two friends laughed and made some joke about the table coming out of nowhere. Keelin did his best to ignore them and continued staring at the not-quite-beautiful woman.

"Now this here," said the drunk to his companions "is jus' the fuckin' thing we're... uh... we need."

Keelin glanced at him and then away.

"The table," said one of the drunken friends. "Seems yer all alone an' this table is better suited to three fine fellows like ourselves."

Paying the men a little more attention, Keelin decided they were most definitely pirates, but he couldn't name either their captain or their ship. "I'm impressed you can count so high," he said with a smile. "Reckon there's plenty of other tables in this little tavern. I suggest you find one."

"I found this one," the man said, placing both fists on the table and glaring at Keelin across the round stretch of wood.

This was the problem with pirates, Keelin had to admit; all they ever wanted to do was drink, fight, and fuck. And if they were deprived of drinking and fucking for any period of time, they tended to resort to the fighting. It dawned on Keelin that perhaps it would be a good idea to give his own crew a fight every now and then regardless of the inherent danger. At the thought of his crew, he looked around the tavern for backup. Of course, there was none. He'd gone ahead of all of his men precisely to be able to spy, in relative privacy, on the woman. In fact, looking around, he realised he knew no one currently drinking in the tavern, and that meant no one would be likely to come to his aid. He had only two options: stand his ground alone, or run away. Running away had never really been an option for Keelin.

Fixing a nasty grin to his face and slowly pushing to his feet, Keelin made a show of resting his hands on his twin cutlasses despite the fact that using them in a simple bar brawl would be something largely considered against the rules.

"I reckon you might have picked a fight with the wrong person," he said. The tavern seemed to go quiet, as though everyone inside sensed what was coming. "Keelin Stillwater." He finished by fixing the drunken man still leaning on the table with a stern stare.

"Never heard of ya," the man said with a shake of his head.

"Captain Keelin Stillwater," Keelin clarified, "of *The Phoenix*."

"Nope."

"Widely regarded as the best swordsman the Pirate Isles has to offer."

"Really?"

Keelin nodded slowly. "Really."

"Well, I don't know much about sword fighting," the drunk said, standing up to his full height and suddenly seeming a lot less drunk. "But I don't reckon you'll be drawin' those fancy stickers o' yours. 'Less ya want ta end up on the end of a rope." As he spoke, his two friends moved to flank him.

The thing about a setup, Keelin admitted to himself right there and then, was that they rarely felt like a setup until after the fact. And the thing about a fist fight, he knew from past experience, was that they were usually won by the man who struck first.

In one lightning-fast motion Keelin kicked the table towards the first man and, not waiting to see the result, launched himself at the man to his left, landing a punch squarely between his eyes. A howl of pain and a fair bit of blood later, and Keelin was fairly certain he'd just broken a nose. He spun around and ran at the third man who, it had to be said, was looking a little shocked by the sudden and unexpected outburst of violence. They connected and Keelin pushed the bald pirate backwards a few steps until they collided with a table and both went careening over the top of it, spilling cups everywhere and no doubt kicking a few bystanders on the way. The bald pirate hit the floor, and Keelin hit the bald pirate. Before either of them could recover, Keelin started raining punches down onto the man's unprotected face.

Strong hands grabbed hold of Keelin under his arms and pulled him back and off the bald pirate, and Keelin found himself flailing at nothing. A punch to the kidney later and he was gasping in pain and wishing very much that he could swap places with the bleeding man on the floor.

Shoving an elbow backwards, Keelin was rewarded with solid contact and a grunt. He shoved free of the hands holding him and spun around to confront his new assailants, almost tripping over the prone form of the bald pirate, who was now very much curled into a ball in an attempt to protect his vulnerables from a man and a woman who had decided to get in a good kicking.

Keelin saw the haymaker coming a moment too late and, despite his rushed attempt at a block, caught at least half the fast-travelling fist with his cheek. Despite the impressive force of the punch, Keelin took it well and recovered quickly enough to give his assailant the most violent kick to the shins he'd ever delivered. He followed it up with a thunderous punch to the face, which put the other man down. He was just about to congratulate himself and look for an escape route when a body slammed into him and Keelin found his world turned upside down.

Lying face down on the tavern floor with the solid weight of a body on top of him, Keelin looked around to see the unmistakeable random violence of a bar brawl in full swing. Multiple small skirmishes were taking place with odds that ranged from uneven to dire. The woman who had been Keelin's sole reason for ever coming into the tavern was well and truly gone.

He watched a giant of a man with Riverlands tattoos trading punches with another man who had arms hairier than most monkeys. A small woman wearing a red bandana picked up a chair and turned it to kindling across the giant's back. The giant turned and, with speed that belied his size, grabbed hold of the woman's neck with one hand. Keelin decided he might just lie there and play dead until it was all over; rejoining the brawl would likely be detrimental to his health. It was just as he reached that decision that his head was pushed forwards, connecting violently with the wooden floor.

The world first turned upside down, then became very bright before resolving into what could only be described as a painful blur. Keelin pawed uselessly at the floor in an attempt to move. Again his head collided with the wooden boards, and this time everything went a dark shade of black.

Keelin felt his body lift, dragged upright by his arms. He prised his eyes open just in time to see a painful blur hit him in the face and close them again. Something else hit him in the gut, then again and again. He tried to bend over and retch, but someone appeared to have a hold of his arms, so instead he just threw up right there. Painful bile tore at his throat and he heard someone swear and curse.

"Told ya it was our table," Keelin heard someone say as he sagged against the strong arms holding him. "Now we're gonna make you eat it."

A distant part of Keelin recognised he was in real trouble. He struggled, thrashing about wildly, but the person holding him had him tight and all he earned for his effort was another punch to the face.

"Put him there. No. Make him kneel."

Keelin's legs were kicked out from under him and he dropped onto his knees. He opened his eyes and saw the edge of a round table right in front of him. Someone pushed his face towards it and Keelin clenched his jaw, struggling as the edge was pressed harder and harder into his mouth. He heard a smash and his arms came free. In one smooth motion he twisted away from the man behind him, rolled onto his back, and kicked at the man, who already appeared to be teetering. The kick sent him well and truly over the edge into sprawling unconsciousness, and Keelin rolled back onto his front and started to scramble away.

"Stillwater?" someone said.

Keelin sprang from his hands and knees, turned, and drew both cutlasses, staring down his attackers with a fierce urge, to kill the first man to come close enough.

The brawl was starting to die down, with many of its participants unable or unwilling to carry on. No doubt the clean up would take the better part of a couple of days, given how much of a mess the tavern was in.

Facing Keelin stood three men he didn't recognise, but each one was sporting his own marks of involvement in the fight. The two men Keelin did recognise – the two who had been attempting to *feed* him the table – were down and out, and looking much the worse for wear.

"Do I..." Keelin slurred, and then proceeded to spit out a mouthful of blood, spittle, and bile. He ran his tongue around his mouth, wincing at the pain, but miraculously found no missing or loose teeth. "Do I know you?" he said around a rapidly swelling lip.

The lead man, a fellow of short stature but with the muscles of someone used to plenty of hard work, tucked his hands into his threadbare suede jacket. "Don't reckon so. Name's Pip."

Keelin nodded. "Well. Thank you." He gestured to the two men lying unconscious on the floor.

Pip laughed. He sounded good natured enough, but Keelin well knew looks, or sounds, could be deceiving where pirates were concerned. Or simply where *people* were concerned, if he was being brutally honest.

"Might be you don't wanna go throwing around ya thanks jus' yet," Pip continued. "Didn't exactly save ya out the goodness of our own hearts."

Keelin tightened his grip on his twin cutlasses. Pip noticed and held up his hands.

"Whoa there. You won't be needin' those. Just got a man who'll be wanting to talk to ya, is all."

Keelin narrowed his eyes. "Who?"

Pip grinned.

For a town, Port Sev'relain was small, but for a pirate town it was almost excessively large. Pip and his two friends led Keelin up the hill that gave way to the forest threatening the outskirts, waiting for the day it could reclaim the pirate-infested portion of the island. As they went, the buildings grew more and more sparse and more and more grand. Here was where the elite of Sev'relain resided, and the most elite of them all was the man who owned most of the island – Loke.

Pip led Keelin past the walled and gated residence of Sev'relain's master. Keelin snatched a glance through the gates and saw green gardens and stone buildings complete with brutish-looking guards who appeared to be armed with the very latest in ranged warfare – rifles. Clearly Loke was rich enough to afford not only luxurious living, but also luxurious protection.

"Just in there, mate," Pip said with a slap on Keelin's back as he turned to leave.

"Not coming in?"

The pirate didn't even turn around. "I fancy continuin' my shore leave, an' they don't much like my kind in there. You'll feel right at home."

Keelin eyed the building in front of him. It was a tall stone structure that boasted none of the obvious merriment of most pirate taverns. In fact, the only indication that it was one was the sign hanging outside that showed a picture of a man with his head through a noose and the words "Never Again". It seemed the elite of the Pirate Isles had their own tavern and, for the very first time in all his years of pirating, Keelin was invited.

It was gloomy inside, with dim lighting – and little of it – that cast the whole room into shifting shadows. A suspicious-looking bartender was sitting by a selection of side-stacked barrels; he looked up from a book as Keelin entered, and quickly pointed to the other side of the room. Keelin followed the gesture and found just the man he was looking for sitting with his boots up on a table.

With a smile that hurt every one of his cuts and bruises, Keelin wandered over to Drake Morrass' table. He was sitting with a woman whose back was to Keelin, but her hair was clearly visible from underneath her hat and it was a stunning shade of blond, almost golden. Keelin would have put good money on the woman being from Sarth.

Drake looked up as Keelin approached and smiled, a single golden tooth glinting in the lamplight. "Quite a shiner you're sporting there, Stillwater."

Keelin touched a hand to the right side of his face; it was tender and swollen and he was certain his eye would soon be black. "Seems I owe you a debt, Drake," he said, pulling a chair from underneath the table and sitting without being asked.

"You do?" Drake had to take his feet off the table to keep Keelin in view. The woman watched through cold blue eyes, and Keelin noticed she was armed with more pistols than anyone could hope to use at once.

"Your men pulled me out of the fight just before I lost a set of teeth," Keelin admitted. "And I happen to be fairly fond of my teeth."

"They are very white," Drake said before raising his voice. "Yron,

Stillwater's buying the next round."

The bartender looked up from his book. "Something from the top row?"

"I reckon so." Drake grinned as the bartender stood and started pulling three mugs from one of the top casks.

"More expensive than the bottom row?" Keelin said.

"You better believe."

"So we're done? Debt repaid?"

"My boys save your life and you think a single drink will cover it?" Drake slowly shook his head. "Is that all your life is worth?"

Haggling was just another form of stealing, and never more so than when it was over a debt. Keelin wondered if he could somehow gain a copy of Drake's charts out of whatever deal they were about to strike.

"Who's the woman?" Keelin asked with a sideways glance.

"Crew," said Drake.

"Not many folk sail with women on the crew. Last I heard you weren't one of the few."

"Times change," Drake said as the bartender arrived with three mugs of something that looked and smelled suspiciously like beer. "She watches my back, makes certain it doesn't get stabbed."

The bartender cleared his throat. "One gold bit," he said pointedly to Keelin.

"Eh?" Keelin exclaimed rather pointedly. "For three drinks? Not unless it came from Pelsing's golden tits."

"Four drinks, actually," Drake said with an easy smile. "Custom is for Yron to get one of what everyone else orders."

"Cheap way to get drunk." Keelin still didn't reach for his purse.

"Actually, I think he just takes the money. I suggest you pay up, Stillwater. Folk who skip out on Yron without paying don't tend to make it out of Sev'relain. Unmarked graves somewhere out in the forest, or so I hear."

The bartender let slip a dirty grin to reinforce Drake's point, and Keelin took the hint, though not without comment. "Fucking robbery, this."

The bartender snatched the coin from Keelin's fingers and snorted.

"And I suppose the folk on the ships you catch willingly hand over their goods."

Drake chuckled. "Folk'll willingly do just about anything at the point of a sword."

"Doesn't taste like it came from anyone's tits I've ever known, golden or otherwise," said the woman, having already drained half her mug.

Drake turned his attention to her and grinned. She kept her gaze firmly on the mug, taking another swig.

"Word has it you burned Black Sands," Keelin said, deciding to try to put Drake on the back foot.

"Whose word?" The captain snapped his attention back to Keelin with a look like fire and thunder mixed into one.

Keelin shrugged.

"Don't be coy with me, Stillwater. There are some slurs to my reputation I will *not* abide, and credit for that massacre is very much one of them."

Keelin hadn't believed for a moment that Drake was behind the burning of Black Sands, and his current state of agitation only proved it. "Don't know whose word. Heard it said in Fango though."

"Tanner." Drake looked like he was about to spit on the floor, but one glance towards the bartender and he seemed to decide otherwise. "There's gonna come a time that old bastard is gonna need dealing with.

"I was there, that much is true. Sailed in just in time to see a few folk all afire trying to save themselves in the sea. Not quite in time to help them though. Sent a few boys ashore to look for survivors, but they didn't find none. They did catch a glimpse of the fuckers that did it. Man of War flying the pretty colours of Sarth."

Keelin glanced at the woman, wondering if there was a connection. "Very convincing," he said. "I'm convinced."

"I'm glad you feel that way, mate. Reckon I'll be calling in that debt now."

"Huh?"

"My crew saved you from… eating a table, was it? Reckon that constitutes saving your miserable life, no?"

"It may not have been fatal." Keelin had the sudden feeling that he was a very small fish in a very large net.

"Well, either way, when you walked in you said you owed me a debt. I'm cashing in that one right now."

"What for?"

"Your help, Captain Stillwater, in saving this town, the Pirate Isles, and every thief, beggar, and bastard that lives here."

Keelin tried to hold it in, but it was too much for him to take and the laughter escaped as a very pointed snigger. The very idea of Captain Drake Morrass wanting to save anybody, let alone the entire Pirate Isles, was almost certainly the last thing Keelin had expected to hear. Unfortunately, as both Drake and his female companion remained stony-faced, it quickly became clear the man wasn't joking.

"Save them from whom?" Keelin said, still laughing. "Themselves? Come on, Drake, you've been doing this for longer than I have. Black Sands ain't the first town burned to the ground and it ain't gonna be the last. That bloody God Emperor of Sarth has to look like he's doing something about all the piracy. So they found and burned a town – two more will spring up in its place within a year."

Drake was shaking his head. "Not this time. It ain't just Sarth coming for us. That new king of the Five Kingdoms is building himself warships. Ain't no need to do that unless he's planning on using them."

"Maybe he's thinking of attacking Sarth?" Keelin suggested, though he already knew that would never happen. The Five Kingdoms and Sarth were far too closely allied.

Drake snorted. "You looked out in the port when you sailed in? Or, not just this port, any of them. What do ya notice?"

Keelin shrugged. "Ships? Water? Can I have a hint?"

"Ships," Drake said in a tone that suggested he was deadly serious. "And a fuck load of them. Or maybe you and yours gone hunting of late only to find another crew has already taken the boat?"

Keelin nodded slowly. "That has happened once."

"There's too many of us," Drake said, banging the table to emphasise his point. "More than ever. More, even, than in Black's evil fucking reign. And what did Sarth and the Five Kingdoms do when the old Black was around?"

"Built ships, sailed in, and murdered everybody they could find," Keelin agreed. "But one town doesn't make this a purge, Drake, and I'm not about to tie my ship to yours." Keelin drained his mug, stood up, and turned to go.

"Why not?"

Maybe it was the beating he'd only recently taken and the subsequent aches and pains, or maybe it was the daylight robbery that the bartender had just submitted him to, but Keelin was feeling particularly angry and more than willing to tell Drake the cold, hard truth.

"Because you're Drake fucking Morrass," he said with more venom than the average sea snake bite. "You really think I'd believe that 'save the Pirate Isles' shit?" Keelin let out a bitter laugh and shook his head. "I don't. I don't believe you. I don't trust you and no one else does either. I'll admit, I don't believe you burned Black Sands yourself, but others will. They'll believe it because they know you're capable of it, same as Tanner Black is, only he started the rumour mill first instead of trying to peddle some shit about Sarth starting a new purge."

"Careful, Stillwater," Drake said behind flashing green eyes.

"Problem is, Drake," Keelin continued, knowing somewhere deep down that he should stop but wanting to drive the point home and hurt someone, "everybody knows that you're only out for yourself, that Drake Morrass never does anything that doesn't benefit Drake Morrass." With that Keelin turned and stormed towards the door. He heard the scrape and crash of a chair hitting the floor but ignored it, hoping he wasn't about to get a bullet in the back from the Sarth woman in the hat. He made it outside before Drake caught up to him.

"How dare you question my motives, you pretend bloody pirate."

They were out in the dust with the tavern and a couple of large houses nearby, the trees of the forest looming overhead, and the vista of Port Sev'relain spreading out below them. There was nobody around to witness the altercation and nobody around to stop any blood being spilled. Drake was close, staring right at Keelin, but his hands didn't stray near the sword attached to his belt. His companion was loitering in the doorway, leaning against the frame, her hands hovering close to the pistols attached to her jerkin.

Keelin decided there was no point in backing down now. "I'll stop questioning your motives just as soon as you tell me what they really are. You say you want my help. To do what? 'Cos it sure as shit ain't saving folk you don't care one drop about, Drake. What do you get out of helping these people?"

Drake looked torn between throwing a punch at Keelin and throwing two punches at him, but to the man's credit, he kept control. "You self-righteous little shit. If I didn't need your help I'd happily put a sword in you. Just my fucking luck, and yours as it happens, that I do need you.

"'Course my intentions ain't wholly pure – no one's are. Greed rules us all, mate. You think because you sail around on that ship of yours and offer – nay – urge folk to surrender so you don't gotta fight – you think that makes you a good man? You're a pirate. You rob people. You kill people. Or am I missing something? Do you then give all your loot away to folk more deserving and less financially acclimated?"

Drake's accusation hit home, but Keelin wasn't about to let that show. He kept his face stony, neutral.

"It's all about greed, Stillwater. Whether the gain is money, power, fame, or even the freedom that being a pirate offers. Fact is, we're all in this game because we want something for ourselves. So yeah, what I'm proposing does in fact benefit Drake fucking Morrass. Doesn't mean I'm not also trying to save these people and the isles."

Keelin wasn't even sure what the man was proposing just yet, but there was something more important he needed to know first. "And just how do you benefit from your plan?"

Drake smiled, one golden tooth glinting in the fading light. "I intend…"

Boom!

The Phoenix

Yanic opened his eyes to dim afternoon sunlight and dark thunderous clouds. The world sounded muted and painful, and he was so tired. His body seemed to agree, so he closed his eyes and let sleep claim him.

Something hard hit him in the arm and he heard shouting, close and far away at the same time. He tried to roll over in his bunk, but the pain got worse so he lay back down. He coughed, and almost gagged on something bitter and metallic.

His bunk felt harder than usual, and that took some doing. A first mate might get his own cabin, but that cabin was small and his cot was packed straw, tough and lumpy. Something shook him, and the pain flashed through his body like lightning.

"Fucking shtop it," he slurred. His voice sounded so far away, which seemed strange. With great effort he opened his eyes to see the blue sky, dim light, thunderous clouds, and the face of a pretty young man who barely looked old enough to grow hair on his stones.

It took a moment for Yanic's mind to realise everything wasn't right. "What's goin' on, Feather?" he mumbled up at the pretty young sailor.

"Ship exploded, Yan," Feather said, his voice so distant.

"*What?*" Yanic sat bolt upright. The world took a turn for the worse and his vision decided it couldn't keep up. Next thing Yanic knew, he was curled up in a ball, retching up his most recent meal, and his entire left side felt as though it were on fire.

"Yan? *Yan?*" Feather's voice was starting to sound a little less muted now, but it was high pitched and urgent.

Yanic opened his eyes again to see a puddle of vomit and blood on the wooden decking. Something about that seemed more than a little worrying, but he didn't have time to sort it out. "*The Phoenix?*"

"Still floating," Feather said. "But *Cold Rain* is gone. Just… gone."

Now the world was coming back into focus, Yanic could hear voices crying and shouting in panic. Boots thumping along decking.

Something that sounded a lot like fire. He looked down at his left arm to find it covered in red and, by the feel of things, most of it was his.

"Bollocks. That don't look too good." He rolled onto his arse and realised for the first time that the thunderous black clouds were actually thunderous black smoke.

"What do we do, Yan?" Feather said, shaking him by the shoulders.

Yanic felt his eyelids growing heavy and shook his head to clear the cobwebs. "Get everyone back on board. Find the captain."

"Aye," Feather agreed, sounding a little more confidant now he had orders. "Aye. Will do. What about you?"

Yanic lowered himself down onto his back, ignoring the searing pain in his left side. "Reckon I might just have a little nap."

A deafening thunderclap rolled over them, cutting Drake off and stunning them all. Keelin shook his head in an attempt to clear the ringing in his ears, but to no avail. Drake looked similarly bemused by the sudden noise.

"Look," the Sarth woman in the hat said, pointing down towards the town of Sev'relain. "The bay."

A great plume of black smoke had appeared off the shore, and it looked like there was burning debris on the water. The distant sound of a scream echoed up out of the town.

"Was that a ship?" Keelin asked, not really expecting anyone to answer.

"Magic?" Drake said.

"Worse," she replied. "That is a black powder explosion."

"How can you tell?" Keelin was struggling to contain the creeping sense of panic descending upon him. "And how is that worse? And how much black powder does it take to do that?" He pointed at the plume of black smoke out in the bay.

The woman didn't appear to be listening to him. Her head was cocked towards the nearby forest, and she was muttering something to herself.

"What in the Hells is she doing now?" Keelin demanded of Drake.

There were people emerging from the nearby houses, staring

towards the bay, including some of the armed guards from Loke's personal estate. Most were wearing expressions tending towards the panic Keelin was suppressing.

"There are men moving through the forest," the woman said eventually. "By the sound of it they're wearing armour."

"Sarth?" Drake said in a harsh voice little more than a whisper.

The woman shrugged. "They're close."

Keelin decided sometimes it was best to give in to the panic. "I have to get back to my ship."

"Aye," Drake agreed as he backed away from the trees. "Folk'll be occupied with the explosion, and nobody comes into town armed anyways. This'll be another massacre."

One of the guards from Loke's estate, a bald man with a perfectly groomed moustache, trotted over to them. "What's going on?" he said.

"Sarth is attacking." If Drake was at all surprised by events he certainly wasn't showing it.

"Shit."

"Fair sums it up. Stillwater, you with us?"

Keelin felt someone grab hold of his arm, and he was turned to face Drake. "I need to get back to my ship," he said.

"How's your hold, Captain Stillwater?" Drake said. "Is it empty."

"Bits and pieces," Keelin said, coming round a little. "Barely worth selling."

"Dump it. Get to your ship, and take on board as many of the townsfolk as you can."

"What?"

A man emerged from the tree line. He was wearing the blue-black uniform of a Sarth soldier with a shiny cuirass over the top, and he was carrying a shield and a longsword. He shouted something behind him when he saw the four people staring his way.

There was a loud bang, and the soldier staggered backwards and collapsed. Drake's companion holstered one pistol and drew another.

"Get back to your ship, Stillwater," Drake shouted. "And take as many folk as you can with you. Anyone left on this island is going to die!" With that, Drake gave Keelin a hard shove in the direction of

Sev'relain. Keelin took the hint and broke into a run just as he heard more shouts from behind. He didn't bother turning to see if anyone was following him.

By the time Keelin reached the docks it felt like half the folk of Sev'relain were at his back. He and the bald guard from Loke's estate hadn't been quiet about the issue of the attack, and while many folk had dismissed the crazed men running through the streets shouting bloody murder, just as many others had heeded the warning. Word of the massacre at Black Sands had left everybody on edge, and some folk, it appeared, had already packed their belongings ready for flight. Those same folk would meet a rude awakening if they tried to take any of their crap with them on Keelin's ship.

He had, at some point during his mad run to the docks, decided Drake was right about one thing, if nothing else. The people of Sev'relain would be murdered to every man, woman, and child if they didn't escape the island. There was simply no way any of them could stand up to a determined force of soldiers from Sarth.

As Keelin's boots hit the wood of the pier he stopped to take in the chaos that was unfolding before him. One ship was a mess of burning debris out in the bay, and by the looks of things it had taken a pier with it. Bloodied bodies had been dragged up out of the surf and now lay upon the beach, draining red back into the lapping waves. Some looked still alive, but just as many looked just as dead. One corpse was missing both legs and an arm; the sight made him sick to his stomach.

Folk were crowding the remaining piers and shouting at the pirates manning the dinghies. Some of those shouts were pleas, some threats, some bribes, and some were simply people begging for their lives. It was hard for even the stoniest of pirate hearts not to be moved by a woman with three young daughters begging for men to ferry them to safety.

Keelin spotted a couple of dinghies in the custody of his own crew, and they didn't appear to be letting anyone on board. They were moored dangerously close to the smouldering wreckage that had, until very recently, been a ship.

"Cap'n?" Keelin spotted the owner of the voice, and pushed through a few people to find Feather looking paler than the ghost fish that haunted the shores of Brie Isle at night. The lad was barely more than a boy, but in that moment he was looking all his years and a dozen more besides.

"Yanic sent me ta find you, Cap'n," Feather shouted over the crowd.

"What do we do?" cried one of the folk who had followed Keelin from Sev'relain.

"We need to get on a ship," shouted another.

"Quiet!" Keelin roared in his best captain's voice. There were times when a bit of stern discipline was needed, and this seemed like one of them. Blind panic would likely get them nowhere but drinking seawater at this point. Some of the folk moved off to find other boats, though most stayed behind and let Keelin speak. "Where's Yanic?"

Feather pointed towards one of the piers, but Keelin couldn't see through the crowd of people. "He's hurt bad, Cap'n."

"Shit. Get to the boats, Feather. Tell the boys to start letting folk on but not so many it'll sink 'em, and nobody that's causing a panic. We're taking people on board *The Phoenix*."

"Aye, Cap'n," Feather shouted, and darted away. The lad always seemed to be calmer with orders.

"Captain Stillwater," the bald guard from Loke's estate said calmly. He was red in the cheeks from his run through Sev'relain but seemed no worse for it. "I think I can be of use to you."

Keelin appraised the man quickly. He was tall and wiry and looked like he knew his way around a fight, but kept himself well groomed. "What's your name?"

"Kebble Salt."

"You know how to sail?"

"I'm a quick learner."

"You know how to use that thing?" Keelin gestured at the rifle slung over Kebble's shoulder.

"Better than any man alive."

"We'll see. Follow me and you'll get a seat." That prompted a chorus of similar claims from the folk surrounding them. Keelin ignored them all. He started pushing through the crowd towards his crew and his longboats.

Halfway along the pier Keelin found his first mate. Yanic left a bloody mess of a body, trampled and kicked and pushed to the side of the decking. His corpse had got tangled with one of the support posts and he lay half in the water. Keelin stopped and stared down at the thing that had been his oldest and closest friend. Yanic's left side was riddled with wooden splinters and deep cuts, and he looked as though he was wearing more blood on the outside than in. His face had obviously been kicked by folk trying to get along the pier, and white skull was showing through the skin in more than one place.

Keelin felt the world recede around him. He stood still and silent in the chaos as people jostled against his back to get past.

Drawing in a deep breath and letting it out in a slow sigh, Keelin closed his eyes. He drew in another breath.

"*Anyone* still between me and my boats when I turn around gets to die!" It wasn't the most poetic of threats, but he delivered it with enough volume to drive his point home.

When he opened his eyes and turned around, he found the people on the pier had crowded to the sides to create a narrow channel down the middle of the already cramped walkway. Some folk had suffered for the threat and were now taking a dip in the warm waters of the bay. A few stragglers still loitered in the newly created path, so Kebble Salt moved along in front of Keelin to shove them out of the way. Keelin, his face a grim mask of anger, stormed along the pier to his crew and his boats.

The members of Keelin's crew manning the nearest boat waited quietly while he leapt down from the pier. Even Smithe seemed to think better than to comment. Kebble Salt followed Keelin into the boat, bringing the complement up to sixteen. The boats could hold twenty at a squeeze, and eight of those were required on the oars. They would ferry as many of the townsfolk as they could out to *The Phoenix*, but there simply wasn't enough space to save them all.

"Twenty people per boat," Keelin said loudly to the waiting crowd. He looked back towards the town. Much of it was now on fire, and the screams of the dying made it an eerie picture. "Anyone pushing gets left behind. Anyone refusing to dump their belongings gets left behind.

Anyone so much as argues with a member of my crew, they get left behind. We'll send back as many boats as we can, but we ain't got time to ferry you all – so any can swim, I suggest you jump in and start paddling." He pointed towards *The Phoenix*. "That there is my boat and your salvation. It ain't big enough for you all, but we'll take on as many as we can."

"Is it Sarth?" a woman shouted from the crowd. "Drake said they'd be coming."

"Aye." Keelin nodded. "It's Sarth." He turned to his crew in the longboat. "Push off and put your backs to it."

As the boat pushed away from the pier, Keelin witnessed many of those gathered surge forwards towards *The Phoenix*'s second boat. Some of the rest took his suggestion to heart and dove into the water to swim to his ship.

"Can't save them all. Can't feed them all," Smithe said as he and the other seven pirates started rowing. Keelin hated to admit it, but the man was right about that. *The Phoenix* had limited supplies, and taking on a bunch of refugees was going to drain them quickly. They'd need to find another port soon, and he doubted he'd receive a warm welcome back at Fango.

"What the fuck is happenin', Captan?" Morley said before Keelin's boots had even hit the deck.

Keelin leapt over the port side railing and stepped away for the others to follow him up. "Sarth is attacking…"

"Did they attack your face?" Morley interrupted.

"No. This was… uh… something else. We're taking on people, as many as can make it. As many as we can fit. Anything not edible or sharp enough to kill a man goes over the side."

"You want us to dump the loot?" asked one of the nearby pirates. Keelin found himself with quite an audience, and it was growing every moment as more of his crew came to find out what was happening.

"Yes. To make room for those coming aboard."

There was a grumble from a few of those gathered, but it was Smithe who spoke up as he finished the climb. "That there's our earnings," the man all but spat. "Ain't right to throw it overboard. Ain't your choice neither."

Keelin rounded on the man, lamenting the fact that Smithe was a couple of inches taller than him. "Long as this is my ship, it *is* my choice, and I just made it. Good?"

Smithe stared back, and Keelin could see true anger in the man's eyes. "No."

The boat below had emptied now, and pirates and townsfolk alike stood on deck watching the confrontation.

"Then it's a good job your opinion doesn't mean shit, Smithe," Keelin replied in a voice as dark and dangerous as a thundercloud. "The captain of this ship just gave an order. If you don't like it, you can always head back to Sev'relain and find yourself another boat. I don't have time for your shit right now."

Keelin turned to his gathered crew. "Get the ship ready to sail. Soon as the *Fortune* leaves, we're following her."

Morley stayed behind as some pirates jumped to their duties and others showed townsfolk to the hold. "Drake Morrass?" he said.

"Temporary arrangement," Keelin assured him. "Yanic's dead."

"What?" Morley's expression was caught between anger and sorrow. "How?"

"You saw that ship explode? He was a little too close when it went up. That makes you first mate now, Morley."

"Aye."

"We gonna need a new quartermaster," Smithe said, still lingering nearby.

Keelin shot the man a glare. "Aye. It can wait though. Right now we need to get ready to leave. Sev'relain doesn't have long left and I don't want to be here when Sarth sails round from the other side of the island."

There were people in the water, boats in the water, hastily rigged-together rafts in the water, and all were heading towards *The Phoenix* or the *Fortune*. Keelin couldn't tell if Drake had made it back to his ship, but they appeared to be taking on townsfolk all the same. Much of Sev'relain was on fire now. As the afternoon light waned it became more and more apparent that the invaders intended to torch the whole town. Ash and smoke drifted into the sky, and the sounds of fighting were all but lost among the sounds of people dying.

The second longboat bumped against the hull, and Keelin's crew set about helping people up onto the deck. Some of those in the water, the stronger swimmers, were arriving too. Before long the ship would be full of those who had no home and no use aboard a pirate boat.

Keelin was just about to order the first dinghy back to pick up more townsfolk when soldiers appeared on the docks. There was little in the way of resistance, and they showed no mercy, sparing neither man, woman, nor child. Keelin was more than acquainted with the sight of death, but he felt a little sick to his stomach as he watched the massacre unfold on the beach and piers.

A few enterprising soldiers pulled out bows and began arcing arrows out onto the water. They were too far away to pose any threat to *The Phoenix*, but the men found their range and one of the boats heading Keelin's way took a couple of shafts. Fresh screams drifted out over the water.

"Poor bastards are little more than target practice," Keelin said, more to himself than anyone within earshot.

"I can help there," Kebble Salt said from nearby. The man unshouldered his rifle and pointed it towards the beach. There was a flash of light and a noise like thunder, and one of the soldiers was thrown to the ground. He lay there, writhing.

"Wind is coming in from the east," Kebble said as he brought his rifle down and started reloading. "Only winged him."

Keelin plucked his monoscope from his belt and looked down towards the three soldiers with their bows. One was on the sand, struggling to crawl away, but the other two were still loosing arrows into the water. Keelin heard another bang from Kebble's rifle and another of the soldiers dropped, but this one didn't move after he hit the sand. The third soldier took note of his two fallen comrades and fled.

"Impressive," Keelin said.

"Thank you." Kebble was already reloading his rifle.

"Keep an eye on the beach. Cover those poor bastards as best you can."

"Aye."

Another boat bumped against the hull of the ship; more and more people were arriving. Keelin's crew were doing their best to get as many of them up on deck as possible. There were still some folk jumping into the water from the piers back in Sev'relain, but the Sarth soldiers were busy murdering by the hundreds and no more boats would make it off the beach.

Only *The Phoenix* and the *Fortune* were left in the bay. The other ships – and Keelin remembered there had been a few – hadn't bothered to take on refugees; they'd fled at the first sign of trouble. Keelin hated to admit it, but he would have joined them if not for Drake's insistence on helping the folk of Sev'relain. It would, however, take more than one good deed for him to rethink his low opinion of the captain.

Something caught Keelin's eye, a woman being plucked from the bay and dragged up onto the deck of *The Phoenix*. She was soaked to her skin from the swim and looked caught between terror and misery, but she was still beautiful to his eyes. It was the serving girl from the tavern, and Keelin found himself staring at her and smiling. He quickly wiped the smile from his face, but he couldn't tear his eyes away from her. Feather moved over to her, no doubt to steer her down into the hold where they would be keeping the refugees. She started to follow the young pirate, keeping her arms held tightly across her chest. Keelin had a brief internal war with his better judgement – he won.

"Feather," Keelin shouted even as he realised that what he was about to do was a bad idea. "Put that one in my cabin."

"Um… aye, Cap'n," the lad said, and changed direction.

The woman looked no more or less alarmed than before; she didn't even appear to notice she was being taken to the cabin of the captain of a pirate ship. Keelin had seen shock lock people down before; sometimes they became little more than living dolls, but most seemed to snap out of it given enough time. Unfortunately, he didn't have time to consider the woman's mental health right now, what with a town burning to ash just a short distance away and plenty more survivors wanting rescuing.

Keelin saw the *Fortune* turn across the bay and her sails billow with the wind. Drake – assuming he had made it to his ship – was leaving even though there were people still in the water. *The Phoenix* was filling up fast, and if they took on many more mouths they simply wouldn't have the supplies to save any of them.

"Haul anchor!" Keelin shouted over the noise of the people on his deck. "Get some sail on and put us after the *Fortune*." Pirates jumped to his orders in an instant, leaving the refugees on deck unsure of where to go.

Morley took up the orders and began putting the ship and her crew in motion while Keelin moved aft to watch Port Sev'relain's death throes. There were still people in the water, dozens of them, screaming for help even as *The Phoenix* picked up speed and left them behind. Some might make it back to the island, hide from the soldiers and survive until it was over, but most would either drown or swim back to shore only to be murdered on the beach.

Once, long ago, Keelin had fancied himself a champion of the people. He would have done anything, sacrificed his ship and crew, in order to save those people. But that was long ago, and things were different now. He turned away from the burning spectacle of Port Sev'relain and focused instead on the ship and captain he was now following.

Fortune

Drake was furious. He'd spent years practising the art of schooling his appearance so that his true emotions didn't show, so that the world only saw the man he wanted them to see, but that didn't stop him from feeling – and right now he was feeling furious.

Losing Sev'relain had most definitely not been part of the plan. It was supposed to be the beginning of his rise, the centre of his empire, the heart of the Pirate Isles. Now it was nothing more than ash and ghosts, and the isles already had more than its fair share of the latter.

The men mourned, some of them for a town that had been good to them and better over the years, and some for the few who hadn't made it back to the *Fortune*, either lost amidst the chaos or in the brief and ill-fated resistance the pirates had given the soldiers of Sarth.

Drake had known Black Sands would fall long before the Sarth Man of War even set sail from its home in the Holy Empire. The Oracle had told him it needed to happen, so Drake had arranged it. But the loss of Sev'relain was more than a shock.

"There's a boat being lowered from *The Phoenix*, Cap'n," said Princess. "Reckon that ponce, Stillwater, means to come aboard."

"Stow it, Princess," Drake said quietly.

"Your words, Cap'n."

"Stillwater saved a lot of lives back there," Drake continued. "Most other captains fled. The man has earned some respect at least."

"Aye. Well, him and his respectable arse are headed over here, by the looks."

"Show him to my cabin."

Drake turned, ignoring any further response, and leapt down to the foredeck, crossing the space to his cabin quickly and sparing barely a glance for the refugees from Sev'relain littering his ship's deck.

It was early morning, with a brilliant sun just starting to peek over the horizon, and both ships were floating in languid waters just a stone's throw from each other. Stillwater would no doubt want to know what happens next, and where they should take the refugees. The truth was that Drake didn't have so much as an inkling, and that angered him even more than the loss of Sev'relain.

Beck was waiting for Drake in his cabin. Despite his fury over the burning of his town and the murder of his people, Drake found himself aroused by the sight of the woman. Unfortunately, as he knew full well, women like the Arbiter couldn't be confronted directly. He would need to be very careful in his approach, and she was definitely the type who needed to feel as though it were her choice.

"The fuck are you doing in here?" he said with a smile that didn't reach his eyes.

"Preparing," the Arbiter said casually, tilting her head just for a moment to look at Drake from underneath her hat. "When I accepted this assignment I believed you would be the target of an assassination attempt by heretical forces. I now believe that may not be the case, and I find myself unprepared for the task. Also, I can't get the smell of peppermint out of Princess' cabin."

"Aye. He uses it to wash his hair. Don't tell the rest of the crew though, eh. We got company coming, so how about you fuck off for a bit."

"The captain of the other ship."

"Aye."

"I killed for you, Captain Morrass," the Arbiter said. She was using Drake's ink, pen, and paper to draw an intricate design Drake didn't recognise, though he guessed it to be a magical rune. "Four men of Sarth died at my hands back in that shit hole you called a town, and you still don't trust me?" Her compulsion failed to take hold of Drake's will yet again.

"If all you had to do to earn my trust was end a couple of lives, the list would be very long and I would be very dead, Arbiter. Stay if you fancy. You might not like what you hear."

The Arbiter said nothing, nor did she show any sign of moving. Drake refused to show his frustration and instead decided to pour himself a drink. By the time the door to his cabin opened he was staring out of the window at the fathomless blue. Even in the roughest of waters, Drake found that the sight of the deep sea beneath him calmed him enough to let him collect his thoughts – and at that moment they truly needed collecting.

"Good to see you survived, Drake," Stillwater said as Drake turned to greet his fellow captain. Two men from Stillwater's ship flanked him, and one of them looked suspiciously like one of Loke's guards.

"Just a day ago I reckon you'd have been just as happy to see I hadn't," Drake replied with a grin. He was starting to feel a little more like himself again, now he had a deck beneath him and a drink in hand.

"Just a day ago I hadn't watched Sev'relain burn to the ground." Stillwater's voice sounded so heavy with grief Drake wondered who the man had lost in the massacre. "We got a problem." Stillwater seated himself in the single remaining chair.

"Who are they?" Drake waved a hand at the two men behind the other captain.

"Morley is my first mate, Kebble is my new shadow. You got another cup of that?"

Drake took a mug from the cupboard and placed it on the desk along with the bottle of rum.

"Is she trustworthy?" Stillwater said as he poured himself a drink.

Drake glanced at Beck, who appeared to be paying the whole conversation little to no attention. "More than less."

"Well, we brought sixty-seven refugees on board, Drake."

"Eighty-two," Drake said with a grimace.

"Our supplies can't support that many," Stillwater continued. "We didn't exactly have time to take any on in Sev'relain, and my crew have to eat first."

"We're gonna be stretched a little thin our own selves."

"There's only one port close enough so that me and mine won't starve."

"Fango ain't an option," Drake said through gritted teeth.

"It is for me."

An oppressive silence settled upon the room and all eyes turned towards Drake. He felt a burning anger in the pit of his stomach, and it took all the self control he could muster not to round the desk and put a dagger in the ungrateful bastard of a captain's eye.

"You siding with Tanner, Stillwater?"

"I ain't siding with anyone," Stillwater objected. "Didn't even realise it had come down to choosing. Fango is the only settlement near enough that our supplies won't run dry, and it's damn near unassailable. Those bastards from Sarth wouldn't stand a chance against the jungle. You really want to save those people we plucked out of that massacre, then Fango is the only real option."

Drake considered his options carefully. It wasn't that he agreed with his fellow captain, but more that the Oracle had told him he needed Stillwater on his side – and this sure as all the Hells felt like a moment he could lose the man. After all the trouble Drake had been through arranging Stillwater's beating and subsequent saving just so he'd believe he owed him a favour, losing him now wasn't an option.

"Back there, before the attack, you asked me what I was getting out of helping the folk of the isles. I intend to be exactly what we all need to save us from those bastards who want to wipe us out. I intend to be king."

Drake would have liked Stillwater to be shocked at the idea, or at least angry. At that point Drake would have settled for an indication that his fellow captain had even heard him, but Stillwater remained still and stony.

"Wish I could say I was surprised, Drake," he said eventually with a shake of his head. "Last time pirates had themselves a king it caused the exact thing you're wanting to stop – a purge. Do you really think what we need now is to give you a crown and piss off Sarth even more? We need to run. Hide. Lay low until they get bored of burning towns, and then come back and resettle."

"You're a fucking coward, Stillwater," Drake said with more scorn than he intended. He was starting to wonder why the Oracle had insisted he needed such a spineless cur. "Your plan is to run away and hide? Let Sarth murder thousands of people, most of whom never done a day's pirating in their lives.

"They're after us, not the folk of Black Sands or Sev'relain. Just, the easiest way to get to us is through them. It's because of us Sarth is out here, and it's because of us the folk of Sev'relain are dead. I ain't about to run away from a fight we started."

"Are you trying to save the folk of the isles because they deserve to be saved or because you can't be king of a sea of corpses?" Keelin said.

"What does it matter? As long as they get saved."

Stillwater stood slowly, holding Drake's gaze all the while. "I'm no coward, Morrass. I just know a fight I can't win, whether I helped to start it or not. We're pirates, not soldiers. We can't beat Sarth."

"Aye, we're pirates and sailors. Maybe we couldn't beat them on the land, but we sure as Rin's wrath can beat them here on the sea. The Pirate Isles has the largest navy in the known world, Stillwater; they just don't know that's what they are yet. We pull all the captains together into one force, ally them under me, and crush the bastards looking to murder us all."

"Then what?" Stillwater said, still staring right at Drake. "You said yourself, they're killing us because there's too many of us. So we unite under your flag and beat them back and keep pirating, and how long till they stop sailing ships through our waters?"

Drake picked up the bottle of rum and refilled his glass. "Why did you turn pirate, Stillwater? Fancy bastard like you weren't born in the isles. Reckon you were Acanthian, maybe? Merchant's son or some such? Fell in love with the romance of piracy and joined up on a crew?"

"Tanner Black's crew," Stillwater said through clenched teeth.

"Aye, bet the romance wore pretty thin pretty quick under that bastard, though fucking that daughter of his probably helped. But you kept on with it, stole yourself your own ship and set yourself up as captain. So why are you still a pirate? Romance has worn off, so… what? You enjoy chasing folk down and killing them for what's theirs?"

"No! I ain't Tanner Black."

"No. I reckon you enjoy the freedom. Sailing the waters to your own schedule and course. Not relying on anyone not on your ship. Every captain is a king of their own vessel, eh? Freedom."

"What's your point, Drake?"

"We beat back Sarth and the Five Kingdoms and any other fucker wants to have a go at us, and then we change the way we pirate them all."

"Huh?"

"Taxes, Stillwater. We let folk travel our waters unmolested, but in return they pay us for the privilege of that protection. Anyone doesn't pay gets robbed blind. Works out best for us all. Unless you're in it for the killing?"

"Tanner is. He'll never agree to it."

"Tanner will be dealt with in time. Right now, Stillwater, I want to know if you're in."

Stillwater opened his mouth, then slowly shut it again.

"Still get to be free, Captain," Drake continued. "Still get to sail where you will, just without the danger of the fight to take the ships. Still answer to yourself."

"And to you. To your rule."

Drake snorted out a laugh. "My rule ain't shit. King in name only, for the most at least. Truth of it is, pirates rule themselves. Remember, every captain is king of his own ship."

A loud banging on the door interrupted Stillwater even as he opened his mouth to retort. Before Drake could speak, the door burst open and one of his men, an old pirate by the name of Link, pointed towards the window.

"Ship ahoy, aft of us, Cap'n. She's a big bitch."

Drake walked behind his desk and looked out the window there. He could see a speck on the horizon, little more than a dot at that distance. He pulled his monoscope out of his belt and extended it to its full length before looking again. It was a ship, alright, and a large one. He couldn't see the colours from this far out, but he didn't need to.

Turning back to the room, Drake found all eyes turned his way. "It's Sarth," he said heavily.

"Back to *The Phoenix*, Morley." Stillwater turned and walked for the doorway.

"Princess," Drake said. "Get us ready to sail, all the speed we can muster. Anyone not on duty, wake them the fuck up."

"I think I'll stay close," Beck said quietly to Drake as he made to round the desk and go after Stillwater.

"You do whatever you want, Arbiter, as long as you don't get in my way."

Where Loyalties Lie

Out on the deck of the *Fortune*, everything was activity. Pirates were crawling over the rigging like fleas on a mangy dog's back, and the refugees who hadn't gone below were busy trying not to hamper their efforts. Drake caught up with Stillwater just before the man followed his crew members into the boat waiting below.

"You still haven't answered me, Captain," Drake said, grabbing hold of Stillwater's arm. The other captain turned and gave Drake a warning look, but it would take more than a stern glare to scare Drake Morrass.

"I reckon it can wait, Drake."

"I don't," Drake said, not letting go of the man's arm. "I'm not running."

"What?"

"I'm turning the *Fortune* around and making sure those bastards don't go burning any more of our towns or our people."

"Any more of your subjects?" Stillwater scoffed.

"Aye. Can't be a king without them. I'm gonna turn and fight. I need your help, Stillwater. I can't do this alone. That Man of War will have twice the *Fortune*'s crew. Can I count on you?"

Stillwater held Drake's gaze another moment before his face softened just a touch and he nodded. With that, Drake let go of the captain's arm and let him descend into his longboat.

"You really think you can take that ship?" Beck said as Drake moved to the stern to watch it approach. He felt her compulsion seek out his will, but as always he slipped away from her.

"You scared, Arbiter?"

"Yes. You'd have to be mad not to be."

"Aye." Drake lowered his voice so that only she would hear. "Me too."

The Phoenix

It wasn't a long crossing from the *Fortune* to *The Phoenix*, but it was one of the most tense trips Keelin had ever experienced. Morley and Kebble kept silent despite their knowledge of the situation, and Keelin used his monoscope to watch the approaching Man of War. As the giant ship drew near, Keelin found himself more and more certain that Drake's plan was madness.

The crew of the *Fortune* scurried about, making the ship ready to sail, and as the dinghy bumped against *The Phoenix*, Drake's ship began to move. A few moments later she started to turn. Meanwhile, Keelin's crew stood at the railing, watching and wondering what was happening.

"He's a bold man, that Drake," Kebble Salt said just as Keelin grabbed hold of the rope ladder lowered to him.

"A captan many would follow," Morley agreed.

"I hear many follow Tanner Black also," Kebble said.

Keelin shot the man a dark glare. "You wouldn't say that if you knew the old bastard." Keelin scaled the rope ladder up to the deck of his ship. He took a deep breath as the others followed him up and his crew gathered around.

"You've all no doubt heard there's a ship behind us…"

"It's the Man of War," Smithe said with challenge in his tone. "Has to be, a ship that big."

"It is. Morrass means to attack them. Pay them back for what they did at Sev'relain."

Everyone started shouting at once. Some voices yelled their support of the plan, others decreed it suicide. Keelin noticed a few faces he didn't recognise in the crowd, those belonging to the refugees they'd saved from Sev'relain. The idea that they'd rescued them from one massacre only to throw them into another occurred to Keelin, and he remembered the woman he'd ordered placed in his cabin.

"Quiet!" Morley roared over the din. "We following the *Fortune* in, Captan?"

"No," Keelin answered quickly. "We're getting the fuck out of here, making for the nearest port, dropping off these poor sods just lost their home, and finding the nearest merchant ship to pillage."

There was a mixed response from his assembled crew, but for once Smithe didn't speak out against his captain.

"So that's the plan," Keelin said, raising his voice. "Anyone with a job, get to it. Anyone without a job, get the Hells out of the way."

As pirates sprang to his command, one remained behind. Morley had a look of disappointment as deep as the sea on his face. "You're condemning him and everyone on that ship to death, Captan."

Keelin shook his head, but he couldn't meet his first mate's eyes. "Drake condemned them to death when he decided to attack the Man of War."

"What about the charts?"

"Damn the charts," Keelin said with little to no conviction. "Right now I just want to get out of here alive."

Fortune

The wind was on their side and so were the numbers, with Stillwater's crew backing them up. The soldiers on that Man of War might be trained for combat, but they wouldn't be used to fighting on a ship. With the deck moving beneath them and cramped confines, the battle would sway in the favour of those with relevant experience, pirates who had earned their salt a hundred times over.

The Man of War was growing steadily now as the *Fortune* flew towards it, and Drake found himself truly grinning for the first time in what seemed like an age.

"She ain't coming," shouted Pip from up in the nest.

"What?" Drake screamed back, his good mood evaporating in an instant.

"*The Phoenix* is turning away. She's running, Cap'n."

Drake stormed to the aft of the ship to find Pip was right. It was clear as day *The Phoenix* was presenting them all her arse and leaving Drake and his crew to an enemy that greatly outnumbered them.

"That fucking piece of shit pretend fucking pirate cunt running off to suck on Tanner's black fucking cock leaving us to fucking die. Fuck!" Drake screamed impotently at the retreating form of *The Phoenix*. He turned to find a number of his crew staring at him with expressions one part impressed at the tirade, and four parts terrified at their captain proclaiming they were all about to die.

Princess appeared, near leaping up the ladder from the quarterdeck. "She really leaving us?"

"The Hells do you think?" Drake was still very much in a rage.

"We turning tail and runnin' then, Cap'n?"

Drake turned, slammed his fist onto the aft railing, and spat a huge glob of spittle into the sea. The Oracle, Drake's own brother, had predicted that he needed Stillwater on his side, and he'd also predicted that Drake would die many decades from now and not in a suicidal attack on a superior force. The possibility that Hironous could be wrong, that Drake might die before establishing his empire, had never even occurred to Drake until now.

Drake turned to find Princess, several members of his crew, and Arbiter Beck all staring at him, waiting for his decision. It was the presence of one of his brother's Arbiters that made Drake's decision for him. He would trust his brother.

"Stay true to the course," Drake hissed. "Someone go below and see to the refugees. Anyone can hold a sword gets one, anyone looks like they can swing one gets to come up on deck and fight for their lives with the rest of us."

"We're gonna fight 'em?" said one of the newer members of his crew, a pirate named Wes, if Drake wasn't mistaken. "That's suicide!"

Drake cracked a rictus grin. "I'm captain, so I'll tell you what is and ain't suicide. You really reckon I aim to die here?"

There was a slight pause. "No."

"Reckon that's settled then. Get to your damned orders."

Beck stayed behind; it seemed she was serious about sticking close to Drake. He wondered how serious she would be once the fighting started. Drake knew he wasn't the best swordsman in the isles, nor on his own ship, but he wasn't one to shy away from a fight no matter how shitty the odds.

"You ready for this?" he said. "Could always put that coat of yours back on. Bastards on that ship are from Sarth – they'd never attack an Arbiter."

Beck shot him a glance. "You might be surprised what men will do when they think they can get away with it. Inquisitor Vance gave me instructions to keep you alive. I can't do that if I'm hiding in a cabin, begging for mercy."

Drake considered making an amorous comment, but the threat of death was too high even for him. Maybe after the battle, when everyone's blood was up, he'd see about getting the Arbiter naked. Drake made his way to the railing overlooking the main deck and looked down upon the gathering pirates and refugees. It wouldn't be long now until that same deck was awash with red, so decorated by those same men and women. He opened his mouth to speak.

"Can't we run?" shouted one of the refugees.

"Ain't time for it now," Drake shouted back. "Wind would be against us. Better or worse, we're fighting our way out of this one."

Princess and Beck joined him at the railing. He spared each of them a glance and found himself sincerely hoping neither of them would die.

"Besides, folk on that ship have killed too many of us. They burned Black Sands. They murdered your family and friends in Sev'relain. They're looking to fucking kill us all, and they ain't about to stop unless we stop them."

"They outnumber us."

"Nah." Drake cracked a grim smile. "We outnumber them. Each one of us counts for ten of those land-loving turds. Ain't a one can stand straight on a boat, let alone fight." He glanced up at the approaching Man of War, and it suddenly looked close. He wagered just another minute and they'd be exchanging pointy projectiles.

"Those" – he pointed towards the ship with his sword – "are Volmar's lapdogs. We" – he waved his sword over those below him – "are Rin's chosen, and we're fighting on *her* sacred waters. Ain't no way she'll let us die. So let's make some noise and show those bastards they picked a fight with the wrong bloody pirates!"

A cry went up, followed by the sound of weapons being bashed upon wood, and Drake had to admit it was loud and, hopefully, intimidating. His pirates went about taking up positions of cover against the immediate threat of arrows, while most of the refugees milled about on deck, believing they were invincible all of a sudden.

"Nice speech," Beck said as she took up her own position, near Drake but behind a mast.

"Rin's sacred waters?" Princess said.

"Fuck knows." Drake grinned, ducking down behind the railing on the quarterdeck. "They might be."

"If it means anything to ya, Cap'n, I really hope you don't die," Princess continued, with what might have been considered a smile.

"Do you find yourself missing that spider, Princess?"

"Hells yes, Cap'n. Bloody great thing terrified the shit out of me, but I always felt she was watching out for the crew."

With all the noise his own crew was making, Drake didn't hear the soldiers on the Man of War loose their arrows, but he did hear those arrows thud as they hit the *Fortune*'s hull; he also heard the scream of one of the refugees not smart enough to find cover. Drake wondered where the arrow had taken the man, but it wasn't really important. Some arrows poked holes in the sails, holes that would soon need fixing, and others cleared the ship entirely. Only one man down from the first volley, and Drake hoped the next would follow suit.

"What's this bitch called, anyway?" Drake asked Princess in as jovial a tone as he could muster.

Princess shifted his position and poked his head above the railing for just a moment. "*Righteous Indignation*. She's pretty close, Cap'n."

Drake groaned even as another volley of arrows embedded themselves into the wood of his ship. One of them impacted into the mast Beck was hidden behind, just a few inches from her arm. By the look on her face she didn't take the near miss well. The Arbiter stepped out from behind the mast; her mouth was moving, but Drake heard no words over the noise of his pirates. She threw something small towards the bigger ship before ducking back behind the mast. A moment later Drake heard a loud bang, accompanied by fresh screams not coming from his ship.

Drake risked a look over the railing. The Man of War was close now – very close. A small portion of its bow was a splintered, smouldering wreck, and in that moment Drake had a little more respect for Arbiter Beck's magic. It was short lived, though, as more pressing concerns quickly took over. The first of the Sarth soldiers swung across the gap between the two ships on a rope, and he was soon followed by more men as well as grappling hooks.

"Repel borders," Drake screamed as he darted out of cover. He turned just as a Sarth soldier in a pristine blue-black uniform landed right where he'd been standing only a moment earlier.

With Princess beside him, Drake rushed forwards and darted a quick jab at the soldier to get his attention. Princess capitalised on the distraction by sticking his own sword into the soldier's groin, before both captain and first mate leapt backwards to meet the next wave of soldiers coming aboard.

For a brief moment Drake considered rushing forwards to cut away the grappling hooks that were pulling the ships together. Soldiers coming across a few at a time they could deal with, but if the gap were close enough to leap across they would soon be overwhelmed by superior numbers. Unfortunately, his moment of procrastination made his decision for him as two more soldiers swung across to protect the grapples. The first died of a gunshot wound – Beck's work – but the second quickly unhooked a shield from his back and stood guard.

Again Drake rushed forwards with a quick jab and Princess followed his captain in, but this soldier was a little more ready and parried Drake's sword only to block Princess' attack with the shield. Another soldier hit the deck beside his comrade, and Drake was forced to retreat a few steps.

Fighting merchant sailors just trying to defend their cargo was one thing, but these soldiers seemed to be trained in the tactics of assaulting a smaller vessel. If anything, they seemed to be using tactics that pirates had been taking advantage of for years.

Princess feinted right and then switched left for a wild swing, which the soldier with the shield again blocked. Drake stepped forward to capitalise and found himself engaged with the second soldier, a man larger than most and wielding a broadsword in one hand as if it were as light as a feather. Drake quickly found himself giving ground, and that left Princess all alone even as more soldiers crossed the gap between the ships. Drake decided his claim that each pirate was worth ten soldiers might need reconsideration.

It was his experience that big men, even if they were as strong as the average ox, were usually slower on their feet, and given that the man currently trying to run him through was definitely bigger than him, he decided to rely on that speed advantage. With a parry that turned the man's sword away, Drake stepped into the soldier's reach and kicked him in the shin and drove the pommel of his sword into his throat all at once. The soldier choked and stumbled backwards, and the lights dimmed for Drake as a meaty fist caught him on the side of the head.

It was a few moments, and then a few more, before Drake's vision returned to him without blinding white spots, and he found himself on hands and knees on the deck getting a good up-close look at the grain of the planks. A shadow fell across him and he turned his head just in time to see the big soldier with the broadsword taking an executioner's swing at his face.

Something punched a hole into the soldier's chest right through his heart, and the man stopped mid-swing, looking utterly perplexed. Drake wasted no time in jumping to his feet and planting his own sword, halfway down the blade, through the soldier's confused face.

The soldier went down heavily, dragging Drake's sword from his grasp. Drake looked around and saw Beck up on the poop deck, fighting two soldiers with only her pistols in hand. She was using them as bludgeons and, judging by the three bodies on the deck around her, Drake guessed she was using them well.

Princess had been joined by two more of Drake's crew and they were busy trying to fight towards the grapples on the quarterdeck, but it was too late. Even as Drake watched, the first of the next wave of soldiers leapt across the shortening gap between the two ships and was quickly followed by more. Things looked little better on the main deck, as more and more soldiers were replacing those that had fallen and the pirates and refugees there were quickly becoming outnumbered. Drake saw Pip go down with a nasty slash across the stomach that, if not fatal, would do nothing to improve the man's disposition.

A body hit the ground just a few feet from Drake, fallen from the rigging with an arrow in the eye. The pirate hadn't even had a chance to scream. With a growl, Drake snatched up his sword from the big soldier's ruined face and charged towards the battle his first mate was losing. Unfortunately, he didn't even manage to make it to Princess' side.

Another soldier, just as big as the last one and with a gruesome hair lip, broke away from the melee and charged at Drake, bringing a shorter, shield-bearing friend along for the slaughter.

Drake neatly sidestepped Hair Lip and launched himself at the big man's comrade, only to take a full-body shield hit that sent him sprawling. He recovered just in time to duck under Hair Lip's sword as it slashed through the air, and Drake scuttled away before the two men could surround him. It was about that time that he sorely wished a couple of his crew would appear to turn the odds, but judging by the number of soldiers pouring over from the Man of War, he knew every pirate and refugee on the ship was as outnumbered as he was.

They were herding Drake backwards towards the starboard side of the ship, the shield-bearer protecting Hair Lip from any of Drake's counter attacks. Pretty soon he'd be up against the railing with nowhere else to go but overboard. Desperate times often called for desperate measures, and Drake was feeling more than a little desperate.

"Last chance to back away from this, boys," he said with a dark grin. "You ain't dealing with some know-nothing pirate. I'm Drake Morrass."

With a roar all of fury, Hair Lip rushed forwards and brought his sword down on Drake, who barely got his own up in time to block. He both felt and heard the crack in his right arm, and the pain that accompanied it made him let loose an involuntary howl of pain. He found himself on his arse on the deck and scrambled away backwards using his left arm. His right was still attached, but felt more than a little broken. The two soldiers advanced upon Drake, and the sudden feeling of wood against his back told him he'd run out of time.

Again Hair Lip brought his sword up, and this time Drake had no weapon of his own to block with. The sword came down, and Drake witnessed a wooden plank in the deck of his own ship break off between his legs and rise up to shield him from the attack. The sword hit the wood and damn near carved the plank in two; the blade stopped just inches from Drake's head.

Never one to stop and marvel at his own luck, Drake seized the opportunity of two stunned soldiers to roll out of the way. He put one foot on the nearby railing and leapt off it to deliver a flying, booted kick to Hair Lip's hair lip. As the big man stumbled backwards Drake pointed at him with his left hand.

"I am going to fucking kill you for that!" he roared, with no idea how he was going to follow through with the threat. There was a bang from nearby that sounded muted in the din of battle, and Hair Lip's chest exploded, showering the deck and the nearby shield-bearing soldier with gore.

Drake turned and caught sight of Beck, bloodied and leaning

against the starboard railing, holding the largest pistol Drake had ever seen, its barrel still smoking from the shot she'd just fired. Even more glorious a sight was the ship sailing up alongside the *Fortune* and the pirates lined up waiting to board the besieged vessel, Keelin Stillwater first among them. Drake was caught between wanting to stab the man for leaving him and hug him for coming back, but now wasn't the time for either. The *Fortune* was still very much under attack, and even with Stillwater's crew the outcome of the battle was far from decided.

The Phoenix

Keelin was first to board the *Fortune*, swinging across on a rope tied to the yard and hitting the deck just a few metres from the wounded Drake Morrass. The infamous captain looked a truly sorry state, with blood leaking from a dozen different cuts and his right arm cradled protectively against his body. His bodyguard, the Sarth woman, loitered nearby, looking almost as banged up as her charge.

More of Keelin's crew followed him across and charged into the battle that raged on the other side of the *Fortune*, bolstering Drake's hard-pushed pirates. "You look like all the Hells, Drake," Keelin said.

"I'll look a touch better when I drive these bastards off my ship." Drake grimaced as he retrieved his sword and gave it a couple of test swings with his left hand. Keelin would have put money on the man never having fought with that hand before.

"You saved my life back in Sev'relain," Keelin said. "Reckon we'll be calling that debt repaid."

Drake grunted. He looked a little like he was ready to pass out.

"Perhaps you should sit this one out, Drake. Let…"

"Ain't happening, Stillwater!" the captain spat. "Ain't nobody leading the charge to take back my own ship but me." With that, Drake stormed off towards the quarterdeck, where the fight had already been won.

Keelin was about to follow his fellow captain when the Sarth woman spoke. "Why did you come back?"

Something reached inside of Keelin, something dark and indomitable, something he hadn't felt for a long time and something he hated with all of his being. He felt the answer to the woman's question, the truth, bubble up from inside and burst out of his mouth.

"For the charts," he said, losing the battle against the woman's magic. Before she could ask another question, Keelin crossed the distance between them and swung a fist at her face. She blocked the attack with ease, catching Keelin's hand and holding it there.

A few of Keelin's crew stopped, but didn't intervene.

"You're a fucking Arbiter," Keelin hissed. There was nothing in the world that Keelin hated quite so much as the Inquisition. He'd happily have taken his hatred out on the woman standing in front of him, but no matter how hard he pushed she held his hand steady. Eventually he eased off, and she let go.

"If you ever use your magic on me again," Keelin said, seething with rage, "I will kill you."

The Arbiter started walking towards Drake, but stopped beside Keelin. "You can find the last eight men who tried to kill me up on the poop deck, Captain," she said in a honeyed voice dripping with danger. "I suggest you take a look and learn their lesson well."

Keelin waited for a few moments after the Arbiter had gone, letting his anger build. He turned to find some of his pirates watching him from a distance.

"Don't just stand around," Keelin snarled. "Fight!"

Kebble Salt watched the battle unfurl from a distance. From up in *The Phoenix*'s nest, the murder down on the deck of the other ships seemed disjointed, almost as if it weren't really happening. He looked down the sight of his rifle and focused on three men trading blows. Two wore the blue-black of Sarth, and they'd herded the other, a pirate, into a corner. The pirate wouldn't survive much longer with nowhere to run. Kebble sucked in a breath and took aim before carefully squeezing the trigger.

One of the Sarth soldiers attacking the fortunate pirate dropped dead in a mist of blood, a hole through his head. The other soldier startled, panicked, and ran, but the pirate wasn't so slow and capitalised on his good fortune, skewering the soldier as he turned. Kebble reloaded his rifle without even needing to look, replacing the black powder and bullet by touch. He settled the rifle butt against his shoulder and searched for a new target.

He could barely see the deck of the Man of War with the masts of the *Fortune* in the way, only glimpses of the battle there as the pirates beat back the soldiers and took the fight onto their ship. Kebble spotted the other captain, Drake Morrass, near the rear of a fight. He was dancing into the fray whenever an enemy looked away, taking wild, left-handed swings with his sword. Kebble noted the man's position, but decided he'd be fine with three other pirates backing him up nearby. Kebble blocked out the sounds of fighting and dying that floated up to his ears, preferring to remain a detached force upon the battlefield, not allowing the chaos below to affect him. He spotted a boy who looked too young to even grow a moustache attempting to fight a much bigger man. Kebble noticed the mismatch too late to stop the boy from losing his right hand, but not too late to stop him from losing more.

Kebble's rifle flashed and the soldier hit the deck, bleeding from his chest and mouth as blood leaked into his lungs. A breastplate might be enough to stop a sword, but it would take much more to keep one of Kebble's bullets out. The boy regained his feet and, despite the loss of his hand, set to kicking the soldier in the head until there was little left of the man's face. Kebble moved his watchful gaze to another part of the battle.

There was the unmistakeable twang of a crossbow, and a bolt struck the outside of Kebble's nest, its tip just protruding through the planking. He didn't have time to take care of the man wielding the weapon; two of Captain Stillwater's pirates jumped the soldier and gave him what was possibly the first and definitely the last stabbing of his lifetime. Glancing down and seeing how close the crossbow bolt had come to ending his life, Kebble let out a sigh; and kept on living.

He was running low on black powder; he estimated a mere four shots remained to him, and after that he would be useless to all those down there still fighting.

It occurred to Kebble that he occupied a strange position on a battlefield. He would never turn the tide through weight of numbers killed, but by choosing his targets carefully, he could make each shot worth much more than a single kill. But right now he felt he needed to prove his value to his new captain, and with that in mind he chose a target close to Keelin Stillwater.

Keelin sidestepped the attack, then sent one cutlass against the man's shield while the second slashed at his belly. It was a wild strike driven more by anger than his usual precision, and it rebounded harmlessly off the soldier's breastplate with a metallic hiss. Keelin cursed under his breath and disengaged, while one of Drake's pirates came up behind the soldier and brained the man with a bloody mace.

The Arbiter had rattled him, and not just with her magic; her presence made him angry, and that rage was making him sloppy. Keelin had changed his mind – he'd been ready to support Drake, to follow him and help him achieve his goal of uniting the pirates – but now he wasn't so sure. He needed to find out just what sort of hold the Inquisition had over Drake Morrass and what interest they had in the isles, and he was certain he wouldn't get that information out of the Arbiter.

No matter how many years passed, the ghost of Keelin's sister still haunted him, and every time he spotted an Arbiter she cried for vengeance. He could no longer remember Leesa's face or her voice, but he could never forget the smell of her flesh burning, the sound of her guttural screams. The sight of her writhing in flames.

Keelin had almost avenged her just a year ago. He'd given a half-crazed Arbiter safe transport in return for the location of Arbiter Prin, but the bastard had lied, and again his sister's murderer had escaped his grasp.

The battle was moving on. They'd all but pushed the soldiers from the *Fortune*, and now the pirates, angered by the events of the past couple of days, were no longer satisfied with the damage already done; they wanted to take the ship. The grappling hooks deployed by the Sarth Man of War were now working against the soldiers, giving the pirates the opportunity to leap and climb onto the bigger ship and take the fight to their tormentors.

A soldier came at Keelin, screaming and brandishing a dagger and little else. Keelin was about to gut the man when something hit the poor bastard in the side of the head and he crumpled to the ground, all sorts of dead. Without even bothering to wonder what had happened, Keelin sprinted towards the nearby railing and leapt the three feet up and across from the *Fortune* onto the Man of War.

It took him a moment to scramble up over the railing, and when he hit the deck he found himself kneeling in a pool of blood. Keelin stood, gave the situation a quick survey, and charged the nearest soldier he could see, barrelling into him shoulder first and sending him crashing to the deck. Keelin wasted no time finishing the man off with a quick sword thrust through his unprotected neck, and turned to the next.

It had been a long time since Keelin had been to Sarth, but he recognised nobility when he saw it. This man wasn't dressed like the other soldiers; he was wearing an impeccable uniform labelling him as Sarth navy and an admiral, if the number of pins on his lapel was anything to go by. He was also flanked by two soldiers bearing both sword and shield sword, who looked as if they knew how to fight and were more than willing to prove it.

Keelin paced in front of them, trying to goad them into coming at him. Their training showed and they held their ground, shields up and eyes alert. A quick glance told Keelin he was alone and could expect no help from either his crew or Drake's. It was almost hard to believe that just a day ago he'd been beaten bloody and nearly killed in a bar, and now he was about to try his luck at three armed opponents.

"Last chance, lads," Keelin said, still pacing in front of the three men. "You can see how the battle is turning. Ship's near as ours already. Now I want that bastard alive, or at least clinging to it. If you two just turn him over and lay down your sharp and pointies, I'll make sure you get to be among those we send back to Sarth alive."

The admiral, a man of no small stature himself, with great bushy eyebrows and a dark gaze beneath them, drew his sabre and laughed. "Cowards and turncoats," he said in a very admirable voice. "We will die to a man before we let you take the ship."

"You won't, but they will," Keelin growled, and rushed the three men.

There was a part of Keelin – quite a large part – that realised how foolish he was to attack three men head on, especially when two of them were brandishing shields. But he was angry, and he didn't make smart decisions when he was angry.

He pulled up short before the first of the soldiers and danced left, sending both his cutlasses clattering against the man's shield. The soldier took the blow with a grunt and stabbed out from behind his cover. Keelin was already gone, twisting away and launching himself at the second soldier. Again he swung both his swords at the shield. This soldier was a bit more savvy; he pushed back while Keelin was off balance and sent the captain stumbling away. Instead of pushing the attack, both soldiers formed up in front of the admiral and stood their ground.

Regaining his balance, Keelin found himself with a chance to reconsider his foolish decision. Unfortunately his blood was still up, and now he was feeling humiliated as well – and that didn't lead to rational choices. Again he charged the three men.

This time one of the soldiers charged as well, and Keelin collided with the man's shield, sending him crashing to the deck. He rolled away just as something sharp bit into the wood where he'd landed, and came to his feet with both swords ready. One soldier was down, quickly regaining his feet, while the other was pulling his sword from the wooden plank of the deck. The admiral strode forwards to join the fight.

Keelin jumped forwards and attacked the soldier retrieving his sword; the man blocked with a wild swing of his shield, turning away one of Keelin's blades, but he slipped his other one around and scored a shallow cut on the soldier's thigh. Something hit the soldier in his shield arm and he roared in pain. Keelin wasted no time capitalising, bringing one of his own swords down in a heavy slash that severed the man's arm just above the elbow.

As the soldier dropped to the decking, rolling and screaming, Keelin found himself beset by heavy blows from the admiral while the second soldier defended with his shield. But now the odds were better, and two to one sounded like they were in Keelin's favour.

With a cheeky feint to his right, Keelin rushed left and jumped onto a nearby railing. Launching himself back into the fight, he slashed out with his cutlasses and the second soldier, still turning to face his flying opponent, dropped to the deck with a deep gorge carved out of his neck. Keelin completed his showy attack by landing on the deck, slipping in a deep pool of blood, and going down hard.

By the time he'd recovered from his unfortunate slip the admiral was upon him with the tip of his blade hovering above Keelin's heart.

"Pirates..." the Sarth officer said, just before his eyes rolled back in his head and he collapsed forwards. Keelin managed to shift just before the man fell, and the admiral's sword merely cut a shallow gash in his chest rather than piercing his heart.

With a grunt, Keelin shoved the admiral aside and pushed to his feet to find Drake Morrass flanked by three other pirates. Keelin's fellow captain looked pale and bloody, but his eyes were bright and his single gold tooth flashed in his mouth.

"Life for a life, Captain," Drake said through laboured breath. "Reckon you'll be owing me that favour after all. That one looks important."

"Admiral, I reckon," Keelin agreed as he finished off the soldier with the severed hand. "How's the rest of the ship?"

"Taken, for the most. Bit of resistance down in the holds. Nothing we can't handle. Reckon we lost a lot for the victory though, my crew more than yours."

Keelin grimaced at the pain in his chest and went to lean upon the nearby railing. The sounds of battle had died down, but the sounds of the dying had taken their place. Men screamed, men cried, and some men were even praying. The deck of the Man of War was awash with blood and littered with bodies. The deck of the *Fortune* looked more than a little similar. They'd have to make a body count to tally the total cost on both sides of the battle, but even if Sarth had come off worse, they had more men to lose.

"If we're going to fight them, we can't lose this many men every battle," Keelin said. He sounded tired even to his ears.

Drake joined Keelin at the railing. The man was cradling his broken arm, and looked ghastly. "That mean you're in? Joining my side of this instead of Tanner's?"

"I'd never join Tanner Black's side of anything," Keelin growled.

"That ain't an answer."

Keelin glanced at Drake, and then back at the blood and bodies on the deck. There would be more battles just like this one before they were done, but for now it was the only way he could see to get his hands on Drake's charts, and that was the only way he could see to get his revenge.

"Aye," he said with a smile that was half grimace. "I'm in. So long as I don't have to call you king."

Part 2 - Wet Winds, Strong Seas

You need a seat of power said the Oracle
Sev'relain will do fine said Drake
Yes, I believe it will said the Oracle

Fortune

Drake sat staring out across the endless blue as the ship's doctor poked and prodded at him. He grunted away the blinding pain and clenched his teeth to stop himself crying out loud as the doc tried to raise his arm. Last thing the crew needed was to see their captain turn into a babbling mess in place of the dashing hero they believed him to be.

All night and most of the morning they'd floated peacefully, too far out to anchor and too badly banged up to sail on until certain issues had been dealt with. Three ships lashed together might make for an odd sight if there were anyone around to see it, but the chances of anyone happening upon them were slim and then some. They'd need to set sail, and soon; the sea might be endlessly blue and calm, but the clouds were looking to take a darker turn, and Drake didn't feel like being caught out in a storm in their current condition.

"It's broke," the doc said eventually.

"Didn't I say the same thing to you just a few minutes ago?" Drake retorted in a tone that could curdle milk.

"Your expert opinion aside, thought I best look at it myself." The doc had a note of challenge in his voice and twice as much in his eyes, so Drake decided to shut up and let the man get on with his job. "Ain't too bad, but we're gonna need to put it in a sling."

"Do it."

"It's gonna hurt."

"It already fucking hurts. Do it."

Drake spent the next five minutes with teeth gritted against the pain, and silently cursing the name four different gods while the doc tried to remember how to tie a proper sling. It was, perhaps, a problem with hiring a drunkard as a ship's doctor. Luckily for the crew of the *Fortune*, the man was a better doctor than he was a drunk. After he was done, Drake levered himself up from his seat at the forecastle and decided it was time to tour the ship.

"How many dead and injured, Doc?" Drake said, deciding it was always best to start with the worst news.

The doc shook his head as he packed up his tools. "Rin knows. Too many. Stopped counting. Reckon Princess got a number for you though. Bastard damn near lost an eye, and he was still going around checking on folk."

Drake nodded and limped away from the doc. Sometime during the course of the battle, possibly when he'd delivered the showy kick to the hair-lipped soldier's jaw, he'd picked up a sprained ankle. It was far from the worst of his current wounds, but it was getting on Drake's very last nerve. He hated showing weakness, and with a pronounced limp and his arm in a sling, he was already showing more than too much.

The two pirate crews – those not dead or too injured to work – had been steadily clearing the bodies from the decks of the two ships. Well over a hundred corpses had already been tossed overboard to the sharks and other beasties below, and there were still more below decks. Many of the soldiers had surrendered once they realised the fight was lost, though some had continued to put up a fight. Some might say it was a testament to either their training or perhaps their belief in their god, but Drake saw it more as a testament to their stupidity. Not that it truly mattered; most of those who had surrendered would never make it back to Sarth. Drake would select a few to send back, and the rest would feed the denizens of the deep.

After a struggle down the ladder to the main deck – Drake didn't feel much like taking the leap with a sprained ankle, and climbing with only one arm proved to be as difficult as it sounded – he found Princess talking to Stillwater. Twenty-one men were bound and on their knees, guarded by armed and pissed-off pirates.

"Cap'n," Princess said with a grin as Drake limped near. The man's right eye was swollen shut, and he had a bunch of stitches on the same side of his head. Despite the obvious injuries, Princess looked in good spirits, though Drake guessed that was as much to do with the good spirits that the doc gave to his patients as anything else. "Got a bit of an issue with the prisoners."

"I don't see it as an issue," Stillwater said. It pleased Drake no end to know that, though his fellow captain was infamous for being the best swordsman in the isles, he'd still taken a wound in the battle. "These sons of arses slaughtered hundreds and tried to do the same to us. All of them should swim. Let Rin pick the survivors."

Drake cleared his throat and pitched his voice so that the prisoners would hear him. "We all know, Stillwater, that if those men are thrown overboard, Rin won't get a look in. Sharks have been lounging around for hours, feeding on the dead, and all it takes is a glance to see things worse than them have started to arrive. Ever seen a man's skin digested from his bones while he's still breathing?"

Stillwater pulled a disgusted look and shook his head.

"I have," Drake continued. "And, judging by the beasties thrashing around down there, that's what these poor boys will see up real close if we make them swim." He lowered his voice and leaned in towards Stillwater. "Besides, Captain, satisfying your bloodlust comes second to what we may still gain from these men."

"We have the admiral," Stillwater protested, his face turning a darker shade of red. "Anything he knows is worth ten times what these men might."

"Sometimes, Stillwater, it's not about what they might know, and more about what they're willing to tell others that they think they know."

"What?"

Drake had already selected his target: a young soldier, short and gaunt, huddled with a few of his fellows on the deck nearby. The soldier was desperately attempting not to make eye contact with anyone, and especially not Drake. Little did the man know he was likely the only one who would actually survive this ordeal. The older soldier to his left certainly wouldn't be so lucky.

"That one." Drake pointed at the older soldier. "Overboard."

As three of Drake's crew moved to obey their captain's order, the man, a handsome fellow with piercing blue eyes, started shaking his head and babbling for help. Rather than helping him, his fellow soldiers shuffled away from the doomed man as quickly as they could with bound hands and feet.

"Please don't do this," the man cried as the pirates hauled him to his feet and started dragging him to the railing. "I'm sorry. I was only doing my job. I have a family..."

"Stop!" Drake approached the soldier, who was now just a few feet from the railing. "You hear that, Stillwater? Man has a family. Wife and kids, I reckon." He looked at the soldier, who nodded obligingly. "Son? Daughter?"

"Two daughters."

"What are their names?"

"Mari, she's five, and Londre is two. I love them and I just..."

Drake held up his hand to silence the man, wincing as his other arm gave a twinge of pain. "What do you say, Stillwater? You wanted these bastards dead. Still set on it now you know you'll be orphaning poor Mari and Londre?"

Keelin Stillwater, the pirate captain infamous for taking ships without any blood spilled, stared at the soldier whose life was on the line. Drake noticed that not only pirates from both crews, but also surviving refugees from Sev'relain, had gathered around to watch and wait on the decision. He had to suppress the smile that threatened to erupt onto his tightly schooled features.

"Black Sands and Sev'relain are gone." Stillwater's grey eyes were as cold and unyielding as stone. "You beg for a mercy you did not show any of your victims."

Drake waited a moment longer for Stillwater to make the decision before prompting him. "Up to you, Captain Stillwater. Over the side or back with the others?"

"Feed him to the sharks."

"No!" the soldier shouted, but it was too late. The pirates dragged him the last couple of steps and tossed him over the railing.

The soldier's scream rang out for a moment, before it was drowned out by a splash; another moment later, Drake heard the sound of pleading again as the man resurfaced and begged for mercy he was never going to receive.

"Shouldn't be long now." Drake smiled at the twenty soldiers still bound and huddled together on the deck.

When the screaming started it was guttural, raw, and it left none that could hear under any doubt about how painful a death it was. Drake kept his face fixed in that dangerous smile, ignoring how ill the affair was making him feel. Death was necessary and, often even more so, the spectacle was needed as well. Now was one of those times. Thankfully, the screaming didn't last long; the creatures of the sea had a habit of dragging their food down below the waves to devour it. There wasn't much like the ocean and the beasties that lived in it for making a man seem small and fragile.

Drake looked at Stillwater to find the man had gone pale. He stepped between his fellow captain and the captive soldiers. "That sated your need for blood yet?" he said quietly.

Stillwater looked up at Drake and opened his mouth to reply, before promptly shutting it again and nodding.

"Good." Drake turned back to the soldiers. "So who's next?"

There was a silence so complete that Drake could hear the timbers groaning and the waves smacking against the hull. Many of the soldiers attempted to keep their eyes locked on the decking, but some of them started looking around for an escape.

"You've made your point, Drake," Stillwater said slowly.

Drake ignored the man. "I recognise you." He pointed to a young soldier and cracked a grin.

The soldier shook his head frantically.

"Aye, I think I do. Seem to remember you had a shield and were dead set on getting me killed."

"I… uh… sorry."

"You and that big bugger with the lip. Tell me something, soldier – what did you see?"

The soldier looked Drake in the eyes, his expression something between awe and terror. He opened his mouth, closed it, then opened it again. "I saw the ship come alive."

Drake heard Beck scoff, and he shot her a dangerous glance before turning back to the soldier. "Go on."

"Aiben was about to put his sword through you, and the ship came alive, protected you. Then you pointed at Aiben and told him to die, and he did. Chest just burst open."

Drake nodded sagely before turning around and approaching Princess. "Make sure that one gets back to Sarth. Drop him off on a trade route, I reckon."

Princess smiled and nodded. "The rest of 'em, Cap'n?"

"Couldn't give a shit. Feed them to the waves or stick them with their mate somewhere. Just want them out of my sight."

"Aye, Cap'n."

As Drake started walking towards the plank that had been set up between the Man of War and the *Fortune*, both Beck and Stillwater rushed to his side. Drake couldn't help but notice that Stillwater was watching the Arbiter through narrowed, suspicious eyes. There was a good chance the man had worked out what she was, and that was an issue that would need dealing with sooner rather than later. Unfortunately, he currently had the more pressing issue of a hundred homeless refugees to house.

"What was that about?" Stillwater said as Drake mounted the walkway between the ships. A quick glance downwards and Drake was assured that whatever had killed the unfortunate soldier they had thrown overboard was still very much about.

"Sometimes a healthy dose of reputation can do a man wonders. That bastard goes back to Sarth and reports to his superiors that the ship was taken by Drake Morrass and Keelin Stillwater, bloodthirsty pirates more than willing to orphan unfortunate children, all the while protected by the very ships they sail. Not to mention possessing of some quite inexplicable magics."

Drake stepped carefully back onto the *Fortune* and waited for the others to make the crossing. "Those superiors, folk in charge, dismiss most of that as fancy, possibly caused by weeks, or months, of exposure to the rough sea and indomitable sun. Problem is, that soldier doesn't stop at just telling those in charge. Problem for them, anyway.

"Back into the ranks and a couple of ales down him and he's telling everyone he knows, soldiers for the most part, maybe some sailors, but they've no doubt already heard their fair share."

Beck was the last over the plank, and she was giving Drake that unimpressed look she favoured so highly; problem was, she was beautiful no matter what look she was giving him, and Drake liked having beautiful things.

"Before anyone can stop him, there's stories floating about saying we rode ships made of fire, shot lightning from our eyes, and sucked the souls from men's bodies. Dread pirates. Morale won't be too high among men who find themselves ordered to hunt down foes like that, eh."

A couple of Drake's crew were waiting to talk to their captain with all the patience a pirate could muster.

"They say similar things about Tanner. Dread pirate, eats souls to stay alive," Keelin said

"Aye, I've heard them all. Ghost of the old Captain Black, made a deal with Rin herself to float him up from his watery grave. Same stories say that Elaina is actually the sea goddess in mortal form, but I reckon you'd know the truth of that one better than most. Ever find seaweed down where there should have been hair?"

Stillwater looked ready to take a swing, and, with Drake's current condition, he would likely land the blow. Drake held up his hand. "Point is, Stillwater, rumours and reputation are mostly shit. I know – I've made up more than a few in my life. You know the truth about Tanner and you know the truth about you. Don't really matter what other folk think, does it?"

Stillwater looked like he was about to protest, but said nothing.

"Good. Now we got some concerns to deal with. What is it?" Drake said to the first of his crew hovering nearby as he started for his cabin. Stillwater's first mate was loitering around the doorway, and Drake decided to give him the staring of a lifetime. The man looked away, cowed.

"Folk from Sev'relain, Captain. Even… uh… with… even with all da boys we lost – ain't enough space for 'em all. 'Less we gone start packin' 'em in like, uh, crates." The pirate laughed; he quickly stopped when no one else joined in.

"We have all the space we need, Heller. Start moving the refugees over onto the Man of War. You should do the same with those on your ship, Stillwater." Drake opened the door to his cabin and walked in, letting his procession follow him. He crossed the cramped space to his desk and lowered himself into the chair behind it, resisting the urge to let out a grateful sigh as his body decided it never wanted to stand ever again. At the same time he truly wished he'd retrieved a bottle of rum from the cabinet before sitting down. Little could make how he currently felt right, but rum would definitely make him feel better.

"Food..." said Stillwater's first mate, a southerner from the Wilds, if Drake wasn't mistaken.

"Same solution, I reckon." Drake leaned back in his chair and put his boots up on the desk, an action he quickly regretted when he realised they were covered in blood. "Anybody bothered to check the Man of War's hold? Reckon it might be stocked with supplies to get us to where we're going. More than enough, if you don't mind soldier's rations."

"And where are we going?" Stillwater was pacing bloody bootprints into the rug. Seemed everybody was tracking in the same mess.

"You two done, or ya got more to say?" Drake said to the two members of his crew who had followed him in.

"Uh, done, Cap'n."

"Then roll up that bloody rug and give it to the sea, then find Princess and tell him to get his arse in here."

"Aye, Captain," said Heller as they moved to obey.

Drake needed one of his charts of the isles; unfortunately, his body needed to not move. In an act of sheer willpower, he pushed himself up out of the chair. Drake was unwilling to show any sort of weakness in front of another captain or, even worse, an Arbiter. He limped over to a locked cabinet and pulled out a key from his pocket. The key was a show and nothing more; the real release on the cabinet door was a small button hidden on the bottom side of the lock. Drake inserted the key and turned it, pressing the button as he did so, and the cabinet door opened. It wasn't that he was paranoid, but more that he occasionally spent extended periods of time away from the *Fortune* and didn't trust any of his crew. Or anyone from any crew, for that matter. There were, in fact, only two people Drake trusted in the world, and one of them was himself.

He picked a specific chart from the cabinet, and then locked it again before taking the old chart to his desk and laying it flat, using two stones to weigh down the edges. He walked around to the other side of the desk, stopping by the cupboard to take out a bottle of rum, and lowered himself back into his chair. The others moved closer. Even the Arbiter seemed curious.

Drake uncorked the bottle and took a deep swig before pushing it towards the others. Stillwater eyed the rum warily, but Beck happily plucked it from the table and took a swig, and Stillwater's first mate quickly followed suit.

"So where are we going?" Stillwater was frowning down at the chart. "Can't ferry these refugees around forever, Drake."

The door to the cabin opened. Princess shuffled in, closed the door behind him, and joined the others at Drake's desk. Now that his full audience was here, it was time to upset them all. Drake pointed at a large irregular shape on the chart.

Princess was the first to respond – with laughter. Stillwater looked stony-faced, Arbiter Beck looked disappointed, and Stillwater's first mate cursed in a language Drake had never heard before.

"You're fucking mad! Captan, he's fucking mad."

"Careful, Morley," warned Princess, still grinning as if Drake had told the funniest joke the man had ever heard. "Opinions aside, you just insulted Drake Morrass aboard his own ship. Crew don't take too kindly to such."

"Blind devotion to your captan aside, Princess, but we just followed you into a foolish attack on a Sarth Man of War, and now your captan wants to feed us to the devils of Cinto Cena."

"A fairly dramatic name, don't you think?" Drake said merrily, reaching across the chart for the bottle of rum.

"Oh!" Morley exclaimed. "I should call it by its common name? The Isle of Many Deaths."

Drake shrugged, spreading his hands. "Also fairly dramatic."

Morley turned to Stillwater. "Captan, the men have already lost so much. Yanic's gone and Smithe's already got a fair number of the crew behind him."

"Not now, Morley." Stillwater was staring daggers at his first mate.

"Sounds like loyalty problems," Drake said.

"Nothing I can't handle."

"Good. Hate for a mutiny to put our alliance to dust before we even get anywhere."

"Morley isn't wrong about Cinto Cena, Drake. It's uninhabited for a reason, and folk have tried to settle there before. Between the flaming cliffs, the sand devils, and whatever the Hells makes all those noises in the forest, Many Deaths is an apt name."

"It's untouched, aye." Drake nodded. "Plenty of resources for building a new town. Getting these folk off our ships, settled and started. Between the flaming cliffs on the south side of the island and the sand devils occupying every beach front, it's the most defensible island we got."

"Except maybe the Isle of Goats."

"Aye, well that one's a whole different kettle, eh. Folk who wander into that forest don't come back out normal. Besides, it belongs to Tanner, and I don't think we'll get far trying to take it by force. Cinto Cena is the best choice we got."

"It's a shit choice," Morley said.

"Your pessimism is starting to piss me off, friend," Drake growled.

"Better you pissed off than all of us dead. Captan…"

Bristling, Drake very nearly leapt over the desk to stick a sword in Morley's guts. Only his better judgement and a lack of anything approaching an energetic response stayed his hand. Instead, he leaned forwards just a little and stared into the man's shit-brown eyes.

"My being pissed off is likely to lead quite directly to your death."

"It would be a dangerous place to settle," Stillwater said quietly.

"Captan, you can't…"

"Ain't a place in the isles doesn't have its own peculiar sorts of danger." Drake spoke over Stillwater's first mate. "That's what makes the folk that live here so damned tough."

"The flaming cliffs regularly set fire to the forest," Morley protested.

"A band of deforested area, well maintained, will make certain the fire doesn't spread," Stillwater countered. It almost made Drake smile, watching his fellow captain argue his point for him.

"And the sand devils?"

"Can be killed," Drake cut in. "I've seen it. Reckon I could teach folk. Just gotta lure them out and don't let them get away. We take the north beach, wipe the beasts out on that one, and leave them on all the others. Natural protection from any and all who might want to repeat Sev'relain."

"What about the thing in the forest?" Princess asked.

Drake sucked his golden tooth and grinned. "I'll deal with that." He forced as much bravado into his voice as possible.

The unfortunate truth of the matter was that he had no idea what called the forest of Cinto Cena its home, and just as little an idea as to whether he could deal with it. Luckily for him, he had an Arbiter as a shadow, and he was relying on her to follow him into almost certain death.

Morley looked sceptical. "You'll deal with it?"

"Aye."

There was a moment's silence as everyone in the room started to wonder whether or not it was truly possible to tame the island of Cinto Cena. It was a turning point. If they believed in Drake, they would follow him – and if they followed him there, they would follow him anywhere. If they didn't believe in him, they would try to run, sail along in someone else's wake, and the only other option was Tanner Black. If they tried to run, Drake would have to stop them.

"Start sending the refugees across to the Man of War, Morley," Stillwater said eventually. "At the same time I want the supplies split three ways, one third for each ship. Pick ten men, those you trust the most, to sail her. I assume you'll do the same, Drake?"

"Aye. Only fair, I reckon," Drake said with a genuine smile.

"As soon as people and supplies are where they need to be we'll set off."

"Good to have you on board, Stillwater."

"I really hope you know what you're doing, Drake," Stillwater said with a cold voice and a vicious glare at Beck, before turning and walking out of the cabin.

Drake waited until the other captain and his irritating first mate had gone. He waited until Princess had reported on the number of dead and injured and left. He waited until only he and Beck remained in the cabin.

"You and Stillwater," Drake said quietly. "Are we gonna have a problem?"

The Arbiter looked at him. There was still dried blood stuck to her face, and her hair was matted with it. She looked on the verge of exhaustion, but stood straight and proud regardless. She seemed to think about the question for a long while before shaking her head.

"I can handle him."

The Black Death

The back of Tanner's hand connected with his daughter's face, and she went down hard and spitting blood. Didn't take long for the little bitch to come springing back up, standing up to her father and looking like she was spoiling for another beating. She was a good head shorter than Tanner, and despite all the fury of a seasonal storm flashing behind her eyes, she backed away when he stepped forward.

"Ah, ya may have bigger stones than the rest o' my gets combined, Elaina, but don't think for a moment ta stand up to ya da." Tanner pitched his booming voice to carry both to his own crew and to the members of Elaina's that had accompanied her.

"I ain't some little girl for you ta bully, Da!" Elaina spat as she rubbed at her cheek and winced. "And if Ma were here…"

"She'd coddle ya an' tell ya 'love be a harsh mistress with harsh lessons', aye. Unlucky, then, that she ain't here an' I am. Ya shoulda told me the second I set foot on the island that Stillwater was here. That boat of his ain't so fast *The Black Death* couldn't o' caught him."

"And done what?"

"What *you* shoulda. Taken the boat back."

"It was my ship. Not yours."

Tanner gave his daughter's other cheek a sturdy backhand that sent her crashing to the decking. "It was my ship, ya little whore. They're all *my* ships. The only reason I was allowing ya ta sail it is 'cos ya got my blood in your shitty little veins, which happens ta also be the only reason I ain't strapping ya down and lettin' me crew teach ya this fucking lesson."

Like a whipped dog yet to learn its lesson, Elaina sprang back up and faced Tanner down. "Ya wouldn't fuckin' dare, Da."

Tanner lunged forwards, his head striking Elaina's face, and he felt her nose crack. His daughter collapsed onto the deck and lay there moaning, her eyes unfocused and blood leaking down over her face to pool on the decking beneath her.

"Mace," Tanner said to his first mate, pointing at his prone daughter. "In the arse. Don't want any of your gets takin' root in her belly."

Tanner watched as his first mate, a small man with arms like tree trunks and a temperament like he had something to prove, grabbed hold of Elaina's semiconscious form and turned her onto her front. Mace twisted her arms behind her back and held them there with one hand while he pulled down first her britches and then his own. Elaina struggled as she started to come around, but Mace was a strong man and he just twisted her arms tighter. Elaina gasped in pain, first as Mace twisted, and then a second time, even louder, when he thrust his cock up her arse.

"Da, get this fucker off me," Elaina screamed. Tanner stared on through pitiless eyes. If she wasn't strong enough to stop the man from fucking her, then she deserved it; and it was only through suffering that people got stronger. Elaina may be the only child of Tanner's worth the squirts he'd put in their mother, but that didn't mean she didn't need to be taught lessons the hard way.

Elaina didn't stop struggling, but Mace held her fast, and every time she tried to rid herself of her rider he only twisted her arms tighter and pushed her harder into the decking. Eventually Mace stopped thrusting and let out a long groan. Tanner heard his daughter let out an accompanying cry full of disgust and humiliation as Mace pulled himself out of her arse and stood up, backing away from the prone woman with a wild grin on his face.

Tanner loomed over his first mate. "Don't remember tellin' ya ta enjoy it."

"Sorry, Cap'n Black." The smile dropped from Mace's face, and his eyes found the deck all sorts of interesting.

Tanner growled and turned his attention back to his daughter. She was still lying face down on the deck, not moving, not making any sound.

"Get the fuck up," Tanner yelled, "before I order another one inside ya."

Elaina moved immediately, curling up into a ball before getting shakily to her feet and pulling up her britches. She turned to face Tanner, but kept her eyes cast downwards.

"That little shit, Stillwater, stole from me," Tanner shouted in his daughter's face. "Stole a ship from me. And instead of guttin' him and takin' it back, ya let him fuck you. An' the first I hear of him bein' here at all is from that dumb lubbard, Quartermain."

Elaina said nothing, but kept her eyes on the deck. Tanner could see his daughter shaking.

"Get the fuck out of my sight, ya stupid little whore." He spat on her.

Elaina didn't run, and Tanner was proud of her for that. Despite the humiliation of being beaten and raped in front of Tanner's whole crew, the girl turned and walked slowly from *The Black Death*. She didn't shed a single tear. Tanner was both proud of his daughter and disgusted with her at the same time.

"We goin' after him, Cap'n Black?" said Neril, the quartermaster.

Tanner took in a deep breath and let it out as a sound somewhere between a sigh and a growl. His crew, renowned for being the most bloodthirsty, depraved, evil bastards to sail Rin's waters, remained silent. They all knew the punishment for interrupting while he was thinking.

"No point," he said eventually. "News he was here is weeks old. Thievin' little shit is long gone by now." If only Elaina had been dutiful as a daughter, even now Tanner would have his hands around Stillwater's throat. But she was a woman, and women were prone to foolish acts – especially where men were concerned.

Some of Tanner's crew winced at an ear-piercing shriek that erupted from up high, as Pilf flew in on his great, dark wings and landed easily on the captain's shoulder. The bird looked around the gathered crew through his one good eye and let out another cry that set Tanner's ear ringing. He shrugged his big shoulders and the bird took flight again, this time landing on the ship's wheel. Pilf's beak was dark red, a testament to the fact that the bird had found something to eat.

"Ain't many places near here Stillwater coulda run ta, Cap'n Black," Neril continued. "We could…"

"He's gone," Tanner said in a voice that brooked no argument. "We lost him this time, but we'll catch up with the traitor soon enough. I feel the need to kill someone. Let's find us some quarry, boys."

Starry Dawn

Elaina ached. Every muscle in both arms hurt, and her nose was a mess of agony. She tasted blood and wiped at her mouth again. She'd limped all the way back to her ship without help, without a word, and without a tear. Elaina had been raised better than to cry in public, to be stronger than that. Now that she was alone in her cabin, the damned tears welled up and rolled down her cheeks like hot wet streaks of fire.

Pulling out a bottle of rum from her bedside cabinet, Elaina ripped the cork away with her teeth and took three unhealthy-sized swallows of the fiery booze. Being drunk would help to dull the pain.

Her arse hurt. It hurt like it had recently had a cock shoved up it, hard. It hurt to stand, and it hurt to sit. She'd wiped and wiped and wiped as soon as she was alone, but still she was finding evidence of the humiliation.

The worst pain wasn't how badly her arse hurt, nor the humiliation of the rape, of being helpless in front of all those men. The worst pain was that her father had ordered it, that he was so disappointed in her that he'd ordered one of his crew to rape her. The tears welled up and rolled down her cheeks again.

Elaina had disappointed her father before. With a man as great as Tanner Black as a father, it was impossible not to disappoint him from time to time. Her feelings for Keelin Stillwater had always been a source of contention between the two of them, but he'd never taken things so far before. She must have hurt him this time. It was her own fault; she'd had every opportunity to kill Keelin. Instead Elaina had let him go, and even worse, she knew she'd do it again, given the chance.

There was a knock at her cabin door, and Pavel's soft voice drifted through the wooden barrier. "Captain. I should look at you. The crew says you're banged up rather badly."

Elaina wiped the tears from her face, wincing at the pain, and took another swig from the bottle of rum before making her way to the door. Her quartermaster was on the other side with Pavel. Corin's face was caught between horror and anger. Pavel's was worse. Elaina hated being pitied. Even worse was that she deserved the pity.

"Captain..." Corin started.

"Tell the crew I'm fine," Elaina slurred, her swollen lips sore and the taste of blood suddenly stronger. "They get a few more days' leave and are not to go anywhere near my father's crew."

Corin looked set to argue, but he nodded and turned away. Elaina stood aside to let Pavel into the room. The man swept past her, his red robe billowing as he went, and headed straight for Elaina's desk, where he deposited a large black leather case. Elaina closed the door and limped after the doctor.

"Your father did that to you?" Pavel said as he rooted through his case.

"Some of it." Elaina stopped beside the doctor and leaned against her desk, wincing.

Pavel said nothing in reply, giving Elaina a disapproving look. Not that the doctor's opinion mattered a damn. He stared into her face, gently took hold of her chin, and turned her head first to the left, then to the right. Even Elaina's neck hurt, and she felt like cursing the names of all the gods to have been born with such poor judgement as to piss off her father so.

"Your nose is broken," Pavel said eventually.

"I can tell," Elaina slurred back.

"It will need setting. It will hurt. You should sit."

"I prefer to stand."

Pavel looked at her disapprovingly again. "You should sit."

Elaina attempted to give the man a withering stare, but considering her black eyes and swollen cheeks and lips, she wagered she missed the mark. "Have you ever had a cock up your arse, Doc?"

Pavel looked uncomfortable. "No."

"I'll stand."

Pavel spent a few minutes poking painfully around her nose before placing one hand on either side and...

"Fuck!"

Elaina couldn't help but shout as the doctor snapped her nose back into position, bringing with it a fresh wave of blood that careened down her face and the metallic taste of more of it at the back of her throat. She pulled away from the doctor just in time to stop him seeing her tears, and banged her fist down hard on her desk. Fat drops of blood dripped down and pooled upon the wood, and Elaina fought the urge to turn and punch Pavel in his nose so he could experience the agony.

Wiping at her eyes, Elaina turned back to face the doctor, who had already riffled through his case and was now brandishing some sort of lotion. "I need to clean the blood away and apply this to your cuts. It will stop them from infecting and should help bring down the swelling."

Elaina perched on her desk, ignoring the pain, and nodded at the doctor. "Remind me never to disappoint my father again."

Pavel began to wipe the blood from Elaina's mouth. "I would prefer to remind your father that Pelsing judges how we should treat our children."

Elaina snorted out a laugh, complete with a spray of blood and a hearty dose of pain. "I don't think you'd survive that sermon, Doc. Your golden god don't hold much sway out here. Our god is wet, cruel, and loves women over all men."

"If that were true," Pavel countered in a frustratingly calm voice as he applied lotion to Elaina's face, "would she allow your father to treat you in such a way?"

"Suffering makes you stronger," Elaina said, repeating the words her father had drilled into all his children over and over again. "A lesson learned without pain isn't learned at all. The pain makes you remember. Stops you from repeating."

"Poor girl."

Elaina snapped out of her reverie and gave the doctor a hard push, sending him stumbling. "Don't ever think to pity me, Doc. Don't you ever. Are we done?"

"Yes," Pavel said quietly as he packed his lotions and tools back into his case. "You should rest."

Elaina did feel tired, but there was no time to rest. She needed to plan where she would take the ship next. Needed to figure out how to regain her father's favour.

The Phoenix

Keelin set foot on his ship for the first time in almost a full day. He'd been over on the *Fortune* or the Man of War for so long it was a breath of fresh air to be confronted by a clean, bloodless deck. Morley was only a few steps behind him, and Keelin could feel the man's frustration. Morley didn't agree with the decision to attempt to settle on Cinto Cena. Unfortunately for Morley, it wasn't his decision to make.

Most of *The Phoenix*'s crew were assembled on deck, far too many for chance. Keelin felt his spirits drop. He was somewhere beyond tired, ravenous as the sharks that prowled the waters below the ship, and sick to the stomach from the weight of death he'd witnessed – and caused – over the past two days. It dawned on Keelin then that he hadn't actually seen the inside of his cabin since they'd left Sev'relain two days ago.

"Captain…" Feather started, but he was pushed out of the way by Smithe.

"Seems we still need a new quartermaster…"

"Not now," Keelin said as he started towards his cabin.

"Aye, now." Smithe sidestepped into Keelin's way and planted his feet.

Keelin stared up at the bigger man, who looked more than ready for another fight. In fact, despite the recent battle they'd been involved in, Smithe looked wholly uninjured. Keelin wished he could make the same claim.

Smithe balled his hands into fists. "We vote. Now."

With a resigned sigh, Keelin nodded his acceptance. "Morley," he said, perching upon a nearby railing. "As previous quartermaster, it's your show now."

Morley looked anything but happy about the affair, but stepped forward nonetheless. "Captan made me first mate," he said loudly to the pirates. "Can't be quartermaster too, so looks like we need a new man for the job." A low grumble went through the gathered crowd, and Keelin saw Feather trying to manoeuvre his way to his captain. Only problem was the boy was too small to get past the bigger men. Keelin focused his attention back on the vote.

"You all know the way this goes," Morley continued. "Candidates need to be recommended, and no, you can't recommend yourself. Nor can myself or the captain recommend anyone."

"I recommend Smithe," shouted a young man called Fiefel Wash. Keelin made a note of the name, as he did with all Smithe's supporters. The recommendation was expected, and if Fiefel hadn't made it, there were others who would have. The unfortunate truth was that Smithe was well liked among the crew.

Keelin sat and watched, waiting for the next recommendation as the pirates talked quietly and some even started jostling others to put names forward. Keelin idly wondered where Kebble Salt had got to. He hadn't seen the man during the battle, but he'd definitely felt his presence. An expert marksman seemed to be a useful crew member to have. Now Kebble appeared to be missing, and Keelin hoped he wasn't among the dead.

"Is there no one else?" Morley said. "Last chance."

Keelin had thought it unlikely that anyone else would attain enough votes to beat Smithe, but he'd hoped it might happen. Dealing with the irritating pirate day in and out as quartermaster of the ship was right up there in the list of things Keelin would prefer not to experience, along with hanging and ever seeing Tanner Black again. Without another candidate, there wouldn't even be a vote; Smithe would simply take up the position unopposed.

"Really?" Morley sounded sceptical. "No one else?"

"Call it, Morley," Smithe said, wearing a victorious grin that said he'd planned such a victory all along. No doubt he and his supporters had been visiting other members of the crew and making certain none would recommend anyone else.

"Alright," Morley said with a heavy sigh. "Smithe is our new quartermaster." He shot Keelin a sympathetic look.

"Congratulations," Keelin growled. "Now if you will all excuse me."

Keelin pushed past the crew and made for his cabin. Smithe caught up with him easily. "Where are we headin'? Crew deserve to know."

"Right now I'm heading to my cabin. After that we're following the *Fortune*."

"Where? Crew want to get paid. Can't pay nobody if we don't have nothin' to pay them with. We need to find a ship to take, not cling to Morrass' skirts."

Keelin stopped outside the cabin door. Behind Smithe, Feather was still waiting, but Keelin didn't have the patience for any of them right now.

"Smithe," Keelin said slowly. "Fuck off." He turned, opened the door to his cabin, and stepped through, quickly locking it behind him. He was immediately hit by the silence. It wasn't a true silence; on board a ship it never was. No matter how calm the ocean, or how empty of crew a boat might be, there was always the creaking of planks, the slap of waves against the hull, and the murmur of voices through the walls and deck. It wasn't real silence, but there were no more sounds of battle, of the dying screaming out their last breaths, or men wanting orders, or a hundred other intrusions.

"Is it over?" A woman's voice, behind him.

Keelin spun around, his left hand instinctively moving towards a weapon. The woman from Sev'relain, the one he'd been watching and obsessing over, was sitting on Keelin's bed with her knees gathered up into her arms and a look of fear plain upon her face. It took Keelin a few moments to remember that he'd ordered her brought to his cabin when they left Sev'relain.

"Aye," he said with a tired smile. "For now. We killed them."

"Oh." The woman's eyes stayed locked onto the bed. "Did you have to?"

Keelin laughed as he walked over to his wardrobe. "Well, they were trying to kill us, so it seemed prudent."

"Prudent?"

"A good idea."

"Oh."

Keelin glanced back at the woman. There was something beautiful and delicate about her that didn't belong in the Pirate Isles. Her eyes were wide and looked almost vacant; it was a type of shock Keelin had seen a hundred times.

"I'm going to change now." Keelin wished he had time to wash as well. "I hope you don't mind. It's just, I'm covered in blood."

The woman made a non-committal noise.

"Don't worry. Only some of it is mine." Keelin opened the wardrobe and selected a new shirt and britches, and a jacket that he hoped would make him look very much like a swashbuckling hero, even though in reality swashbuckling heroes only appeared in children's stories. He'd learned the hard way that most swashbucklers are actually murderous pirates, and he was very much one of them.

As he changed, Keelin watched the woman in the mirror attached to the wardrobe door. She never moved, not an inch; not even her eyes shifted from their fixed position.

"What's your name?" he said as he pulled his new shirt on over the bandages.

"Aimi." Her voice was soft and warm.

"I'm Keelin..."

"Captain Stillwater. We're required to know all the important people."

Keelin felt his pride swell a little. Not usually one to indulge in his ego, a little flattery was always nice. He pulled on his jacket. "Required for what?"

"Work. Important people get served first. Keeps the captains happy."

Keelin nodded and started arranging his dirty clothes. He gathered them all into a neat pile and briefly considered throwing them overboard, but good jackets and shirts were difficult to come by in the isles, so he decided he'd clean them the next time he found a spare moment. He noticed that his boots were soaked in blood as well – and he desperately needed to not be wearing any more bloody attire.

"There should be a spare pair of boots under the cot. Would you mind fetching them for me?"

"I'm not a whore," the woman said with venom, lifting her eyes for the first time and gazing furiously at Keelin.

"Uh..." Keelin attempted to think of a reply. He failed, and settled on staring at her as though she were a wolf about to attack. She stared back, and for a long time silence held between the two. "I'll, um… fetch my own boots then."

Perhaps it was the lack of sleep, the sheer exhaustion from recent events, or perhaps it was Keelin's strange fascination with the woman, but too late he noticed the shards of his little clay rum mug swept underneath the bed. As he drew close the woman uncoiled and pounced in one fluid movement, her body crashing into his. They both went down. The world turned as Keelin fell, and he reached out, grabbed hold of the woman's arms, and held her above him so that he wouldn't land on her. Then he hit the wooden deck, his head bouncing, and white spots twinkled in and out of existence. The world seemed muggy and slow. Distantly he heard the sound of a woman crying.

With effort, Keelin pushed the woman up off him. That was when he noticed the shard of baked clay sticking out of his chest.

"What the fuck?" Keelin all but shouted, more than a little shocked by his recent, if rather unorthodox, stabbing. He was also a little worried that the pain hadn't yet kicked in.

"I told you, I'm not a whore!" the woman shouted back, retreating to the cot and resuming her curled-up position.

"I wasn't trying to screw you, woman. I was trying to get dressed." Keelin gripped the shard and, with a grimace that was all pain, pulled it out of his flesh. Luckily the fragment was small and hadn't gone in too deep, but it was starting to hurt like all the watery Hells.

"Please don't do that again." Keelin got to his feet and debated changing his shirt again – there was already a deep red patch on it that would likely get bigger – but he needed to get the wound seen to first.

"Then why did you bring me here? Why am I the only one in your cabin?"

Despite her recent attack and accusations against Keelin's moral character, he still found himself inexplicably attracted to the woman, and it didn't put him in the best of moods.

"To protect you," he growled. "From people who actually might be trying to fuck you."

"What?"

"There's a lot of men on this ship. Some haven't been ashore in a while, and that means they haven't seen a cunt in a while. Not to mention those that have recently lost their homes, families, and livelihoods, and may be looking for a little fun to make things seem a bit less worse. Not all men care about whether or not the woman feels the same way." Keelin looked at himself in the mirror; the shirt was ruined and the wound was still bleeding.

"Are you saying you can't control your crew?" The woman stared at Keelin over her knees.

"What? Of course I can... most of them. Look, if you'd rather take your chances out there with them..." Keelin stormed over to the cabin door, unlocked it, and threw it open. Feather was waiting on the other side, and he jumped to attention. "Then go ahead."

"Captain?"

"Shut up, Feather," Keelin growled, still waiting for Aimi's response.

"You promise you won't try to fuck me?"

"I honestly can't think of anything I'd rather do less," Keelin lied.

"Then I'll stay."

"Wonderful," Keelin shouted. He stepped over the threshold and slammed the door behind him, only then realising that he still wasn't wearing any boots.

"Captain?" said Feather.

Keelin buried his head in his hands. "What is it?"

"Just thought ya should know that woman ya ordered put in ya cabin is still there."

Fortune

The man let out a groan, and his eyelids fluttered. His mouth worked open and closed, and he tasted the wooden deck he was lying on. A moment later, a confused expression graced his previously peaceful face. His eyes slowly opened and blinked away the blurry confusion.

"Good morning," Drake said with cheer. "I was starting to wonder if you were ever gonna wake up."

"What…" the man started. He coughed.

"Probably a little thirsty, eh?" Drake placed a water skin in front of him. "Go on, have a drink."

The man reached out for the skin, but stopped short when the shackles around his wrists clattered on the deck. He looked down at the cold iron for a moment, before Drake saw realisation light in his eyes.

"You…" He coughed again.

"Go on, Admiral." Drake pointed towards the water skin with his good hand. "Just water. You'll feel better after a slurp, and then you can insult and threaten me as much as you please."

The man hesitated for a moment before the needs of the body won out. He reached forwards, grabbing the water skin and squeezing mouthful after mouthful down his throat.

"I hear you're supposed to sip when dehydrated," Drake said, earning a glare from the admiral. "Isn't that right?" Drake looked at Beck, who was leaning against the wall next to the door.

Beck shrugged and went back to cleaning one of her little pistols. Drake had no idea how she could do such delicate work in the dim light of the little cabin, but there were many things about Arbiters he didn't entirely understand.

"My men?" The admiral pulled himself up into a more gentlemanly sitting position, placed his back against the wall, and smoothed down his naval jacket – which, Drake had to admit, had seen better days.

"Dead," Drake replied with an easy grin. "Most of 'em, anyway. Couple of them are going to live, I'll see to that."

Having smoothed down his jacket as well as he could manage, the admiral set about running his fingers through his moustache and bedraggled hair.

"I like that," Drake said to Beck. "Even in chains and certain peril, he takes the time to smarten up his appearance."

"That's the difference between gentlemen and rogues." The admiral sneered. "No matter what you do to me, I will always be a gentlemen. No matter how high you might rise, you will always be a rogue."

Drake mulled the statement over for a moment. "I think I prefer being a rogue." He glanced at Beck. "Think she does too." Beck snorted.

"So let's get down to business, Admiral. You're done. Ship captured, crew killed, and ain't nobody expecting you back home for a while at least. Ain't nobody going to come rescue you. It would be… sensible for you to answer my questions."

"You will get nothing from me, pirate."

"Do you know where you are?"

"Aboard your ship?"

"Aye, a small, dark cell on board the *Fortune*. Right at the bottom, so when we get sailing seawater will slosh in and out and in and out. Do you know who I am?"

Drake saw the man hesitate before nodding.

"Good. This lady behind me is Arbiter Beck."

The man's face twisted in disgust. "No Arbiter would ever work for a pirate."

"He's not wrong," Beck said sweetly. Drake turned to find her grinning at him. She may have saved his life more than once already, but Drake truly wished she'd be a little more cooperative. Just once, he would like people to do as he wanted with being manipulated, coerced, or threatened into it. Of course, he had to admit, that would remove the pleasure of bending them to his will.

"We got three ways of doing this," Drake continued. "You can either answer my questions willingly – that'd be the gentlemanly way of doing things – or you can answer her questions." He nodded towards Beck. "Or we can do this the old-fashioned way."

"I won't be asking him any of your questions," Beck said. "I'm not a member of your crew, Drake. And I don't take orders from you." She pulled the door open and stepped outside.

The admiral let out a very noble-sounding laugh that made Drake want to punch the man – and he might have if his right arm hadn't been hanging in a sling.

"I don't know why you have an Arbiter on your ship, Morrass, but as you can see, the servants of Volmar are not easily corrupted."

Drake cracked the admiral a golden-toothed grin over his shoulder. "We'll see about that."

Beck wasn't angry; she was indifferent. It was the curse of being a beautiful woman; all of her life, men had been trying to take advantage of her. After she'd earned her coat, things had been a little different. No matter how much the average fool might be attracted to her, most would pale at the prospect of spending prolonged periods of time with an Arbiter. Of course, that had angered her at first. The only thing worse than the attention of men had been losing that attention, but she'd got used to it mostly because she'd realised it didn't truly matter. Their desire for her and knowledge that they could never have her gave her power over them and, whether they ignored her or not, she retained that power.

Drake was different. He wanted her – any fool with eyes could see that – but he didn't pursue her, and neither did he act like a man who knew he would never have her. It was all frustrating to the point of murder, an act Beck was not beneath, but she had given Hironous Vance her word that she would protect Drake Morrass.

With a frustrated growl, Beck stopped and levelled a punch at the door to her cabin. The wood neither gave an inch nor cared at the unsolicited violence.

"You got an issue, take it out on me, not the ship," came Drake's voice from behind. That he'd followed her, after she'd quite clearly stormed away, only served to make Beck angrier. She turned, and as soon as the pirate captain was within reach, she grabbed him and shoved him up against the wall. Beck was smaller than Drake, but with a whispered blessing of strength, and his back pressed firmly against the wooden wall, it was an easy thing to lift the pirate off his feet with just her left arm. With her right, she sent a punch into his stomach before stepping away and letting him collapse onto the floor.

"Fuck," Drake wheezed out between coughs and splutters. "You hit… hard."

In truth Beck had pulled her punch significantly. With her blessing of strength she could likely kill a normal man with one strike, but she wouldn't break her promise to Inquisitor Vance. She pulled open the door to her cabin.

"Obviously I touched a nerve," Drake said from the floor.

Beck stopped. "My magic is not some tool to facilitate your torture of a man. It is not a plaything, and it is to be used only in the service of Volmar." Beck might have imagined it, but it almost felt as if the ship shook at the mention of her god's name.

Drake slowly pushed himself to his feet with his one good arm. "But it's alright for you to use that magic to beat up unsuspecting pirates, especially one obviously too injured to protect himself?"

Beck glared at the man. "Sometimes it serves Volmar to remind people that…" Again the ship seemed to shake a little at the name of the god, and this time even Drake seemed to notice it. The man looked truly worried, far from his usual arrogance.

"You say that name again, Arbiter," he said, more earnest than Beck had ever heard him, "and I swear to Rin, I will throw you to her. I'll not risk my ship, my crew, and my life because you don't understand the rules here. There's power in names, Arbiter Beck. Things greater than us hear them when spoken, and not all of those things like that name you keep throwing about. There's a reason folk refer to their gods as *he* and *she* and *her* and *him*. It's not always wise to gain the attention of a creature powerful enough to name itself a god."

"Captain!" A grizzled old pirate with more grey hair than black leapt down from a ladder that led up to the deck.

"What is it, Ollie?"

"The sea, Captain."

"Aye, still there, is it?"

"It's… um… ah, shit. Captain, you best come look fer ya own self."

Drake wasted no time in running for the ladder, and Beck followed in close pursuit. The older pirate had gone ahead, and as Beck emerged into the waning light of the day she could see him, and what looked like most of the crew, crowded around the railings of the ship and looking down at the water below them.

Beck followed Drake as he mounted the ladder to the poop deck and crossed to the side of the ship. Many of his crew were looking to him now, asking what they should do, while others were making crude signs in the air.

As Drake reached the railing his face paled, his mouth hanging open. The man was clearly speechless – for the first time in his life, Beck suspected. She reached the railing a moment later, and looked down to see why. The sea was black.

It took Beck a while to realise that it wasn't actually the sea that was black. There was something darker than night just below the surface of the water, and whatever it was, it seemed to stretch the entire length of the ship and then some. Judging by the reaction of the crews on the other ships, it spanned all three of them. With a whispered blessing of sight, Beck could just about make out scales on the black surface.

"What is it?"

"It's a leviathan," Drake said, his voice full of awe and dread.

"Shall we get the poles, Cap'n?" shouted one of the pirates to a cacophony of replies from other crew members.

"Anyone so much as spits into the water, and I'll personally sacrifice ya to Rin," Drake shouted over the din. He gestured downwards to make his point. "Stillwater," he yelled across to *The Phoenix*. "Same goes for your crew. Let's try to not make any aggressive moves, eh."

"How big is it?" Beck said. She'd never seen a creature so large. She'd never even imagined anything living could grow so monstrous. Even a dragon would pale in comparison to the beast that floated beneath them.

"Big enough that it could sink all three ships with barely a flick, and it wouldn't even notice the carnage it caused." Drake grabbed hold of Beck's shoulder and turned her around to face him. A part of her realised she should be insulted by the manhandling, but something about the size of the creature beneath them shocked her into inaction.

"You know why there's so few tales about these bloody things?" Drake hissed.

Beck shook her head. Drake's face was different; all the usual smug self-confidence was gone, replaced by earnest fear.

"Because nobody tends to live through a sighting. They ain't just your average beastie come up from the depths for a glimpse of sunlight, Arbiter. They're Rin's damned servants. Sent by an angry goddess to punish those who earn her wrath," Drake added in a whisper.

"I'm sure people must have said Vol…" Beck was silenced by a slap from Drake. For a moment she was too shocked to react. But only for a moment.

"How dare…"

"I just saved your life, and that of every other man, woman, and child on these three boats. I'm sure your god's name has been said over the sea before. For one reason or another, she" – he pointed downwards – "has decided to take offence, and trust me when I tell you this, Arbiter. Your god will not be able to save you from her. Not here."

Beck thought about arguing for a moment. One last glance over the side of the boat convinced her that, though it might all be shit, sometimes it was better to be cautious. Instead, she leaned forwards so that her face was close to Drake's, and attempted to still her shaking.

"If you ever slap me again, you will lose that hand."

"Captain," shouted a pirate from the lower deck. "What do we do?"

Beck held Drake's gaze for a few moments more, until a grin erupted onto his face and he turned to face his crew.

"Do?" Drake shouted loudly enough to carry to the adjacent ship. "We do nothing. That beastie down there is one of Rin's, and we are her fucking chosen!" A cheer passed through the pirates below, and Drake leapt up onto the railing that overlooked the main deck, steadying himself by grabbing hold of a low-hanging rope.

"You really think she'd send a leviathan to kill us? No. She sent it to inspire us. To congratulate us on our victory. Her victory. And to remind us that out here on the blue, we live and die by her leave.

"Today we did the impossible, boys. Today we took on Sarth and we *fucking won*!" Again a cheer erupted from the gathered pirates; this time it wasn't only Drake's crew. Beck looked across to Stillwater's ship to see the captain and many of his crew standing at or on the railing, leaning out to hear Drake's words and cheering along.

"They burned our towns, slaughtered friends and family members, and they tried to murder us. But did we let them?"

"No!" the pirates shouted in unison.

"They tried to take away our freedom, but did we let them?"

"No!" The atmosphere was so charged that Beck almost found herself joining in. After all, she'd fought to keep these people alive and free as well.

"No!" Drake screamed back. "We fought and we won!" Pirates from both the *Fortune* and *The Phoenix* cheered even louder than before, complete with stamping on the decks and wooting calls from up in the rigging. Beck watched Drake from behind as he strutted back and forth on the railing, inciting the crowd to even more noise. Eventually the captain raised his hand, and the crews fell silent, waiting.

"Today was historic." Drake didn't shout. He pitched his voice to carry, and Beck saw that the sudden lowering of volume worked. Crew members on *The Phoenix* were hanging dangerously far out over the stretch of water between the two vessels to hear the man's next words. It was almost as if they'd forgotten about the giant sea creature below them. "And the thing about history is you either watch it pass, or you make it happen. Well, today we made it happen."

Again a cheer went up, and again Drake strutted back and forth for the pirates before holding his hand up for quiet. Beck caught herself in a smile, and quickly replaced it with a much more fitting scowl.

"Now, it ain't over. Not by a bloody long shot. In fact, this right here is just the beginning. They're gonna send more, a lot more. They're gonna come at us with every fucking thing they have."

Drake paused and swept a gaze over all those gathered before him. Beck tore her eyes away from him and risked a glance at the pirates. They were rapt, hanging on his every word and looking at Drake Morrass as if he were their saviour – or, Beck realised, their king.

"So we're gonna answer with everything we have. The *Fortune* and *The Phoenix* and all of you are just the start. By the time they next come at us I intend to have every pirate that calls the isles their home, and every ship they sail, ready to fight alongside you.

"This is our home," he shouted. "This is her kingdom. And we are Rin's chosen!" Again the crews cheered, and again Drake strutted for them.

"Break out the rum," he said when the noise had died down enough that he could be heard. "Two portions per man, and then back to work. I want these ships ready to sail by nightfall."

Beck realised she was standing behind Drake, but couldn't recall moving from the port side railing. She quickly rectified the situation by crossing back to the railing and arranging herself as if she'd never left it. The problem was that Drake was compelling, and his words were inspiring. Beck found herself caught up in them and wanting to help. It was unusual for her, a woman who had built a reputation of indifference.

"Is it still there?" Drake said as he approached.

"Yes." Beck took care to keep her voice neutral. "Although only a couple of people seem to care anymore. Fancy words, you said. Were they for their benefit?" Beck waved towards the two ships. "Or for hers?"

Drake smiled. "Both. They needed something else to think about, and it never hurts to appease the local deity, eh. So you believe in her now?"

Beck ignored the question. It was difficult not to believe in Rin, given the timely appearance of a leviathan directly below her, but she certainly wasn't about to admit that to Drake Morrass, nor convert. She did decide it would be prudent to refrain from speaking Volmar's name when over water in the future.

"Thought so," Drake said. "Well, if you'll excuse me, I have to go torture a man."

"I can help," Beck said before she could think of a reason to stop.

"Eh?"

"You need to know what he knows."

"Might help save lives. Might help win the war that's coming."

Beck turned and pinned Drake with a stare. "I'll help."

"Why?"

"Does it matter why?" Beck attempted to seize hold of Drake's will but, as always, it proved to be as slippery as the man's reputation. "You want my help. I'm willing to give it."

Drake walked out of the little cell, leaving a broken wreck of a man behind. The admiral was kneeling on the wooden floor with his head buried in his hands and great, racking sobs escaping from his lips. It appeared he could be made to be less than a gentleman after all. Drake knew the man's breaking had been inevitable the moment Beck had entered the room, the moment he realised that his faith in the Inquisition had been a lie. The moment he realised that Drake had *corrupted* an Arbiter. The subsequent questioning, during which Drake had learned everything the admiral knew about Sarth's invasion of the Pirate Isles, had reduced the man to tears. To see him struggle to resist Beck's compulsion and fail, to see the man's will subverted by such a small woman – Drake would be lying to himself if he tried to deny the whole situation had turned him on.

"Did you get everything?" Beck said from behind. Drake felt her compulsion wash over him and take hold of nothing. That he was one of the few people who could resist her subversion of a person's will only turned him on even more.

Drake stopped and turned on his heel so suddenly that Beck almost walked into him. She was mere inches away from him, close enough to touch, close enough to smell. He smiled at her, making certain his one golden tooth showed.

"Not yet," he said with a wink.

He expected her to hit him, or insult him, or hit and insult him – but she didn't. For a few moments Arbiter Beck just stared up at Drake. Then she snorted, pushed past him roughly, and stormed away to her cabin. Drake watched her go with a smile plastered to his face. Not for the first time, he caught himself imagining what she'd look like naked. His imagination was not left wanting.

Climbing ladders was not the easiest thing to do with one arm in a sling. Nor was it the first time Drake had done it. An unfortunate consequence of being a pirate was that he spent much, if not most, of his life on board a ship. It was impossible to sail without climbing ladders, ropes, and rigging, and occasionally free-climbing up the outside hull even as the ship was cresting and falling through thirty-foot waves. Drake hoped he'd never have to repeat that experience, but if it had taught him one thing, it was to not complain at the relatively simple climb of a six-foot ladder leading to the main deck.

Up top he found his crew had ceased their celebrations and were well into the act of getting the ship squared away. Refugees were being led onto the captured Man of War, and supplies were being moved the other way. The wounded were all gone from the deck. Those that were likely to live were recovering in the mess, while those that weren't were also being moved to the Man of War. There was still plenty of blood on deck, and it was impossible not to notice the smell of it along with the stench of loosened bowels – an unfortunate side effect of death.

"Princess," Drake shouted over to his first mate as he limped his way to the captain's cabin. There was nothing in the world Drake wanted to do right now more than sleep – with the one possible exception of Arbiter Beck – but sleep would have to wait. He had more pressing concerns.

"Aye, Cap'n," Princess said as he fell in line with Drake. The man looked terrible, with one eye swollen shut and a larger, darker bag than Drake had ever seen under the other.

"How are preparations?"

"Could be better," Princess admitted. "We're down a few men and they took a spell off their feet with the rum, but they're all back up to it now. We should be ready to sail by night. Hopefully, Cap'n."

"Good enough." Drake nodded. "Princess, I need you to get over to the Man of War and find the ship's charts. Bring them to me as soon as you find them, and under no circumstances is anyone else to see them. Good?"

"Aye, Cap'n. Something wrong?"

Drake stopped outside his cabin and fixed his first mate with a blank stare. "Get to it, Princess."

Starry Dawn

"Sail starboard!"

Elaina threw the rope she'd been fixing aside and leapt to her feet. She sprinted to the starboard side and reached for her monoscope. Sure enough, there was the tell-tale white of a sail at the very edge of visible range.

"Change course, put us on her," she shouted to Ed the Navigator. "Pollick, The moment you get a glimpse of what she is, you yell."

"Wouldn't ya rather it be a surprise, Cap?" Four-Eyed Pollick called down from the nest.

"Don't get smart with me! Remember where the Hells we are and keep all four of your eyes peeled."

Elaina went back to her rope. It was tangled, frayed, torn, ripped, and mouldy, but if there was one thing she'd learned growing up in the Pirate Isles, it was that no matter how much like shit something seemed, it could be made near good as new with a lot of hard work. She sat back down on the deck and took one of the knotted sections in hand, working it back and forth against itself to loosen the salty crust that formed on all knots. Some captains didn't like doing this sort of work; they preferred to distance themselves from their crew and sit in their cabins, staring at charts and pretending they were busy when really they were just plain lazy. Elaina was not one of those captains. If there was a job to be done, she was the first to sign up for the task, and her cabin was little more than a place to sleep. She preferred to be up on deck, to be able to see the ocean and the sky.

Corin hovered nearby, watching and chewing on his lip. Elaina had noticed him even before she sat back down on the deck, but decided to wait for her quartermaster to make his move.

The knot in the rope loosened just enough for Elaina to start threading it through, and within a minute she'd untangled it entirely, leaving only a stiff, salt-encrusted kink in the rope where it had been. Unfortunately the kink would need to be ironed out before the rope could be used again, but that was a task for later, once all the knots had been removed. The loosening of the knot had also revealed yet another mouldy strand of rope that would need to be cleaned. Elaina pulled out her boot knife and started scraping away at the green-blue filth.

"Elaina…" Corin said after what seemed like an age of waiting.

Familiarity with the crew was something her father disagreed with, but whatever his misgivings, he let Elaina run her ship as she pleased, and she preferred to breed trust through friendship. Most of her crew still referred to her as "Captain", but Corin had known her since birth; they had in fact both fed off the same tit as babies, after Elaina's mother had run dry. An unfortunate consequence of having eight previous children, Elaina wagered.

"Your concerns, or the crew's?" Elaina interrupted him

The quartermaster squirmed a little, then walked to the aft railing to stare out at the sea. "Mine. Crew would follow you into the port of Sarth if you led them there. Probably."

"Because they know I never would," Elaina countered as she cut away a decaying thread of rope. She heard Corin spit over the side of the ship. "Point is, they trust you, perhaps more than they should."

"Have I ever done wrong by them before? Haven't I earned that trust?"

"Earned it and more, Elaina. You know that. But I got responsibilities, as quartermaster, to them, to you, and to the ship. Ya know?"

"It's OK, Corin. Out with it."

There was silence, a little too long a silence. Elaina looked up to find her friend staring out across the blue behind them with a vacant look on his face that went beyond peaceful and into serene. Elaina was up in flash, the old rope once again discarded. She grabbed hold of Corin and shook him hard, until his eyes came back into focus.

"Are you using on board my ship?" Elaina hissed as she held the man close. Close enough to smell it on his breath.

"Um…" Corin glanced downwards, and Elaina realised she was still holding her boot knife – only now it was pressed up against the quartermaster's neck.

With a curse that was more fury than words, Elaina drove the knife point-first into the aft railing and took a step back from Corin. She could feel a choking rage inside that was attempting to blot out all rational thought, but she took control and refused to let it out. Her temper was a horrible thing, and it ran in the family. Hers was second only to her father's; even so, it was nothing in comparison to his.

Elaina had once witnessed her father beat a man to death with his bare hands, and keep on swinging until there was little left of the man's head but bloody mush and bone. Even then, he'd ordered the corpse strung up so he could continue to beat it. The mere memory helped Elaina to calm her inner rage.

"I don't care what ya do on your time, but I told ya not to use that shit while on my ship."

"I don't," Corin protested. "Not usually. I mean, I just… I needed something to take the edge off before I came to speak to you."

"Take the edge off?"

"It helps me relax."

"You weren't just relaxed." Elaina gave him a hard shove before sitting back down with her rope. "You were one shitting step away from being asleep."

"I wasn't. I was…" Corin paused, fiddling with his locks of matted brown hair. "Contemplating."

"You ain't boarding."

"Elaina, that ain't…"

"No," she said firmly. "You just damn near fell asleep during a conversation. What happens if ya do the same during a fight? You ain't going anywhere near a fight till that shit is out of ya."

Corin made a whining sound, but didn't argue any further. After a few moments Elaina looked up to find her friend chewing on his lip again. He looked very much like he had something to say.

"Concerns," Elaina prompted.

"You sailed us south-west, Elaina. Towards Acanthia."

"I'm well aware."

"What if that's an Acanthian ship?"

"I hope it is."

"And what if it's one that's got protection? Not even your da goes against the Guild."

That was precisely why Elaina had ordered the crew to sail towards Acanthia. She needed to regain her father's favour, to prove she had stones as big as his own. That wasn't something Corin needed to hear. He, like the rest of the crew, was a pirate, and the language they spoke was loot.

"Acanthian merchants are pretty much hands down the richest in the world, right?" Elaina said as she used brute force to try to work a knot free. The salty rope didn't budge.

"Right."

"Because those bastards over in Truridge don't just trade in normal goods. They have access to exotic shit, the likes of which can't be got anywhere else. I don't know how they do it, but they sell and ship Drurr-made items. Glass swords that glow with the light of a candle and don't ever chip or break. Leather armour harder than steel. Cloth that changes colour depending on who's looking at it. Shit like that is worth more than its weight in gold, and they're the only ones that sell it. Guess they must trade with the Drurr, or something. That's why they're so damned rich, and that's why they can afford to pay the Guild for protection."

"But the Guild…"

"Fuck the Guild," Elaina spat. "If that ship's a trader, and if it is from Acanthia, and if it is one with Guild protection – who's gonna tell the Guild it was us that took 'em when all their throats are cut? We kill everyone on board, no exceptions, and whatever fancy loot we take off 'em is gonna make us all rich. Even my da will have to be impressed then."

"I don't know, Elaina…"

"Well I do," she snapped. "And as it fucking happens, I'm captain. We're taking that ship, and you aren't going anywhere near the fight. Get yourself below decks and don't let me see you again until that shit is out of your system."

Corin opened his mouth to say more, but quickly closed it when Elaina shot him an acid glare. With a nod, the quartermaster turned to slink away. It was a harsh way to deal with a friend, Elaina knew, but she wasn't about to have her decisions questioned – not over this, and especially not by a man so drugged up on Lucy his teeth likely shone in the dark.

With a growl, Elaina threw the tangled rope aside and leapt to her feet. Feeling the need to expend some energy all of a sudden, she ran all the way to the forecastle as fast as her bare feet could carry her.

Three hours later, and not only had they confirmed the ship was a trading fluyt, but they were quickly gaining on her. The *Starry Dawn* was not the fastest ship in the isles, nor the fastest in Tanner Black's little fleet, but she was sure as a watery grave fast enough to outrun a merchant vessel that was clearly riding low in the water. Elaina's crew had piled on as much canvas as they dared tie to the ship, and she was cutting her way through the waves in leaps and bounds.

Elaina grinned into the spray as it whipped up in front of the ship and washed over the deck. With her black hair plastered to her skull and a rictus grin distorting her features, she no doubt made a terrifying sight as she hung onto the front of the boat. Elaina didn't care. The thrill of the chase would be over all too soon, and she intended to enjoy it while she could. They only had a few hours of daylight left and would need to catch the fluyt before it disappeared, or they'd lose her in the night. A single, slight course change and the two ships could pass within a hundred feet of each other and never know it in the dark. Or even worse, the two could collide, and they could both be dragged down into the depths. No, night-time piracy was a fool's game, and Elaina was brave, not stupid.

"Cap." Elaina didn't have to turn to know it was the bosun, Mitsurgory. He was the only one on the ship with an accent from the Dragon Empire.

"What is it, Surge?" Elaina shouted as another wave of spray hit her in the face. She laughed away the salty water and turned. "Can we get another knot out of her?"

The bosun flinched. "Actually, Cap, I was hoping we could slow her down. She's straining at the mizzen. Wind is up and she's catching it fine, but… too much is dangerous."

Elaina felt her mood darken a little, and another wave of spray hit the back of her head; this time it did little to lift her spirits. "She'll hold, Surge. She'll fucking hold. We have precious little time left to make this catch, and we are going to make it. Keep the canvas up, and make certain my ship doesn't falter. Good?"

"Aye, Cap." The bosun sounded anything but in agreement.

"Sail!" Four-Eyed Pollick's cry came from the nest. "Port side."

Elaina turned back to the sea just as another sheet of spray whipped up. She fought to wipe the ocean from her eyes as she scanned the port horizon, looking for the tell-tale signs of a ship. She saw nothing.

Shrugging off another sheet of froth, she took a deep breath and shouted up to the nest as loudly as she could. "I don't see it."

There was a moment of palpable hesitation before Pollick replied. "The sail is blue, Cap."

Elaina let out a groan and found herself swallowing a mouthful of seawater – one more thing she'd blame her brother for when she saw him. Tanner's eldest living son, and a permanent thorn in Elaina's side, Blu Black was the only man alive self-obsessed enough to sport blue sails on his ship, the *Ocean Deep*. He claimed they masked the boat's existence at a distance, allowing him to close on potential prey long before they knew he was coming. In reality, the man was obsessed with himself and with his own name. He even went so far as to dye his beard a horrid shade of blue.

Elaina pulled out her monoscope and scanned the port horizon, moving away from the bow of the ship to avoid the spray. Now she knew what she was looking for, it didn't take her long to spot the sky-coloured sails.

"Cap?" Rovel the Weird was so named because he preferred the company of other men, and made no attempts to hide it. It had caused a few problems with some of the crew when Elaina had made him first mate, but the man was big enough and tough enough to crack the skulls of those who expressed those concerns.

"He's onto the same prize we are," Elaina said without lowering the monoscope. "And he has a better line on her."

"*Ocean Deep* ain't near as fast as *Starry Dawn*," Rovel said confidently.

It was true, and then some. Blu's ship was a juggernaut, heavy and slow, but with a crew compliment like no other pirate vessel sailing the waters of the isles. Blu liked to claim he'd stolen the ship right out of Land's End while the local Five Kingdoms navy men slept. Elaina knew the truth though; he'd commissioned the ship out of his own pocket and had never so much as set foot in the Five Kingdoms.

"He has a better line on her," Elaina repeated. "If the wind keeps up like it is, *Ocean Deep* will catch that ship long before we're in hailing range. We need her to turn."

Elaina snapped her monoscope shut and tossed it to Rovel. She leapt down onto the main deck and sprinted across to Ed the Navigator, at the wheel. The man had a wild grin on his face as he watched his captain approach, which only made his abnormally large chin appear even bigger.

"Fifteen points to port, Ed," Elaina said.

"Aye, Cap."

"That'll put us on a course to intercept your brother," Rovel said, coming up behind her. "Can't say I know what ya planning, Cap, but that don't seem wise. The *Deep* has to have at least twice our crew – no way we can take her. And besides, ya brother…"

"Don't be simple, Rovel." Elaina sneered. "We ain't taking on Blu, just trying to get the fluyt to change course. A few more points starboard and we can get as good a line on her as my useless fucking brother, and then the bitch is ours. We'll be in and picking the carcass clean before he even knows we're there."

"What if he decides to treat us like the prey? A lot more folk on that ship of his."

"He won't." Elaina was confident. "Blu's got no stones. Hates a real fight, too much chance of losing, and that's exactly what we'd give him, outnumbered or no. He'll do what he always does – tuck his mangy tail between his maggoty white legs and tell our da I stole his toys." Nothing would give Elaina greater pleasure than Tanner Black's favourite son running home to his father to whine about how his younger sister had stolen a prize from him.

It didn't take long for the merchant ship to take the bait. Within ten minutes the cry came from above that the fluyt was changing course, swinging further to the starboard side, and Elaina ordered Ed to put *Starry Dawn* between the fluyt and Blu's ship. Thirty minutes later, Elaina's ship was cutting through the waves parallel to *Ocean Deep*. Squinting though her monoscope, Elaina could just about imagine Blu making obscene gestures her from the deck.

They were moving much faster than *Ocean Deep* now, and Elaina wagered they would catch the merchant fluyt in a few hours, long before Blu's ship caught up with them.

When *Starry Dawn* was just a few hundred feet away, almost within hailing distance, the fluyt gave up its impotent flight and its sails were brought in. No doubt the captain would order his men to stand down and allow the pirates to loot the ship unmolested. It was quite often that way at sea; piracy was more about the chase than the battle.

"*Ocean Deep* will be on us in no time, Cap," Rovel said, joining Elaina at the railing as they sailed alongside their prize.

"Best stake a claim quickly then. Get aboard, find anything worth having, and take it quickly."

"Aye, Cap." Elaina could now see down onto the smaller ship's deck, and as predicted the captain had ordered his crew up on the main deck, where they were huddled together, unarmed and at the mercy of the pirates who had just caught them. She allowed herself a savage grin.

"Pull her close and get some planks across," she ordered.

As always, Elaina was one of the first to board the captured vessel, and with her came half of her crew. Pirates swarmed onto the fluyt, some of the men immediately heading below decks to see what was worth stealing while others took to harassing the surrendered crew, shouting challenges and waving sharpened swords at them. In a real fight it would be embarrassing, but this was anything but, and right now intimidation and fear would serve the pirates well.

She found the captain of the fluyt hunkered down with his men on the main deck. The man's two front teeth could rival a goat's, and his eyes seemed to bulge out of his face. It was clear that he was in charge from the worried glances his crew kept sending his way. That, and the ostentatiously large hat he wore. Elaina abhorred hats, for the way they obscured her vision; she much preferred to wear a bandana to keep her hair in line. Aware that she had limited time to do what needed to be done, Elaina decided the direct route was better than the cat and mouse game she usually liked to play.

"You." She pointed at the man. "You're the captain?" He took a step forwards, his eyes still bulging in a way that made him look more than a little hostile. One of Elaina's crew moved closer and waved his sword at him. Elaina laughed and gestured for the pirate to stand aside.

"You're in control of these men?" the captain said.

"Aye, I'm their captain."

The man glanced down quickly and ran his tongue across his overly large front teeth. Elaina felt her lip twitch in disgust.

"A word if you please, Captain," he said, looking up into Elaina's eyes.

Elaina pretended to think about it for a moment before nodding and stepping backwards, waving for the man to follow.

"I'd make it quick if I were you," Elaina said with a grin. "That other ship ain't here to help you."

"But is it here to help you?"

Elaina laughed at the man's arrogance. "Do I look like I need the help? But before ya go thinking it might be some sort of saviour in disguise, it happens that my brother is captain of that ship." Her smile vanished. "Ya wanted a word, time ya spoke ya piece."

The man nodded. "My name is Captain Marvle Tel'touten." An Acanthian name, and no mistake. "I sail for the Bal'rio merchant family." Elaina nodded along sagely, as if any of those names meant a damn to her. "The head of the Bal'rio family is the Lord Merchant Dellin, a long-time supporter of Thom and contributor to his cause."

Finally, a name Elaina did recognise. She plastered a conspiratorial look onto her face and winked. "Ah, the Guild."

Tel'touten nodded. "Indeed. So, you see, we are... guaranteed against situations just such as this."

Elaina knew she shouldn't string the man along, but she just couldn't help herself. "Got any proof?" She made it sound hopeful, as if robbing the ship blind was something she really didn't want to do.

"Well, no. Of course not." Captain Tel'touten looked worried for the first time. "While any sort of proof would help to facilitate the immediate cessation of hostilities just such as this, if we were to carry any, its discovery by a naval vessel or even by a legitimate port authority would mean almost certain death, as well as confiscation of the ship's wares. Not to mention, the implication towards the Bal'rio family would be a scandal."

"Well, we wouldn't want that," Elaina agreed. "Only problem is, without proof, how do I know you're not just some two-bit Acanthian pissing himself and trying to worm away from a rightful robbing?" Tel'touten took a step backwards, fear now plain on his face, and opened his mouth to speak just as Rovel appeared from below decks.

"Not a bad haul, Cap." Rovel's grin was as wide as a mast is tall. "Some interesting shit down there. Got the crew hauling it over to the *Dawn* as we speak."

"This all of them?" Elaina said, gesturing to the crew of the fluyt huddled together on the main deck.

Rovel nodded. "Checked all over, this is the entire crew."

"Good." Elaina grinned at Captain Tel'touten. "No survivors." She lurched forwards, drawing a dagger from her belt and plunging it up to the hilt into the captain's belly. The man stumbled backwards, his face caught between shock, horror, and confusion. He collapsed onto the deck, his blood spreading over the planks. His last few breaths came out as an undignified moan. Elaina knelt down, pulled the dagger from the man's belly, and used it to slit his throat, while her pirates set about the murder of the fluyt's crew. In just a couple of minutes they were dead to a man and already being hauled over the side of the ship.

Rovel joined Elaina by one of the boarding planks set up between the two ships. "Dirty work, that."

Elaina shrugged. "Couldn't leave any of them alive."

"Ah," Rovel said, pointing behind her. "Your brother."

Elaina looked up to see the *Ocean Deep* pulling alongside them. Up close, the ship truly was monstruous. Blu was looking down at her from the upper deck, and even from a distance Elaina could tell the bastard was grinning. Blu Black swung down onto the deck of the fluyt from a rope tethered to his own ship. He was tall and broad, just like their father; unlike Tanner Black, however, Blu sported a scraggly beard dyed blue and a wide-brimmed hat of foolish proportions complete with a sapphire cock feather. He also had a nasty habit of showing his teeth when he talked, as if everything he said was a challenge to everyone around him. It made Elaina dream of punching the idiot so hard he'd swallow those teeth.

"Ho there, little sister," Blu said as his boots hit the deck, followed quickly by another couple of pairs as two of his crew flanked him. "I see you've taken me prize."

Elaina squared up to her brother, annoyed as ever that he was so much taller than her. "Don't remember givin' ya permission to come aboard, Blu."

He smiled down at her. "I don't remember askin'."

"Ya really wanna make this a fight? Don't ya remember what happened last time? Dyed that fluff on your face red, didn't I."

"Crude, little sister." Blu showed his teeth. "You always wanna be takin' it ta fists. We ain't supposed ta fight no more. Da says we're ta work together."

"Da ain't here," Elaina hissed. Ever since they were young, Blu had always hidden behind either their father or mother. The only times he fought his own battles also happened to be the times he lost.

"Well, I suppose I'll be the bigger man then," Blu said, wearing a dirty smile.

"I doubt that."

"Permission ta come aboard, Captain Little Sister," he continued, ignoring Elaina's jab.

Elaina nodded. "Aye. Granted. Might as well, seein' as you're already here."

"How cordial. So did ya have ta kill 'em all?" Blu waved at the blood on the deck.

"Seemed prudent. You saw the flag they were flying. Some merchant or other from Acanthia is gonna be missin' a ship and crew, an' they ain't exactly gonna be too happy 'bout it. Reckon the Guild won't either." Elaina started to walk towards the plank to her own ship, but paused. She turned to find Blu and his two crew members close on her heels. "Why are you here, Blu?"

"Huntin'. Just like you."

"This far out towards Acanthia?" Elaina sniffed; the air smelled of lies. "Ain't your style."

Blu shrugged, smiling toothily. "Ain't yours either, little sister, an' yet here ya are. Hard to believe we had the same idea. Pickings are slim an' all, these days. Too many pirates, not enough prizes, an' always the crew need their pussy money."

Elaina narrowed her eyes, unable to contain her suspicion, but Blu forged on before she could accuse him of anything. "Fancy lettin' us have a look around? Take anythin' you an' yours don't want. I'll let ya take anythin' ya do."

There was a veiled threat there, the possibility that if she refused Blu might order his own men to attack Elaina's smaller force. "What is it ya lookin' for? Might be we already found it."

Blu's eyes twitched to something over Elaina's shoulder, and she knew full well the captain's cabin was behind her. It was fair to say whatever her brother was looking for was in there, but that meant this wasn't a random act of piracy. He was after this ship specifically.

"Listen, Elaina," Blu started with a wide smile. "I'm willin' ta let ya loot the whole damned ship, an' all I ask is…"

"Sail! Stern!" The cry went up from two different sources, almost at the same time.

Elaina and Blu shared a look, then both ran for the stern of the fluyt. When they reached the railing Blu pulled out his monoscope, and Elaina cursed herself for handing hers to Rovel and not taking it back.

"What the fuck is it, Blu?" she said after a few moments of tense waiting.

"Five Kingdoms galleon," he replied, still looking down the monoscope. "Looks like navy. I need ta get back ta my ship an' run."

"Run?" Elaina scoffed. "Together we can take 'em."

Blu looked down at his sister. "Why?" He sounded incredulous.

"One less navy vessel in the waters will make Da all sorts of happy." Elaina grinned.

"You're mad, little sister." Blu snapped his monoscope shut and started towards his ship. "There's no loot ta be had here. Ain't riskin' my ship or my men for nothin', an' neither should you."

"Together…"

Blu stopped by the rope and turned on his sister, towering over her. "Listen ta me, ya crazy little bitch. There ain't no together. There ain't nothin' here worth getting killed over, so we ain't stayin'. Now, if you wanna fight those fuckers, go right ahead. I'm headin' home, an' I'll be sure to tell Da ya died tryin' to make him proud."

"You're a rotting coward, Blu," Elaina spat, but her brother paid her no more attention as he climbed the rope back up to his own ship.

With a growl of rage, Elaina stormed back to the *Starry Dawn* to find Rovel and Corin waiting for her. Ignoring her drug-addled friend, Elaina pulled Rovel aside.

"Get everyone back on board and cut us loose. We're runnin' for home as fast as the wind'll take us."

It wasn't until they were well under way and making good speed that Elaina realised she'd never looked in Captain Tel'touten's cabin, and she still had no idea what Blu had been looking for.

The Phoenix

Keelin looked furtively into his cabin one last time – the same cabin he'd only entered three times in the past ten days – and swung his foot over the side of the ship. He climbed down the rope ladder and into the boat waiting below. His crew weren't blind, and they'd have to be to not notice that he wasn't even sleeping in his cabin anymore. He'd been the butt of no end of jokes regarding the woman who had taken over his domain. Worse than the jokes, though, was Smithe's endless undermining of his authority.

It wasn't that he was scared of her. It was that the woman was quite clearly crazy. All attempts at conversation between them seemed to end in an argument, even the most mundane, and Keelin always seemed to find himself looking very much the villain. He didn't like looking like a villain, despite his profession.

"Sure ya wanna do this, Cap'n?" said Bronson as he sat down with the oars. "Got rid of some of them sand monsters thanks ta Cap'n Morrass, but there's still plenty left hiding. No need for ya ta come ashore."

"I'm sure."

A part of him hoped they'd get the little town set up and thriving soon and sooner. That way he could be rid of the woman. Another part of him, deep, deep down, didn't want her to leave. It was the same part of him that wanted to solve the puzzle that was Aimi.

"You have the ship, Morley," Keelin shouted up to his first mate before signalling Bronson to start rowing.

Cinto Cena loomed up in front of them, looking much like any other island in the isles. Broad, expansive sandy beaches framed by rocky cliffs with a steady rise that led into a thick jungle of giant trees.

A roar went up, so loud it hurt Keelin's ears, accompanied by a distinct shaking of both land and trees. Everybody turned to look up at the forest, and many of those standing on the beach began to back away towards the water, instantly forgetting their sand prodding duties. After a few moments the shaking stopped, and the chatter of birds resumed in the forest. The men chosen as taskmasters set about getting their workers back into order, and it was as if the ground-shaking roar had never happened.

"Many deaths," Bronson said quietly as he pulled on the oars.

Keelin looked at the big man and, for the first time since he'd known him, saw real fear in his eyes.

"But not ours," Keelin said. "We'll tame this place, don't you worry. Drake has a plan. That bastard always has a plan. I doubt it involves any of us dying here."

Bronson nodded, seeming a little emboldened, and for the first time Keelin realised just how much faith even his own crew had in Drake Morrass. Even more worrying was how much faith Keelin now placed in his fellow captain.

The boat drifted into the shallows, and Keelin leapt out and began to drag it up onto the beach as Bronson stowed the oars. A couple of *The Phoenix*'s crewmen rushed to help, Smithe among them.

"Captain," Smithe said, somehow managing to fill the word with scorn, hate, fury, resentment, and challenge. "I see ya've decided to brave the beach with the rest of us. Shame we've already done most of the dangerous work, aye."

Keelin glanced towards the stretch of the beach where the sand monsters had been laid out. He counted five of them, and they were monstrous. Each of the beasts was fifteen feet from mouth to tail, with a wingspan almost as long. They were beige nightmares made all of skin, bone, and teeth.

"You have a slack definition of work, Smithe, if you believe that to be most of them. On a beach this size I would expect there to be easily three times that number." It was a lie, but Keelin was sick of being undermined, and it was about time Smithe found his own authority in question. "So how about you stop flapping that mouth at me, pick up a spear, and go back to combing the damned beach with your team before I have you flogged for insubordination."

Smithe let go of the boat and squared up to Keelin, proving once again he was the taller man. "You wanna try puttin' me to the whip, ya damn well better have the stones ta do it yaself, Captain."

Where Loyalties Lie

Keelin let go of the boat as well, letting his hands fall on the hilts of his twin cutlasses. "Careful, Smithe, you shouldn't test me. I honestly think I'd enjoy it."

Smithe said nothing, but stared at Keelin, almost as if daring his captain to break out the whip – an act which Keelin had never once had to perform.

"Back to work it is then," Keelin said cheerily. "Off you go, quartermaster."

Smithe spat into the sand and turned away, storming off to his hunting group. Keelin found Bronson watching him with a strange look on his face.

"He's got more pull with the crew than you might think, Cap'n," Bronson said quietly once Smithe was well out of earshot. "Most of us are loyal to ya, but he's got a fair few folk riled up. Now I ain't saying he's like to call a vote anytime soon, but… some of us, him included, were around when you took the ship from Elaina, and it didn't sit right with 'em all."

"Got a point, Bronson?" Keelin said a little more tersely than he'd intended.

"Only that Smithe ain't the type of man ya want as an enemy, Cap'n."

"Well, I sure as a watery grave don't want him as a friend."

At that Bronson sat back in the little boat and shrugged his big shoulders. Keelin decided it was time to take his leave, and moved off towards the little camp that was destined to grow into a town if Drake and the rest of the pirates had their way. A few shacks had already been erected and were being put to a variety of uses ranging from storage to recreation. They were little more than three walls, a roof of sorts, and a sheet of canvas to provide privacy. Judging by the sounds coming out of one such recreational shelter, Keelin could only assume that at least one entrepreneurial whore had survived Sev'relain and was busy charging every pirate she could entice into the tent through their teeth for what was between her legs. There was a hastily painted sign embedded in the sand outside proclaiming the shack was in use, and a queue forming next to said sign. Keelin walked on by quickly, without giving too much thought as to which of his men would likely be needing a consultation with the ship's doctor before too long.

Further along, there was a fire pit furnished with a large cauldron pinched from the Man of War, in which some sort of stew was bubbling away to itself. Neither the pirates nor the refugees had any idea what sort of wildlife lived on the island, and none were willing to brave the jungle to find out, so there was no fresh meat to be had, only ship's stores and rations – and neither of those was ever particularly enthralling. Still, the chef from *The Phoenix* was collaborating with a man from Sev'relain who claimed to be well versed in culinary delights. Keelin had been to Sev'relain more times than he could count, and he was fairly certain he'd never once seen the port offer anything approaching delightful.

Combing the beach in teams of six men apiece, each carrying iron-tipped spears, short swords, and crossbows, were no fewer than sixty workers. Drake had given them all strict instructions on how to find the sand monsters and how best to deal with them, and as yet they'd apparently killed five of the beasties without losing a single man. Though one woman from Sev'relain, a former guard in the employ of Loke, had taken a nasty gut wound that was likely to put her off her feet for a couple of weeks.

Kebble Salt stood watch over it all from a rickety wooden tower, where his gaze could cover every corner of the beach. His hawk-like vision and precision aim with his rifle had already become something of a legend – one with many different versions, most of which ended with him killing half the crew of the Man of War single-handed, all from the safety of *The Phoenix*. Keelin was as happy as Drake to let the stories persist if they meant order was kept in the fledgeling town, and nobody had to know that the man was currently able to fire a total of one shot before his store of black powder would run dry.

"Is she still refusing to leave your cabin?" Kebble said quietly as Keelin mounted the steps of the little wooden watchtower.

Keelin laughed. "I just thought I'd come and take a tour around our new little town."

Kebble glanced at Keelin knowingly.

"Fine. I haven't asked her to leave yet." Keelin reached the platform at the top of the tower, where he was greeted by an accusing silence.

"I know," Keelin continued, feeling strangely guilty. "I'm the captain and it's my ship and my cabin. I should just ship her here to shore."

More silence.

"But what sort of life is that condemning her to?" With a dramatic sigh, Keelin shook his head and stared out towards the jungle. Drake and his Arbiter were close to the tree line, though what they were doing there was a mystery.

"She'll just have to stay aboard for now." Keelin waited for an argument and got none. "Until we find somewhere better to drop her off."

Still no argument.

"Well, I'm captain, damn it, and that's what's happening."

Kebble pointed out westward over the sand. "Over that way, between the palm tree and the jungle. What do you see?"

Keelin squinted. He saw nothing but sand and a bit more sand. "Sand?"

"Exactly. Sand." Kebble nodded sagely. "Do you see how it moves?" Embarrassed, Keelin coughed and pulled out his monoscope. He looked again. The sand was moving very slightly, grains being flung up into the air and thrown a few feet at a time like sea spray on the wind.

"The wind," Keelin said, automatically trying to feel the breeze. There was none. It was a warm day with air as still as death.

"That's what I thought at the beginning," Kebble said. "Nothing but a cool breeze yet to reach my face. But the longer I looked, the more I saw beneath the surface of the event. The more I saw a pattern and understood what it meant."

"What does it mean?"

"There is a creature there." Kebble spoke with the air of a man absolutely certain of his words. "As it breathes, underneath the surface of the sand, grains are thrown into the air in such a way that it looks to be just a breath of air on an island which is strangely still."

"You're certain there's a sand monster there?"

Kebble laughed and smoothed down his moustache. "I wouldn't call them monsters, just animals looking to find their next meal. It's a lure, you see. On a hot, humid day, what do men and animals alike look for on a beach such as this?"

Keelin thought about it for a moment. When it came to him, the answer seemed obvious. "A breeze to cool down."

"Exactly. An interesting adaptation in an attempt to lure in potential prey, or just a byproduct of the inescapable need to breathe? Maybe both."

"What does that have to do with my problem of the woman in my cabin?"

"Maybe nothing." Kebble sighed. "May be that the more you look at a thing, the more you see of it, and the deeper your understanding goes."

It seemed to Keelin that there was definitely more to Kebble than met the eye. It was hard to believe the man had been working as a guard for a small-time stolen goods dealer just a few days ago.

"Perhaps you should tell the teams about your little discovery regarding the sand monsters," he said, deciding to shift the subject away from his own problem. "Might be it could help them clear the beach faster."

"You're the captain, Captain." Kebble laughed. "Though I do think someone should warn that man of the danger he is in."

Fortune

"What the fuck is he doing?" Drake didn't expect an answer, and he didn't get one.

Keelin Stillwater was charging across the beach, his arms waving in the air, towards a pirate who looked to be heading over to a palm tree; no doubt the man was searching for a cool place to rest in the afternoon heat. The fact that the pirate was wandering across an uncombed area of the beach was alarming enough, but Stillwater running blindly towards him seemed far more dangerous.

"You spent a lot of time courting his alliance to let him risk his life like that," Beck said. She was smirking, which only served to make her more beautiful.

Drake snorted. "You sound a little jealous, Arbiter. Besides, what should I do? Go running after him and put my own life on the line? Reckon I'd rather him die than me no matter how much work went into getting him on my side."

A bang echoed through the still air of the beach. The pirate walking towards the palm tree paused, looked around, and stopped when he saw Stillwater running towards him. A few moments later the two men met. Keelin pointed towards the palm tree, and both of them started backing away quickly.

"What was that noise?" Drake said.

"Gunshot. That rifleman of Stillwater's fired a shot into the sand in front of the pirate. No idea why though."

"Reckon there's one of them sand devils over by the tree. Bastard must have figured out how to spot them." Drake silently cursed that he wasn't there to take credit for the discovery, but he had a more important task to deal with.

The jungle loomed up large and close in front of them. The trees were tall, green, and buzzing with all manner of insects. Occasionally a hooting call from some animal or other sounded, usually followed closely by more, similar cries, but they always fell silent after a while. Then there was the roaring. Whatever beast called the jungle its home must be large and then some to make a noise like that, not to mention the shaking of the trees.

Drake glanced sideways at Arbiter Beck and prayed to Rin that she was as capable as Hironous gave her credit for. With Drake's right arm in a sling he would be less than useless in any real fight, and he didn't want to leave the world as a nameless meal in some great monster's belly. That being said, wandering into the trees to slay the beast that threatened them all was exactly the sort of heroic deed he needed folk to think he was capable of.

"Ya ready?" Drake said with a grin he didn't really feel.

"Me?" Beck shook her head. "You're the one who volunteered to slay the beast. I'm just coming along to watch."

Drake ignored the creeping feeling of doom. "Well, at least I'll have an audience to recount the tale. Saves me having to embellish it my own self. Remember, if you happen to mention my cock at all, it's at least two feet long."

Beck let out a disbelieving sigh, but she also glanced down at Drake's crotch. He smiled at the little victory. Without another word he set foot into the forest and started walking as if he had an idea of where he was going.

It wasn't long before both Drake and Beck were coated in a layer of sweat, swatting away biting insects every couple of seconds and spending every bit of willpower they had hating the jungle. It was far from Drake's first foray into a dense island jungle, but that made it no less irritating. He felt sticky, dirty, itchy, in pain, and pissed off. Even the company of a beautiful woman, usually enough to lift his spirits no matter the situation, was doing nothing to alleviate his stress.

As he stumbled over yet another overgrown root looping out of the dirt and hidden by a handful of leaves, Drake glanced sideways at Beck. The woman was labouring as hard as he was, and it didn't appear that any of her magical Arbiter powers were helping her through the ordeal. Her skin bore the unmistakeable sheen of sweat, the few strands of hair that escaped her wide hat looked wet and lank, and, judging by the way she kept pulling at her jerkin, she was dangerously overheated. Drake, wearing nothing but a thin cotton shirt over his chest, felt just as hot.

"Need a rest?" Drake said, attempting to sound smug and failing utterly as he stumbled over yet another hidden root. The tree it belonged to mocked him by looming up high to his left and disappearing into the dense canopy above.

"No." Drake could hear the strain in Beck's voice. "Do you?"

Drake attempted to laugh, but it came out as a cough. "I can go all day, Arbiter."

"Wonderful. I can go for two."

The jungle seemed to close in on Drake, moving both further away and closer all at once. He closed his eyes to avoid the wave of vertigo, but it was no use, and he felt his balance go. Remembering something his old captain had once said, long before Drake became master of his own ship, he let his knees buckle rather than take the full fall on his face. He didn't even feel the impact.

When Drake opened his eyes the forest was dimmer and the air felt cooler. He didn't remember lying down, but he was definitely on his side now, staring ahead into the darkening jungle. It seemed to stretch on forever. With a groan that sounded loud in the silence, Drake pushed himself into a sitting position and looked around for Beck. He found her splayed out on the forest floor, not moving.

It took a monumental feat of effort for Drake to attain his feet, yet he managed it. There was a strange sense of stillness in the air, and breaking that stillness by moving felt wrong, almost as if the only correct action would be to lie back down and sleep forever. He stumbled over to where Beck had fallen. It took only a moment to confirm she was still alive; he could see her lips were just slightly apart, and her chest rose and fell with each shallow breath.

A line of ants, the only things still moving as far as Drake could see, had made a path over her right hand and were busy collecting leaf debris. Beck's hat had fallen away, and her hair spilled out around her head, creating a golden halo – even if it was playing host to all manner of dirt and dead leaves. She looked so peaceful and serene that Drake didn't want to disturb her; in fact, all he really wanted was to lie down next to her and join her in oblivion. Before he knew what he was doing, he was down on his knees and getting ready to do just that.

A thought occurred to Drake then. If he was going to lie down and drift away into nothing with this woman, he at least wanted to taste her first. With a gentleness the pirate captain had never known he possessed, he bent down over Beck's face and placed his own lips to hers. A moment later she kissed him back.

Slowly Beck's eyes fluttered open, and her icy blues locked gazes with Drake's emerald greens. It was at that moment that he realised he was poking her in the leg, just as something equally as hard, but ultimately more dangerous, poked him in the stomach.

"What the fuck are you doing?" Beck murmured drowsily as she detached her lips from his. He felt her compulsion wash over him, and even though his will escaped hers as it always did, the fact that she was holding him at gunpoint compelled him to answer truthfully.

"Kissing you." He smiled.

"Why am I on the ground?" Beck said, as if she'd only just noticed that she was horizontal. She shoved Drake away and sat up quickly; a moment later her eyes went vacant and she collapsed backwards.

"What did you do to me?" Her voice sounded far away, dreamy.

"Ain't me. There's something in the forest. Magic, I reckon." Drake was finding it hard to concentrate. The only reason he wasn't lying right next to Beck was that he wanted to be lying on top of her, and even with his head feeling as fuzzy as it did, he didn't think she'd let him without her pistol going off.

"Mhm." The soft noise escaped Beck's lips even as her eyes closed again and her hand dropped, the pistol spilling from her grasp. "Magic." Even though his head felt as if it were full of sea foam, Drake saw his chance and seized it. He swung one leg over Beck's body and pulled his other one close, straddling her.

There were more ants now; the forest floor almost seemed alive with them. They were running over Beck's arms and hands and leaving little red footprints there. As Drake bent in closer to look, he realised it was blood. Her blood. The little ants were slowly eating her alive as she lay in a stupor. It should have been horrifying, Drake knew, but he just couldn't seem to bring himself to care. All he really wanted to do was lie down, and it all just seemed as if it were happening to someone else.

With the last remnants of consciousness, Drake raised his one good arm and brought it swinging down, slapping Beck hard across the face just before his eyes closed again and he embraced the darkness.

The Phoenix

"Should we keep going or stop?" said the bare-chested pirate, one of Drake's men.

Keelin thought about it, and came up with no good answer. With Drake and his Arbiter dog missing – it had been hours and more since they'd walked into the jungle, and neither of them had been seen since – it appeared that everybody accepted Keelin as in charge of the entire colonisation. Unfortunately, there were decisions to be made, and Keelin had no idea what the correct choices were.

The light, or the rapidly approaching lack of it, was the problem. They'd so far combed significantly less than half of the beach in an attempt to wipe out the monsters, and that left a whole lot more sand for them to hide beneath. If they kept going in the waning light, the teams would need torches to see, and even with those the task would be more dangerous. However, if they stopped now, there was no guaranteeing the creatures wouldn't move around beneath the surface during the night, and then the pirates would have to start the task all over again.

Keelin mulled over the choice while those close by waited for him to make the decision. That nobody else offered an opinion only served to further indicate how impossible a choice it really was.

"Pull the teams back," he said. "We'll set up a camp just above the high tide line and surround it with torches. Send half the teams back to the ships for the night; no need to keep everyone here."

"Why keep anyone here?" Smithe asked with a sneer.

"Because Drake might come back tonight, and if he does I want somewhere on the beach he can aim towards."

"Aye," agreed the bare-chested pirate. "Cap'n could come back." It was almost a dare for Smithe to disagree, and Keelin truly hoped his quartermaster would. There was no easy way for Keelin to rid himself of the antagonistic fool, but one of Drake's crew stabbing him seemed a decent solution.

"Well done, Smithe." Keelin smiled. "You've just volunteered to sit first watch. You two will sit it with him." He pointed at the bare-chested pirate and another of Drake's crew.

"Anything I can do to help?" Drake's first mate said from his position by the cook fire.

"I want twenty men here on the beach, a mixture from both crews, and the rest sent back for the night. No rum for anyone staying and weapons close to hand all night. A line of torches leading up to the edge of the jungle wouldn't go amiss either, placed in a line that's already been combed. If Drake does make it back tonight I want him to be walking a safe path."

"Done," the man said as he stood up, the firelight gleaming off his milky white eye. "You'll be staying yourself, I imagine."

"Aye."

"Good. I'll be heading back to the *Fortune*. You be sure to signal if Drake does turn up during the night."

"You don't seem too worried about your missing captain," Keelin said as the man made to walk away.

Drake's first mate laughed. "Don't reckon there's enough deaths even here on Cinto Cena to keep Drake Morrass in the grave."

Fortune

Drake's eyes snapped open to reveal the concerned face of Arbiter Beck staring down at him. It was dark, the sort of dark one gets in a cage locked deep underground. The memory was more than a little disturbing, so Drake shook it away and focused on the woman watching him. There was rock behind her and the rhythmic sound of dripping water; it didn't take long for Drake to realise they were in a cave.

Opening his mouth to speak, Drake found his throat as dry as sun-baked sand and ended up coughing instead. A water skin appeared in front of him, and he reached for it instinctively. Beck moved away, leaving Drake staring at dark rock.

As he sipped at the water, Drake scoured his memory for how they could have ended up in a cave. The last thing he remembered was… ants. Ants and the thought of Beck naked. It seemed a strange combination of memories.

"Thank you," Beck said from somewhere in the darkness.

"Eh?" Drake barely managed to mumble between swallows of water.

"You saved us both."

Drake struggled into a sitting position and took note of all the aches and pains the movement caused; it seemed there wasn't much of his body not currently bruised or battered. He could just about see a small figure sitting alone in the darkness, and he guessed it was Beck.

"Don't remember saving anyone," he protested, though a part of him disagreed and claimed that it must be true despite how unlikely it seemed. Drake Morrass never passed up credit for any feat.

"You managed to bring me out of my slumber long enough to realise it was magic causing us to sleep." She sounded subdued. "Luckily the Inquisition teaches us counters to all sorts of things." She waved her wrist in the darkness, and Drake thought he saw a bandage wrapped around it. He looked down at his own wrist and saw a similar strip of cloth. He held it up for closer inspection.

"As long as you're wearing that you won't be able to sleep," Beck said. "I would not advise taking it off; I don't have any others right now, and I've no way to fashion any more until we get back to the boat."

Beck fell silent for a while. "I should have noticed it sooner. Too damned distracted. I…" She trailed off.

"What's your name?" Drake asked the woman sitting in the darkness.

There was a significant silence before the answer came. "Beck."

"Oh, I got that. Arbiter Beck, to use your full title, I'm sure. But that's only one name. Strikes me I should know the other one."

"I don't have another name," Beck said quickly. "I used to, I think, but I don't remember it. Did you know the potential is passed down family lines, from parent to child? Though not all children are guaranteed to inherit it."

"Aye," Drake said, remembering his own mother. "I happen to know a little about that myself." There was a moment of silence before Beck spoke again. Drake thanked Rin his little slip hadn't piqued her curiosity.

"Well, it appears the potential can also show up in families who have no history of it. I started showing signs at maybe five years old. I don't remember much from back then, but I know my parents were happy about it."

"Happy about sending off one of their children to be a witch hunter? Feared and despised the world over? Seems unlikely."

Beck let out a bitter laugh and leaned forwards. Drake could just about see the outline of her face in the darkness of the cave. Her eyes looked like dark voids.

"Careful, pirate," she spat. "What we do in the service of Vol… our god is righteous. He knows the best course for this world, and we carry out his will. We are his eyes, ears, and left hand, and…"

"Spare me the zeal, Arbiter. I'd rather not get into another bout of 'my god's better than your god'. I ain't saying I don't believe in him, just that I don't trust him."

"Well, anyway. You might not believe it, but it's a great honour for a noble family of Sarth to provide children to be trained as Arbiters. The Beck family is one of the oldest and noblest. Before me they had never had the chance to give a child to the Inquisition. When I was given, the instructors called me Beck, and the name stuck. I honestly cannot remember what my full name was before."

"What about you – is your real name Drake Morrass?"

Drake felt her compulsion wash over him; it was almost becoming comforting now. "Aye."

"Really?"

"Aye. My ma named me. Said a special man needed a special name."

Beck snorted in the darkness. "She called you a special man?"

"Of course she did. She had a gift, my ma. She could…" Drake stopped. It was common knowledge in the Inquisition that Hironous Vance's mother had been a witch possessed of the sight. It was not, however, common knowledge that Drake's mother was the very same witch, and it was something both he and Hironous wanted no one else to know.

"What type of gift?"

Drake had long ago learned that the best way to hide a lie was within the truth. Actually, his first lesson had been that the best way to hide a lie was with silence, but he had a feeling that if he fell silent, so would Beck, and he was enjoying listening to her.

"She could talk to Rin," Drake said. "Actually, she was the one taught me to do it. Don't know where she learned it from, but then there's plenty most folk don't know about their parents. When I popped out between her legs she used her own fluids to contact Rin, and asked her what my name should be."

Beck laughed. "You're really trying to sell me the story that you were named by a sea goddess?"

"Certainly seems that way, doesn't it." Drake laughed along with her, deciding some truths were too hard to swallow. He wondered if the woman would believe him if he told her that he and Hironous were brothers.

"I never realised you pirates were so religious."

"Most pirates ain't. There's a big difference between religious and superstitious, Arbiter. Most pirates wouldn't know a protective sign" –

Drake held his right hand in the hook of Rin and crossed it from the left side of his chest to the right – "from a useless waving of the hand."

"I thought you weren't supposed to make those signs on land," Beck said, her voice a challenge.

"Well…" Drake shrugged. "I can get away with all sorts. Besides, we're surrounded by rock on all sides here. She can't see us. Can't help us."

"So she presides over all water?" The question sounded genuine enough, but Drake couldn't forget the woman was loyal to Volmar, and he very much doubted Rin would be happy if he gave away all her secrets.

"Not all water. Her powers stretch to most large bodies, at least those connected to the sea in some way, but they're strongest here around the isles. This is her domain. Her portion of the world."

"And it just so happens that this is where you pirates built a home for yourselves. Also happens to be pretty close to the main trade routes running from Sarth to the Five Kingdoms. Not to mention, any ships from the Dragon Empire have to come close too, or trade only with Acanthia."

"You think that's a coincidence?" Drake snorted. "Your god does like to keep you in the dark. They're only as powerful as the people worshipping them. Rin came to the isles because there have always been people here, living off the sea. Maybe once they weren't even pirates, just fishers and traders. She made them believe, made them worship her. Now there ain't a seaman worth his salt around the isles that don't make regular tributes in her name to keep himself safe in her waters."

"Your god would punish you for not giving her tributes? She sounds…"

"Harsh? Vengeful? Capricious?" Drake let out a laugh. "Aye, she is all of those things. Not quite your benevolent, forgiving god, eh? Though Rin never ordered her worshippers to wipe out an entire race, or enslave another, or burn folk alive."

"Careful, Drake."

"Just making a point." Drake held up his hand to placate the angry Arbiter. After a few moments of silence he decided it was best to change the subject.

"So what are we doing hiding in this cave?"

"Waiting for you to wake up. After a while I wasn't sure if you would, so I put a sleepless charm on you. The magic out there is… old, and strong. I couldn't see the source of it. I don't think it came from the ants; they were just capitalising on its effect."

"Is it natural magic?"

"Is there such a thing?" Beck sounded unsure of whether Drake was spinning more tales.

"Not in your world, Arbiter. Your Inquisition spent most of its early years removing it. But here, out in the places where folk don't usually tread, all sorts of old magic and beasties can be found."

Beck was silent for a long time. "I think we should wait here until morning. It's dark out there, and we could easily get lost or split up."

Drake lay back down on the rock. It was uncomfortable at best, but he'd rested on far worse in his time. The Drurr did not treat their prisoners kindly.

"Didn't think to bring any food, did you?" he asked without much hope.

"No."

"Guess we're gonna have a hungry night then."

The Phoenix

The boats were already in the water by the time Keelin woke to find the first rays of daylight forcing themselves upon him. He'd personally sat two watches during the night – his and Smithe's, for lack of trust in the man. Inadequate sleep, along with the anticipation of the day ahead, had the unfortunate effect of putting him in a mood which could only be described as grumpy. A boatload of folk were being shipped over from the *Fortune* and, just a few strokes behind them, another from *The Phoenix*. The Man of War floated in its anchorage, dwarfing both the other ships and making the bay look more than a little crowded. Keelin was still staring out towards the Sarth vessel, taking a much needed piss into the sea, when someone tapped him on the shoulder.

"Lost a man durin' the night," one of Drake's pirates said. "Nilly stepped out fer a piss, just like ya doin' now, an' didn't come back."

"Any sign of him?" Keelin finished up and tucked himself back into his britches.

"Blood on the sand a little bit that way." The man pointed down the beach, and Keelin thought he could just about make out some discoloured sand. "Looks like his hat too, but no one wanted ta get close enough ta check. Whatever got him might still be there. 'Neath the sand."

"Then we best find out," Keelin said sternly. "Get a team together and comb the sand around the blood. Kill anything under the surface and try to find Nilly."

The pirate looked uncomfortable, and on the verge of arguing. He evidently decided against it. "Aye, Cap'n," he said with a grimace, and set off towards the fire where his crewmates were gathered.

By the time the boats arrived, Keelin had found the cook pot and was busy eating a cold bowl of last night's left over stew. Kebble Salt had found him, and the two were busy eating in companionable silence when Princess jumped from the front of his skiff and made his way up the short stretch of beach to the makeshift camp.

"Drake didn't show up then?" Princess sat down opposite Keelin, brushing a few lank, wet strands of hair away from his face.

Keelin shook his head and spooned another mouthful of stew. "You don't sound concerned."

Princess laughed. "Hear we lost a man during the dark. One of ours or yours?"

"Yours," Keelin replied solemnly. "He wandered off to take a piss, didn't come back."

"Nilly, was it? Poor bugger never could piss with an audience. The Cap'n will be sad. He always liked Nilly."

"I want you to send the boats back and get every able man and woman down on this beach."

"That so?" Princess didn't sound too certain about the order.

"We're starting again. Combing the beach over."

"What?" Princess snorted. "Took us most of yesterday to do as much as we did, and ya want us to start over?"

"Yes."

"Mind sharing ya thinking?"

"Your man was killed close to the camp, an area we'd already combed. That makes me think the sand monsters move around during the dark. Can't be certain those areas we checked yesterday are still safe. So we start again."

Princess thought about it as Kebble handed him a bowl of underwhelming stew. "Aye, sounds solid reasoning."

"I also want any man or woman with real carpentry experience reporting directly to me by the time this pot of food is empty. And I want preparations drawn up to beach the Man of War as soon as we're confident we've killed most of the sand monsters."

"Outfitting?"

"Repurposing. That ship burned down two towns. Now its bones are going to be the foundation of a new one."

Fortune

No sooner had light begun to creep in through the forest canopy than Drake and Beck struck out of the cave and resumed their hunt for the creature in the forest. Both of them were hungry, and that had led to a sullen couple of hours cooped up together, surrounded by rock. When the opportunity had presented itself to escape, Drake had leapt upon the chance. There was no shortage of berries, leaves, and shrooms in the forest, all of which could possibly be eaten, and all of which could potentially be fatal. Drake wasn't about to risk death by fungi just to quell the rumbling of his stomach.

He walked like a man who knew where he was going, even though that was far from the truth. They were lost, pure and simple. The encounter with the ants and the sleeping magic had had a greater impact than the implicit peril. Thinking back, Drake couldn't remember much of the time leading up to the moment when they both collapsed. He couldn't remember how long they'd been walking, or in which direction. They could have got turned around any number of times and not been any the wiser. With that in mind, Drake had done the only thing that had seemed sensible; he'd turned his feet to the sun and walked east. Beck followed.

A sharp pain in Drake's neck made him wince, and he slapped at it. His hand came away bloody, with a squashed insect the size of a large coin. Already Drake could feel his neck beginning to itch where the pain had been, and it wasn't the only place he wanted to scratch. The sooner they got out of the damned forest and back onto the ships, the better. He may be intending to settle the island and turn it into a stronghold for his people, but that didn't mean he wanted to spend any time here.

"Do you hear that?" Beck asked, her compulsion washing over Drake.

Drake looked at her with impatience, but stopped and strained his ears. He heard nothing. The impact of that revelation hit him only a moment before the roar ripped through the forest.

Trees shook, birds took flight and fled, and both Drake and Beck dropped to the ground, covering their ears as best they could.

Considering Drake's injured arm, that wasno't very well. The noise was deafening as close as they were, and almost sounded like a dragon's cry. Drake had first-hand knowledge of how loud those could be up close.

The noise rumbled to a halt, and a few moments later the near-constant call of island birds and the monotonous drone of buzzing insects started again. Drake looked over to Beck to find her crouched on the ground with two pistols drawn and a face as white as canvas despite the heat and humidity. Wild eyes peered out from beneath the rim of her hat, darting everywhere as they searched for the threat. Scared only began to cover it, and Drake had to admit he wasn't feeling much better. Of course, unlike Arbiter Beck, Drake was determined to put on a show of bravado. His fearless reputation would let him show nothing less.

"That way, ya reckon?" Drake whispered, pointing with his good hand.

Beck's eyes snapped to his, and she nodded.

"Good." Drake smiled at her. "Let's go slay this monster."

He strode away in the direction of the roar, confident the Arbiter wouldn't let him go alone. Beck counted herself a warrior, and a proud one; there was simply no way she'd allow Drake to appear fearless as she cowered away from the creature, even if it meant her own death.

Never having been one for flights of fantasy, Drake refused to let his imagination run wild. There were any number of beasties that could create a noise like that, and each was as dangerous as the last. If he started listing them all in his head he'd likely find himself paralysed by fear, so instead he forged on through the trees, slapping away flying insects and keeping his footfalls as quiet as possible.

Eventually the trees gave way to a large clearing walled in on the far side by an outcropping of rock with a dark cave that housed an opening as large as a ship. Not much light penetrated the mouth of the cave, and there was no way to tell how deep it went. Beck shuffled up beside Drake at the edge of the clearing, and they crouched behind a giant of a tree, peering around its trunk.

"It must be in the cave," Beck said, staring towards it. The Arbiter started whispering something under her breath, but soon stopped and shook her head.

Drake looked more closely at the clearing. To one side of the cave was a small steaming pool no larger than a dinghy, and to the other side there appeared to be a hole in the ground much larger than the pool, only with no steam emitting from it. There were also no trees near the hole in the ground, and those that were closest almost seemed to be leaning away from it.

"Have you any idea what it might be?" Beck said in an urgent whisper.

Drake wanted to laugh at the question, but it would have given the game away and he wanted to drag Beck's vulnerability out a little longer.

"Surely you'd know better than I, Arbiter. It was your Inquisition that hunted all the old monsters into extinction. Far as I know, only dragons, sea beasties, and trolls are left. But I reckon the Inquisition has all sorts of books and shit on all those terrors they wiped out, eh?"

"I was never one for spending much time in the Inquisition libraries," Beck hissed. "Waste of time. The world is out here, not in a bunch of dusty old tomes." Drake laughed and stood up. He casually wandered out of his hiding spot and into the clearing.

"Drake! What the fuck are you doing?"

Drake turned, but continued to stroll backwards so he could see the Arbiter's face. Much to his pleasure, she looked genuinely worried, and that was very much a victory in his book.

"There is no monster, Arbiter Beck. At least not here."

Beck stood, clearly unsure whether Drake was right or not. Drake couldn't help but grin at the look on her face; it was almost as if she expected something to reach up out of the hole in the ground and swallow him whole at any moment.

"What about the cave?"

"It's just a cave." Drake laughed. "Likely got bats in it and little else, I reckon. See the two holes in the ground?" He pointed first to the pool and then to the much larger hole.

Beck took a few steps into the clearing and nodded.

"This one..." Drake moved closer to the steaming pool and looked into it. He could see a definite bottom only about ten feet down, and warm, clear water coloured green by the rock around it. "Aye, this is a hot spring, warmed by the earth around it to" – he dipped his finger into the water – "a very pleasant temperature."

Beck moved to stand next to Drake and looked into the pool.

"The other one," Drake continued, "is much larger. No water, but the rock around it is wet. Well, that one is a geyser."

"A what?"

"Boiling water from deep underground occasionally rises up and shoots out of it," Drake clarified. "Makes a hell of a noise too, much like a roaring beastie. And the force of it, if it's powerful enough, can shake trees. Best not get too close to that one. Those things can be pretty dangerous."

"There is no monster," Beck said, echoing Drake's earlier words.

"No."

"Did you know this before?"

Drake felt her compulsion and shrugged it off. "No. Wouldn't very well be out here if I did. Got far better things to be doing with my time. Nice surprise though, eh? Instead of fighting a ferocious beastie we get to have a nice relaxing dip in some warm smelly water."

Again the look of disbelief. "You can bathe in it?"

Drake nodded.

"You're sure it's safe?"

Beck's compulsion wasn't just washing over Drake now; it almost felt like a permanent fixture hanging over him. He'd never experienced an Arbiter asking him so many questions in such a short time before. As Arbiter Beck seemed to be reluctant to use her compulsion – most of the time – Drake wondered whether she was enjoying the company of a person she couldn't dominate so easily.

"Aye, it's safe." Drake smiled as he knelt and dragged his good hand through the water. "Folk bathe in these things all the time. Shit, there's a town in the Wilds that sells time in them, charges a bloody fortune for the privilege too. Folk travel from all over to take a dip in the bitter springs of Bittersprings. And look, we get our own one here for free. Best take advantage of that, I reckon."

Beck looked at the steaming water, and Drake could see longing written plain on her face. It was likely a good long while since she'd last

Where Loyalties Lie

had a chance to bathe, and there came a point in most civilised folks' stay in the isles where they just wanted to feel clean. Still, in Drake's experience, sometimes people needed an extra incentive and a little push.

"I hear it does wonders to stop the itching too," he lied expertly.

"What?" It was likely Beck hadn't even realised how badly the insect bites were itching, and now that Drake had mentioned it, he could see her become uncomfortable as all those little irritations made themselves known.

"See how there's none of those little bastards around the pool?" Drake said. "Seems they don't like something in the water. Keeps them away and relieves the damned itching." To drive his point home he scratched at his neck. There was no bite there – he was smart enough to know not to scratch at bites – but it had the desired effect on the Arbiter, and a moment later she was scratching.

"And you're just going to stand there and watch?"

Drake grinned, his golden tooth glinting. "I was thinking of joining you."

Beck looked as though she was considering the idea, and leaning towards telling Drake exactly where he could go.

"You first," she said. "And if you try to touch me when I get in, I will drown you."

Unbuttoning his shirt proved to be fairly difficult with a broken arm, but Drake guessed that asking Beck for help would result in a less than favourable response, so he laboured alone, dropping the shirt to the ground along with the sling that held his arm in place. He had to sit to remove his boots, and then pulled his belt free, letting his britches drop and stepping clear of them. Naked as his name day, save for the charm attached to his wrist and the ring on his finger, Drake stood in front of Arbiter Beck, grinning. She didn't return the smile. He saw her eyes dart all over his body, a frown forming on her face as she took in his scars and tattoos.

"These things safe to take a dip?" He nodded towards the charm on his wrist.

"They're waterproof," Beck said, her eyes momentarily dropping to Drake's crotch.

"Good." Drake tucked his right arm close to his body, an act which brought eye-watering pain, and leapt into the pool. He plunged into the hot water, and the sudden change in temperature threatened to take his breath away. With his eyes closed he could see nothing, but he didn't need to see. Water had always been Drake's element, and his mother had used to say that she couldn't believe he'd been born without gills. The Drurr had used all sorts of water-based tortures on him, and although they still hurt and ached, and had almost broken him, they'd never seemed as bad as the ones involving fire.

Drake used his left arm to propel himself to the bottom of the spring, and his feet soon touched the rock. He could feel the heat coming up from the earth, warming the water. He pushed off the bottom, swimming upwards quickly until his head broke the surface.

Kicking lethargically to keep himself at the surface, Drake used his good hand to push his hair back and wipe the water from his eyes. He found himself looking at the cave, so he turned back to find Arbiter Beck undressing next to the hot spring. Her hat was on the ground and her golden hair was spilling down around her face, lank and grimy from many days of poor treatment. Her jerkin, along with the brace of pistols, had been discarded, and she was busy undoing the last button on her blouse when she noticed Drake had resurfaced and was staring at her.

Without a word, Beck popped open the last button and dropped her blouse to the ground. Drake gawked at her breasts. He'd seen a fair few pairs in his time, and he'd happily admit that the Arbiter's were very close to being the best. Some sagged, others were too perky, but Beck's were right there in the middle, and large enough for a handfuls a piece. He'd already pegged Beck as a woman who enjoyed the attention of men, and he was more than happy to give her his, full and undivided.

"Are you done?" She raised an eyebrow, and Drake barely even felt her compulsion.

"Oh, I could happily stare at those all day." He grinned, and spared a moment to quickly lock eyes with her. Unfortunately she chose that same moment to drop her britches, and Drake couldn't help but drop his gaze again.

Treading water was becoming difficult with only the one arm, so

Drake swam backwards a little and grabbed hold of the wall of the spring, spitting out some of the foul-tasting water.

"Very nice," he said as Beck stood before him as naked as he was, putting herself very much on display.

With a snort she stepped forward and disappeared beneath the surface of the pool. Drake looked down through the clear waters and saw Beck below him. She'd swum down to the bottom, just as he had, and now appeared to be looking up at him.

When Beck resurfaced, Drake treated her to one of his more genuine smiles. He could still just about see her breasts, distorted only a little by the rippling water, and it wouldn't have been untruthful to say he was finding it hard to calm himself. She pushed her hair back and smiled – possibly the first real smile Drake had ever seen on her face.

"You were right," Beck said, her voice a little softer than usual. "It really does feel good. It's been so long since I've felt anything close to clean. Honestly, how do you pirates live like this?"

Drake laughed. He was leaning against the wall of the hot spring, kicking slowly, with his good arm draped over the side. He watched Beck clean a month of dirt, sweat, and grime from her skin.

"This is nothing," he said. "Few weeks, maybe a month at sea, with minimal bathing opportunities broken up with some time on land, where bathing is pretty much required. Besides, you oughta try getting yourself locked up in a dungeon deep, deep underground. Soon changes ya values on what exactly 'clean' means."

Beck looked at Drake as she wrung water out of her hair; it was fairly obvious she didn't believe him. "I can't imagine who would want to lock you up."

"Let's just say your Inquisition did a piss poor job of wiping out the Drurr."

Beck laughed. "This is where you tell me it was a Drurr matriarch who locked you up because she was in love with you."

Drake tried to laugh but couldn't quite force it out. "Aye. That'd make for a fine fucking story."

Beck turned different eyes on him then; not the iciness that he was used to, but deep blues filled with endless pity. "I'm sorry, I thought…"

"Reckon you'd prefer to bathe alone." It took more willpower than Drake would have liked to admit, even to himself, to turn away from the naked Arbiter. But he did, and then proceeded to scramble, claw, and roll free from the hot spring, earning himself a few scrapes along his good arm. His body protested at being out of the water, and all the aches and pains the soothing spring had been suppressing made themselves known again. Drake heard the Arbiter swimming across the pool towards him. He ignored her and started walking towards the cave.

"Wait." Beck grunted as she pulled herself out of the pool. "Drake, I'm sorry."

Drake stopped, and let out a sigh. It took some effort, but he wiped the frown from his face before turning around.

Beck stood there naked and dripping wet, with an expression so earnest it was almost painful to see. Drake had seen many attractive women in his time, and until that moment he would have named Rei Chiyo the most beautiful, but the little Empress of the Dragon Empire was only seventeen and, in many ways, still a child. Arbiter Beck was no child, and her body proved it. Drake found himself at a loss for words. He stood there staring at the beautiful sight before him, and the earth moved beneath his feet.

Beck's eyes went wide and she dropped into a crouch, her hands going to the sides of her head. It took a moment longer for realisation to dawn on Drake, even as the geyser erupted behind him.

The noise was a deafening roar that blasted all thought from his head and scrambled his senses. Drake felt his legs buckle just as the force of the eruption hit him, and the world twisted. For a brief moment he caught a glimpse of boiling steam rushing into the air, and then he hit the rocky ground hard, and the pain brought on a whole new set of problems.

The world was still twisting above Drake, swaying from side to side in a manner that usually only the truly dedicated drunkards would experience. There was a persistent and loud ringing in both his ears that wasn't only painful, but was also making him nauseous. Drake punctuated that particular torment by retching up what little was left in his stomach. His body felt like bread dough, beaten, battered, flipped, beaten again, and finally left to bake at an uncomfortable temperature.

He would have expected the experience to have brought back painful memories of his time in Drurr captivity, but his memory was in open revolt and refusing to take orders.

Warm water started raining down upon Drake, and a moment later a beautiful, and very naked, woman appeared before him. She was saying something, but no sound could penetrate the ringing in his ears, and Drake couldn't keep his attention on her mouth to attempt to read her lips. His eyes rolled downwards and he saw her breasts hanging there, swaying back and forth a little as she shook him. Drake focused every bit of strength and willpower he had left, managed the heroic feat of lifting his arm from the ground, and cupped Beck's left breast.

Starry Dawn

Elaina had been pushing her crew for days now, and it had paid off. Not only had they successfully escaped the Five Kingdoms naval patrol vessel, but they'd outdistanced *Ocean Deep* and Blu to make it back home to Fango at least a day ahead of the useless blue-bearded fool. Elaina would explain things to their father long before Blu could have his say, and she'd also present him with some of the more decadent items they'd pilfered from the Acanthian fluyt.

"Should be able to taste dry land in just over an hour, Cap," Corin said from behind Elaina. "Pollick says he spies a ship looks a lot like *The Black Death*, so reckon ya da's there."

"Good," was Elaina's only reply. She'd been cold and then icy on top to her friend since they'd taken the fluyt, despite Corin's apparent sobriety, but damn if the man didn't deserve it. He was quartermaster aboard a pirate vessel – and not just any pirate vessel, but one belonging to Tanner Black. He should know better than to attempt his duties while high on Lucy. It wasn't something Elaina was willing to accept from any of her crew, even her best friend, and her displeasure needed to be well known.

"Ya won't, um…" Corin let out a heavy sigh. "Ya won't tell him, will ya?" Corin had grown up with Elaina, and he'd seen the things Tanner Black was capable of. He'd seen that family and friends were spared no leniency just because of their ties to the man. Elaina's father believed in gaining strength through pain and hardship, and he was no stranger to doling them out either.

"All of my crew's discipline as well as their punishments are my responsibility, Corin," Elaina said without looking at her friend. "This has fuck all to do with my da, and even if it did, the last thing I'd do is let his men get their grubby fuckin' hands on ya."

"Thanks, El."

"I told you not to call me that anymore."

"Sorry, Cap."

"Is it a problem, Cor?" Elaina said quietly before her quartermaster could leave.

There was a significant silence. "No. No problem."

"When was the last time you used that shit?"

"Day we took the fluyt. Day you found out." Elaina knew her friend too well; the quiver in his voice betrayed the lie.

"Corin, if..."

"It's fine, Cap. As you said it. What I do on my time is my affair, long as it don't affect ship's business. It won't. I swear."

Elaina turned, but her friend was already sprinting away across the deck in search of a job to do, and that was well and truly the end of it.

"What do we do with the loot, Cap?" said Rovel as Elaina leapt out of the boat and onto the pier.

"Nothing yet. Not until my da has had a chance ta look it over."

"What the fuck?" Ylander shouted. The pirate was known for her shrill voice. "That loot is ours, not his. Why should..."

Rovel gave Ylander a hard slap across the mouth to quiet her – and not soon enough. Bad-mouthing Tanner Black on his own island was a feat only for the brave and foolish.

"We're on his island," Elaina said quietly. "He gets tribute, and that means his pick. Good?"

Ylander nodded, but she didn't look pleased.

"I'll be back soon," Elaina said with a grimace.

Rovel folded his beefy arms across his equally beefy chest. "Do you need an escort?"

Elaina snorted and walked away.

Most people feared the Isle of Goats. They'd crowd around the populated places and only tread in "safe" areas marked by wards Tanner claimed were magical. It was true that men and women had been known to wander off into the jungle never to return; or perhaps they'd return, but changed beyond recollection. But the Isle of Goats held no secrets for Elaina.

She'd been born on the island, and raised both there and at sea. Early on in her life folk had warned her not to go out into the jungle, that it was dangerous – but that had only spurred her on. By the age of ten she'd explored every tree, every cave, every secret, and every mystery the island had to offer. It wasn't that what she'd found hadn't terrified her – it had – but Elaina wasn't the type to be terrified into inaction, so she'd kept up her exploration and the secrets of the Isle of Goats were no longer secrets. They did still terrify her though.

Her mother lived in the island interior, far beyond the protective wards and well into the territory of the spirits that called the isle their home. She lived apart and alone save for the army of monkeys that she raised and fed and called her friends. Oljanka Black wasn't entirely sane, and that was something Elaina had long ago come to terms with. Despite her obvious instability, the woman was strong and kind, and the only person in the world who could get away with upsetting Tanner Black. She'd given the man nine children, though only five had survived birth, and had the honour of being the only thing in the world that he truly loved. Elaina envied her mother for that.

She looked up at the tree house that her mother called home, squinting against the glare of the sun that glanced through the canopy above. The house was no more than fifty feet from the forest floor, certainly not the loftiest in Fango, and there were a few ways to reach it. A series of wooden planks had been nailed into the tree to form a makeshift ladder, and two ropes hung down the full length from house to ground. Elaina smiled as she remembered racing Keelin up those ropes. Stillwater was the only person who didn't share their blood that Tanner Black had ever allowed to visit Oljanka's home.

Ignoring hooting calls from above, Elaina set first her hands to the rope, then her feet, and started climbing. The climb was taxing yet didn't take overly long. Elaina was well used to scaling ropes; it was almost second nature for her. Her brothers used to tease her, saying she'd been born with a tail and was actually the daughter of a monkey, not Tanner Black. Insults like that had created more than their fair share of fights, and Elaina had won most of them despite being smaller than all three of her brothers.

As she finished her climb and set her hands to the solid wooden decking of the tree house, Elaina found herself face to face with a monkey no larger than a cat. The little beast sat on its haunches, barring her way and staring down at the intruder with a curious expression on its almost-human face. Its eyes were big and round, and the diminutive creature held its tail in its hands, nibbling on the end of it in such a way that made it seem nervous.

"Move," Elaina said as she held herself half in the tree house and half on the rope.

The monkey opened its mouth, showing a large number of sharp little teeth, and screamed at her.

Elaina sighed. "Mother."

Oljanka Black wandered out of one of the tree house's side rooms, nibbling on what appeared to be nuts much in the same way the monkey was chewing on its tail. She was grey and wrinkled, plump in a matronly fashion, but she had a piercing stare that could skewer a person at an impressive distance. Despite her appearance Oljanka wasn't actually that old; years of hard living had taken their toll, and Tanner Black was, by all accounts, hard to live with.

"Oh, Elaina, it's you. Up you come." Her mother's voice was soft and caring and full of warmth.

"I'm not sure I'm allowed," Elaina said, staring pointedly at the monkey blocking her way.

"Zsheizshei," Oljanka said firmly. "Come away from there. That's my daughter."

The little monkey bolted at its name, and only a second later was up Oljanka's leg and disappearing into the voluminous folds of her patchwork dress.

"How long has it been, Elaina?"

"Too long, Mother." Elaina pulled herself into the tree house and stood up, rolling a kink out of her shoulder. "Long enough not to have met that one before."

Looking around, Elaina now saw more monkeys – many more. She gave up counting at twenty. Some of them lounged around, sunning themselves in patches of light. Others cleaned themselves or their comrades, and others watched the intruder with cruel, beady eyes. Elaina felt very vulnerable with so many sets of little teeth and hands close by.

"You won't have met Zsheizshei then. He's a little protective of me." Oljanka Black stopped nibbling on the nuts long enough to embrace her daughter, and was then away into the room that served as a kitchen. "Doesn't yet have the teeth or stones to be very formidable though."

One of the monkeys let loose a mournful wail.

"Don't argue with me," Oljanka reprimanded the little beast. "Come. Sit down, Elaina. Tell me how you're doing."

With exaggerated care Oljanka began to sweep debris from the table in the centre of the room. Much of it was monkey hair, but there were also a number of wooden carvings that made Elaina's eyes itch just from looking at them. Each one was placed in its own spot, no matter how insignificant it looked. Elaina couldn't help but laugh. She'd grown up here in this house; for the first few years of her life it was all she'd known. She'd missed how meticulous her mother could be about even the smallest of things.

"I've missed you, Mother." Elaina pulled out a rickety stool that was likely older than she was and sat down.

"Well, of course," Oljanka said as she moved about the room, putting trinkets and tools away or moving them into new positions. "You wouldn't be a very dutiful daughter if you didn't. Have you seen the kettle?"

Elaina was about to ask why she would have seen it, when one of the monkeys let out a low noise that almost sounded like a husky whistle.

"You're right. The fireplace does seem like the most likely spot for it, and – oh, look, you're right." Oljanka stopped next to Elaina for a moment. "You remember Rolo, always has to be right even when he's wrong. Tea?"

"Aye."

"And this time he's right." Oljanka walked to the fireplace, a reinforced stone monstrosity common in many houses on the Isle of Goats.

Elaina felt something tug on her britches and looked down to find a tiny, grey, bent-backed monkey staring up at her through milky eyes. She didn't need her mother's prompting to recognise Tchewie. The old female had been ancient even when Elaina was a child, and now she looked even more frail. Carefully, Elaina reached down, picked the little beast up, and set it on her lap, where it curled into a ball and promptly fell asleep.

"How many of these little monsters do you have these days, Mother?" The woman was pottering about by the fireplace, dropping all manner of crushed leaves into two cups.

Oljanka laughed merrily. "You know I can't count past my fingers, Elaina."

One of the monkeys hooted a few times. "Ptiti says there's fifty-four of them, however many that is, but I wouldn't take her word for it. I found her eating her own dung just this morning."

Elaina's mother returned to the table with two mugs of steaming broth, and set them down before moving away to find some other small task. The woman was incapable of staying still, and it was something that had driven Elaina near to madness as a child. It was having a similar effect now, but she knew there was nothing she could do to stop her.

"So, how is the world?" Oljanka said. "How are you? Still at daggers with little Blu?"

Elaina grimaced. "Blu ain't so little no more, Mother. He's pretty big now, in fact, and the spitting image of Father. Only he dyes his stupid beard blue."

"Oh, I don't remember him having a beard." Her mother sounded sad. "I suppose it's been a while since he came to see me."

Elaina blew on her tea before taking a sip. She grimaced at the bitter taste. "I'm good, and the world is dangerous as always. Maybe a little more so these days."

"Tanner came by the other day," Oljanka said happily. "He said he would be gone for a while. I wish you would all just come back to me here. It's so much safer in the forest."

Elaina laughed. Most folk who set foot on the Isle of Goats were of the exact opposite opinion. Oljanka turned at the sound of her daughter's amusement and crossed the room, cupping Elaina's chin in her puffy hand and smiling down at her.

"Oh, my daughter. The dead are only dead until they're not, and kings and queens are made of lust before love. The heart is black now, the light forgotten, but not all fortunes are made of gold. Winter wilts even the darkest of flowers. Walls. Where did I put the walls?" Then she was off into another room, cleaning, rearranging, and talking to her monkeys as though she hadn't just said something utterly crazy.

Elaina sipped at her tea for a while, mulling over her mother's words. The woman had been launching into such outbursts for years now, and Elaina had always wondered whether she even knew what she was saying. She looked down at the sleeping monkey in her lap and let out a long sigh. It wouldn't be long before her mother fell into a shaking fit; they always followed the outbursts, and Elaina hated the thought of the woman being here alone when she collapsed.

It was hours later, and quickly approaching dark, when Elaina sauntered out of the jungle and into Fango. Some folk might find it hard to navigate in the dim light, but she knew her way around the Isle of Goats better than most men knew their way around their own bodies, and definitely better than any man knew his way around a woman's.

An elderly seaman, long past retired, was sitting on a withered old stump and smoking a pipe. He squinted at her curiously for a few moments before cracking a rotten-toothed smile and greeting her by name. There weren't many residents of Fango who didn't know Elaina Black, and those that didn't had, at the very least, damned well heard of her.

Elaina had put off going to see her father for long enough. Her visit to her mother had been a calculated delay, and she would need to present herself before the day was out or earn yet more of his disapproval. That was not something she could bear. She also needed to speak to him before *Ocean Deep* arrived and Blu got his say, or her idiot brother would no doubt poison their father against her.

Tanner Black always kept court at the same place whenever he set foot in Fango, and his choice wasn't random. The Nymph was the town's only brothel – and Tanner had seen to it that it remained that way. Nearly every pirate who set foot in Fango would frequent The Nymph, or at the very least pay a fleeting visit, and Tanner had eyes and ears in every nook, cranny, and whore. It was all part of his iron-clad control over the island and its people. And it worked.

The brothel was in the centre of town, a monster of a building spreading out across three of the largest trees in Fango. There were multiple entrances, all complete with ropes, ladders, and even donkey-powered cages for those that couldn't manage – or couldn't be arsed with – the climb. There were, however, far more exits from The Nymph than entrances, and many a drunken sailor had stumbled to find themselves on the fast track to the ground.

Elaina, never one to shy away from a little physical exertion, set hands and feet to rope for the third time that day and started climbing.

She'd been to a few brothels in her time – sometimes the places even had boy whores to her satisfaction – and one thing she hated about all of them was the smell. Stale perfume, stale booze, and stale sex filled the air, turning it thick with the stench. The noise was almost as bad. From the common room she could hear the clatter of badly played instruments and general revelry, but there was also the noise behind that. The grunts and gasps, the squeals and screams. Some men liked their women to be noisy and would happily pay extra for the fantasy that she was enjoying their clumsy attentions. The whores, being what they were, were always accommodating.

As she finished her climb, Elaina found one of her father's men waiting at the top of the rope. It wasn't uncommon for him to post sentries at each of the ways up, but Elaina instantly wished she'd picked a different entrance. Tanner Black's first mate, Mace, was leaning against the outer wall of The Nymph. He leered at her with everything he was worth, which in Elaina's opinion was less than nothing. The bastard didn't say anything; he didn't need to. They both remembered what had happened the last time they'd seen each other, and the memory sent shivers of rage coursing through Elaina's veins every time she thought about it.

She had to restrain herself from attacking the leering bastard. She was armed with a sword and he only a wooden kosh, but even if she did prevail and send the monster stabbed and bleeding over the edge to his death below, her father would find out and punish her for it. Sometimes it was better to forget and live on no matter how difficult, and now was unfortunately one of those times. Elaina strode past the man, feeling his eyes on her the entire time, and fought the urge to hurry. Fought the urge to scream. Even worse was the knowledge that she would have to suffer him again later. If she used a different exit the bastard would think she was scared of him, and she couldn't have that.

Pushing open the door and stepping over the threshold, Elaina was struck by everything she hated about brothels all over again. The smell inside was tragic, and the noise was viscous, but the atmosphere was contagious. Pirates sang, pirates danced, pirates fucked their way through a dozen prostitutes, and pirates paid respects to the man who allowed it all to happen around him.

Tanner Black sat in a large alcove, surrounded by whores and pirates all hanging on his every word and drinking on his generosity. The rest of the world may hate him, but here in Fango he was a king, and soon the rest of the isles would see him that way too.

An effeminate young man with plucked eyebrows, oiled hair, and a shaved chest sauntered over to Elaina. He was dressed only in shallow britches, and his sun-bronzed chest was hard with muscle. Some might mistake Quell for just another male whore attempting to stake a claim on a newly arrived customer – they would be wrong, and then some. He was the host, and management of both the house and the whores was his responsibility. Those who knew Quell respected him, and those that didn't soon learned their mistake. There was some debate as to whether Quell preferred the company of men or women, but those that shared his bed, if any, kept quiet on the matter.

"Elaina," he said softly. "Wonderful to see you again. Would you like a drink brought over to your father's alcove?"

"Do ya have any mulled spirits? Rum can get a little tiresome, living aboard a ship."

"Thankfully not all of the patrons share your misgivings," Quell said with a practised smile of his silky lips. "We have some spiced whiskey from the northlands of the Five Kingdoms."

Elaina narrowed her eyes at him. Goods from the Five Kingdoms were becoming rarer and rarer out in the isles. "The big bastard here just a couple of weeks ago?"

Quell nodded. "Captain T'ruck Khan. Apparently he still has some contacts from his homeland."

"Aye, bring me a mug."

"As you wish. And…" He flashed Elaina a genuine smile, though it was laced with pity. "I heard about… well, you know. Please try not to anger him here; I have a business to run, and violence is not it."

Elaina stepped close to Quell, close enough to smell the sharp perfume he wore and see the individual hairs on his head.

"Oh, don't you worry your pretty little face about that, mate. I'll try not to get myself raped in your establishment." It was all she could do not to spit at him, a man she usually got on very well with.

"I never meant to imply…" Elaina had heard it said that it was hard to make a whore blush, so what it said about *her* that the host was now turning an uncomfortable shade of red, she'd rather not know. Without waiting to hear the rest of his apology, she turned and approached her father's court.

Tanner Black, never one to miss a beat, had likely been watching Elaina since she entered the brothel. Now, his eyes followed her all the way to his alcove, where any number of his men stood ready between him and any newcomers. It was a carefully chosen position within the brothel, as defensible as a fort, with high wooden chairs either side and a table as sturdy as a bulkhead that could be tipped up to provide extra cover. Elaina thought about speaking first, before her father could greet her in his usual derogatory way, but Tanner Black always had to get in the first and the last words. To deny him either would only rouse his anger, so Elaina waited for him to acknowledge her.

"Well, boys, will ya look at that," Tanner said, ignoring the two whores and the female pirate all crowded into his court. "Arrived this mornin', me daughter did. Sailed right up next ta me own ship, an' only now does she think ta come an' see Cap'n Black." Her father had an annoying habit of talking about himself as if he were someone else. It was something Elaina had always hated.

"Rude, is what that is, Cap'n," said one of Tanner's crew, a burly pirate with a mouth full of rotting teeth.

"Careful, Flow." Tanner glanced at the pirate. "That's me daughter ya speakin' of, an' she's worth ten of all of ya."

Elaina almost smiled, but her father would turn on her if he caught it, and she was counting on staying in his good graces this visit. "I went ta see Ma."

"Aye?"

"Aye."

All of Tanner's court went silent, and the music and singing and fucking nearby seemed all the louder for it. Everyone knew that Elaina's mother was cracked in the head and crazier than a deep blue storm, but no one dared mention that fact with Tanner around. The last man who had had found himself staked down and cut open from groin to collar, left to rot for a week until maggots erupted from the open wound and ate him from the inside. It was the first and last time anyone but family had mentioned Oljanka's illness to Tanner's face, and even family only spoke of it in private.

"Is she well?" Tanner's dark eyes searched Elaina's face for any hidden message. She gave none.

"Strong as a woman half her age," Elaina said proudly, knowing that much was true at least.

"Aye. Well, she misses you."

"She asked after Blu."

Tanner growled. "Ungrateful cur hasn't been ta see her in years. Carried an' raised him, an' he don't even know he's born."

This time Elaina did smile; turning her father against Blu had always been one of her favourite pastimes. Unfortunately, turning Tanner right back against Elaina had always been one of Blu's.

"I've a hold full of goods ya might like, Da," she said, deciding not to push her luck. "Fancy spice wines from the desert. Some rugs look like they're made of snake skin. And a bunch of gems right for the cutting."

"Aye? Well, girl, ya best take a seat an' get ta drinkin' that shit Quell's brought ya. Cap'n Black ain't nothin' if not generous ta those that are generous ta him."

Just like that, Elaina found herself back in her seat at her father's court and back in his good graces. She knew full well the trick would be staying there.

The Phoenix

Everybody always said Drake Morrass was the man with the plan; this time it was Keelin Stillwater's plan, and he was more than a little proud of it. That it seemed to be lifting the spirits of everyone involved, both pirates and refugees from Sev'relain, only deepened his satisfaction.

The beach had, as far as they could tell, been cleared of sand monsters, and sixteen rotting carcasses littered the far west end as a grim testament to the sacrifice of the seven folk who had died making the landing safe. The fact that the smell of decaying flesh drifted all the way down the beach, even in such little wind, was a small price to pay for the reminder of how dedicated everyone was to establishing a new home for the dispossessed folk of Sev'relain.

The Man of War had been beached, and her hull now rested on the sand, keeled over and attached to nearby trees by its rigging. Carpenters and their work crews were taking it apart piece by piece. It was hard work and hot, but it would be worth it once a town and harbour were built from its bones.

Water was fast becoming an issue, and Keelin was debating sending some folk into the jungle to find a fresh source. The stores they kept aboard ship could only last so long, and with the heat and distinct lack of breeze, folk were already bordering on dehydration. But the jungle scared Keelin. Even in the height of the day it looked dark and dangerous, and he knew just how perilous the forested areas of the Pirates Isles could be. Elaina Black had shown him the terrors of the Isle of Goats, and he had no wish to repeat the experience on an isle named after a multitude of deaths.

There was also the issue of Drake's crew. The men of the *Fortune* were beginning to get anxious, and they weren't alone. Keelin shared their worries.

It had been three days since Drake and the Arbiter had entered the jungle, and they had yet to return. Their disappearance along with the continued roaring from whatever beast called the interior its home, everyone was starting to come to the same conclusion. Drake had failed, and the monster had eaten him.

It was hard to gauge how the *Fortune*'s crew would react if their captain didn't return, and soon. They might elect Princess as the new captain and continue Drake's plan to become king of the isles, or they might simply sail away to resume their life of piracy. Given how zealous the crew were when it came to their captain, they might storm the jungle and attempt vengeance on the creature.

The biggest problem, Keelin was quickly realising after only a few days in charge, was that he was the captain of a pirate ship, not the governor of a fledgling town.

"Accommodation," said Breta, a large woman with an even larger voice and a distinct Five Kingdoms accent. "We can't camp out under the stars forever. We're not beasts, and the women need their privacy. We can't walk five paces out here without being leered at by some pirate, or by some bereaved fool thinks the death of his wife is a boon."

"Aw, fuck, Breta. I loved my wife, ya know that. But she's gone now, an' I'm still of a givin' age." This from Po, a former slave from the Wilds who had earned his freedom by way of mutiny. Keelin knew this from the tattoos along his arms and chest.

"The only thing you have to give is the pox. We need houses."

Keelin wiped sweat from his forehead and glanced out over the bay towards his ship. A large part of him was tempted to pack up, sail away, and leave the refugees and Drake's crew to themselves.

"Captain Stillwater. We need houses," Breta insisted.

"Twoson's team is working on housing…" Keelin started.

"Not quickly enough. All of your teams should be…"

"There are other concerns, Breta," Po said, leaping to Keelin's defence with a wink towards the besieged captain.

"Oh, I'm well aware you want that whore house up and running as soon as possible." There was more than a little venom in Breta's accusation, and without intervention the argument threatened to turn to violence. Unfortunately, Keelin was sick to his gut of all the arguing.

"By Rin's watery minge, Stillwater, what the fuck are ya doing to my prize?" The shout came from somewhere up the beach, and Keelin couldn't help but smile at the sound of it. Despite any misgivings he had

Where Loyalties Lie

about the man, he found himself more than a little glad to see Drake had survived the jungle.

Keelin stood from the barrel he'd been using as a chair as Drake drew closer, Beck behind him. He looked sweaty, pale, and weak, and when he was only a handful of feet away he stumbled. The Arbiter caught Drake before he could hit the sand, and helped him back to his feet. He struggled forwards, into the middle of Keelin's meeting; all the gathered pirates and townsfolk were silent as the captain took his rightful place. Keelin couldn't help but notice that all work on the beach had stopped as pirates and refugees alike quit their jobs to catch a look at Drake, as if he were some returning hero.

"Don't take this the wrong way, Drake, but you look like shit." Keelin smiled as he stepped aside to let Drake take the barrel.

Drake let out a noise somewhere between a grunt and a sigh and lowered himself onto the makeshift seat. "Water and food wouldn't go amiss," he croaked. "For Beck too."

Keelin glanced over at the Arbiter and realised for the first time that she didn't look much better than Drake, save she didn't have a broken arm or a black eye swollen to the size of a fist. They were both dishevelled and sweaty, and looked in dire need of a few months' sleep.

"Why is my prize beached?" Drake said before any water or food could appear. "Refurbishing?"

"Repurposing." Keelin smiled. "Folk here need a town, a port, a place to live and make a living. Figured that beast could provide it, since it took it all away in the first place."

Drake seemed to think about that for a moment, and Keelin watched the anger drain out of him, leaving only weary acceptance.

"Aye, sounds good. First thing's first, get a tavern built, just up the beach but before the jungle."

Breta stepped forward. "We were just discussing…"

"And pull that nameplate off the hull. Hang it above the tavern door." Drake grinned. "Show those bastards what we think of their ships, eh?"

"Housing must be a priority," Breta forged on, undeterred by Drake's interruption.

Drake turned a tired smile on the big woman. "Housing can wait. Ain't none of you gonna hurt from a few more days camping out under the stars. What you folk need – what we need – is a place to relax a little. Ease tensions, you might say. Aye?"

Breta looked stunned by Drake's earnest appeal, but still pressed her point. "The women need privacy for women things."

Drake nodded as a pirate handed him a mug of water. He took a few small sips. "You'll have it. We'll get you some temporary shelters set up. Any bilge scum who gets a bit over eager with any of you can answer to me. Ain't gonna have any rape here in… Let's call it New Sev'relain." He paused and swept a gaze over the gathering. "That includes throwing a couple of bits at a woman and telling her she's paid. All manner of ways to punish men who are a bit too amorous, eh?"

A nervous laughter rippled through the crowd, yet no one argued with him.

"Now if you wouldn't mind, I need a word or two with my fellow captain here." Drake left it in no uncertain terms that everyone else was dismissed, and as people started to wander away, the taskmasters took control and directed their workers back to their jobs.

Princess sauntered into the little clearing carrying a small, unmarked barrel no more than a foot high. He carefully set it down on the sand and stood in front of his captain. He looked relieved.

"Good ta see ya, Cap'n." Princess almost sounded choked with tears. "Safe ta say, me and some of the boys were starting ta get a little worried. Reckon ya've proved us all fools now."

Drake grinned back at his first mate. "You should know never to bet against me, Princess."

"Hell of a shiner though," the pirate said, looking at Drake's black eye. "That beastie give you a pummelling?"

"There is no monster in the jungle." Drake sighed.

Keelin noticed Kebble Salt drifting into the clearing, silent and watchful as always. He found himself glad of the man's presence, but wished Morley were there. Unfortunately the man was needed on board *The Phoenix*, as Keelin didn't entirely trust every member of his crew.

"The roaring and shaking is just a geyser," Drake continued.

"Erupts every so often. Nothing to be worried about. It even comes with a hot spring, if anyone fancies a nice dip."

"So how'd ya get the black eye, Cap'n?"

Drake's face soured, and he paused to take a long swig of water, glancing at the Arbiter. "I tripped."

"There are some dangers in the forest," Beck said. "Magical traps would be the best way to describe them. We triggered one and it almost cost us. I found another few as we were returning and disarmed them, but there may be more."

"Of course you would know how to disarm a magical trap," Keelin spat.

Drake seemed to perk up a little then. He looked between Keelin and the Arbiter and let out a heavy sigh. "Like that matters. Question is who set 'em and why, and how many more are there?"

"Got a solution, Cap'n?" Princess said.

"Of sorts. Beck here says she can make us some charms that'll warn folk when one of these traps is nearby. For now it'll have to do. Nobody goes into the jungle alone, and not without a charm."

Keelin felt the anger burning in his chest. He already knew the Sarth woman was an Arbiter, but now it appeared that Drake knew as well.

"Found this when we started gutting the Man of War," Princess said, pointing to the barrel. He pulled a small cork from the lid and tipped the barrel at a slight angle. Black powder spilled out of the hole, and Princess quickly put the cork back in and kicked sand over the small pile.

"Would you mind moving that barrel into the shade," Kebble said. "Black powder is unstable and best kept away from any heat sources; I would suggest that includes the sun."

Princess looked at the barrel sceptically, but moved it under the shade of some hanging canvas all the same. "How much do ya reckon a barrel like that is worth?"

"A small fortune," the Arbiter said. "A pouch can cost upwards of five gold bits, depending on the merchant. A barrel that size, hundreds at least."

Princess grinned. "We found ten of them."

There was a stunned silence. Keelin could hear the work crews hammering and sawing, and even the jungle birds cawing from far away.

"How many barrels would it take to explode a ship?" Drake sounded beyond tired.

Kebble and the Arbiter exchanged a glance, and it was Kebble who answered. "That depends on how you mean. One barrel, placed correctly, would put a hole in a ship large enough to sink it. To turn a ship into debris, such as at Sev'relain… five might suffice. More likely ten or more."

Drake sat in silence for a while, his eyes closed. Keelin was about to check whether the man had fallen asleep when he sat up straight and the ghost of a grin passed his lips.

"Well, I reckon those bastards have given us a hell of a weapon there. You two take as much as you need to replenish your stocks," he said to the Arbiter and Kebble. "The rest I want storing somewhere safe, here on the island. I want as few folk as possible knowing about it. Good?"

"Aye, Cap'n," Princess said.

"Good." Drake stood from his barrel, swaying on his feet. The Arbiter rushed forwards to hold him upright. Keelin couldn't quite figure out the relationship. If the Arbiter was Drake's keeper, making certain he kept to whatever agenda the Inquisition had, why did she seem to care so much for him? "Now, if you all don't mind, I need to rest. Princess, I'll need a boat back to the *Fortune*."

Starry Dawn

The beer was bitter and warm and foul, but Elaina swigged it down nevertheless. Courage was what she needed now, and while that was something she usually had in spades, and then some, the matter at hand was sensitive, and she had a bad feeling about it.

Three days ago Blu and *Ocean Deep* had arrived at north port, and three days ago Corin had gone missing. The quartermaster of *Starry Dawn* was known well in Fango, and not least of all because he could put it back and pass out under a tavern table as well as any sailor, but his disappearance had set Elaina's mind ill at ease.

Fango was a large town with many buildings stretching across multiple trees, from jungle floor to canopy. Elaina had searched as many of them as she could, but to no avail. Even Quartermain hadn't seen the man. Elaina supposed it was possible Corin had wandered off into the jungle, but that seemed unlikely given the fearsome reputation of the place. Much more likely was that Corin had turned on his friend and captain, turned on his crew, and told Tanner all about the ship they'd taken. The possibility of such treachery made Elaina sad and angry at the same time, and she couldn't decide whether she'd hug her friend or stab him when she finally caught up to him.

The shade of the tree and the slight breeze should have been enough to keep Elaina cool, but her blood was boiling and no amount of wind could take away the heat she felt in her cheeks. She finished off the mug of vile beer and threw it into a nearby bush, her eyes fixed on the last place she could think to look for her friend: The Nymph. If she found Corin sitting in Tanner Black's court, the betrayal would be undeniable.

Elaina set off at a sprint and leapt just before she reached the nearest climbing rope, taking it mid-jump and beginning her climb long before the rope had stopped swinging. She went hand over hand as quickly as she could, forsaking finesse for pure power. It was a waste of energy, but she felt like she had energy to burn, and releasing it in this way might make her less hotheaded in a confrontation.

Sweat was dripping from her face by the time she reached the ground floor of the brothel and pulled herself to her feet. As always, one of Tanner's pirates stood guard at the entrance. Luckily for both of them, it wasn't Mace. Elaina wasn't sure how she'd react to the man's presence in her current state. The pirate gave her a cheerful greeting; Elaina ignored the bastard and barged into the brothel.

It was the middle of the day, and though the music was absent, the activity in the brothel was no less vigorous than ever. Pirates drank and pirates fucked and whores earned their pay. Elaina had no time for any of it, and she headed straight to her father's alcove, ignoring Quell's attempt to detain her with flowery words.

Tanner Black was absent, but his court was not. Many of his pirates – and many of Blu's – lounged around drinking and fiddling with their coin purses, trying to decide whether they should buy another fuck now or save their money for later. Blu himself was collapsed in a chair, with his head resting on his shoulder and a thin line of drool wetting his fancy shirt. One of Blu's crew leaned over and poked his captain, and the fool woke with a start, his eyes going wide with shock and fear.

"Where's Da?" Elaina all but shouted.

Blu made a sleepy, non-committal noise, and then shrugged. One of the other pirates was more awake and not so useless.

"Takin' a piss."

Elaina waited, but not patiently, pacing and sighing and snorting and growling, all while Tanner's court and Blu watched her through bemused eyes. When Tanner entered the brothel, still in the act of fixing his belt, he didn't seem surprised to see his daughter. The infamous pirate wandered back to his alcove and picked up a mug from the table, draining it in one large gulp.

"Elaina," Tanner Black said eventually, giving his daughter permission to speak.

"I'm looking for my quartermaster." Elaina decided to skip the pleasantries. "No one has seen him in days."

"Can't keep track of ya own crew," Blu said with a nasty smirk.

"Quiet," Tanner said sharply, and the entire brothel seemed to obey the command. "Follow me." He set off towards the brothel's far exit, leaving Elaina to catch up.

Following him outside, Elaina couldn't hold it in any longer. "Where is he, Father?"

Tanner glanced impatiently over his shoulder, but said nothing. He wasted no time mounting one of the wooden bridges that crossed from the brothel to another nearby tree house, and quickened his pace. Elaina had to all but jog to keep up with him.

After crossing two more bridges they came to a giant tree that had three houses attached to the outside, all connected by a platform. An old one-eyed man sat in a rickety chair outside one of the buildings, and it took only a moment for Elaina to recognise him as a retired member of her father's crew. From a distance he looked as though he were simply sitting, watching the world go by below him, but with an old sword laid on the table next to him and a set of keys attached to his belt, it quickly became clear he was guarding the building.

"Ya lied ta me, Elaina," Tanner said as he took the keys from the old man and slotted one into the lock.

Elaina had the sudden feeling that she didn't want to know what was on the other side of the door. "No, I didn't." Her voice was shaking.

"That ship ya took was Acanthian."

Her father was staring at her now, his eyes dark and accusing. Some things she could get away with lying about, others she couldn't – and this was one.

"That what Blu told ya? Aye, it was Acanthian."

"An' it was protected by the Guild."

"No, it wasn't." Elaina immediately knew the lie was a mistake.

Tanner Black threw open the door to the house, grabbed hold of Elaina, and dragged her inside. She didn't try to resist; her father could easily overpower her, and Elaina knew he might punish her, but never would he do her any permanent harm. At least, she sincerely hoped that was true. Despite her belief in her father, fear flowed through her veins, and she couldn't stop herself shaking. The blood rushing through her ears was as loud as a turbulent ocean.

Inside, the house was dimly lit and stank of the stale straw that littered the floor. The room was empty, but Elaina could just about hear a low moaning coming from the other side of a closed door. Tanner let go of Elaina's arm and closed the door behind them. The house grew dimmer still, but there was a flickering shard of light coming from under the door to the other room.

Tanner opened it, and lantern light flooded out. Elaina could see her father clearly now, as he stood there, staring at her. Never one to be timid, Elaina wasted no time in striding forwards. The second room was smaller than the first and just as poorly maintained, but there was a single storm lantern hanging from the wall. Corin was lying on the floor.

Forgetting her company, Elaina rushed forwards. Corin was moaning softly. His shirt had been ripped open, exposing his chest, and there was barely enough of it left to qualify as clothing. His britches were missing, and Elaina saw them balled up in a corner of the room. Worst, though, were the serene smile on her friend's face and the distant look in his eyes.

"Corin." Elaina shook him by the shoulders, to no response. "Corin!" she shouted, but still received no reply.

"What did ya do to him, Da?" Elaina turned furious eyes on her father.

"Nothin'," Tanner Black said, stepping into the doorway. He filled the space. "He did it to himself; I jus' supplied the means. He begged for it. Oh, the things he said, the things he did. Were you aware your quartermaster is addicted to Lucy?"

There was no safe answer to that question, and Elaina knew it. If she admitted to knowing, she'd seem a sentimental fool for letting an addict serve aboard her ship. Feigning ignorance would make her appear an incompetent captain. She settled on sending a poisonous glare towards her father.

"The ship you took was under the protection of the Guild." Tanner folded his arms across his chest.

Right then Elaina wanted nothing so much as to defy her father.
"No, it wasn't."

Tanner Black took two steps into the room and sent a heavy boot into Corin's midsection. The man barely seemed to notice; his only response was a moan that sounded more pleasure than pain.

"What are you doing?" Elaina shouted, rising to her feet and positioning herself between her father and Corin.

"Punishin' you for lyin' ta me," Tanner growled. "I already know the truth, girl. Ya quartermaster told me everythin' ta get himself another fix."

"Fine, they had protection. But we didn't leave no one alive ta get back ta the Guild."

Tanner shoved Elaina aside, and she staggered away. Before she could get back between the two men, her father sent another boot into the prostrate man's side. This time Corin coughed and attempted to roll away, but Tanner put his boot on the quartermaster's belly to stop him.

Elaina rushed forwards to push her father away, but stopped at the last second as she realised it would only make matters worse. There was only one way to get both herself and Corin out of this situation, and that was to appease Tanner Black.

"I know about the navy ship, girl," Tanner spat. "Provides its own set o' problems. Means that shit Morrass probably wasn't behind Black Sands and Sev'relain."

"What about Sev'relain?"

"Gone. Same way as Black Sands, by the sound of it. Sarth's handiwork, but I hear Morrass thinks the Five Kingdoms is in on it too. Last fuckin' thing we need is the Guild financing the whole shitting thing."

Elaina felt her stomach curdle. Keelin had fled Fango, and it was possible he'd made his way to Sev'relain. It was possible he'd died there. "I'm sorry, Da," she said quietly.

Tanner watched his daughter for a moment, his boot still firmly on Corin's belly; by the looks of it he was pressing down fairly hard. The addict didn't seem to notice; he was stoned long past any sort of conscious thought.

"I'm takin' ya loot," Tanner said eventually. "All of it."

"What? Ya can't, Da. My crew..."

"I can't?" Tanner sent another kick into Corin's side.

Elaina couldn't fathom how he could do such a thing. Tanner had known Corin for as long as she had. They'd grown up together, served on *The Black Death* together under Tanner. Now he'd drugged Corin and was beating him. Elaina nodded, resigned.

"I'll have it sent to Quartermain on your behalf."

"Good." Tanner removed his boot from Corin's belly. "An' you'll be needing a new quartermaster."

"What? Da, please…"

Her father had always been quicker than his size should allow, and his hand shot out and grabbed hold of Elaina. He dragged her out of the room, and she didn't bother to struggle; it would have been useless.

"The boy will stay right here," Tanner said as he dragged Elaina away. "Wouldn't want ta deprive my crew of their new pet." Elaina's last glimpse of her best friend showed Corin lying motionless on the floor, with deep red swelling already starting to discolour his side and a stupid grin on his face.

The Phoenix

Standing outside his cabin aboard *The Phoenix,* Keelin though back to something his brother had said to him a long time ago. "When you're faced with a great many tasks, pick the most arduous and complete that one first. The rest will appear easy by comparison." Right now Keelin was taking that advice very much to heart.

"She ain't in there, Cap'n," Feather said. Keelin turned to the boy with a hopeful grin, though he had a strangely sour feeling in his stomach.

"She's vacated my cabin? Did she go ashore?"

Feather paled and scratched behind his ear. "Nah, Cap'n. She's... um... up in the nest. Taken to spending some time up there, when not teaching the cook to... cook."

Keelin looked upwards to the nest, then grabbed hold of some rigging, readying himself for the climb.

"She don't like to be disturbed, Cap'n. Says it's her place of peace."

Keelin stopped and turned on Feather. "How long have I been gone?"

"F... few days, Cap'n?"

"And you staged a mutiny to put her in charge?"

"No!" Feather looked shocked and terrified all at once.

"Then I think I'll go disturb her. Gods know she's disturbed me enough." Keelin leapt, took hold of a tied-off rope leading up to the main mast, and started climbing.

Just that morning the work crew had finished construction of the *Righteous Indignation,* and before anyone else could claim ownership of the tavern, Keelin intended to rid himself of his squatter.

Halfway up to the nest, Keelin took a moment to look down upon the beach and the fledgling town of New Sev'relain. The massive hulk of the Man of War, still being cannibalised for its wood, was the most visible landmark. A trail of people walking to or from the ship almost looked like ants scavenging a giant carcass.

On the beach front, just up from the tidal line, sat the shacks, shanties, and tents of the temporary settlement. The majority of the refugees were still living in those makeshift shelters, along with many of the pirates from both the *Fortune* and *The Phoenix*.

Further up the beach, towards the tree line and on firmer ground, sat the first true buildings of New Sev'relain. The tavern was the largest, and while it looked impressive from the outside, Keelin knew first-hand it was still all but empty inside, little more than a shell. Smaller buildings were dotted here and there nearby, housing or food stores; some were even occupied already.

In the little more than fourteen days since they'd landed on Cinto Cena, the island had begun to take the shape of Drake's dream. Keelin wanted nothing more than to set sail and get back out onto the ocean. He reached the nest and hauled himself up over the lip and into it. Aimi was staring not towards the island, but out to sea, her back to him. The nest was barely big enough for two people, and Keelin found himself huddled to one side in an attempt to minimise contact. He cleared his throat softly, finding he didn't truly want to disturb the woman.

Aimi looked over her shoulder, gave Keelin a brief but warm smile, then turned back towards the ocean vista. Keelin couldn't entirely blame her; with the sun high and hot and sending glinting shards of light off the waves, it was a truly beautiful sight.

"The tavern is finished," Keelin said, deciding to jump right into the matter. "Down in the town."

"Mhm." Aimi gave no other response.

Keelin opened his mouth to say more, but realised he had no idea how to broach the subject.

"I was born at sea," Aimi said, as if talking to herself. Keelin decided to shut his mouth and listen. "My parents used to love telling me the story. They were fisher-folk from the coast of Tseronei, just south of Larkos in the Dragon Empire. My mother was pregnant with me, and they were out fishing one day when a storm hit. My father used to say it was the largest he'd ever seen, a fitting storm to herald my coming. My mother went into labour and popped me out right there in the little cabin."

"How did you end up in Sev'relain?"

"Fishing villages are small places, Captain Stillwater," Aimi said. "Too small and too confined. I wanted to see more of the world. My older sister taught me how to bind my breasts and dress to look like a boy, and I booked passage on a trader. I learned to tie knots, climb ropes, and piss in secret. I visited some wonderful places, until pirates took the ship." She gave Keelin a dark look over her shoulder. It seemed to dim the brightness of the day, and made him feel guilty for his chosen profession as he never had before.

"Captain Iolin of the *Ferryman* took the ship in a mostly bloodless chase."

"He was a fair man, Iolin," Keelin said. "Until he sailed into Land's End and they stretched his neck." He rubbed a hand across his throat; the idea of hanging was not a pleasant one.

"Seemed so," Aimi continued. "Took me on as ship's boy for a while, but by then it was getting harder to hide my breasts." She looked over her shoulder again, piercing Keelin with a challenging stare. "The problem with growing into a woman. One of many, actually, at least when trying to pass as a boy.

"A few years back he stopped the *Ferryman* at Sev'relain, and I jumped off, bought some clothes more fitting to my figure, and begged for some work at the tavern. I learned to cook, serve drinks, and avoid lecherous pirates. I never meant to stay there."

Keelin sighed.

"Oh, I'm sorry." Aimi turned back to the sea. "I didn't mean for my life story to bore you."

"It didn't, it's just…" Sometimes the best way was to simply dive in. "The tavern is finished, and it needs an owner. I thought that you…"

"No."

"Well, at least you considered it."

"I just told you I never wanted to get stuck in Sev'relain," Aimi hissed, "and now you want me to strand myself here, wherever this is."

"We're calling it New Sev'relain."

Aimi rolled her eyes at him.

"You're going ashore," Keelin said firmly.

"No, I'm not."

"Well, you can't stay here."

"Why not?"

"Because I want my cabin back."

"Done." Aimi grinned, and Keelin realised he'd just walked right into a trap.

"Wait…"

"I'll move down with the rest of the crew; I assume you can still vouch for my safety among them. I'll vacate your cabin immediately and take on some of the ship's duties. For a start I'll replace that idiotic cook of yours; he wouldn't know a spice from an herb. And you'll start paying me a sailor's cut from the ship's earnings."

"Wait…"

"I know my way around a ship, Captain Stillwater. I was born on one, remember. I can sail as well as any man you have on your crew and a fuck lot better than you, I'll wager."

Keelin was still trying to understand exactly what had just happened. He was fairly certain this slip of a woman had just hooked him, reeled him in, gutted him, and cooked him. He needed to regain some semblance of control over the situation. "Can you fight?"

Aimi narrowed her eyes. "No."

"We're pirates. From time to time we're required to board ships and kill folk. It's part of the job. Can't fight? I've got no space for you."

"The cook doesn't fight."

"I can't afford to lose him."

"Now you can't afford to lose me."

Keelin growled. "You're not replacing Mondo; he's been with us for years. You can work alongside him." The words were already out of Keelin's mouth before he realised he'd made the concession.

"Fine. If you want me to fight, you have to teach me how." Aimi's jaw was set like steel and her eyes were as lively as fire.

"Fine. Get your shit out of my cabin, now."

Aimi smiled then, and Keelin realised he'd lost.

"And from now on," Keelin growled as Aimi clambered over the side of the nest, "you can call me captain."

She grinned at him. "I already do, Captain Stillwater." Then she was gone.

Aimi scuttled down the rigging as fast as any monkey, leapt the last six feet, and landed on the deck in a crouch, all while wearing a grin she couldn't even begin to hide. With nothing but her guile, she'd successfully escaped the mediocrity of what would probably have been quite a short life tending a tavern in a run-down pirate town. That she'd traded in those particular boots to become a pirate was another matter altogether, and a decision she hoped she wouldn't regret down the line. Aimi had never seen a man, or woman, hang, but she'd heard it was the popular way for civilised society to deal with their ilk, and like or not, she was now one of them.

"How did it go?" Feather said, matching Aimi's stride as she made for the captain's cabin.

"Exactly as I planned." Feather was a sweet boy, innocent considering his line of work, and quite gullible. She'd used him to a degree in her manipulations, but he seemed none the wiser and more than happy to help.

"I thought he'd throw you off the ship for sure."

Aimi shrugged.

"I mean, you did stab him."

"Only a little." It was a weak defence at best. "But I'm part of the crew now, and soon to be an invaluable part. I need somewhere to sleep."

"With the rest of the crew?" It was clear from Feather's tone that he thought it a bad idea.

Aimi chewed on her lip, her hand on the door. "For now," she said idly, already forming a plan to work her way back into the captain's cabin.

Kebble Salt was an easy man to find, and the reason for that also happened to be the reason Keelin needed to talk to him. The refugees and the crews of the pirate ships alike respected him, and even feared him to some degree. His rumoured exploits during the battle with the Man of War had grown and grown to the point of idiocy. Keelin had even heard that he'd called down lightning bolts to smite his enemies rather than shoot bullets from his rifle. Added to the renown brought by the battle was his watchful diligence over the fledgling town and the fact that he had indeed killed a sand monster on his own with a single long-range shot. People were in awe of Kebble, and that awe was founded on respect.

The little watchtower the refugees had built for Kebble was growing, and now stood a good ten feet from the sand. The better vantage point gave the rifleman a full view of the beached Man of War and the growing settlement, and everyone felt safer with him watching over them. Keelin called up the tower before starting the climb; a man as dangerous as Kebble Salt was not a man he wanted to surprise.

"Everything quiet?" Keelin said as he gained the floor of the watchtower. Kebble was scanning the beach through squinting eyes. Despite the heat and humidity, the man had somehow managed to maintain his moustache perfectly. Keelin, on the other hand, had nearly a week of patchy stubble loitering around his chin and neck. He decided he'd take the time to shave once he was back on board his ship.

"More or less," Kebble answered in a frustratingly calm voice.

"Fair enough," Keelin said once it was clear Kebble had said all he was going to. "I have a proposition for you, Kebble. This little town of New Sev'relain needs a governor. Someone who can run things, keep the peace, and make decisions while Drake is gone. I think it should be you. Everyone looks up to you, they respect you. They'll follow your orders…"

"No."

"Why not?"

Kebble took a few moments to answer. "I'll stay on board *The Phoenix*."

"Why is it nobody is willing to leave my ship?" Keelin said with an exaggerated sigh. "First Aimi tricks me into letting her stay, and now you simply refuse to leave. I might as well go ask Smithe to piss off and make my day complete."

Kebble let out a deep chuckle. "I cannot speak for anyone else, but for me. I will go where you do, because I believe near you, I may find my death."

Keelin sighed again; his life appeared to be taking a turn for the unusual. "I can see you probably think that's the craziest thing I've heard today," he said with a healthy dose of sarcasm. "But you're wrong."

Kebble turned towards Keelin with sad eyes. "I am older than you think, Captain Stillwater. I have seen family and friends born, grow old, and die. I have lived long enough to see old magics disappear from the world and new ones take their place. In this unnaturally long life I have lived, I have done things that no man should ever do, and I am forced to live with the memories of those actions. And the reasons for them."

"Huh?"

"I am cursed, Captain Stillwater. Cursed with immortality. And I have done everything short of taking my own life to cure myself of that curse. I have thrown myself into wars that had nothing to do with me, choosing to fight for the losing side only to survive and turn the tide. I have challenged men and women many times my equal to single combat only to best them and facilitate their deaths instead of my own. I have tended plague-stricken folk guaranteed to be contagious and caught no disease. I once even stormed a burning building on the point of collapse simply to find an old woman's blind cat." Kebble let out a weary sigh. "The cat leapt out of a window just before the building came down, and I had no choice but to follow it. Always I have skirted the issue of taking my own life, and always I have survived. With you, I…"

"Why not just take your own life?"

"The world has strict rules on the issue, and I have no wish to become a wraith, waking once more to find myself serving aboard the *Cold Fire*."

"The ghost ship?" Keelin laughed. "It's a children's story."

"It is not. I have seen it many times. A ship so light it could almost be smoke, it sails the ocean and leaves no wake."

"Or it could just be mist on the water."

"Crewed by wraiths, the souls of those who have committed suicide over water. It haunts the oceans. It haunts those who should be dead."

Keelin would have liked to say he believed Kebble, but instead he was just beginning to doubt the man's sanity. Of course, there were many insane people in the world, and some of them were too damned useful to dismiss.

"So you're not leaving the ship then?"

Kebble laughed and shook his head. "I believe with you I may find a god willing to take pity on me and cure my curse." Keelin sighed heavily, then turned and began his climb down to the sand. It had already been a long day, and he had yet to see Drake.

By the time Keelin found himself on board the *Fortune* it was fast approaching dark, and he was in no mood to decline when Drake offered a glass of something stronger than rum. No matter that the town might be running low on booze, it appeared the captain who had built that town was more than amply stocked. Taking a deep swig of what appeared to be a particularly fearsome peach brandy, Keelin settled in to hear what was to be said. That both Morley and Princess were present didn't encourage Keelin to predict good things.

"The town is coming along well," Drake started. "But there's issues. Expansion into the jungle is one. A real town needs to be sunk into solid earth, not sand. Now, we ain't sure how the forest is gonna react to that, but every island here in the isles has its quirks, right?"

Morley let out a barely audible groan, and Keelin silenced him with a stare.

"Putting New Sev'relain on the map is one thing," Drake continued. "Folk need to know the place is here if we're ever wanting them to visit and trade. Ain't exactly a pirate town without the visitation of piratical elements, and we need the influence this place has to grow, not shrink and lose folk to Fango."

"The pirates need a reason to come here," Morley said. "And pirates put into port in the isles for two reasons – dicks in a whore, and to offload the loot. One look outside, Captan Morrass, and it's obvious we have two problems. There's barely enough whores to service a sloop, let alone a couple of ships or more, and there ain't no one to pay them for their hauls."

"Reckon your man's hit on the issues pretty directly there,

Stillwater." Drake smiled. "The town needs a legitimate front, some crook like Loke or Quartermain who can buy the loot from us at a discounted price, seeing how the goods are slightly less than legal, then ship and sell it on to civilised folk in Sarth, the Five Kingdoms, Acanthia, and anywhere else that might want it. Now we sure as a watery Hell can't do that. Any of us sail into any port bar a free city, and we'll be swaying from our necks in no time."

"I can't see us tempting Quartermain from Fango," Keelin said. "And Loke probably died back in Sev'relain."

"Wouldn't matter even if he hadn't. A legitimate front needs two things – money and ships not linked to piracy. By this point he would have neither, and would therefore be little to no use to anyone."

Keelin took another deep swig of the peach brandy and sighed. "What do you suggest, Drake?"

Drake held up his hands. "We set someone up as a front and bankroll them."

"Cap'n..." Princess started, but was interrupted by Morley.

"The crew will never agree to that."

"It ain't their money," Keelin growled.

"Cap'n..." Princess started again.

"It ain't fucking yours either, Captan," Morley all but shouted. "Ship's money is there to pay for repairs and to give advances to the crew in times of hardship, just like right now."

Drake grinned. "Need a lesson in controlling ya crew, Stillwater?"

Keelin ground his teeth and glared at his fellow captain before rounding on Morley. "Ship's money is to be used at the captain's discretion for matters pertinent and the good of the crew."

"And how is this good for the crew, Captan?"

"Cap'n..." Princess tried once more.

"Because I fucking say it's good for the crew," Keelin shouted. "We need a place to port, Morley. And we can't exactly keep going back to Fango unless you want Tanner to use your hide as a rug."

"Ship don't have enough money, Cap'n," Princess shouted.

"Eh?" Drake grunted, his cup stopped halfway to his mouth, the amused smile gone.

"I spoke to Byron earlier, Cap'n. Ship's coffers are running low, real low."

"How low?"

"Empty low."

Drake fell silent, his eyes fixed and far away.

"How low are ours, Morley?" Keelin said.

"Low enough to be a worry, not so low as to inspire mutiny, Captan." There was an extra edge to the way Morley spoke the title, and not for the first time Keelin wished Yanic had survived Sev'relain. He still hadn't even said a proper goodbye to the man, because proper goodbyes required a dangerous amount of rum and at least a day to recover.

"Reckon the whores are the richest folk on the island at the moment," Morley continued. "With no pimp and Drake's protection, the few girls that are working are earning double the going rate and keeping all of it."

"I knew that 'no raping a whore' shit was gonna bite us on the arse, Cap'n," Princess said with a deep frown. "Girls don't need a pimp, so they ain't gonna have one."

Still Drake said nothing, his expression blank.

Princess turned to Keelin. "What about that rifleman of yours? He go for the governor gig?"

Keelin laughed. "He refuses to leave *The Phoenix* on the grounds that he believes himself to be immortal and thinks I might be able to convince a god to kill him." He expected shocked silence, but instead Princess nodded and shrugged.

"The immortal ones are always arrogant bastards," Drake's first mate said. "There was that one we picked up off Truridge, Cap'n, you remember. Righteous shit told us we were all mere drops in the ocean compared to him, and he was the lord high ruler of some kingdom don't exist no more."

"The Forgotten Empire?" Keelin was suddenly curious.

"Nah, though reckon he'd said he'd been there…" Princess drifted off, his face creased in concentration. "Fucking awful place. Anyway, Cap'n put his immortality to the test, and to be fair to the poor bastard, he wasn't lying. Took enough to kill ten men ten times over and lived through it. So we dropped him off somewhere in the deep ocean and let nature deal with him. Drop in the ocean." Princess chuckled.

"We're gonna need warehouses and credit notes," Drake said quietly, and Keelin looked over to find a determined expression on the captain's face.

"Warehouses we can do, Cap'n," said Princess. "But credit notes? Here on the isles? Nobody'll trust 'em."

Drake shook his head. "They will if they have my name on them. We need to leave as soon as possible, Princess. The quicker we get the money and the ships to set up the legitimate front, the quicker we can make this all work."

"You're leaving?" Keelin said.

Drake nodded. "Unless you can provide, say, ten seaworthy legal vessels with no history of piracy, and enough bits to pay everyone involved on salary until this little venture becomes self-sustaining."

Keelin nodded back. "Leaving it is, then."

"I need you to stay here, Stillwater."

"Here as in New Sev'relain? Indefinitely?" The very last thing Keelin wanted was to be left floating at port for an extended spell.

"Here and about," Drake conceded. "I need someone to look after the town, protect it while it gets on its feet. Beat down any dissidents and keep the townsfolk in line. I need someone I can trust." He paused, then stood and made his way over to a nearby cabinet. "And I need someone to warn the others." Drake opened the cabinet and riffled through its contents before pulling out a roll of vellum that was unmistakably a sea chart. Keelin felt hope spring to life once again in his chest. Now he knew where Drake kept his charts, he was one step closer to finding the one he needed, and that meant he was one step closer to taking his revenge on Arbiter Prin. Unfortunately, there were still a lot of steps left to take.

Drake tossed the roll of vellum to Keelin before sitting back down behind his desk. It was too much to hope the man had just given Keelin the chart he so desperately desired, but he dared to hope anyway. Keelin unrolled the vellum.

"It's the Pirate Isles," he said uncertainly.

"It's the chart I took from the Man of War," Drake said. "They didn't just know where to find Black Sands and Sev'relain. They know about Utringdon, Fair View, Rockwater, Lillingburn. Every colony, town, and outpost in the Pirate Isles except two."

Keelin searched the chart, and it didn't take long for him to see what was missing. "Fango."

"Your friend, Tanner Black, appears to have been making some nasty friends, Stillwater."

Keelin looked back at Morley, who seemed as shocked as his captain. "Tanner would never… He's an evil bastard and no mistake, but he hates Sarth, hates all the kingdoms. As far as he's concerned, the only kingdom that matters a damn is his own."

Drake raised an eyebrow. "And what would be a better way to get rid of all the competition in the isles to make that little dream a reality?"

Keelin shook his head. It simply wasn't possible that Tanner Black would sell out his fellow pirates. "Quartermain, maybe?"

"Maybe. Either way, the others need to know their towns ain't safe. Sarth sent one ship, they'll send more. New Sev'relain, on the other hand… Well, now that ain't on the map either, is it?"

"You want me to sail *The Phoenix* round the other pirate settlements and tell the townsfolk to gather here."

"Townsfolk, pirates, everyone." Drake nodded. "Tell them all Cinto Cena may well be the last safe island in the isles."

Fortune

"Dead man walking."

Drake walked beside the man with members of his crew both in front and behind. They trudged their way up the hot sand towards the tavern; somehow it seemed the most fitting place for the event, given that its bones had been taken from the Man of War.

It didn't really seem like there was much to say, and the man wasn't exactly in the chattiest of moods. He hadn't spoken to anyone since the day he broke. When Drake had pulled him out of the hold of the *Fortune*, he'd been unresponsive at best and pitiful at worst. His uniform was faded and stained, stinking of sweat, his moustache was an overgrown bush, and his eyes looked like they belonged on a dead man. Soon they would.

It was a rare thing to see a man so broken after so little. They'd taken his ship and killed most of his men, but that was something every experienced sailor had to keep in the back of their mind as a possibility. The former admiral had given up his secrets under duress, but again that was rarely enough to truly break a man. To crack a man to this degree, to the point where he was little more than a walking, eating, shitting doll, wasn't easy. But Drake had seen it before. Long ago, down deep under the earth, Drake had seen it.

The Drurr were masters of torture the likes of which even the Inquisition couldn't match. Drake had seen men and women mutilated, cut up and put back together wrong, made to live with the monsters they'd become. He'd seen tortures of the mind, folk balanced on the edge of terror for so long they actually craved the pain, because the waiting – the expectation, the anticipation – was just too much.

Once Drake had asked the matriarch why they tortured their slaves, and she'd told him with venom. Those Drurr who had taken him hated humanity. They were bitter beyond madness, and all that bile and contempt was directed towards mankind. The humans had once been their slaves, but the Dread Lords had changed all that by decimating the Drurr population, destroying their greatest kingdom and corrupting their dead. Then came Volmar and his Inquisition, and what was left of the Drurr became hunted, persecuted, and driven from the world above. The Drurr had once ruled the world; thanks to humanity, they now ruled nothing. Even their homes deep underground were ruled by terrors far older and more powerful than they.

"Dead man walking," a woman's voice called out. It snapped Drake out of his morbid revery.

Scanning the crowd gathered to watch the admiral's final walk, Drake recognised a lot of the people, both refugees and pirates. It seemed almost everyone on the island was waiting up ahead, near the tavern, to watch the man die.

"Sorry about this," Drake said quietly.

The admiral didn't respond.

Maybe it was the memories of his past, but Drake was feeling more than a little hesitant at the thought of killing the broken man. "What was it that did this to you?"

The admiral lifted his head a little and turned empty eyes on Drake. He said nothing.

"Wasn't giving up your kingdom's secrets, was it?"

Still no response.

"Was it Beck? The Arbiter?"

The admiral turned his head away, and Drake thought he saw tears welling up in his eyes.

"That's it, isn't it?" Drake stopped and turned the admiral to face him. "You believe the Arbiter should save you. One of Volmar's faithful should put us all to the torch. Instead you find her working for me, using the magic of her faith to pull the truth from you."

"How could she use her magic," the admiral said, sounding resigned, "if she wasn't still faithful to him?"

Drake nodded. "So now you're wondering which side of this conflict Volmar is truly on?"

The admiral nodded and his shoulders sagged, his body shaking with sobs.

"Well, then I guess I'll let you in on the truth of it," Drake said in little more than a whisper. "Your god doesn't care. We ain't heretics, just

Where Loyalties Lie

folk trying to survive. Your attack on us, your murder of our people, wasn't divine judgement, Admiral. It was politics, plain and simple."

"Everything we do, we do for Volmar," the admiral protested. "The order came from Emperor Francis, and he *is* Volmar."

"No." Drake shook his head. "The order came from the merchants we steal from. Your God Emperor just mouthed the words. Is the Arbiter by my side not proof enough for you?"

The admiral buried his head in his manacled hands and sobbed.

"You need more proof?" Drake said. "Fine." Drake nodded to one of the pirates waiting nearby, and the admiral was driven up the beach towards the tavern, where the angry mob of refugees and pirates waited to lynch him.

Drake and the admiral stood in a circle of hundreds of people. The entire town of New Sev'relain crowded around them, and they were shouting for the Sarth officer to die. Drake basked in the attention for a while before waving for silence.

"For most of you this is your first look at Admiral Tattern, the man who commanded the ship that burned Black Sands and Sev'relain. The man responsible for the deaths of so very many of us."

An angry cheer circulated through the crowd, and a stone flew out of the back ranks and landed in the sand near the admiral.

"Hey," Drake shouted. "That could have hit me. Next person who throws something gets to drink a pint of the sea."

The crowd quieted.

"Now, I know you all want him dead. You want to see him strung up and turning purple. Well, I'm suggesting a different punishment. I reckon you should let him live."

Shouts erupted from the crowd, and they weren't just from the refugees. Pirates from both crews added their voices to the argument. Drake almost changed his mind when he realised his own crew were against the idea, but again he held up his hand and waved for silence. This time he didn't get it.

"Death is a shit punishment," Drake roared, and the crowd slowly quieted. "You want to send this cockstain to the grave. All that does is release him." Drake gave the admiral a heavy push, and the man stumbled and collapsed to the sand. He remained there on his knees.

"He tried to wipe us all out, but here we are. What better way to punish him than show him how useless his efforts were? Make the bastard watch us rise back out of the ashes. Let him live. If he wants to wander off into the jungle and seek his own death, he can. But if that drive to live we all possess makes him want to eat and drink and keep going, then make him work for it."

Drake turned a full circle, sweeping the entire crowd with his gaze. "Either way, it's up to *you*. I won't kill him." He started off down the beach, back towards the *Fortune*. He grinned as he heard others taking up his advice.

Part 3 - The Storm

*You will need the Rest said the Oracle
That's my fallback, my insurance said Drake
Either you commit it all, or you fail said the Oracle*

The Phoenix

Inactivity didn't suit Keelin. It grated on him, frayed his nerves, and wore down his patience. Day after day, night after night, they floated in the newly built port of New Sev'relain and waited for Drake's return. After three months, Keelin was beginning to wonder whether it was coming. Every day the temptation to haul anchor and set sail for some good honest pirating grew stronger, and not least because of his crew's temperament. Deprive a pirate of a few days ashore, somewhere with a tavern and a brothel, for a couple of months, and they will happily incite a mutiny. Give a pirate a couple of months ashore, somewhere with a tavern and a brothel, and they will drink and fuck themselves broke and then demand their captain take them away from the temptation.

Keelin had yet to pick a governor for the town and, as such, was taking on the responsibility himself. He'd also taken on the responsibility of purchasing loot from passing pirate ships, depleting his own ship's stores and gifting a fair few credit notes signed by Drake. He was managing both the brothel and the tavern, and seeing that the townsfolk were looked after with all their most pressing needs met. If one of the crew didn't mutiny soon, Keelin was fairly sure he'd stage the damned thing himself. Within the first two months, Keelin had found himself dealing with everything from food shortages to food contamination, disease to dissidents, sand monster attacks to magical seduction, lumber shortages to riots over housing. The townsfolk had formed themselves a council, and the members of that council brought their problems to Keelin every day. Every day he imagined running them all through, setting fire to the town, and sailing away into the molten-gold sunset.

Keelin had to admit, as he supped on a mug of what was currently passing for ale in the tavern, it could have been worse. The arrival of Daimen Poole and *Mary's Virture* had been a godsend. If Keelin had worshipped any of them, he'd have given them the praying of a lifetime. Captain Poole was very much in Drake's corner, and had thankfully undertaken many of the day-to-day tasks that would otherwise have fallen to Keelin. Unfortunately, after six weeks ashore, Poole's crew were also becoming anxious to get back on the water.

Scratching at his chin, Keelin caught a finger in a knot of hair and ripped it free with a grimace. He needed to shave. He'd needed to shave for months now, but his razor was back on *The Phoenix*, and he hadn't been back on his ship for… Keelin couldn't actually remember how long it had been. Most nights he found himself getting so drunk he passed out right there in the tavern, and then, when he woke in the morning, he could just pull another mug of piss poor beer and listen to the new list of problems.

There was a stain on his once bright blue jacket. The jacket had cost a small fortune, and Keelin had thought of it as his best, favourite, and smartest garment. Now it looked drab, worn through, and sweaty. Even Keelin had to admit that he smelled. In a town full of folk who stank like weeks-old eggs, that was an accomplishment.

Not even during his time on *The Black Death* had Keelin taken so little effort to smarten his appearance. Back then he'd been young and brash, but he'd also taken pride in being the cleanest member of the crew. Despite some early beatings, Keelin had quickly established himself as more than competent with a sword. There were definitely some benefits to having spent many of his childhood years training with his older brother. More important than his reputation for being clean or dangerous with a pointy object had been his relationship with Tanner Black's daughter. They'd fucked and fought in equal measure, but despite their disagreements, back then Keelin would have drained the sea for her.

A small part of Keelin argued that he would still do anything for Elaina. He chalked it down to the booze and ignored the little voice. He seemed to be finding it very hard to organise his thoughts these days.

"I need some fresh air," Keelin said to no one. A couple of the other tavern patrons, those too drunk to stumble back to their homes or their ship, glanced at him and then away. Keelin struggled with his chair, using the table to pull himself out of it. He promptly staggered, sending both the table and himself careening to the floor. It took some effort to get back up, and even the town drunkard was laughing by the time he managed it.

"Fucking table's a death…" Keelin stopped, realising that no one was listening and even fewer folk cared. He lurched over to the door.

The world that greeted him outside the tavern was too bright and too blurry. The sun was up high, beating down mercilessly, and, as always, there was barely a lick of wind to be had, unless you counted the hot air the merchants wasted on passing pirates. New Sev'relain may have been well on its way to being called a settlement, but it was far from becoming a prosperous one for those who wished to sell any wares.

They had moved the town further up the beach since first establishing the settlement. Trees had been cleared away and more permanent buildings erected on more stable ground; sand was no place to be counting on structural support. The tavern had been taken apart and moved up the beach in what could only be described as a pointless but monumental effort, and now sat in the dead centre of the growing town. There were homes, warehouses, shops, a brothel, two inns for those pirates wishing to sleep in a real bed for a night or two, and even a gallows. Luckily the gallows had yet to be tested, but with Drake outlawing both rape and slavery, it was only a matter of time before someone found themselves swinging.

When Drake had decreed slavery would be outlawed and any passing slavers caught and confiscated, their wares freed, Keelin had asked why. The only reply he received was a dark stare and oppressive silence.

As Keelin's vision adjusted to the new lighting situation, he noticed a drunken pirate passed out half against the wall of the tavern and half on the leaf-littered ground. It didn't look like a comfortable place to rest a face, but the poor bastard was doing it anyway. After a moment Keelin recognised the pirate as Jotin Breen, one of his own men and, until recently, one of the most respected members of his crew. It appeared the long period ashore wasn't doing anyone any good.

Across the street was the brothel, the Merry Fuck. It certainly wasn't the most eloquent of names, but then Keelin had made the mistake of allowing the whores to name it themselves. Shrewd the whores may be with their profession, now they had the protection of Drake Morrass, but their command over the common language was far less savvy.

Outside the brothel lay another unconscious pirate, this one not of Keelin's crew and bleeding from a head wound that didn't look encouraging. The poor bastard was propped up against the wall of the Merry Fuck, and unless someone did something soon, it was likely he'd die there. Though the whores were under Drake's protection, the brothel and the other inhabitants were not. As such the whores had hired themselves a couple of hard-headed, heavy-fisted brutes to keep order within the confines of the building. Unfortunately the two men had turned out to be rather vicious in the beatings they handed out; it was one of the many things the council had recently brought to Keelin's attention.

The streets were busy with folk going about their daily business. Work crews were still felling trees and working their magic to turn them into serviceable wood for construction. A small team of reliable types had been conscripted by the Arbiter before she left with Drake, and they were even now searching the forest and marking off areas protected by magical traps. A fresh water source had been found out in the jungle, and it was currently a full-time job to ferry water down to the town. That was one of the most harrowing jobs the island presented, as the water source was also home to a group of monkeys who would sit in the trees, silently watching any and all who dared trespass on their domain.

There was something slipping Keelin's mind. He realised it as he stood there in the middle of the street, with folk passing him by on their daily errands. There was something he was supposed to be doing, the reason he'd bothered to leave the tavern in the first place.

"Fresh air," he said aloud, much to the surprise of a passing woman carrying a basket and an expression of utter distrust. He'd felt the need for fresh air and the sea on his toes, and the only place he was going to get either of those was down on the beach.

He'd elicited quite a few stares by the time he reached the sand, where he squinted down towards the newly constructed pier. There were four boats sitting out in the bay, but that couldn't be right unless he was seeing double – which, he had to admit, was a distinct possibility. There was also a flamboyantly dressed man wearing a round hat barrelling up the beach towards the town.

"Stillwater," Captain Daimen Poole said, breathless from his charge in the morning heat. "Fuck me, but it's hot today." He doubled over in front of Keelin, sucking in huge breaths of air. "What I wouldn't give for a little breeze, eh?"

Keelin focused on the man and burped.

"Not exactly what I meant. C'mon, got a'selves a new arrival. Big bastard. I reckon we gonna want him on the team. Here, are you drunk, Stillwater?"

Keelin considered lying, but decided he was definitely drunk and he didn't care one bit who knew it. "Only a little," he said, fairly certain he was swaying.

Poole made a face as he took off his hat and fanned himself with it. "Aye, well ya'll 'ave to fuckin' do. Best behaviour, aye?"

Keelin moved his head in a way that might be considered a positive affirmation before gesturing down the beach. "Lead the way."

"Why's that now? Can't find the sea? Aye, it's fairly well hidden behind all the water." Poole laughed, replaced his hat, and started off down the beach.

With most of the buildings now beyond the sand, it was rare to see the beach as busy as it was, but then a new arrival was bound to cause a fair bit of upheaval. From merchants attempting to offload onto water-weary sailors to dispossessed pirates requesting a place on any ship that would take them, there was no shortage of hustle and even more bustle.

A new galleon sat in the bay, and it was quite a large one at that, with three masts and more scars than it was worth paying attention to. Keelin couldn't say he recognised the ship. At this point he was having trouble recognising his own feet.

A crowd of folk were gathered around the end of the peer, no doubt requesting news and showering impotent praise on whoever had come ashore first. Keelin noticed a head poking up above the crowd and let out a weary sigh. Only one man could be that tall and that bearded, and the black bandana was even more of a giveaway.

"His name's…" Poole started.

"Khan," Keelin finished for him, digging around in his memory for the captain's first name and coming up blank.

"You've met then?"

"Aye." Keelin staggered as a dizzy spell hit him, steadying himself on Poole.

"Ah, shit, Stillwater. Don't ya be passin' out on me now."

"I'm fine." Keelin pushed away from Poole even as Captain Khan spotted them. "I'd just rather not deal with that big bastard right now."

"Stillwater," boomed the giant.

"Little late for that, I reckon, mate," Poole said with a smile, then turned just as Khan pushed his way through the crowd. "I'm told ya already know…"

Captain Khan ignored Poole's torrent of words and stepped in front of Keelin, staring down at him; the huge man's belly was very nearly on a level with Keelin's chest. The strange scent of black powder washed over Keelin, reminding him of the final moments of old Sev'relain. It already seemed so long ago.

"Hi," Keelin said, smiling upwards. "Nice to see you again."

"What do you think of my ship, Captain Stillwater?" the giant said. "Not so little now, eh."

Keelin shuffled sideways to look around the man and squinted towards his ship. There were skiffs going to and fro and cargo being unloaded even as they spoke.

"I remember," Keelin said as his memory agreed to function. He waved a finger at the big man. "You were captaining a little sloop last time. Congratulations on trading up."

Captain Khan didn't look impressed.

"Ya used ta pilot a sloop, ya say?" Poole said, stepping between them. Khan looked at Poole as if noticing him for the first time. He gave a curt nod.

"An' ya took that ship" – Poole pointed at the four-masted galleon – "with a sloop?"

Again the giant nodded.

"Do ya mind if I have a quiet word with me fellow captain here?" Poole put an arm around Keelin's shoulders and steered him away. If Keelin had been a little less drunk he might have found it insulting.

After they'd walked far enough up the beach to be out of earshot, Poole stopped. "Ya got any idea what ship that is, mate?" He nodded behind them.

Keelin looked over his shoulder and squinted towards Khan's new vessel. "Can't really make it out from here," he slurred.

"Oh, well let me be ya eyes for a moment. Her name is the *North Gale*. Not terribly awe inspirin', I know."

"Never heard of it," Keelin said after a moment.

"An' ne'er should ya have, mate. A new name is a new name, but it's a fair bit harder to hide a ship's scars, an' those scars tell ya more about the ship's history than the fuckin' log books do."

Keelin was barely listening. He wanted nothing more than to slop back down into his chair at the tavern and nap the heat of the day away. A large part of him rebelled at the very idea of such sloth, but that voice was getting quieter and quieter with each passing day.

"I know that ship better than most, because I've been chased by it enough times. That there is the *Victorious*."

The name instantly gave Keelin a measure of sobriety, and he took a second squinting look at the ship. There weren't many pirates in the isles who could say they hadn't been chased by the *Victorious*, and even fewer could say they hadn't heard of her. She was the pride and flagship of the Five Kingdoms navy.

"Aye," Poole continued, "captained by Bartimus Peel, the most decorated an' most feared captain our enemy has at their command. Bastard has brought over twenty captains, our fuckin' brethren, ta his own personal brand of bloody justice. He's been the scourge of the isles since before I learned ta tie a knot, an' that there is his ship."

"And Captain Khan took it with a little sloop."

Poole nodded. "Reckon that might be one bastard we want on the team, an' I reckon Drake'd agree."

Keelin let out a weary sigh. He wasn't built for this sort of work.

His brand of leadership came with people following him because he was their captain, not because he was courting their favour. He sorely wished Drake had stayed behind and sent *The Phoenix* out instead.

"What should I do?"

"I don't fuckin' know," Poole hissed. "Drake left you in charge for some reason, so get down there an' do whatever it takes ta get that big, glorious bastard on board."

With Poole at his back, Keelin staggered back down the beach, the giant Captain Khan watching him. He tried desperately to think of something to say to convince the man to fight with them. It was hard not to notice Khan's scars, mainly because he had so many of them. He wore no shirt, and the only thing covering his torso was the leather strap that fixed his sword to his back. His skin was so bronzed it was almost brown, and his scars stood out, criss-crossing both his belly and chest. Keelin also couldn't help but notice the man appeared to be missing his left nipple.

"So…" Keelin began, fully intending to launch into a grand tour of the town, complete with a stop at the tavern.

"Fight me, Captain Stillwater," the giant said without a hint of humour.

"I'd really rather not." Keelin laughed. "Look, we need folk like you, Captain. Drake is…"

"Drake?" Khan narrowed his already beady eyes. "Morrass is here?"

"Not right now, no. See, he and I built this town."

"I hear he destroyed Sev'relain."

Keelin shook his head and immediately regretted it, as his hangover chose that exact moment to make his brain feel too large for his skull.

"I was there, and honestly there was no man who did more to save Sev'relain than Drake Morrass. We took the survivors and brought them here. We took the damned ship that burned Sev'relain, and…"

"That ship?" Khan pointed towards the bones of the Man of War. Much of the warship had been scavenged and picked over, but it was still just about possible to see how big the beast had been.

"Aye."

"An impressive catch." Khan glanced back at his own ship. "I would have kept her."

Keelin laughed. "Why? Is your own ship not big enough?"

Khan's head snapped back around so fast his beard took a moment to catch up. His eyes were dark and angry. "Are you again mocking the size of my ship, Stillwater?"

Poole stepped between the two of them, with plenty of open, calming hand gestures. "I think what Stillwater here meant was that ya new ship is pretty fuckin' big, eh?"

"Pretty much," Keelin said, squinting against the light and wishing his headache and the huge captain in front of him would both sail back out to sea and never come back.

"Fight me, Stillwater," Khan repeated.

Keelin let out a frustrated sigh. "What the fuck is it with you and challenging me to duels? Is it just me, or do you challenge everybody you meet?"

"Just you." Khan grinned. "They say you're the best."

It wasn't exactly something Keelin liked to admit, but he was secretly quite proud of his reputation as the best swordsman in the isles. "And if I accept, will you side with Drake against Sarth?"

Poole shook his head. "Hang on a fuckin' minute…"

"Aye," Khan said with a grin that showed teeth even through his beard.

"If that's what it takes, then." Keelin struggled to disentangle himself from his jacket.

"Now hang the fuck on," Poole shouted, his glare taking in the crowd that had quickly started to gather around the scene. "An' before either of you piss poor excuses for deck scrubbers thinks ta ignore me again, how's about ya realise I got far more of me boys down here on the beach than either of you."

A rare silence drifted across the beach, and all eyes turned to Captain Poole.

"Out-fucking-standin'. Now, in case either of ya haven't noticed, Stillwater, here, is past the point o' pickled…"

"I am not!"

"Ya can't even get out of ya bloody coat, mate."

Keelin thought about arguing further, but he was still struggling to remove his right arm from the damned thing.

"Now you wanna challenge the best, right?" Poole said to Captain Khan. "He ain't really the best when he's like this, now, is he? Fairly certain a crab could take him."

Khan rumbled an agreement.

"Two days," Poole said. "We'll sober this bastard up, an' in two days ya can have ya fight, an' when ya lose, everyone will watch ya swear ya allegiance to Drake Morrass. Good?"

Khan smirked through his beard and nodded.

"Good." Poole grinned, and before anybody else could say a word, he turned, grabbed Keelin by the shoulder, and pulled him away towards one of the dinghies.

"I had that under control," Keelin protested, knowing full well the situation was anything but under control.

"You're a disgrace, mate," Poole spat. "Ya meant ta be in charge 'round here, an' everyone just saw ya toasted as Admiral Tatters an' ready ta get cut in half. Now you get back ta ya ship, ya sober up, an' ya get ready ta fight that fuckin' giant."

Keelin put on an arrogant grin that he really didn't feel. "Easy."

"Oh, really?" Poole asked as they arrived at the skiff. "Because his arms are as big as my legs, an' here's the real kicker, mate. Ya can't just win. Ya gotta survive, an' make fuckin' certain he does too."

Starry Dawn

Elaina had never seen the remains of a town burned to ash and bones. It was a devastating sight, and no mistake. She'd taken ships, slaughtered crews, and seen dead bodies piled high on decks awash with blood, but this was something else. Men, women, and children all cut down in the streets, in their homes, in the taverns and brothels, on the beach, and in the surf. Lillingburn would never have claimed to be the biggest of the pirate settlements, but by the number of dead littering its carcass, it couldn't have been far off.

"Don't like it here, Cap," said Pollick, and Elaina couldn't help but agree.

"There's nothing left to fear, Pol." Elaina said with a sorrowful sigh. "They're all dead."

"Don't mean it ain't rightly creepy, Cap."

For months Elaina and her crew had been sailing the seas around the isles, attempting to find some prey. When they'd finally caught a little cog, with barely enough plunder worth taking and all of it perishable, she'd taken *Starry Dawn* straight to the nearest port, only to find the nearest port was no longer there.

"This reminds me of me old soldiering days," said Alfer Boharn, the ship's new quartermaster.

Elaina poked at the lifeless body of a child with her boot. She liked Alfer, and he made for an excellent, fair quartermaster, but the loss of Corin had left a hole in Elaina's chest. It made it worse that she knew what sort of Hell her friend was being put through day after day. After three months, Elaina wondered if there was even anything of her friend left. Lucy had a way of destroying a person's mind, and her father had a way of destroying a person's body.

"Why's that?" Elaina stared at a grisly picture of a woman and two young boys still hand in hand, lying dead on a bed of red sand.

"Notice how all the bodies have been decapitated?" Alfer said.

"Creepiest fucking thing about it all," Pollick said, taking off his eye glasses.

"Five Kingdoms folk did this," Alfer said confidently. "Bastards always chop off the heads of the dead to make certain they don't come back."

"This ain't makin' it any less creepy, Alf." Pollick spat into the sand and backed away from the nearest body, as though it might reach up and grab him if he didn't.

"This?" Alfer pointed at one of the bodies and took a step towards Pollick. "This ain't nothing, lad. You wanna see creepy, you go visiting the Land of the Dead. I been there." He took another step. "Seen an army, must be a thousand strong, all dead and rotting. Some of 'em little more than bones, but they marched on all the same."

Pollick was holding his ground, staring at Alfer through watery eyes. Elaina found the scene funny despite the carnage all around them. It was doing wonders to cheer up her dark mood.

"The walking bones ya think would be the worst, what with the lurching steps, chattering teeth, and the lack of any flesh holding 'em together. But no. Worst is the recently dead children, lad. Toddlers, some looking only just off their mother's tits." Alfer was just a few steps away from Pollick now, and his face had taken on a long, drawn, colourless aspect. "They travel in packs, only as high as ya knees, and they let out little person-like cries, as if they just want to find their parents. But they're strong, ya see, stronger than they ought'a be. And once they got hold, they bring ya down, little mouths biting, eating at ya flesh."

"Fuck, Alfer, stop," Pollick wailed, turning and staggering away to empty his stomach of its most recent meal.

They were joined by the three pirates Elaina had sent deeper into the small town. "Find anything?" she said.

Ed shook his head solemnly. "Nothing but corpses. Seems whoever did this…"

"Five Kingdoms," Alfer interrupted.

"Fair enough," Ed said. "Seems they killed everyone. Pinched anything worth having, and burned everything not."

"Third town they've done this to," Alfer said, and Elaina glared at him. The last thing they all needed to be reminded of right then was how they were being hunted down. "Just saying what we're all knowing,"

Alfer muttered.

Pollick let out a strangled scream and stumbled backwards, tripping over the body of a dead man and landing face down in the breasts of a nearby dead woman. They all turned to stare at the spectacle, Ed pointing and laughing. Ignoring the mockery, Pollick scrambled away from the bodies and pointed towards his friends. "The fucking dead. They're walking. Just like ya said, Alf!"

As one, all the pirates looked about at the bodies littered around the town square. Elaina saw plenty of corpses, some dead in the street, others little more than charred hands poking out of the ashen bones of a burnt-out building, but none of them appeared to be moving.

"Uh, Cap." Ed's voice was unusually high. "He ain't wrong this time."

Elaina followed her navigator's shaking hand and finally saw what Pollick was talking about. People were coming towards them from the island side of the town; they looked dirty and gaunt, and some of them were definitely injured.

"They dead?" Elaina asked Alfer, who appeared to have some experience with walking corpses.

"Fucked if I know, Cap. Why don't ya ask 'em?" Alfer whispered, apparently finding some courage as he stood behind his captain.

"Right bloody brave, the lot of ya," Elaina said, summoning every ounce of bravado she could muster.

"Are you all dead?" she shouted out to the approaching figures as loudly as she could.

There was some dissension among the ranks as a few of the townsfolk turned to the others, as if they were debating the answer to the question. Elaina had never met any living dead, so had no idea how cunning they could be, but if they could pass themselves off as living it could present a real problem.

"Um, no." The answer was shouted by a man at the front of the group, which was around fifty strong. "Are you?"

"Do we fucking look dead?" Elaina yelled back.

"Do we?"

She sighed. "This ain't getting us nowhere. Pol, go up there and see if they're dead."

"Bugger off."

Elaina laughed, and after a moment her crew joined in. "Don't know much about the dead, Pol, but I'm fairly sure they don't talk." She looked at Alfer, but the man only shrugged back at her.

Elaina started forwards, striding up the corpse-littered street towards the survivors and trying not to look at all the bodies that lay in her way. At one point her boot caught on something, and she glanced down to see a little girl's head, her eyes blank and lifeless, rolling away. Refusing to dwell on the horror, Elaina kept walking.

As she got within talking distance, a young woman, dishevelled and looking barely old enough to bleed, rushed forwards despite a nearby man's attempt to catch her and pull her back.

"You're Captain Black, aren't you?" the girl said in a rush as the man caught up with her.

"Aye," Elaina said warily, her hand resting on the hilt of the short sword buckled at her hip.

"I knew it. Get off me, Da. She's come to save us."

Some fifty sets of eyes turned Elaina's way, and most of them had that pleading look about them that she'd often seen on the dying. She had no idea how she was supposed to go about saving them; she couldn't exactly magic a town back into existence or bring the corpses back to life. Whatever they wanted from her was far beyond her ken or her ability.

Elaina raised her voice. "We just stopped by to sell some loot. Saw the place... well, like this. Figured we should see if we could fathom what happened." She stopped to clear her throat and found it a little dry. "We ain't come to save any of ya."

Murmuring erupted through the crowd. The young woman didn't seem deterred; she wrenched away from her father and ran up to Elaina. There was the sound of old, battered metal clearing a scabbard behind Elaina, and she held up her hand to stay her crew. Whatever the woman was about, Elaina would put money on it not being threatening.

"But that's how she works," the girl said. "She gave you the reason to come here just when we needed it most."

"She?"

"Rin."

Elaina laughed. "I ain't exactly a priest of the sea bitch or owt, but far as I've seen it, she ain't really that cunning. She wants ya somewhere, she don't dangle a carrot on a stick, just beats ya with the stick 'til ya bloody well go."

The young woman stared on in silence, her big brown eyes pleading and hopeful.

"So what happened here?" Elaina raised her voice in the hope that anybody else might respond. If there was one thing she couldn't abide, it was zealots who believed everything that happened was the will of some god or another. "How did all of ya survive?"

"Sally saw the sails on the horizon a few days ago," the woman said, still staring up at Elaina as if she were her own personal saviour. "We thought it was one of ours, or possibly one of Django's traders come to pick up from the warehouse."

A young man with a pretty face took up the story. "It wasn't until she launched her dinghies full of soldiers that we realised she was flying a Five Kingdoms flag. By then it was already too late. Even if we'd had the men and the weapons, there was no way we were fighting them off in those numbers."

"We hid in the caves," the woman chimed in, directing a baleful glare at the young man, "while they were swarming the beach and murdering everyone. Lilling is a desolate little island, but we got caves that are hard to find if you don't know they're there. Those of us could make it took what we could and hurried there."

"We didn't have time to gather supplies though," interrupted the young man, "so we've been starving ever since. The soldiers took everything they could and burned the rest. There's no food left on the island. When Lille here spotted your sails, she said she knew it was you, and you'd come to save us."

"I saw you when you stopped by last year," Lille continued. "I'd know *Starry Dawn* anywhere. She's so beautiful, just like her captain."

Elaina groaned. She now understood the look in the little woman's eyes; it was awe. The foolish girl looked to Elaina as a hero. The truth was, she was anything but.

"I ain't come to save no one," Elaina repeated. "We're only here…"

"We should have gone with Captain Stillwater when he warned us," said Lille's father.

Elaina reckoned there was little else the man could have said that would have cut her off quite like that.

"What?"

"He warned us this might happen and offered to take as many of us as he could to New Sev'relain."

"What?" Elaina repeated, her voice breaking.

The man looked confused; it was the look of someone talking to a simpleton, unsure of quite how to get their point across. Elaina realised she had a hand on her sword hilt, which undoubtedly wasn't helping.

"Stillwater was here?" she said slowly. "When?"

"Couple of months back," Lille said happily, and Elaina's stomach turned to butterflies at the confirmation that Keelin had survived the massacre at Sev'relain.

"He warned us that Sarth and the Five Kingdoms were burning towns here in the isles," the pretty young man said. "Said he had a safe town, one they didn't know about. Called it New Sev'relain."

"Where?" Elaina took a menacing step forwards.

Lille started to answer, but the young man rushed towards her and clamped a hand over her mouth. For her part Lille looked terrified, and Elaina had it in mind to save the poor girl, though not entirely for her own benefit.

"You take us there and we'll tell you," the man said, hope and desperation giving his eyes a strange, feral light.

"Deal," Elaina said without thinking. She didn't care about the terms. If Keelin was alive, she wanted to see him. Needed to see him. He at least would understand her pain over Corin's fate.

"Cap," Alfer said from behind her. "There's a good fifty folk here, an' we ain't exactly flush on supplies."

"Then ration them, quartermaster."

Elaina turned back to the group of Lillingburn refugees. "Ya know who I am?" She waited for their nods of assent. "Ya best not be lying ta me over this, or I swear I'll find the nearest sea beastie and feed all of ya to him."

The Phoenix

"You're mad," Aimi said with conviction. Keelin considered arguing with her, but in truth he wasn't entirely certain she was wrong.

"The bigger they are…" Keelin said, though it sounded far more like a damning statement than a consolidatory one.

"He's stronger than he looks."

"He can't be."

"In old Sev'relain I once saw him hit a man with another man."

"What?"

"Picked him up and used him as a club."

Keelin glanced down at her. She was grinning up at him. "For a minute there I thought you were serious."

Aimi laughed, a pleasant noise that made Keelin want to hear it more often. "I was," she said, and Keelin found himself once again facing imminent death and once again wishing he'd never laid eyes on the woman.

"Well, good luck, Captain," Aimi said after another awkward silence.

"Call me Keelin," he replied as he loosened his cutlasses. After a moment he realised Aimi was quiet, and he glanced over to see her scuffing the dirt with a foot.

"That wasn't part of the deal," she said eventually.

She was right, of course. It was in fact contrary to the terms of the deal, but Keelin had been wishing for a while now that he'd never made the deal. "Just a name," Keelin lied.

"No, it ain't. I've seen the way you look at me, Captain. I've seen the way you avoid your own ship since I come aboard."

It wasn't really a conversation Keelin wanted to have, and certainly not given the situation he was about to find himself in. If he was really lucky, the giant he was about to fight would kill him and he'd never have to have that conversation.

"Just wish me luck."

Aimi looked from Keelin to his opponent and back again. "Good luck."

He had to give the folk of New Sev'relain one thing, if nothing else: they were quick builders. In just two days they'd managed to build an arena in the centre of the little town. Stands rose on two sides of the dust bowl that had been decreed the combatants' colosseum, and both were full of people, young and old, male and female, pirate and townsfolk. Bets were busy being taken, and those industrious enough to declare themselves bookies were greedily rubbing their hands at the imminent prospect of financial gain at the cost of blood.

For two days Keelin had been dreading this fight, and they hadn't been the most pleasant of days. The first had been the worst, and mostly because the hangover he'd been suffering had been the most painful of his life. One month of solid drinking, without the prospect of sobriety, had taken its toll. On that first day Keelin had been a shaking wreck barely able to hold a sword, let alone swing one.

The second day had been almost as bad. He'd stood on the deck of *The Phoenix* with two blunted cutlasses in hand and given an open challenge to every member of his crew. Some no doubt found it therapeutic to be handed a weapon and told to swing it at their captain. Keelin had still been sore, aching, shaking, and sweating from the alcohol in his system. He was sporting the cuts and bruises to prove that he was in no shape to be taking on a battle-ready behemoth.

Morley and Daimen Poole were waiting for Keelin near the little arena. Khan stood just a short distance from the two, looking frustratingly relaxed.

"This is foolish, Captan," Morley said as Keelin drew close. "I hear the man once wrestled an elephant."

"Aye?" Poole asked. "An' exactly how the fuck would one go about wrestlin' an elephant?"

"Regardless," Morley continued undeterred, "the rumours say he did, and he won."

"Sounds like a mighty tale it was too," Poole said. "But it don't matter a drop. There's too much ridin' on this fight, an' ya can't be affordin' ta back out now. Ya gotta get in there an' teach that big bastard just why your name is known across the isles as the best swordsman dares to step foot on a boat."

Keelin let out a groan and stepped away from the two, approaching his opponent. Captain T'ruck Khan watched him all the way, his dark eyes betraying nothing.

"Are you ready, Captain Stillwater?" Khan rumbled.

Keelin let out a sigh. "Why are you doing this?"

Khan nodded. "You are an easterner." It was a statement.

Keelin considered lying. It was a fact he'd been hiding most of his life, and it was one he wanted to hide doubly so these days. The fewer people that knew he'd been born and raised in the Five Kingdoms, the better, and if they found out he'd been born into nobility he would lose all respect any of them had for him.

"As long as I'm alive, that's a fact I'd like you to keep to yourself," Keelin said eventually. "Though if you do kill me, feel free to shout it to the world."

"I would not," Khan said. "Your secret is safe with me. I come from the clans beyond the World's Edge mountains. You should know we follow strength, not weakness. If you want me to follow you, then show me you are stronger."

Keelin snorted out a laugh. "Ain't me I'm asking you to follow – it's Drake Morrass."

The giant shrugged. "You follow him, so he must be stronger than you. If you fail to best me, perhaps I shall seek out and challenge him instead."

The crowd were starting to get restless. They'd come to see blood, and so far not a drop had been spilled. It never ceased to amaze Keelin that normal men and women could get so worked up over the prospect of witnessing death.

In the Five Kingdoms most towns and cities sported an arena, and pit fighting was an everyday occurrence. He remembered going to see a fight between two champions long ago. His father had taken Keelin and his older brother, Derran, to Land's End to see how the family business worked. Afterwards they'd gone to the arena and watched one man slaughter another. At the time it had seemed heroic, and Keelin had cheered with the rest of them. Derran had watched quietly, counting the mistakes each of the warriors made. Later that day, after returning home, they'd recreated the fight, and Derran had shown Keelin each mistake in meticulous, painful detail. They had both always been gifted with a sword, but Derran was an unbeatable terror.

"Should we set some rules then?" Keelin said. "To stop either one of us dying for no good reason."

Khan laughed and started towards the arena. "I will be trying to kill you, Captain Stillwater. If you want to survive, I suggest you not let me."

The crowd let out a cheer, happy to see the fight about to get under way. It didn't lift Keelin's spirits at all to see that he knew every face and every name of the people in the crowd. Over the last few months he'd saved most of their lives at least once, he'd helped build them a town, helped secure them a future, and now here they all were, cheering on a man who was going to kill him. "Ungrateful" only began to cover the bastards. He'd given so much to all of them, and now they wanted his life as well. Then he saw Smithe's face in the crowd, cheering along with the rest of them and watching Keelin with greedy eyes. Keelin spat into the dust and swore that even should Khan kill him in the arena, he would rise from the grave and take Smithe down to the watery Hells with him before allowing the bastard to captain *The Phoenix*.

Khan lifted the leather strap that held his sword in place up over his head and drew the weapon, throwing the scabbard away into the dust and planting his sword in the ground. It was a monster of a weapon best suited to huge, cleaving blows, but the giant looked like he could use it much like most normal men would use a longsword. Keelin, on the other hand, had his weapons of choice: dual cutlasses. They were heavy and sharp and deadly, but he wasn't looking to be deadly today. Khan began stretching and, with his chest completely bare barring his dangling beard, Keelin could see the man's muscles and reckoned he was outmatched at least twice over. With such strength and such a sword, blocking attacks would be useless. Keelin would have to rely on dodging and parrying, and somewhere along the line he might look at getting in a few strikes of his own.

Khan raised his sword and held it ready in front of him. The crowd cheered. With a heavy sigh Keelin slipped out of his jacket, letting it fall to the dust, and stepped into the arena, drawing both his cutlasses in one smooth motion.

Khan charged.

It took only a moment for the giant to cross the stretch between them. He slid to a halt, planted his feet, and swung his sword around in a deadly, neck-height slash that could have decapitated a bear made of stone.

Reacting on pure instinct, Keelin dropped into a crouch, rolled forwards into the giant's reach, and thrust both swords up into the pirate captain's unprotected belly. Khan gasped, his mouth dropping open. He made a pained mewling sound, slumping forwards onto one knee with much of his weight resting on Keelin. They remained there for what seemed like an age as Khan fought to regain his breath and Keelin fought to keep the bigger man from collapsing on top of him.

"If I were trying to kill you," Keelin said eventually, still struggling to support the giant's weight, "you would be very dead right now."

Khan let out a grunt that left Keelin none the wiser to his future intentions.

"Is this over?" Keelin said.

"Stop fuckin' huggin' an' fight," someone shouted, and Keelin realised the crowd was still there, and that the cheering had been replaced with a dissatisfied murmuring.

"Aye," Khan growled as he pushed his weight back onto his own legs and used his sword as a crutch. Very little sapped the strength from a man's limbs like a good winding, and two sword pommels to the gut would do just that. "You win, Captain Stillwater."

Keelin stood, still watching Khan warily. He seemed the honourable sort, but honour among thieves was ever a fluid definition, and they were all nothing if not thieves.

"Is that it?" shouted another member of the crowd.

"Yes," Khan roared back so suddenly that Keelin had to fight every instinct he had not to jump backwards and take up a battle-ready stance. "Stillwater bested me."

Keelin resheathed his cutlasses and sent a prayer of thanks to Rin that he'd had the sense to reverse his grip on his swords at the last moment.

"Nobody's even fuckin' bleedin'." Keelin recognised the antagonist as Smithe, and scanned the crowd for the ugly bastard's face.

"You want blood?" Khan shouted. "Then step down here and fight me. I will drain yours and drink it from your skull."

The crowd fell silent, and many even started to slip away.

Keelin wiped sweat from his forehead. Now he was confident the giant wasn't about to swing for him and catch him unaware, he wanted nothing so much as a bottle of rum and the company of an infuriating woman.

"Morrass is stronger than you?" Khan said quietly, still staring down members of the crowd.

Keelin thought about it. In a fight he was certain he could dispatch Drake even quicker than he had the giant, but not all strength was measured in skill with a blade, and Keelin knew for certain that no other captain in the isles could unite the pirates. Like it or not, Drake was the strongest candidate for king they had.

"Aye. You said you follow strength. Drake's the mightiest we got." Keelin smiled. "And we need you. We need that bloody great ship of yours, and we need your crew."

Khan turned to Keelin with a toothy smile beneath his midnight-black beard. "You have all three."

Keelin laughed. "I reckon that deserves a drink, eh? And if you wouldn't mind telling me, how the fuck did you take the *Victorious* with only a sloop?"

Fortune

Most folk thought there was some kind of magical trick to locating the Rest, and in truth, there was. Fortune's Rest wasn't just the largest pleasure house in the known world; it was also the only mobile city. It was capable of packing up, raising sails, and moving at the drop of a hat. The majority of Drake's fortune was housed at the Rest, and he didn't like the idea of it being in one place for too long lest unsavoury folk get bright ideas about pirating a pirate, or the more savoury of folk get ideas about liberating a pirate's wealth. So the Rest moved every month or so, sailing away to tempt a new locale of clients with its innumerable pleasures, and Drake always knew where it was.

Long ago he'd had his brother fashion a number of charms like no other. The first of them was a stone about the size of a child's head, with powerful runes chiselled into almost every bit of its surface. The stone acted as an anchor, and even half the world away, would always draw the other charms to it. The slave charms, as his brother had named them, were ten in number, and each was hidden within a compass. To most observers the compass would simply appear broken, as its needle rarely pointed north, but those few who owned one knew the real reason; the compass needle would forever point to the anchor charm and to the Rest.

Unfortunately for Drake, his compass needle was currently pointing directly into the heart of a developing storm front that, judging by the purple-black horizon, spanned every bit of the water between him and his Rest.

"I don't like the looks of it, Cap'n," Princess said with a terrified shake of his head.

The purple clouds in the far distance lit up a touch brighter for just a moment, signalling that the lightning had just begun. If he was honest with himself, Drake didn't like the look of it either, but he wasn't about to be honest to anyone when being honest meant admitting fear, especially not while Beck was watching.

"We'll be fine, Princess." Drake forced a grin. "Rin'll see us through."

Where Loyalties Lie

"Meaning no disrespect, Cap'n, but we both know that's a bunch of shit," Princess said. "She might have some pretty terrible powers when it comes to the sea, but we both know she can't do fuck all about the weather. If she could, Soromo would have been a touch less terrifying."

Drake couldn't argue with that. His escape from the Dragon Empress' dungeon had almost ended in death thanks to that storm, but they'd all survived then and they would survive again now.

"We've been becalmed for weeks, Princess. Now we finally have a bit of wind, I'm not about to waste it because of a touch of bad weather. You said it yourself just yesterday; supplies are running low."

"There was an island just half a day back, Cap'n. I reckon we should turn tail and head back there for shelter. We've tempted fate once too often of late."

Drake laughed at that. "You heard the Oracle's telling, Princess. It ain't my fate to die in that storm." He pointed at the dark clouds and hoped Hironous had been truthful about his brother's destiny.

Princess looked anything but mollified. "Ain't exactly your fate I'm worried about, Cap'n. Rest of us got lives too, an' we ain't looking forward to wasting 'em by trying to sail through that." Princess pointed his own bony finger at the storm.

"Shame that, cos it's exactly where we're fucking sailing."

Princess stood face to face with his captain for another few seconds before letting out a loud sigh, and the lines on his face crumpled into a smile. "If I die, ya best say a prayer for me, Cap'n."

"Oh, aye," Drake agreed. "I'll make sure Rin sits you down at her court with some merfolk, the ones with the really big tits."

Princess groaned and started walking. "Just my luck, bloody merfolk and their bloody teeth."

Drake spotted Beck looking sceptical. "Merfolk," he said with a smile. "Tail of a fish, body of a woman. Entice men into the water with the promise of tits and more, but they've got mouths full of sharp, pointy teeth to tear a man to bits." He shook his head. "Ain't never seen horror 'til you've seen a merfolk smile." He bared his teeth to make his point. The Arbiter still didn't look convinced.

"Is sailing into that storm really a good idea?" she said.

Drake shrugged. "I've had worse."

Just a few hours later, Drake found himself reconsidering his statement. Sailing into the storm was quite possibly the worst idea he'd ever formed. Wind whipped in a hundred different directions all at once, and every lick of it was accompanied by salty spray that felt like it could tear flesh from bone. The clouds overhead were dark and roiling, thundering together with claps so loud they rattled the teeth and loosened the bowels.

The *Fortune* levelled out for just a moment before her bow tipped forwards at an alarming angle and she started down the crest of the wave. There was little so frightening as seeing nothing but water in front of a ship, and the fact that it was too dark to even see that did little to alleviate the terror coursing through Drake's veins. He trusted the ship to get them through, and he trusted the crew to help her, but even the sleekest of ships and even the most experienced of crews could be lost during a storm – and this was one hell of a storm.

As the *Fortune* crashed into the base of the wave she started levelling out again, and a sheet of water rose up above the bow, soaking everyone and everything on the deck. Drake shook away the wet hair that clung to his face and stared out into the dark churning waters, hoping to see the next wave before it hit.

"She's tuggin' hard, Cap'n," screamed Huin, the ship's navigator. Drake looked back to see the man clearly struggling with the wheel, and wasted no time in ordering the second navigator on deck to lend a hand.

The storm canvas helped; smaller and thicker, it could catch the wind without pulling the ship down, and it was likely the only thing keeping the *Fortune* sailing over the monstruous waves.

They started the ascent up another wave just as a cry sounded from above. A moment later a screaming body crashed into the stairs leading up to the poop deck, turning the railing into kindling. One stolen glance told Drake the unfortunate pirate was dead, and he thanked Rin the man hadn't landed on anyone else.

"Rope loose!" The shout drifted down from above, and Drake looked up to see the canvas flapping.

"Get that rope tied off or we're all dead and worse!" Drake bellowed even as two pirates startled scuttling across the rigging to do just that.

The *Fortune* was rising now, her stern well and truly below them all. Drake saw the body of the dead pirate start to roll backwards up the stairs before it snagged on the splintered railing. Higher and higher they rose, until ahead of them Drake could see nothing but dark, boiling cloud. Then the *Fortune* lurched forwards and tipped the other way. Up became down, and down became up. There was a crash from somewhere below as something in the hold came free of its anchorage, but there were more important things for Drake to think about, and he trusted that someone below decks would see to the loose cargo's proper stowing.

Lightning flashed, forking down from the sky into the water, and for just a moment Drake witnessed the sea around them. Waves taller than any building he'd ever seen surrounded them on every side, and the water churned white on every side. Sheets of rain crashed down, and the clouds blotted out all light from the stars and moon above. They were truly in the thick of the storm now, and in all his years at sea he'd never seen another like it.

"Drake!" Beck stumbled across a sloping section of deck, using her fingernails as claws to hang on to the planks. As she reached the railing Drake was holding on to, the Arbiter almost flung herself into his arms, such was her enthusiasm to find something secure to cling to.

"Best get below deck, Arbiter," Drake shouted over the noise of the storm. "This is gonna last…"

"I saw a sail!" Beck pointed off the starboard side of the ship.

Drake stared at her for a moment before shaking his head. "Light playing tricks on ya."

The *Fortune* hit the water as it completed its descent, and a solid sheet of ocean rose up towards them. Drake attempted to shield Beck from the spray and only ended up dragging himself down to the decking with her on top of him. He lay there for a moment, staring at her as she attempted to remove her sodden hair from her face and the *Fortune* started tipping again. Already they were climbing another wave.

Pushing the Arbiter away, Drake surged to his feet then hauled

Beck to hers next to him. She looked a little dazed from the fall, or maybe just from the storm in general. Drake was feeling a little blurry himself – not that he'd ever admit it to anyone.

Something smashed into the ship and she lurched to port. Drake managed to hold both himself and Beck upright. Judging by the shouts and crashes, there were plenty of his crew who hadn't been so lucky, the navigator included. The man was back on his feet in a moment, but by then the damage had been done. With only one man on the wheel, it had got away from them and the ship was listing to port.

"Get her under control," Drake roared, "or we'll all drown at the crest."

Another sheet of spray whipped across the deck and Drake took a faceful, blinding and choking all at once. Strong hands gripped his arm even as the ship lurched again, and Drake tore his eyes open to see Beck holding him close and tight, her eyes unusually dark in the poor light. For a moment they just stared at each other, then she looked past him and Drake saw what little colour was left drain from her face.

"What the fuck?" Drake heard the navigator scream.

Slowly standing from its resting place amidst the broken and battered port railing was the corpse of the pirate who had fallen to his death. The ship was still tipping backwards as it climbed the wave, yet the dead pirate seemed to have no problem finding his balance. His neck was obviously broken, resting on his shoulder, and Drake could see bone protruding from the left arm. With an inhumanly loud groan that sounded clearly over the storm, the corpse staggered towards the navigators holding the wheel.

"Don't you dare move from that wheel," Drake roared as he fought for balance and stumbled towards the dead pirate.

Another flash of lightning lit the corpse's face in a horrible grimace that resembled nothing human. Again the ship levelled as it crested a wave, and Drake, already with sword in hand, found himself fighting for balance. He knew he had to find something to hold on to before they began the descent. The dead pirate fell, hitting the deck, and began crawling towards the navigators.

The deck fell away from Drake as the ship tipped downwards, and without anything to hold on to, he fell as well. Something as hard as iron clamped around his wrist and held him fast while his feet scrabbled for purchase on the water-soaked deck. Drake opened his eyes to find Beck holding on to him with one hand while the other gripped, white-knuckled, some rigging attached to the mainmast. Chanting furiously, she pulled Drake up to the rigging, which he gratefully grabbed with both hands, only then realising he'd let go of his sword.

"The dead," Drake shouted, pointing up towards the wheel, where he could see the dead pirate still crawling slowly across the deck.

"I see it," Beck yelled back, whipping her head to the side to get her sodden hair out of her face.

The mast above Drake gave a worrying groan, and he sent a quick prayer to Rin that it would hold. If the main mast snapped now they would all likely follow it into the cold dark below them.

"Shoot it!" Drake shouted at Beck.

The Arbiter shook her head just as another flash of lightning made plain the fear on her face. "Powder's wet!"

With a growl that was half frustration and half determination, Drake dropped to his hands and knees and began a painstaking climb up the deck towards the navigators still straining against the wheel. The dead pirate continued his own slow crawl just a few metres away. All it would take was one of the men on the wheel to let go, and the ship would careen and be lost beneath the waves.

Hand over hand, his boots scrabbling for purchase on the soaking deck, Drake edged closer and closer to the dead pirate until he was almost close enough to grab hold of his foot and pull it away. Someone shouted his name, but he was too intent, too focused. The ship jolted and a wave of water swept across the deck, spinning Drake around and washing him away. He hit the railing hard and felt the gradient lessen as the ship levelled off. Something slammed into his chest, forcing the air from his lungs, and he gasped in cold, salty water. For what seemed like forever, Drake's world was one of coughing and gasping and trying to desperately rub water from his eyes.

Drake heard a groan, and the thing that had slammed into his chest started to move. Without thinking, he reached out and wrapped his hands and legs around the figure, pulling it close and holding on with all the strength he could muster even as the ship started to tilt into its ascent of the next monstrous wave.

The dead pirate started to pull away. Even with another man encumbering it, the thing was able to claw its way across the deck towards the navigators. Drake kicked and punched at it, and still the monster kept going.

Teeth sunk into Drake's right arm, and he screamed. Unable to hold on anymore, he rolled away down the deck, cradling his bitten arm, and slammed into the stairway where the pirate had died.

One of his crew members skidded and slipped down the railing to Drake's crumpled position and tried to help him up.

"Fucking kill that thing!" Drake pointed at the dead pirate with his bad arm and saw for the first time just how much blood he was losing as it mixed with the sea spray and soaked into his clothing.

"Who? Merle?" the crewman shouted back.

With a growl, Drake shoved the man away, picked up a nearby splinter of wood no longer than his hand, and leapt after the corpse. It reached for the terrified navigator, who was busy trying to hold the ship's wheel steady while kicking away the monster attempting to chew on his ankle.

Roaring out every bit of pain and frustration he was feeling, Drake drove the shard of wood down into the base of the dead pirate's neck. The creature spasmed and groaned, but kept reaching for the navigator's foot. Drake planted his feet as firmly as he could and started dragging the corpse backwards, inch by inch, away from the wheel. Somewhere along the way the ship levelled off, then tilted back the other way, beginning its terrifying descent down a wave. Drake tightened his grasp on the creature, ignoring its attempts to turn and snap at him or pull itself free, steadying himself with one leg hooked through some rigging. Finally, after the ship had hit the bottom of the wave and a fresh wall of water had slapped them all about, Drake dragged the dead pirate to its feet and gave it an almighty push towards the railing. It stumbled, tripped against the railing, and toppled backwards overboard.

Drake sank down onto his knees amidst the ship and the raging storm and let out a groan. His arm felt like it was on fire where the pirate had bitten him, and he was somewhere beyond exhausted. There was no time to rest. A fresh sheet of sea spray whipped his face, and it was all the wakeup he needed.

Forcing himself back to his feet even as the ship started her next ascent, Drake stumbled his way over to the main mast, passing pirates hanging on for dear life and others scrambling to their jobs. If any of them needed direction, Drake was too exhausted to give it.

He found Beck still clinging to the rigging on the mainmast, her knuckles white and a fearful look in her eyes. Drake doubted it was the dead pirate walking that had frightened her so, and guessed it was more the dubious motion of the ship as she raced up and down the waves. It wasn't uncommon; some folk simply couldn't handle the raw power of a churned-up ocean tossing them about like flotsam.

"You saw a sail?" Drake screamed over the storm.

Beck nodded.

"What did it look like?"

Beck seemed to think about it for a while before opening her mouth to answer and receiving a lungful of salty water for her troubles. After a few good retching coughs she managed to speak.

"Like overlapping scales. Lots of sails all together." She shrugged as though it was the best she could do, but it didn't matter. Drake already knew what ship it was: a Drurr corsair. And unless he was very much mistaken, they were carrying a necromancer on board.

Mary's Virtue

There weren't many people who could keep up with Daimen when it came to a drinking contest. He was one of the few folk to have been born and raised on the isles, and his mother, bless her eternally resting soul, might as well have breastfed him grog, he'd started drinking the stuff at such a young age. Of course, it also didn't help that her suitors had quickly taken to giving Daimen a bottle of something strong and incapacitating to keep him out from underfoot when they came a-calling. All in all, Daimen had been drinking booze since before he was able to stand, and that, along with his natural tolerance for the stuff, made him nigh on unbeatable when it came to any sort of contest that relied on the ability to consume vast amounts of intoxicants.

Of course, his ability to quite literally drink most folk under the table had made him something of a legend among the people of the isles. And along with any reputation of being the best at something, as Stillwater had very recently learned, came challenges from those who thought themselves better.

Daimen's current opponent, a boy with a prolific amount of hair on his neck and none on his face, named himself Caster Shallows. The lad claimed more feats, accomplishments, and miracles than Drake Morrass himself, and Daimen had never met another man quite so enamoured with himself as Drake.

"I shailed with..." Caster paused to let out an inhuman belch that wafted sour, fishy breath into Daimen's face. "With Peregrew Fin out of Korral. Privateers, we named ourselves."

"Aye, is that so?" Daimen put his feet up on the table and signalled the serving wench for another round of piss-flavoured grog. The tavern was merry, the music lively, the shanties were bordering on obscene, and Daimen felt like stringing the poor boy along for a few drinks longer. "I met Peregrew once. Had a face as long as me arse and looked like he'd been usin' it to scrape barnacles off his ship."

"Uglier shunofabitch ya never did see," Caster agreed with a grin and a slow shake of his head.

Daimen laughed. Captain Peregrew Fin was a retired, ex-Acanthian navy officer who had been discharged for alleged piracy and had decided that if he was to be branded as such, he might as well make the claims true. He'd captured a total of one ship before a mutiny had made him governor of his own little island somewhere in the southern isles where, to this day, he remained and screamed bloody murder at any ship that came within hailing distance. For that brief career in piracy though, Peregrew had been known as "the Pretty Pirate", due to his stunning good looks and total ineptitude in command of any vessel larger than a bucket.

The next round arrived and Daimen paid the serving wench, with both coin and a healthy slap on the arse. He pushed one of the mugs towards Caster, who looked down on it as though it were an old friend with a grudge, come to stick him with the pointy end of a five-year-long estrangement.

"I must, uh… must be ahead of you," he slurred.

"Aye? Ya reckon?" Daimen smiled, raised the new mug to his lips, and proceeded to gulp down the entire contents before signalling the nearby wench that he required another. Caster swayed in his chair and let out a painful moan before toppling sideways and hitting the floor, already unconscious.

Daimen lifted his empty mug. "A drink to the fallen," he shouted.

"We'll be joining them soon," called back a fair few of the folk nearby.

"Ya got anything stronger than this swill, darlin'?" Daimen winked at the serving wench as she came over with a new mug. "Not that I don't enjoy a good bit o' grog, but this stuff is weaker than piss and makes ya do just that after every mug."

The wench shook her head. "We ain't exactly at the forefront of many deliveries. We're all waiting for Captain Morrass to get back an' fix it all up."

"Aye, we are. Well, I reckon I need to drain the monster out back. Fancy holdin' it for me?"

The wench's face went from all smiles to seething disgust in the blink of an eye, and Daimen took the hint well. "Reckon I'll manage it alone then, eh."

Without so much as a stumble, Daimen stood up and, leaving two full mugs of grog at the table, headed for the door. It wasn't that he trusted folk in the Righteous Indignation not to help themselves to his booze, but more that he didn't care. He'd already made more than enough from out-drinking Caster and, if he was going to drink himself into a hangover, he preferred to do it with something worth drinking.

Outside, the air was still and stagnant. Drake might have picked the most dangerous and defensible island in the Pirate Isles, but he also appeared to have picked the only one without a single breath of a breeze, even at night. It made for oppressive days followed by sticky nights, and made New Sev'relain a place Daimen would be glad to get away from.

The tavern's outhouse was just next to the main building and set back a little from the dirt street that ran through the town. Daimen was within a few paces of the outhouse when he changed his mind about using it to take a piss. Judging by the smell that enveloped the place, it was either occupied or had recently been occupied by a dead cat, and in Daimen's opinion, there was little that smelled worse than a dead cat. There were plenty of places for a man in need to relieve himself – a nearby building, a nearby tree, the middle of the street – but Daimen sometimes found his bladder needed a bit of coaching, and nothing made a man feel he could let go quite like the sound of the sea.

New Sev'relain was a busy little place no matter the time of day or night, and even the stagnant air couldn't keep the people from the streets. Some might be heading to the tavern, or to the brothel, or to some midnight tryst. Daimen knew full well he had a few weirds on his own ship, but as long as they didn't go screwing each other while at sea, he didn't care what they did ashore. All men had needs; women had them too, as far as Daimen was aware, and whether or not he had the same needs didn't make another man's any less important. Even as Daimen considered the weirds among his crew, he saw one of them walking along the street with a pretty young lad from Stillwater's ship. They looked deep in conversation and didn't notice the approaching captain. Daimen grinned and decided to give them a bit of a ragging.

"And exactly what the shit do we think is goin' on here?" Daimen

Where Loyalties Lie

said as the two men made to pass him without once looking away from each other. His own crewman, a man-mountain named Hert, blossomed red around the cheeks upon realising his captain had caught him in the act. Stillwater's lad looked more worried than embarrassed.

"We was… jus' headin' ta the tavern, Cap'n," stuttered Hert, his eyes downcast.

"Aye, that so? Cos I reckon…"

A distant scream drifted down the street, and Daimen paused, straining his ears for its source. Most of the folk on the street kept walking; either they hadn't heard or didn't care. Daimen wasn't one of those folk.

"You hear that?" he said to Hert and his boy.

"Hear what?" asked Hert.

"Aye, Cap'n Poole," said the boy. "Sounded like a woman's scream, from down that way." He pointed to an avenue leading towards the beach.

Daimen decided to take him at his word; it was likely his young ears were sharper anyway. With a hand on his sword hilt to stop it from flapping about, Daimen set off at a jog. He found it comforting that both the boy and Hert didn't hesitate to follow.

They passed through an alley and then across another street before climbing a hillock, and still Daimen saw no sign of whoever had made the noise. He cast his eyes first back towards the town and then down towards the beach, but the clouds were thick and the darkness was thicker.

"Down there, Cap'n Poole," said Stillwater's crewman, pointing at the beach.

Daimen squinted, but saw nothing. He decided to trust the lad's judgement and set off again. It didn't take him long to see what the lad's sharper eyes had picked out: two figures, one on top of the other. As Daimen drew closer he could see that it was a woman lying face down in the sand, her hands drawn up behind her, and a man thrusting away on top.

"You'll have ta correct me if I'm wrong there, matey, but that don't exactly look consentional," Daimen said as he came to a panting stop, deciding he was a little out of shape.

"Eh?" the man grunted. He was a pirate and no mistake, yet not one Daimen recognised – which put him as one of Khan's men.

"Consentional," Daimen repeated. "Consent... *ing*? Ah, fuck it. Looks like ya rapin' the poor lass."

"I paid her," the pirate insisted, but judging by the woman's tied hands, the gag wrapped around what was visible of her face, and the rest of that face buried in the sand, Daimen doubted the truth of the man's words.

"Hert." Daimen motioned to his burly crewman. "If ya wouldn't mind removin' that bastard from the girl."

Hert surged forwards, and the pirate quickly jumped up and away, fumbling to put his cock back in his britches. Hert paused.

"Might be best ya grab hold of him for now," Daimen said, "'til we can reason out the truth here."

Approaching the lass, Daimen could see dark marks on her face; he'd seen the like before, on many a whore. A good, solid backhanded slap left a very distinct wound, and hers was certainly distinctive. With a tender touch, Daimen first untied the woman's hands and then helped her sit up before removing the gag from her mouth.

He'd seen the woman around the town and, more often, inside the brothel. She was one of the few whores the town could boast, and definitely the prettiest of them all. With a swollen mouth and a newly missing tooth, she looked a sorry state at that particular moment.

Daimen pulled a kerchief from his pocket, accepting that it was at least mostly clean and certainly the cleanest thing any of them had on them at the moment, and handed it to the sobbing whore. He looked up at the pirate, who was currently being manhandled by Hert, and frowned.

"Now generally, mate, when ya pay a whore, and she accepts that payment, there ain't really no need ta go beatin' on her. Well, actually, I don't reckon there's ever really a need for that sort of behaviour."

"I did pay her." The pirate was attempting to wriggle out of Hert's grip, and only making the big man hold him tighter. "Three bits, going rate."

The whore attempted to spit at the pirate, but with her lips so swollen only managed to dribble the spittle down her chin. Daimen wiped it away. "That true, luv?"

The woman was staring at the pirate with burning eyes. "Shoved three bits down my top and said I was paid," she slurred. "I tried to give 'em back, an' he hit me. Next thing I knew, I was tied and gagged."

Daimen sighed. "Were the rules not explained ta you all when ya docked here, mate? 'Cos the penalty for rape is fairly…"

"Captain's law," the pirate blurted.

"Ah, fuck." Daimen shook his head, wishing he'd never left the tavern. He looked up into the clouds and weighed his options. He could kill the pirate here and now, and Khan would want an explanation, or he could take the stupid bastard to his captain as he'd asked and see how the man dealt with him. Not much of a choice as far as Daimen was concerned; either way he had an angry piratical giant to deal with.

"Captain's law says…" the pirate started.

"I fuckin' well know what it says, mate. I am a captain. Got me own ship an' everything. I'm tryin' ta decide whether ta just kill you an' tell your big bastard of a captain you fell onto me sword."

The pirate's eyes widened. "I'll scream."

"How manly you are. Real fuckin' hero. First you rape a poor lass, then you go an' scream like one."

"He's invoked cap'n's law, Cap'n Poole," said the boy. "Only right to give him to his…"

"Well, aren't you a sweet little conscience. I can see why you picked this one, Hert. Arsehole as tight as a miser's purse strings, I'll wager." Daimen barked out a laugh and carried on before anyone could further argue the pirate's case. "Come on then, let's go give him ta his captain an' see what the big bastard says."

They marched the pirate to the *North Gale*, where the ship's first mate informed them in no uncertain terms that Captain Khan was sleeping and didn't like to be disturbed. After a few choice insults, along with the threat of drowning the rapist right there in front of his own ship, the first mate went to rouse his captain. Khan eventually appeared on deck, wearing nothing but his black bandana to keep his hair in check and rubbing sleepily at his eyes. He put one giant foot upon the railing of his ship and looked down at Daimen and his captured pirate.

"Fuck's sake, T'ruck," Daimen said. "You mind puttin' some britches on?"

"Why?" the giant pirate responded sleepily. "Does my cock intimidate you."

"Fuck yes, mate. That thing would intimidate a horse, an' a well endowed one at that. Tell me, have you ever tried stranglin' someone with it?"

T'ruck Khan let out a deep belly laugh and squinted down at the men standing at the gangplank to his ship. "Why are you holding Oppen?"

"You can let him go now, Hert," Daimen said, and his crewman obeyed instantly. The pirate didn't waste a moment in charging up the gangplank onto the safety of his ship and getting behind his captain.

"Found the dumb bastard up the beach, rapin' this here poor girl. Seems your man didn't like 'no' as an answer."

Captain Khan looked slowly from Daimen to the whore to his crewman. "Is this true, Oppen?"

"I paid her!"

Captain Khan took in a deep breath and sighed it out. "You were aware of the rules of this town, Oppen."

"Captain…"

"They were explained to you all."

"Captain…"

"Either you wilfully disobeyed or you were too stupid to listen to me when we arrived here."

"Captain…"

"Did you rape that woman?" Khan roared.

Oppen staggered back a few steps, and even in the dim light Daimen could see tears in the man's eyes. He nodded. "Aye."

Khan turned to another member of his crew, several of whom had gathered nearby. "Rope."

"Please, Captain," Oppen said. "I didn't mean to. I…"

Khan levelled a punch at the pirate's face, flooring the man and, judging by the silence, knocked him out cold. Another crewman arrived carrying some rope and scurried up the rigging to hang it over the mast. The captain knelt down, out of Daimen's sight, and after a few moments stood again, one end of the rope now in his hands. The giant nodded once to Daimen and began pulling on the rope.

All by himself, T'ruck Khan hanged his unconscious crewman, pulling on the rope until Oppen's feet were dangling high above the deck. He held him there while staring down at Daimen and the whore. It was impossible to tell when the pirate finally expired – he never woke from his captain's punch – but after a while his skin turned pale and lax. Still Khan held the rope.

"Good riddance," the whore spat, and wandered away.

Daimen was vaguely aware of Hert and Stillwater's boy quietly slinking off, but he felt compelled to stand there and watch until Khan considered the matter complete.

Fortune

Fortune's Rest was Drake's creation. He'd built the floating pleasure house from the ground up, taking captured or derelict ships wherever he could and outfitting them not for long voyage sailing or combat, but for housing and entertainment.

Drake had made use of any and every ship he could find, from whalers to sloops, galleons to carracks. He'd even found a couple of gargants all but wrecked along a stretch of the Sarth coast; the vessels were slow at sail, dangerous in a storm, and even more dangerous around shallows, so they'd fallen out of favour. He'd hired a small army of shipwrights to restore them, and now they formed the centre of the Rest, easily twice as large as any of the other ships.

The Rest was the beginning of Drake's empire, and, far more than piracy or his trading contracts, it was the source of his substantial income. Many folk wondered just how a pirate could become richer than a king, and the answer was floating around right under everyone's noses.

It was said a man could purchase any pleasure he could think of at Fortune's Rest, and any that didn't already exist there could be found for a price. Aristocrats, merchants, warlords, and even the good folk flocked from all around the known world to the Rest, and many wasted their fortunes there, lining Drake's pockets even as they emptied their own.

It was widely accepted that the Rest was out of bounds for those authorities within the empires of man who knew it existed. Why would the noble folk of Sarth, or the Five Kingdoms or Acanthia, agree to sinking a place they all enjoyed visiting? For many of those in positions of power, the Rest was the only place they could find the pleasures they wanted and the secrecy to enjoy them.

Drake heard of all the requests, of course, and over the years since he'd commissioned the flotilla he'd discovered some insane fetishes. Sable, of the merchant family Fre'tre of Acanthia, requested baths filled with the blood of still-born infants, claiming they gave him eternal youth. Drake had to admit the man looked young for his sixties.

General Tchar from the southern wilds had a penchant for eating the most dangerous creatures known to man. That had been one of the harder requests to accommodate, as the general had once asked for the thigh meat of a troll, and only the Drurr were crazy and skilled enough to breed those monsters.

Everson Breen, captain of the *Malevolent*, had once requested a duet sung to him by female conjoined twins. Drake had never even heard of two people stuck in one body until that one had been put in.

Despite its wonderful profitability, the Rest was hellish to maintain. With all the ships forever at sea and lashed together with so little individual movement, the hulls had a habit of rotting through. One unfortunate sinking could bring down the surrounding ships, so Drake had ordered a rotation. Every six months, groups of ships were sailed to the nearest shipwrights, where they were given a full inspection and time to undergo any necessary maintenance. Thankfully none of the vessels were flagged as piratical, so they could visit any port in any civilised society, but the costs involved were beyond lavish.

For five years Drake had run and maintained the Rest, and for five years he had raked in the profits. Now he needed the money, and he needed the ships. Those that could cross deep waters would be put to use as legitimate fronts for the booty that pirates delivered to New Sev'relain. Those that couldn't cross the deep would be gradually outfitted for war. And he had to manage all of it while keeping the Rest operational. It would be no small feat, and he dreaded the task almost as much as he dreaded leaving New Sev'relain and the Pirate Isles in the care of Stillwater, but Hironous had told him to trust the man as his second in command, and Drake knew better than to ignore his brother's future-tellings.

"Debris in the water." The shout came from one of the pirates tending to the mizzenmast. The *Fortune* had taken a couple of knocks in the storm a few days back and was in need of some urgent repairs.

Limping across to the starboard side, Drake peered over the railing and wished, for the hundredth time that day, that his dead crewman hadn't bitten his damned arm. The wound, the ship's doctor assured him, wouldn't fester, but that didn't stop it hurting like eighteen Hells.

A couple of planks of wood floated past, attached to each other with a length of rope, a dark stain on the otherwise crystal blue waters. Drake peered out across the sea for any other signs of wreckage. There was an ominous feeling coiling its way through his gut, and either something bad had happened or last night's salt beef was about to give him the shits.

"More up ahead, Captain."

Drake fished his compass from his pocket and flipped it open. The Rest was dead ahead, and judging by the minute changes as the ship drifted a little here and there, it was close.

"Any bodies?" Drake shouted.

"I'm seeing plenty of gulls, Captain."

Gulls were a bad omen, and then some. The birds meant carrion, and this close to wreckage, carrion meant bodies. Drake almost ordered more canvas to speed their approach, but the ship was in a bad way and he had a feeling that no matter what they were about to encounter, there was little any of them would be able to do.

It was only a few hours later when Drake caught his first glimpse of Fortune's Rest, and what he saw didn't put him in a merry mood. There was a sombre aura surrounding the ship as it sailed ever closer to its home. Even those pirates not on duty had come up on deck to see the cause of the foul atmosphere. For a while now they'd been seeing more and more debris. Planks of wood, barrels, even a whole mast still dragging canvas as it rode the waves. Even worse than the debris had been the bodies, so many Drake had given up counting. Some were just plain dead, and others looked like they'd been mutilated – and recently, judging by the colour of the skin.

Drake no longer cared for watching the debris or the bodies; his entire attention was on what was left of Fortune's Rest. Only six months had passed since Drake had last been home, and back then it had stretched out wide and long. Over three hundred ships all lashed together and floating as one. Now, as Drake looked out over the start of his empire, he wagered the Rest held just half that, and he itched to find out exactly what had happened and why so many of his ships rested at the bottom of the sea.

Princess had known his captain for a good six years or so. He'd served as second mate while Zothus was Drake's first, and it had seemed a natural progression to step up once Zothus was given his own ship. The point was, he'd known Drake for a good long while, and though he trusted his captain, there were times when the man scared him. For a start, it was impossible to know where the truth began and ended when it came to Drake Morrass.

Princess had seen enough to know Rin was real, and more than enough to know she was a power best avoided. In Princess' experience, women had a habit of being capricious, vindictive, and even vicious, and Rin was undoubtedly female. So when Drake went about claiming he'd met the sea goddess and even hinted at fucking her, well, Princess simply wasn't sure what to believe. Part of him wanted to trust Drake's stories, wanted to believe that his captain was roguish enough to charm the pants off a goddess. But another part of him wanted to think otherwise, because the less he had to do with Rin, the better. In all the years he'd known Drake, however, Princess had never seen his captain quite so angry.

The captain hadn't said a word for hours, letting Princess run the ship, set the course, and order the *Fortune* brought in to dock with what was left of the Rest. Drake stood at the bow, leaning over the side almost as though he was talking to the figurehead – which, now Princess thought about it, depicted the sea goddess he wanted so little to do with. As the crew tied off ropes and secured the *Fortune* to the Rest, Drake hopped across to the ship they'd docked to and strode away without a word, a host of folk from the Rest trying to keep pace and no doubt make apologies in the hope he wouldn't have them killed.

Princess watched his captain storm away, then turned to find a fair few members of the crew waiting for orders or, more likely, waiting for permission to go and find somewhere to drink themselves unconscious.

Princess winced at the sudden responsibility and tried to decide what Drake would do in the situation. "Stay ready, lads," he said. "Nobody leaves the ship 'til the captain figures what has occurred."

There was a resounding groan from the men, and just then Beck emerged from below decks, looking equal parts beautiful and dangerous.

Princess distrusted beautiful women; they tended to be so much more dangerous than the less pretty ones. Not that his experience with either was that extensive.

"Where's Drake?" Beck said, sparing only a momentary glance at the spectacle of Fortune's Rest.

Princess pointed out across the ship they were tied to and half smiled, half grimaced at the woman. "He went that way."

Beck waited for a moment, clearly hopeful Princess would say more, then sighed and leapt across to the ship. Princess considered letting her go; in fact, he put some real thought into it, and hoped she would manage to get herself lost or killed. Unfortunately, Princess was as loyal to his captain as anyone would ever be, and he knew just how disappointed Drake would be if the Arbiter found herself an untimely end. With that thought, and admittedly a desire to be off the ship – even if off the ship meant on another ship – Princess hopped across the gap and set off at a jog after Beck.

He didn't manage to catch up to her. The Rest had a number of problems when it came to navigation, and especially so for anyone who, like Princess, believed they knew where they were going. The further in towards the centre of the floating pleasure house one ventured, the more connections to other ships each vessel had, and it didn't take long for a ship to have up to six different avenues of escape. There was also the fact that the configuration of the ships was always shifting.

Princess clearly remembered *The Ajax* being lashed firmly to *Fires in the Sky*, but now he found himself standing on the deck of *The Ajax* and recognising none of the ships it was connected to. He hated to admit it, but not only had he lost track of Beck, he himself was now lost. Luckily he found some consolation to his failure; unless the interior of *The Ajax* had changed, right below his feet was a tavern that specialised in getting folk very, very drunk.

Just as Princess remembered, the tavern on board *The Ajax* was dark and dirty, and smelled of stale beer and sweat. It was exactly the sort of place that made him feel right at home. Princess had grown up in a tavern just like it, serving drinks, collecting empty mugs, getting beaten for stealing dregs. It all seemed like someone else's life now it was so long ago. The smells brought it all back and put a wide grin on his face.

Despite whatever had happened aboard the Rest, the tavern was busy. Plenty of drunkards lay about on tables with forgotten drinks resting in their unconscious hands, and even more folk were still awake and still buying booze. In one group sitting around a large table near the bar, Princess counted twelve folk in all, and their conversation seemed lively, if a little one-sided. Princess sauntered over to the bar, ordered himself an ale, and took the opportunity to eavesdrop.

"I hear he's a devil," said a man who looked like a sailor by trade and a drunkard by choice. "That's why they're after him. Killed more folk than most men have hot meals."

One of the two women in the group, a tall wench with the tattooed face of a Riverlander, snorted. "Ain't a devil, jus' a man. Fuckin' dangerous one, aye, but a man is all."

"Can't be," said the sailor. "Way I hear it, blooded folk are droppin' like shits in a privy. Ain't no way a normal man could do that. Must be enchanted, or some such witchery."

"Well, my dear men, women, and… I'm afraid I'm not entirely certain of your particular alignment, but nevertheless I shall include you anyway," slurred a man in well-worn green trousers and a coat to match. "I had the profound pleasure of very recently being located within the Wilds and knowing the man in question by sight."

"You seen the Black Thorn?" The woman leaned over the table, sloshing a little ale from her mug.

"I did, in fact, *seen* the Black Thorn," the man in the suit said with a wave of his mug, spilling some of his own booze onto the table. "Oh, bugger, what a waste. Another round."

A cheer went up from all the folk gathered around the table except for one, a large man dressed in a white shawl, with a white turban on top of a bronze half-helm. It might have been that the man hadn't cheered because he wasn't drinking, but Princess found the fellow's eyes too disturbing to pay closer attention to him, and looked away.

"So what's he look like?" the sailor pressed.

"Who?" said the man in the suit.

"The Black Thorn."

"Oh. Right. Well, he's a giant, you see. Ugliest monster you've ever laid eyes on. Well, except maybe for you. If any of the gods truly exist, they were not kind to you."

"Fuck you."

"Have you ever heard the saying 'a face only a mother could love'? Well, I'm guessing she hasn't seen yours in a while, eh?"

The group fell silent for a moment.

"What?" the ugly sailor looked like he might have been angry if not for the free booze headed his way.

The man in the suit sighed. "It really doesn't matter. I sometimes wonder how you pirates are able to tie a rope so well when the simple concept of language so easily escapes you. No matter. So, he's big and ugly…"

"Who?" asked the sailor.

"The Black Thorn. Please do keep up."

Princess grinned and sipped his ale. He'd seen the Black Thorn once, when Drake had taken a ship the sellsword had been a passenger on; he couldn't really claim to have met him though. Thorn was big and ugly, and no mistake, but he wasn't really a giant. Still, he was plenty scary.

"I heard he sacked Carsington all on his own. Ran that bastard D'roan right out of his own city and left him poorer than… well, us," said the sailor.

"Well, yes, that's more or less the way of it. He may have had some three thousand men behind him, but he was certainly the first through the walls, and he cut a very striking figure in the process. Honestly, there are songs about it. I'm especially fond of the lyrics from 'Fire in His Eye', but then I've always been partial to dirty limericks. Say, does anyone know a rowdy shanty we could sing?"

"What about Jogaren?" The sailor seemed to have completely forgotten his earlier anger.

Princess saw the man in green exchange a glance with the man in white before answering. "What have you heard?"

The sailor looked uncertain. "Was a few months back, might have been shit. Lad came by from that way an' said the Black Thorn camped

Where Loyalties Lie

his army right outside o' Reingarde an' challenged Willem Jogaren to a duel, what with him bein' such a famous fighter an' all. So Willem trots out on this big horse, wearin' all shiny armour the likes o' which ya find on Five Kingdoms knights, all plate an' mail. Turns out the Black Thorn is as dark as his own reputation, an' he had the blooded lord feathered with arrows before cuttin' off his head an' stakin' it outside the city."

The man in green paused his consumption of ale for a brief moment. "Yes, that's the truth of it."

"But the folk o' Reingarde refused to surrender, even with their ruler dead, an' a couple o' days later every one of those blooded Jogarens turned up bloody in their beds. Word has it Thorn snuck in an' cut 'em all up while they slept. Murder, plain an' simple."

"I believe Thorn is calling it pre-emptive revenge, actually." The man in green nodded. "Regardless, Black Thorn and his Rose have vowed to rid the Wilds of the blooded and unite everyone under their rule. Who's to quibble over the nefarious methods they use, so long as they get shot of those who have been choking the life out of the Wilds for generations, hmm?"

"That include the Brekoviches?" Princess said with a wide grin.

"I'd say it almost certainly does." The man in green turned to the bar. "They are, after all – oh, fuck. Hello, Princess. I'd say it's nice to see you, but I'm trying to cut down on the lies, you see. I presume it would be far too much to hope that you're here alone?"

"Aye, Anders, far too much, mate. Sailed in just now. Gotta say, I'm surprised to see you here."

"Well, no one likes surprises, Princess. May I suggest pretending I'm not here? Most people tend to find their lives so much more fulfilling upon taking that course of action."

Princess shook his head. "I reckon Drake might want to see you."

"Of course he doesn't." Anders' smile looked about as genuine as a pickpocket's fingers. "I'm such a terrible wastrel that no one is ever pleased to see me."

Princess knocked back the last of his ale and stood. "Come on, mate. Don't make this hard on me. My life is already a right fucking chore these days."

The big man dressed in white rose slowly and positioned himself between Anders and Princess.

"Pern here seems to agree with me, and he's a very worrying person." Anders grinned as he peered around his bodyguard. "You know he killed six of those Drurr all on his own."

Princess opened his mouth to reply, but stopped short of threatening the bigger man. "What Drurr?"

Fortune

There was a hole in the Rest. Actually, there were quite a few, and Drake couldn't give a damn about most of them, but the one he was staring at now changed everything. That hole, where once a ship had floated, meant that while he had once been one of the richest men in the known world, he was now no better off than an average merchant. Drake couldn't abide being average.

Coloured Sky had been more than just another ship in the Rest; it was the only one that hadn't offered pleasures to the public, and the only one that had boasted a seasoned crew and a veteran guard. Drake wasn't so stupid as to put all of his eggs in one basket – his fortune was spread out over many of the vessels he owned – but the majority of it had been right there, where now there was only water. Millions of bits down in the drink, where no one, not even him, could ever go.

None of the nearby ships had been touched, none of them sunk. Reports from his men aboard the Rest claimed that while most of the inhabitants had been fighting against the Drurr and the living dead, a small band had crept inwards and found *Coloured Sky*. They had apparently pierced the hull with magic. Just how they knew which of his ships housed his vast fortune was still a mystery. His men had killed the Drurr who had sunk his treasure ship and, even better, they had captured one of the bastards.

"Drake."

"It's about time you found me," Drake said as Beck joined him. They stared down at the ocean where the *Coloured Sky* had been. The Arbiter had been furious, and then some, when he told her he suspected the Drurr had a necromancer aboard their ship. Even after Drake had explained that they had no way to find the corsair after the storm, Beck had been beside herself. Now they could both get some answers. "Reckon I could use some of that magic of yours again."

"What?"

"Got one of the fuckers that did this trussed up and awaiting interrogation." Drake turned a hungry grin on Beck. "Drurr bastard from that ship we passed in the storm."

"Where is it?" The fury in Beck's voice matched Drake's own. He found it curious that she was so angry. The Drurr had done so much to Drake, they'd taken so much from him, that it was natural for him to hate them. As natural as it was to draw breath. He wondered if Beck, too, had suffered at their hands, or if it was just the hatred the Inquisition peddled to all its followers.

"In the cabin," Drake said. They were aboard *Rising Night*, the largest of the ships in the Rest and far larger than any but a Man of War. It was also a ship devoted to some of the more vicious, carnal pleasures. People paid to be tortured aboard *Rising Night*, or sometimes paid to watch others tortured – maybe even take part themselves. It was a ship devoted to pain and blood, and once he was finished with the bastard in the cabin, Drake intended to have him pinned to the front of the ship as a grisly warning to all Drurr.

The Drurr's eyes flickered open, and there was a moment of pure panic as he realised where he was and how much trouble he was in. He was a handsome one, and no mistake, but he wouldn't be by the time they were through with him. Like all Drurr, he was paler than any man had cause to be, and his skin seemed just a little too tight across his face. His eyes were black – not just the pupils, but the irises as well – and his mouth was too wide and full of too many teeth. There was very little difference physically between Drurr and humans, Beck reflected, but enough to mark them out as what they were. Heretics.

With a groan, the Drurr closed his eyes and slumped in his restraints. Beck itched to start questioning the creature, but she would follow Drake's lead. The man seemed to have an intimate knowledge of the Drurr and a history with them that Beck needed to know more about.

"Do I know you?" Drake said.

The Drurr opened his eyes again and stared at Drake. A smile slowly spread across the creature's face, a smile that would have seemed too wide upon human features. But the thing bound and kneeling on the deck was not human. It shook its head.

"Do you know me?"

The Drurr nodded. It looked around at the others on the deck, first gazing at Beck, then the men and women who had captured it. It was impossible not to feel uneasy under the intensity of that dark glare, but Beck hid her discomfort as well as she was able to.

Drake grinned. "That'll make things a whole bit easier then."

"*You*... were... here all the time?" the Drurr asked in a voice clearly unused to the common language.

"Nah," Drake said. "Just arrived. Passed you bastards in the storm just back."

The Drurr laughed, a haunting sound of disjointed melodies that would make a strangled cat ashamed. "That was... *you*. If only *we* had known."

"You came here for me?"

Again the Drurr shook its head. It let out a groan and slumped down to the deck.

"Bastard took a couple of blows to the head. Only way to put him down," said a scarred sailor.

"Anything you can do, Beck?" Drake said.

"Concussions are a problem of focus, not consciousness." Beck didn't take her eyes off the Drurr, in case it should be feigning ailment and try to escape. They were devious, hateful creatures, and heretics one and all. It was well within her right to put the creature down right then, but she wanted answers as much as Drake. The Drurr had never before been known to use necromancy. It had, after all, brought down their entire civilisation long ago.

"No spells or charms then?"

"Arbiter!" the Drurr lurched upwards onto its knees and spat at Beck. The insult fell short and did nothing but wash the deck. There was no denying the hatred plain on the creature's face.

"My presence appears to vex it." Beck smiled, enjoying how easily she could enrage the creature.

The Drurr attempted to stand, but the scarred sailor put two big hands on its shoulders and forced it back to its knees, where the creature continued to seethe, mumbling to itself in a language Beck didn't understand.

"He's cursing you and your entire order," Drake said.

"I don't feel very cursed," Beck replied, meeting the Drurr's hate-filled eyes.

"Oh, aye. The thing about your god, Arbiter, is he protects you from more than you know. But let's try this again." Drake turned his attention back to the mumbling Drurr. "So you came here looking for me?"

"*We* came here to… destroy *you*." The Drurr seemed unsure of its words, and it was trembling with rage.

Drake spoke quickly in the Drurr's language, and the creature responded in kind. Beck hadn't thought it was possible that a human could not only understand the Drurrs' language, but also replicate it. There was certainly more to Drake that she was yet to uncover.

Drake appeared to be growing angrier and angrier as the Drurr spoke, and once it had finished, the pirate turned and let out a wordless scream. The Drurr laughed.

"They came here to destroy me by sinking my fortune," Drake said, turning back around. "And they picked the worst possible fucking time to do it. Pissing bad luck, they got here just before me."

"Why?" Beck's compulsion passed through Drake, but as usual found no purchase. "Why are they coming after you?"

"Because *she* will never let *him* go," the Drurr said.

"Shut up," Drake snapped.

"Who?" Beck asked, her compulsion once again proving ineffective.

"*You* were *her* favourite," the Drurr hissed. "And… *she* will never let *you* go. *She* will destroy *you* over and over again until *you* come crawling back on *your* knees… and beg to be *hers* again."

"Who?" Beck leaned closer, her fists clenched.

Even as the Drurr opened his mouth to speak, Drake snatched one of Beck's pistols from its holster and, before she could stop him, put a bullet in the creature's chest. The Drurr collapsed, writhing and struggling to breathe. No one made any attempt to save its life. They all stood there and watched it die.

Fortune

The Drurr gurgled his last breath, and Beck turned to Drake. "Who?"

"Don't." Drake's nerves were long past shredded, and the reminder of his years with the Drurr had put him in a mood fouler than a week-old corpse. "Some things are better left buried, Arbiter."

"Like why the Drurr have themselves a necromancer?" Beck moved in front of Drake as he made to leave, blocking his path. "I needed to question that thing." She pointed at the body of the Drurr.

Drake shook his head. "Your boss sent you to watch my back, protect me, aye?"

Beck nodded.

"Ever think this might be why? These bastards are coming for me. Don't much matter why. All that matters is that you're right by my side to set the heretics on fire when they do come." For all Drake knew it might even be true. Hironous was his brother, but the man kept his cards even closer to his chest than Drake did.

Beck seemed to mull it over for a minute. "I still want to know who *she* is."

"It ain't pertinent," Drake growled. It was bad enough that he had to live with the memory of what he'd endured, and even worse that she was still alive and looking for him. The very last thing he wanted was anyone else to know, especially Arbiter Beck. For a while they stared at each other, neither willing to be the one to back down.

"Was it the matriarch?" Beck said quietly. She sounded concerned. "The one you mentioned at the spring?"

"Yes," Drake conceded, hoping it would shut the woman up.

"What did she do to you?"

"Drake," called a voice from the next ship across.

"What?" Drake roared, venting all his fury at the hapless fool who had chosen to interrupt them.

"I can see you are busy, and I would hate to cause any undue stress. I'll come back later. Lovely seeing you again."

"Anders. What in all the watery Hells are you doing here?" Drake almost felt like grinning again; the interruption was a welcome one after all. Anders Brekovich was as slippery a serpent as Drake had ever known, but he was also one of Drake's best agents. Even if he had died twice.

With a dramatic sigh, Anders bridged the gap between the two ships, and Drake spotted Princess just behind the drunkard along with a man dressed in white. "Well, Pern here…" Anders paused. "You remember Pern Suzku?"

Drake nodded. "Seem to remember you working for that little shit Swift."

The warrior shrugged.

"Indeed," Anders continued. "Well, he was also directly responsible for Swift's death, which is something his old clan frown upon."

"The Haarin becomes a Honin," Drake said with a smile. "Dishonoured and a death sentence all in one, I hear."

The warrior stared down at Drake. "The true dishonour would have been continuing to protect that man," he said calmly. "My clan chose to serve his evil; I chose otherwise."

"Oh, yes, you're the most honourable pariah I know." Anders shook his head. "His old clan have thrown three Haarin assassins at him in the last year. The fools only come at him one at a time, luckily, or he'd already be dead. After the third, Thorn decided it was best to put Pern out of reach for a while, and here seemed the best location for such a task."

"And you?" Drake said.

"We couldn't very well send Pern to the altar of temptation and decadence without an escort, could we? He's very impressionable. Sheltered life and all that. No, I was the obvious choice to protect him from the seductions this place offers."

"Of course you were." Drake glanced over his shoulder at Beck, but she was paying the conversation little attention, instead riffling through the dead Drurr's clothing. "You were here when these bastards attacked?"

"Oh, yes. We valiantly fought off a score of invaders. Why, some of the Rest's crew attribute their eventual retreat solely to the efforts of myself and Pern here. In fact, he killed a good six of the bastards single-handedly – with me watching his back, of course."

"Of course."

"It didn't help that they kept getting back up though. I've not seen anything like it since Absolution…"

Drake turned to the sailor who had captured the Drurr. "That true?"

"Aye." The sailor raised an eyebrow at Anders. "More or less. They sunk a good few boats, but we turned the tide when we got ourselves organised. These two helped. So did releasing some of the nastier beasties we keep for fights. Ever heard of a killapede?"

"No."

"Well…" The sailor looked a bit embarrassed. "Don't reckon that's its real name, jus' what we call 'em cos they look a bit like a centipede, only bigger an' killa'rer."

"Go on," Drake said, intrigued.

"Well, they got a load of body, uh…"

"Segments," Anders said, apparently recovered from his brief loss of words.

"Aye," the sailor continued. "Each with two sharp, pointy legs. They can grow up to six feet, I've heard, an' the adults have skin harder than steel. They got poison that paryl… parily…"

"Paralyses." Anders tipped the sailor a magnanimous nod. "And I believe you mean venom."

"Yup, that's the one. An' they got these big fucking, uh, jaws, more like swords really, that can slice through bone. Seen one take a man's foot off before. Poor bastard. Anyway, we released a bunch o' them right as those Drurr cunts were comin' at us. We haven't got 'em all back yet."

"You're saying there are still some giant centipede killing machines loose aboard the Rest?" Anders said.

"Aye, reckon so."

"Well, that's damned unnerving." Anders produced a hip flask from his jacket and took a few long sips.

"Get 'em found and caught." Drake ran a hand through his hair as a thought struck him. "Can they be trained?"

The sailor looked uncertain. "Most anything can be trained if caught young enough. No idea how ya might go about it though."

"Get me one just hatched and have it brought to the *Fortune*."

"They don't exactly hatch so much as eat their way out of the mother…"

"Just get one as young as possible." Drake dismissed the sailor by turning his attention back to Anders and the Honin. "I hope you have some good news, Anders."

"I do," Anders replied cheerily. "So good I think I'll write it down, hide it somewhere in your cabin, and then quickly jump on a ship bound anywhere but near you."

Drake sighed. It seemed the fates had decided to heap shit upon him and watch him flounder. Having an oracle for a brother was useful for the long game, but short-term problems were his to deal with through and through.

"Out with it, Anders. Unless it's your fault, I ain't about to burn you for it."

"Oh, sure, you say that now. The Five Kingdoms are building a fleet."

"Something I don't know would be better, Anders."

"Well, they've built a new ship as well. A warship."

"Man of Wars ain't new. Dealt with one just a while back."

Anders shook his head. "Those monstrosities are built to carry troops; this new ship is built for war. As big as a Man of War but as fast as a galleon, and bristling with all manner of nasty machines."

"Such as?" Drake could feel tendrils of worry creeping up his spine.

"Catapults, scorpions, a big steel ram on the front, and more black powder than an army of alchemists could make in a year." Anders swallowed. He looked nervous. "Rumour says it's been designed by the engineers of Sarth and built by the shipwrights of the Five Kingdoms, and it's heading your way soon, if not now."

"It don't look good, Cap'n," Princess said. He looked as worried as Drake felt. The pirates of the isles weren't ready for a war, and wouldn't be for a while yet. Drake had only managed to unite two captains and already his enemies were throwing titans at him, while others were doing their damned best to cripple him. Worst of all was that folk looked to him to have a plan, to know everything that happened and how best to turn it to his advantage, and right now he had nothing. If he wasn't careful, everyone would soon figure that out.

"Find Ruein," Drake said to Princess. "Have him brought to the *Fortune*, and tell the lads they have three days for drinking and fuckery. After that we're leaving."

"What about us?" Anders said, grinning foolishly.

"I want you to go back to Rose and her Thorn and tell them I need some help. Feel free to remind them that they owe me."

Anders sighed out a laugh. "Sure. Give me the easy job." He turned around and started to walk away, the Honin on his heels. "What could possibly go wrong with telling the future king and queen of the Wilds…" His voice trailed off, and Drake stopped caring.

Beck had finished going through the dead Drurr's pockets and was staring at Drake with care in her blue eyes that was even more damning than the more usual ice. "I still want to know, Drake."

"More important things right now, Arbiter. Besides, not everyone gets what they want." Drake made a show of leering at the Arbiter before walking away.

Ruein Portly was a former pirate captain who had sailed under the flag of a Sarth privateer until he boarded the wrong vessel. A Five Kingdoms princess had been secretly aboard, and upon her eventual arrival home, she had demanded Ruein be branded a true pirate. Two years on the run later, and unwilling to take the isles as residence, Ruein had received an offer he couldn't refuse; Drake hid given him control of Fortune's Rest and a healthy cut of the profits. Now Ruein was a fat old sailor with a balding head and a beard that stretched down to his expanding waist.

"About the attack, Drake," Ruein said as soon as he opened the door to the *Fortune*'s cabin.

Drake cut the man off with a raised hand and a laugh. "Ain't your fault, Ruein. As it happens, it appears to be my own. Though quite where those bastards got hold of one of my compasses is another matter."

Ruein ambled over to the nearest stool and sat down with a groan – and without permission. The man had always seen himself as Drake's equal, despite working for him, and that was just one of the reasons why Drake didn't entirely trust him.

"Are we drinking to drowned treasure?" Ruein was eyeing both the rum bottle on Drake's desk and the hulking form of Byron standing to Drake's left.

"Help yourself." Drake pushed the bottle a little further across the desk with his feet.

As Ruein grabbed the bottle and tipped a measure down his throat, Drake glanced at the door to the cabin. He'd expected Beck to be back by now, and had become so used to her presence that the lack of it had him worried. The last thing he wanted was to tell her about his time with the Drurr, but he found himself wanting her trust.

He looked back at Ruein. "Did you bring the ledgers?"

"Oh, aye." Ruein gave the bottle a shake before apparently deciding he deserved another mouthful. "Outside in a chest."

"A chest?"

Ruein shot Drake a glance. "There's a lot of books, Drake. Took two men to carry it here."

"You weren't one of them, I assume."

Ruein laughed. "Volm…" He coughed. "Gods, no."

"Fetch them in and have a look, Byron," Drake said, and the giant scuttled away before returning a moment later with a large chest between his arms. Ruein's eyes widened.

"That lad could crush a man's head in one hand," he said. "I could put him to use here."

"He has his uses right where he is."

Byron sat down on the floor with the chest and slowly started emptying its contents, carefully sorting the books into piles and then leafing through the pages, his beady eyes roving over the numbers contained within. Drake sat patiently, waiting for Byron to finish and for Ruein to give his report.

"He alright?" Ruein took out a pipe and starting to pack it with leaf.

"He's fine," Drake said with a predatory smile. "He has a head for numbers. Would you like to tell me how the Rest is doing? Or would you like him to tell me?"

"Well, we have just lost a number of ships. Initial count puts it at about fifty or so." Ruein paused to light his pipe. "Maybe a hundred. It's a set back and, uh…"

"*Coloured Sky*," Drake prompted.

Ruein winced and looked at Byron. Drake followed the fat pirate's gaze and found Byron frowning at the books.

"How are they looking, Byron?"

"The Rest has been operating at a loss for a while now," Ruein said in a rush. "Your orders were that almost any desire, with very few exceptions, be catered for. Well, there are some expensive tastes out there, and prices have had to be lowered of late."

"Have they now?"

"Competition," Ruein said with a hasty smile. "Why sail halfway around the world to the Rest when the same… desires can be fulfilled closer to home, and cheaper?"

"What competition?"

"The Slavers Guild." Ruein sucked on his pipe.

Drake could ill afford a war on a financial front as well as the other wars he was already fighting, and there was simply no way he could win against the Slavers Guild. They had too much money and too many people, and they could operate legally in cities Drake couldn't even be seen in. It was a war lost before it had begun.

Byron finished looking through the books and started neatly packing the leather-bound tomes back into the chest.

"So?" Drake said.

"Numbers add up," Byron mumbled.

"But they don't look good?"

The giant simpleton shook his head.

"How much is left in the coffers?"

"One million one hundred and twenty-two thousand gold bits and…"

"Um…" Ruein looked like he very much regretted the interruption. "With the sinking of *Coloured Sky*…"

"How much?"

"We kept most of the money on the ship." Ruein quickly dragged at his pipe, then snatched his fingers away from it; he'd been smoking it so hot that he'd burnt them.

"How much?"

"One million bits were lost."

"I see." Drake drummed his fingers on the desk. "What you're saying is, I'm practically a pauper."

"You still have more than most men would make in ten lifetimes," Ruein said with a pathetic smile.

Drake banged his fist down on the desk. "I am not most men," he shouted at the pathetic excuse for a captain.

Ruein paled, his pipe all but forgotten and heavy beads of sweat springing from his bald head to run down the creases in his fat face. Byron started humming to himself.

"Shit." Drake stood from his desk to calm the giant down. "It's all savvy, Byron. I'm not angry with you. Why don't you take those ledgers down to your bunk and memorise them? That'd be fun, yeah? Then you can store them with all the others."

Byron stopped humming and nodded eagerly.

"Off you go then." Drake waited for the giant to make his way from the cabin, carrying the heavy chest as though it weighed nothing.

"I need eighty thousand bits brought to the *Fortune*."

"The Rest won't be able to operate with no…"

"I'm breaking up the Rest. Any ships already able to cross the deep will come with me to the isles, same as any sailor wants to come. Any that don't will be put ashore at Korral. Sell off anything that can be sold, and use what you get to get the ships that don't come with me repaired and outfitted for battle."

"Battle?" Ruein sounded incredulous.

"Aye," Drake said, showing Ruein his golden tooth. "Don't you know? We're at war."

The Phoenix

Her hands were raw and red with blisters that sported their own blisters, and hurt more than childbirth, which, Aimi had been assured many a time, was about as painful as torture. Years of working as a serving girl had made Aimi's hands tough and leathery, but the calluses were long gone and needed to be earned all over again. She didn't mind though. She was once again out on the ocean and sailing the world. It was a glorious feeling to see new sights, experience new things, and meet new people. Aimi had been born at sea, and she was more than a little certain that the sea was where she belonged.

The sea ranged from crystal blue to emerald green, and was usually clear enough that Aimi could see down beneath the waves. There, she might spot any number of animals and monsters that called the water their home. Some of those creatures were fairly dangerous, and many were large enough to pose a real threat to a person's life, but they were also beautiful.

Aimi let out a contented sigh, which quickly turned into a curse as the rope she was desalting popped another blister and deposited a stinging build-up in the wound all at the same time. She clenched her teeth and blinked away the tears of pain, biting her lip to stop herself shouting out a whole myriad of curses. She failed.

"Maggoty cock-swallowing fuck-monkey!" A couple of nearby pirates laughed, and one even applauded her.

"There's a trick to it," Captain Stillwater said from above. Aimi looked up to see him hanging from the rigging, looking down at her with a smile. He was nothing if not clumsy in his obvious advances, but Aimi didn't truly mind. The captain was easy on the eyes and charming despite himself.

"Really? Oh, master of sailing, please enlighten me." Aimi grinned up at the captain and turned her attention back to the devious length of rope.

"You don't think much of me as a sailor, do you?" Aimi thought she detected a note of disappointment in the captain's voice. He'd likely come down in an attempt to impress her.

"I don't think much of any captain as a sailor," she said. "Most are good at giving orders and sounding like they know a cleat from a grommet, but…" She paused and rolled her eyes at him. "Ask 'em to actually haul up a mizzen and tack the yard, and they'll probably just end up dropping the anchor."

The captain shook his head. "I didn't catch a word of that." He dropped from the rigging and landed easily on his feet, before leaning against the railing and staring out across the sea.

Aimi was young, not even twenty years, and the captain was older, but at that moment she reckoned him younger than he looked. Life at sea had a habit of ageing people before their time. Too much wind and sun and salt was the most likely cause of it.

The captain glanced Aimi's way and caught her staring. She curled her lip at him and went back to the task of scraping the damned salt off the rope.

"I was a sailor long before a captain," he said.

"Uh huh." Aimi may have been interested, but it was much more fun to let the man think he had no chance.

"I spent a good few years as ship's boy aboard *The Black Death*."

Aimi had heard of Captain Black, and she'd heard a great many horror stories about his ship and her crew as well as the captain himself. If even half those tales were true – and she knew it was likely a good half of them weren't – being a young boy aboard *The Black Death* must have been a harrowing experience.

"Sounds jolly," Aimi said, digging her knife into the rope and narrowly missing cutting her own finger open. Trouble was, she was paying far too much attention to the captain and the attention he was paying her.

"Anything but, actually." Aimi sneaked a glance to see the captain once again staring out over the ocean.

"Captain Black ruled his ship by terror and pain. The crew had to fight for the best jobs, for the best bunk, for the first servings at meal time, and to keep that food once we had it. I can't tell you the number of times I took a beating and had my cut stolen from me just as we made port. And by men I was supposed to rely on during a fight."

"Well, I certainly can't think of a worse life," Aimi said with a grin. "Tell me, have you ever tried imagining what it's like to be a young girl of fucking age in a town full of pirates?"

The captain looked at her then, with eyes wider than a whale's. "Uh... no. I haven't."

In truth, Aimi had never fucked a man she didn't want to. There had been a few and then some more that had tried it on, but she was smart enough to stay away from the ones that looked like they might get a bit rapey, and quick enough to outrun the more persistent bastards. Still, it hadn't been fun, living with the fear of it hanging over her head for three years. Some pirates had morals, that much was true, but when a man killed folk and stole their goods for a living, there weren't that many that were above taking what they wanted.

"I just meant to say," the captain said, "I do know how to sail and how to do a sailor's job."

Aimi grinned at Stillwater and gave him a wink. "I was only messing with you, Captain. So what is this grand trick to not fucking up my hands on the rope?"

He was staring at something out in the ocean, a wild grin on his face. "Oh, it's simple really. Give the job to the lowest-ranked sailor on the boat."

Before Aimi could think of a retort, the captain rushed away, calling for a course change. She couldn't believe she'd let him suck her in like that. As she started to come up with ways to get her own back, she glanced over the railing and saw a sail in the distance.

The ship turned out to be a merchant carrack, and it was carrying a complement of guards as well as sailors. It was a nice prize for any pirate, and likely to contain quite a few treasures. The chase was long and a forgone conclusion, *The Phoenix* both sleeker and faster in the wind. The fight to take the carrack was vicious and bloody; at least, it certainly sounded vicious from below decks, and afterwards the deck of the carrack was certainly bloody. Aimi was no slouch with a knife in close quarters when the poor fool on the pointy end wasn't expecting it, but she wouldn't know where to begin in a battle with a sword or axe, so she kept well and truly out of the fight and sent a prayer to Rin for it to go well and for the captain to remain unscathed.

Once the cheering started she knew the crew of *The Phoenix* were victorious. Nobody cheered quite like a group of ecstatic pirates. Emerging onto the deck, Aimi was surprised to see the sky had darkened considerably, the daylight almost over. The deck of *The Phoenix* was all but empty, but the captured carrack was swarming.

Aimi could see the crew of *The Phoenix*, weapons still in hand, were moving about with a purpose. Some were descending below decks while others were securing the ship and keeping the prisoners under guard.

As she mounted one of the makeshift bridges between the two ships, Aimi felt her stomach lurch, and she counted herself lucky that she was over water because a moment later her most-recent meal evacuated her body in a torrent of foul-tasting vomit. She wasn't certain what sickened her more – the bodies, the blood, the scale of carnage, or the men standing over it all admiring and celebrating their gruesome work. It didn't take her long to decide. It was the smell. Blood and shit and sweat and fear and death all mingled together to form a nauseating miasma. In that moment of realisation, Aimi feared she'd made a horrible choice in signing on with Stillwater's crew.

After finishing throwing up and wiping her mouth with her hand, Aimi continued on to the carrack. She found the whole scene sickening, but she'd be damned before she ran away and hid from it all. Looking down onto the ship's deck, there seemed no safe place to step; it was awash with blood as it mingled with the water from the sea. Though her determination to join her crew on the carrack drove her to the ship of death, she was not yet ready to wash her bare feet in the blood of their victims, so she leapt onto the nearby rigging and scurried up a few feet before slotting her legs through a couple of loops where she could watch the scene on the deck below. By force of will she managed to stop counting the bodies and focusing on those still writhing in pain as *The Phoenix*'s crew finished off any unlikely to survive.

Captain Stillwater presided over the brutal scene, standing on the sterncastle deck while he cleaned his twin swords on a strip of cloth. Of all the pirates swarming across the decks, only the captain retained his usual demeanour. His hair was tousled and his jacket was speckled with blood, but his suit remained neat and his attitude calm. Aimi had to admit he cut quite the handsome figure, even amidst the carnage.

She saw one pirate emerge from the hatch that led below decks and run towards the captain, while Feather, sword in hand and a wild grin on his face, burst out of the navigation cabin with a couple of prisoners in tow. Neither the man nor the woman Feather had found looked like they had any fight in them. Both were short and leaning towards overly fed, and the woman was clearly heavily pregnant.

Feather led them towards the rest of the prisoners. Aimi had spoken to the boy just a couple of hours earlier to find out how the captain usually handled taking ships, and he'd assured her that Captain Stillwater preferred bloodless encounters. This one was anything but. Aimi had also learned that Feather had yet to kill a man. Judging by the blood on the boy's blade, he could no longer claim such a thing.

The pirate who had emerged from below decks wore an insane grin as he approached the captain and whispered in his ear. Stillwater nodded solemnly and pointed towards the ship's quartermaster, Smithe, and the pirate eagerly went to spread the news.

Aimi glanced back towards *The Phoenix*. Morley, the first mate, had stayed behind to man the ship, along with a number of other crew including Kebble Salt, who sat up in the nest casting his watchful eye over the surrounding sea.

Kebble was a mystery to Aimi. The man took no part in the sailing of the ship and bunked with the other pirates, yet all of the crew showed him great respect. She'd seen Kebble shoot and knew just how deadly he was with his rifle, but Aimi knew full well how disrespectful pirates tended to be to any who didn't know how to sail.

"Ho there, little one," someone said from above.

Aimi looked up to see Jojo Hyrene sitting in the rigging above her. Jojo was from the southern wilds and a true veteran of the seas, with more years on the ocean, and more exciting stories from those years, than most sailors were ever likely to see. Jojo was also one of the most likeable and friendly folk Aimi had ever met, despite being a pirate.

"Come to see how we do things?" Jojo said in his deep, raspy voice. He held out a small clay flask, which Aimi took gratefully. She swallowed a mouthful of burning rum before answering.

"Figured I best get to know the ropes." She grinned, shaking the rigging as she handed back the flask.

Jojo laughed. "Well, the real work's done already. After the killing comes the looting, then the captain will send the bastards lucky enough to survive on their merry way. You look a little pale – need another hit?" He offered the flask again, and Aimi shook her head.

"Just not used to the blood yet."

Jojo nodded, his pale eyes full of understanding. "Pray you never are, little one."

"Keelin?"

Aimi turned back to the scene on the carrack to see one of the prisoners on his feet. The man was short and bald with a hook-like nose and the dark grey robes of a priest. Judging by the blood soaking into the man's robes, he had, until just now, been kneeling with all the other prisoners. Aimi realised he was the man Feather had escorted from the cabin, and she saw the woman he'd been with shaking her head and trying to pull the man back down onto the deck.

The captain glanced at the man once and then went back to what looked like a frustrating conversation with the quartermaster.

"Keelin Fowl?" the man in the grey robe said again, louder this time. "I'm not imagining this, it is you. I'd recognise you anywhere, boy. I watched you grow up, taught you your numbers and letters."

Again the captain looked at the captive, and this time, after a moment, he crossed to the ladder and descended to the main deck, approaching him with a menacing step.

"Your father was convinced you were dead," the man continued.

"Listen, mate." The captain's accent was more heavily tinged with the Pirate Isles than usual. "Reckon ya got me mistaken for some other bastard. So sit back down before I put ya back down."

Again the pregnant woman pulled on the robed man's hand, but he shook her away.

Aimi looked up at Jojo. Jojo shrugged down at Aimi, and they both returned their attention to the main deck of the carrack.

"No mistake," the robed man said. "Don't you remember me? Orin Syú, your father's steward."

Captain Stillwater was a few inches taller and broader than Syú, but he seemed to tower over him. Aimi realised that both the crew of *The Phoenix* and those who remained of the carrack were deathly silent; only the sound of the waves lapping against the hull and the creak of the rigging breaking the stillness.

"Last chance, mate," Stillwater said in a voice as cold as his grey eyes. "Ya obviously got me mixed up with someone else. So how about ya stop trying to save ya worthless skin and sit back down with the rest of these smart folk."

The captain turned and started back towards the sterncastle. Both crews relaxed.

"Your brother is still alive," the robed man said.

Captain Stillwater let out a long sigh and shook his head. He turned back to the captive.

"They call him the Sword of..." Syú said before the captain's fist collided with his face.

A couple of pirates cheered; most just watched in silence, and Aimi was no different.

The captain grabbed hold of the robed man by the neck before he could fall, and started dragging him towards the starboard railing. The pregnant woman was crying and begging for his forgiveness. The man seemed to regain his lucidity just as the captain drew his dagger and stabbed the poor fellow in the gut, then hauled him overboard. Aimi didn't even hear the splash as the man's body hit the water, and there were no screams other than the pregnant woman's.

Captain Stillwater spent a minute looking over the starboard railing before turning back to the prisoners gathered on the main deck.

"Anyone else reckon they taught me to read?" he said, to a chorus of silence. Without another word the captain mounted the ladder to the sterncastle deck and resumed his conversation with the quartermaster.

Aimi looked up at Jojo, who appeared unconcerned by the murder.

"Sometimes there's a bit more killing to be done," he said with a shrug, and again offered her the clay flask.

With night quickly approaching, lanterns were lit on both ships and, while *The Phoenix* floated leisurely nearby, the captured carrack was cleared of bodies and made ready to sail. It appeared the ship was to be taken back to New Sev'relain, where its goods could be offloaded and the ship itself could be repurposed into the pirate fleet. The prisoners – those that were in a healthy enough condition to serve – were quickly press-ganged into service, split between the two ships. The quartermaster was tasked with keeping all the men so busy they'd have no time to think about an ill-thought-out mutiny.

The captain had disappeared into his cabin soon after the capture of the carrack and had yet to emerge. Aimi was on the verge of going to see him when Morley caught her and put her to work scrubbing the deck of the carrack. Despite her wish to remain bloodless, Aimi found her hands and knees stained red. Never before had her decision to turn pirate and join *The Phoenix*'s crew seemed so real.

Now, with her shift over a good hour ago, every bone in her body aching, a weariness that would put the restless dead out of sorts, and the knowledge that her next shift was only a few hours away, Aimi wanted nothing so much as to crawl into her bunk and forget the world existed. She stopped halfway across the deck of *The Phoenix* and glanced towards the captain's cabin.

Aimi's better judgement screamed at her to keep walking, to drop down the hatch to the crew quarters and reward herself with some much earned sleep. Aimi had made a habit out of ignoring her better judgement. Her knock on the captain's door was not well received. After a moment's silence, Captain Stillwater barked out a couple of words, and though Aimi couldn't entirely understand them through the wooden slab, she was fairly certain they weren't an invitation to enter. She tried the handle and found the door unlocked.

"My mistake," the captain said, glancing up from the bucket he was hunched over. "I didn't realise where you're from, 'fuck off' means 'please come and interrupt me'. I'll remedy the situation immediately.

Unless the ship is on fire, there's a mutiny in progress, or Reowyn himself has appeared on my ship to reap his fill of souls – go. Away."

Aimi shut the door behind her and leaned against it. Captain Stillwater stared at her and sighed. "Part of the agreement of you serving aboard this ship is that you follow orders. My orders."

Aimi nodded. "I thought you might need to talk."

"I don't."

"I think you do."

The captain lifted his hands from the bucket and dripped red-tinged water onto the deck of his cabin. "Do you even... I mean, you are actually the most... argh!"

"Good." Aimi forced a cheerful smile onto her face despite her exhaustion. "Now we're past the denial. You shouldn't wash your clothes in salt water."

The captain nodded. "I don't exactly have spare fresh water to hand. What we do have is for drinking, not for washing."

"Well, you'd be better off using spit than salt water."

"Oh, really? Well, as you're obviously the expert, would you like to come over here and wash the blood out of my jacket?"

Aimi held up her hands to show the blisters she'd earned scrubbing the deck for hours. "Not really."

"You're the one wanted to join the crew. Don't go complaining just because Morley actually puts you to work."

Aimi raised an eyebrow. "I didn't complain."

Captain Stillwater went back to washing his jacket.

"You know you murdered that man today?" Aimi knew she shouldn't have mentioned it, but she needed to know why it had happened. The rest of the crew may be content to shrug off the murder, but she wasn't.

"I murdered a lot of men today," the captain said distantly. Aimi realised she was tense, gripping the door handle behind her with both hands. "We all did. You too. You might not have dealt the killing blow, but you helped us catch up to them, and that puts you as responsible as the rest of us. Congratulations, you're a pirate and a killer."

Aimi didn't like to think of herself as a murderer. She'd dealt out a few cuts and bruises in her days, but nobody had ever died from those wounds. The idea that she might be responsible for another person's death sat leaden in her gut.

"When I was young," Stillwater continued, "I used to think I could be a real heroic rogue. Stealing from those that deserved it and giving to those that needed it, and no one would get hurt. Doesn't work quite like that.

"We may steal from merchants, kings, and noble folk, aye, but they can afford the losses. The people that get hurt, they're the sailors hired to transport and protect the cargo. I steal from those that deserve it by killing those that need it, and don't have a single bit left over to give away to anyone. And I'm still no closer to Prin."

Aimi bit her lip, but her curiosity won out. "What's Prin?"

The captain fixed her with a cold grey stare so intense Aimi had to look away. "He's a man I need to find," he said eventually.

"How mysterious." Aimi grinned.

"Have you any idea how frustrating you are?"

"Yes," Aimi said, nodding. "Have you any idea how conflicted you sound?"

"Yes."

They stared at each other in silence for a long while. Aimi found it hard to tell what the captain was thinking behind his steely eyes, but he didn't look like he was about to try to throw her out again.

"I used to know exactly what I was doing," he said quietly. "Where I was going. Now I feel like a ship without a course. I'm just following Drake Morrass blindly. Honestly, I'm still not convinced I'm not following a demon right into a watery Hell."

Starry Dawn

If someone had asked Elaina just a few weeks ago, she would have quite firmly stated Cinto Ceno was the most uninhabitable island in the isles. She was glad someone hadn't asked her a few weeks ago, because now she would have to admit the mistake and would look a right fool to boot.

As the refugees from Lillingburn rushed down the gangplanks, they were greeted with open arms by folk who usually would have been suspicious, cautious, and downright hostile. Now they were welcoming and bordering on friendly.

"What in all the watery Hells is going on here?" Elaina asked of no one in particular.

"Fuckin' creepy, if ya ask me," Four-Eyed Pollick said. "Nobody in the isles is this welcomin'. We've got generations of breedin' to make us untrustin' bastards. Can ya imagine steppin' off the dock on Fango an' someone welcomin' ya with a clap on the back?"

"Depends if they had a knife in the other hand," Elaina said, watching the refugees being welcomed to their new home.

Elaina recognised one of the other ships floating out in the bay, *Mary's Virtue*. That meant the insufferable Daimen Poole was somewhere in the town, unless – and Elaina dared to hope – he'd been killed and someone else was now captain of the frigate. The second ship she didn't recognise. Elaina had never even heard of a boat called *North Gale* before.

"What do ya think?" she said to Rovel, to her right.

"I don't see *The Phoenix* anywhere. Stillwater ain't here. I think we should throw the rest of these mouths off our boat and sail back to Fango. Ya da won't be pleased we're here."

"Screw my da," Elaina said, and hoped none of her crew were secretly his. "I'm curious. Want to know what's going on here and how they managed to settle despite the burning cliffs and the sand monsters."

"Recognise the hat?" Pollick said with a sneer.

Elaina did recognise the hat that was strolling down the beach towards the docks. As far as she knew, only one man in all the isles wore a round-topped hat. Most preferred flat-tops or tricorns these days, but Daimen Poole liked to stand out.

"Reckon I might need a translator," Elaina said, grinning. "Bastard's accent is thicker than Gurn's porridge."

Poole reached the docks and greeted the refugees from Lillingburn; Elaina heard none of what was said from her position on *Starry Dawn*, but she got the distinct impression Poole was in charge of the town. After a brief conversation with some of the refugees, Poole started weaving his way through the bodies up to Elaina's ship.

"An' what brings the Lady Black ta our little town? Other than droppin' off these fine folk, that is."

"Lillingburn is gone." Elaina stared down at the man, refusing to join him on the dock and refusing to extend him an invitation onto her ship.

"So I hear. Reckon that evil bastard you call Da would prefer you took these folk ta Fango, but, well, here ya are."

Elaina ignored the insult to her father. Poole would get what was coming to him in due course. "They wanted to come here. I wanted to see if you really had colonised Cinto Cena."

"Aye? Well, as ya can see, we've colonised the fuck out of it. Bye now." Poole turned to walk away.

"We have goods to sell." Elaina smirked down at the man. "Assuming your little town does actually facilitate our profession."

Poole stopped, and Elaina could tell by the slump of his shoulders that he'd let out a sigh.

"Cap," Rovel hissed. "Ya da won't be pleased if ya sell here."

"Shut up. I have a plan, and you will fucking well follow my orders."

"Aye," Poole said without turning around. "Little building attached to the tavern is where you'll find the man with the money. He'll buy ya crap off ya."

After Poole had walked away, Elaina turned on Rovel like a storm cloud. "Next time you try to contradict me like that I'll have you mounted onto the keel of the ship. Folk here are in straights, just look at the town up the beach. Plenty of mouths, and I don't reckon they got near enough supplies. That means they'll pay over the odds for any old loot we can give them. That and the longer we're here, the more shit we can dig up to take back to my da." Elaina didn't mention that she wanted to wait for Keelin to come back.

Rovel didn't look convinced. "You heard the folk from Lillingburn, Cap. This here is Drake Morrass' town. What'll he do to us if he comes back?"

"Likely he'll wet himself," Elaina spat. "Morrass is a coward. Only reason my da hasn't already gutted him is the bastard is too good at running away."

It was three days before Keelin returned to New Sev'relain, and in that time Elaina sold all *Starry Dawn*'s loot, allowed her crew the run of the town, and drunk herself into a stupor twice. She was back aboard her ship, stark naked and enjoying a saltwater wash when the call went up. *The Phoenix* had been spotted rounding the shore line and was heading into the bay.

Elaina didn't rush; she wouldn't let her crew see her excitement. She calmly finished scrubbing herself down, doused herself with another bucket of salt water, and walked back to the cabin. Once inside with the door closed, however, she became a flurry of activity.

Elaina wanted to be waiting on the docks when Keelin stepped off his ship. He'd know she was here by now – it was impossible to hide *Starry Dawn* – but she wanted to see his face as he docked with his town and saw her waiting. After that she'd drag him to the nearby inn, or to her ship, or maybe back onto his, and they'd pick up right where they'd left off. It had been a while since Elaina had had a good fuck, and it was fair to say she was looking forward to their reunion.

Elaina dressed black on black, with britches, a shirt, and a long jacket over the top. She bound her breasts a little higher than usual and buttoned her shirt a little lower. After running a brush quickly through her hair, she decided to leave it down instead of in her usual tail, and after pulling on her newest pair of boots, she delved into her oils, powders, and scent kit. Elaina was not one to make herself up regularly, but she knew how to when it suited her, and knew she would turn heads. She ran some scented oil through her hair and wrapped a black bandana over it, sprayed a similar scent onto her clothes, and ringed her eyes with a black powder to make her icy blues stand out.

When she was finished she emerged into the morning light and buckled a rapier onto her belt before leaping down to the docks and making her way to the free berth, just as *The Phoenix* was being towed in by her dinghies.

Keelin spotted her. She could see him standing at the railing, and when he looked her way it was obvious. Elaina cut a striking figure on the worst of days, and right now she was on one of her best. She fixed a wry smile onto her face and waited. Keelin was the first ashore, leaping down onto the docks as soon as *The Phoenix* was in place and long before any gangplanks had been extended. Behind him, his crew rushed to get the ship tied and docked, and a few of them jumped down to follow him, but he was far ahead. Elaina knew he'd missed her as much as she had him, even if neither would admit it.

"Elaina…" Keelin started as he stopped just a pace from her.

She gave him no time to continue. Closing the gap between them with one easy stride, Elaina went up onto her toes and kissed Keelin, grabbing his cock through his britches at the same time.

For a long moment Keelin kissed her back, and Elaina felt him going hard. She leaned into him and wondered which was closest, her cabin or his. Then Keelin stepped backwards, breaking the kiss and making Elaina stumble to catch her feet.

"Elaina…"

"What?"

"We're not doing this," Keelin said, and it didn't look like he was joking. Elaina felt an anger pulsing up from somewhere deep down, but it did nothing to stop her feeling horny.

"Why not?" she asked stupidly. "Felt like you were up for it."

Keelin glanced behind him quickly. "We're just not anymore."

Elaina looked past Keelin to see a few members of his crew securing the ship, others in the dinghies, and one just a dozen paces back trying desperately not to look interested in her captain and Elaina.

"Really?" Elaina felt her cheeks go hot, as well as a pressing need to hit either Keelin or the bitch. "That mousy waif?"

The girl looked up at the insult, and there was a fire in her dull brown eyes, but it was nothing compared to the inferno raging in Elaina's chest, choking her breath and making her want to scream.

"She's not..." Keelin started, but Elaina wasn't about to stand around to let the bastard finish.

Elaina gave Keelin the full force of her anger in a glare that could have boiled the sea. "Fuck you, Stillwater." She turned and strode away.

Her anger filled her like a furnace, and it was all she could do to not stab the nearest man she came across, but Elaina kept her sword firmly in its sheath. She couldn't go back to her ship – it would look too much like running away, both to Keelin and her crew – so she headed for the next best place. The tavern.

Starry Dawn

Elaina wanted to get drunk. She wanted the sweet bliss of intoxication to dull the pain. The only problem was she didn't feel like drinking. After ordering one mug of what passed for ale, it now sat untouched on the table, both tempting and repulsing her.

It was a lively place, the Righteous Indignation. Men and women drank, sang, danced, and drank some more. Her own crew mingled with those from *Mary's Virtue*, *North Gale*, and *The Phoenix*, and with the townsfolk as well, and it was both merry and rowdy.

Some men and women paired up and slipped out, while others stayed to keep the money flowing in the direction of the tavern owner. A number of competitions started up, tests of strength or durability and even a brief wrestling match. Pirates and sailors alike spent most of their lives aboard a ship with only brief interludes ashore where they could truly unwind, and unwind they did. Elaina didn't join them. While most of the tavern was loud, lively, and filled with song or laughter, Elaina's corner was a void of merriment. She sat alone, her boots up on the table, scowling at everything and everyone. No one dared approach, not even the serving boy, and those that glanced her way quickly moved their eyes elsewhere. All but the giant of a man she remembered from Fango. Khan, she seemed to remember his name was, and he wasn't subtle about his interest in Elaina – though even he didn't dare to come near.

Elaina didn't want to be there. Not in the tavern, not in New Sev'relain, not even in the isles. Right now she wanted to be anywhere but, yet there she was and there she would stay. If *Starry Dawn* sailed out now, it would look like she was running away, and that wasn't something she could live with. She'd already run away from her father and from Fango, and she couldn't run away from Keelin and this shit hole as well.

Why he'd choose that little slip of a girl still didn't make any sense to her. Elaina had known Keelin since they were children. He'd walked onto *The Black Death* at just thirteen years old and demanded a spot on the crew. Tanner wasn't the type of man to take demands, especially aboard his own ship, so he'd had Keelin beaten to a bloody mess. But

Where Loyalties Lie

Tanner had seen something in the boy, something that made him stop short of killing Keelin, and he'd given the lad what he wanted. Elaina was eleven at the time, and she'd seen something in Keelin too, though it was likely a very different something.

For years Elaina and Keelin had been inseparable whether on the ship or off, and it hadn't been long before they were far more than just friends. Elaina's father had known what they were doing, but Tanner didn't care who she fucked and he'd liked Keelin, treated him almost as another son. Elaina even got pregnant once, but long before she'd told Keelin and before she'd even decided whether to keep it or not, she lost the wretched thing.

Then came *The Phoenix*. Tanner captured the galleon, and a true prize she was, even more beautiful than *The Black Death*. Blu already had his ship and Elaina was just old enough to take her own command, so Tanner gave her the boat and let her pick a few crew members to go with her. Of course she'd taken Keelin, though her father had almost refused that request. It was no secret he wanted Keelin to have a ship of his own under Tanner's command.

Elaina still didn't know how Keelin had managed it, but the bastard turned a few of the crew, and before Elaina even had a chance to sail her new ship, Keelin and Yanic stole the damned thing and ran.

Tanner had been furious, threatening death and worse as soon as he caught Stillwater, but Elaina hadn't been angry in the slightest; if anything it only made her want Keelin more.

It wasn't like they were promised. They'd never made any commitments to each other, and they both knew they'd fucked others, but Elaina had always thought they had a connection. No matter what happened in-between, every time they ended up at the same port, the sparks flew and left them both feeling sore. Every time one sailed away from the other, Elaina found it harder and harder.

Elaina's mother had once told her that some people were born to be together and that fate would guide them to each other again and again until they fulfilled their destiny. Elaina had thought it a tale full of shit. Deep down, though, she'd honestly believed she and Keelin were being pushed together by fate. Never had she chosen another man over him and, until now, he'd never chosen another woman. It was maddening, and Elaina knew full well that madness ran in her family.

As her mood spiralled darker and darker, Elaina finally decided it was time to stop before she did something stupid. She downed half the mug of ale in one go and was just thinking about vacating her lone table and joining the festivities when the tavern door opened and Keelin walked through, followed closely by the little girl he'd chosen.

Elaina relaxed back into her seat, all thoughts of enjoying her evening forgotten, and sent an icy glare towards Keelin and his new lover. The girl was the first to notice, perhaps sensing hostile eyes following her, and whispered into Keelin's ear. Elaina felt her rage surge as the woman clearly laid claim to her captain.

Keelin pointed towards a group of men from his crew, and the girl reluctantly left his side. Elaina watched as he approached her table.

"Mind if I sit, Elaina?"

She considered kicking the spare chair into his legs. It would be a petty thing to do and would never cause any real damage, so she refrained. She nodded just once by way of reply.

Keelin pulled out the chair and sat slowly, never taking his eyes from Elaina. "About earlier…"

"You work for Morrass now?" Elaina said. An idea had popped into her head, a way to punish Keelin and a way to get back into her father's graces all at once.

"I… We work together," Keelin said awkwardly. "He has a plan for the isles, Elaina. I think it might be a good thing."

"Aye?" Elaina glanced towards the girl, to find her staring right back. Elaina let slip an ugly grin and turned her attention back to Keelin.

"He wants to unify the folk of the isles. All of us. He wants us to stand up against the other kingdoms, not just hide from them."

"Can't unify shit without my da on his side."

"We know."

"What if I can do that?"

Keelin looked confused. "You really think you can get Tanner to talk to Drake?"

Elaina smiled and held Keelin's eyes until he looked away. "My da knows we're in the shit as well as you do. Bastards are burning our towns, killing us. Best way to stop that is together. He knows it. Just don't wanna be the one to make the first move. Now, if we were to say that Drake asked for a parley – well, that'd look like Drake was coming to my da, not the other way round."

"Drake isn't here," Keelin pointed out as if Elaina didn't already know.

"But he will be soon?"

"Any time now." Keelin sounded far less than certain.

"Seventy days from now," Elaina said. "On Ash."

Ash was a small island far away from both New Sev'relain and Fango, and it could be considered neutral ground. The island was too small to be habitable; it was little more than rock and sand with a few overgrown weeds daring to call themselves trees, but it was a good place to spring a trap. If she could convince Keelin to drag Drake to his own execution, her father would have no choice but to accept Elaina back into his good books. She might even be able to ask for Corin's release.

The thought of Corin tugged open the wound in Elaina's chest, and at that moment she wanted nothing so much as to tell Keelin about it. He would understand her pain; he'd always understood her.

Keelin appeared to be mulling it over in his head, but eventually he nodded. "Seventy days from now on Ash." He hesitated. "Elaina, about earlier. Aimi…"

Elaina pulled her feet off the table and leaned forwards to give the bastard a good view of her cleavage. She barked out a savage laugh. "I don't care who you fuck, *Captain* Stillwater."

Before Keelin could say anything else, Elaina stood and walked away. She crossed the room to where Captain Khan was sitting, and with two words whispered in his ear he followed her back to *Starry Dawn*.

Part 4 - Parley

You need Tanner said the Oracle
Drake laughed
He'll come to you said the Oracle

Fortune

"As you can see, Drake, in your absence we've made a few improvements."

Stillwater wasn't wrong about that. By Drake's estimate, the size of New Sev'relain had more than doubled in his months away, and not just in the land it now claimed. Hundreds of people were living in the town, and it was a busy, thriving settlement that already came close to rivalling the size of old Sev'relain.

The bones of the Man of War still sat tall and proud on the beach, but it was no more than a skeleton left to remind the folk of the isles just what they were capable of. And the folk of Sarth just what they were up against.

Halfway up the beach, towards the tree line, the docks ended and the town began with stalls set up by enterprising merchants already dotting the sand, and even a few poorly constructed tents offering pirates "Cheap Hores!". Fire pits, old and new, darkened patches of the sand where those men without enough coin for the tavern kept themselves happy and lubricated.

A large warehouse rose up just apart from the town. It was marked by a number of armed men loitering around the exterior and a raised guard tower to its rear.

One of the first things Drake noticed as they approached the town was a raised wooden stage in what could possibly pass as the town square. Beyond the stage, rushed buildings stretched off in almost every direction with alleys that snaked between in a twisting maze of dirt, trees, waste, and the occasional unconscious pirate.

"What's that for?" Drake nodded towards the stage.

"Folk built it for a duel," Stillwater said. "Afterwards, they reckoned it'd be worth keeping around. Public declarations and what not are held there so everyone can hear the news. Lillingburn is gone. Five Kingdoms soldiers took it and burned it to the ground. Bunch of survivors fled here, swelled the population some. We've had extra houses knocked up, a second tavern and brothel, but we're finding problems supplying the taverns with booze and the brothels with whores."

Drake groaned. He'd been back on dry land for all of five minutes and already he was being saddled with the problems Stillwater was too single-minded to solve.

"What about the whores on the beach?" Drake asked. "The ones in the tents."

"They ain't clean," Stillwater said, sucking on his teeth. "Fuck with them and you're like to find your cock dropping off. Can't stop them trying to sell their wares, but we can try to put folk off buying them."

"How many sailors?" Drake mounted the stage and looked around the town square. A few shops had opened, but they were barely more than well-dressed stalls. Lots of homes and a rough-looking tavern were new. Nearby he could hear the sound of sawing as felled trees were turned into planks of wood for more buildings.

"Three ships' worth and a few more. Captain Poole and Captain Khan are with us. They're out pirating right now. Most folk that know how to sail are with one of the crews, except for a few fishermen, but we're short on those and on boats for them. Besides, I reckon anyone who knows how to fish is more useful than a pirate right now. We're fine on water, but food is short."

"How many fighters?"

"We've got a few acting as authority around town just to keep the peace. Most folk who can fight are already aboard a ship."

"Shit." Drake shook his head.

"What?"

Drake waved towards the port. "I've got ships and more coming, but each one is sporting a skeleton crew and even fewer folk who know how to fight. We've only had two captains sign up so far?"

Stillwater laughed. "About that. A few others have stopped on by. They ain't picking sides just yet, Drake. Not while Tanner is on the other one."

Drake spat. He would happily have cursed Tanner Black if he'd known any that would work. The bastard had been a thorn in Drake's side for too long, and he needed dealing with sooner rather than later. Before more captains settled on his side.

"Elaina Black stopped by a couple of weeks back," Stillwater said.

Drake glanced at the man to find him staring out to sea. "That so? We all know about your history with that little snake."

Stillwater ignored the jibe. "She said Tanner wants to meet you. Too many of our settlements are being destroyed, and too many of our people are being killed…"

"Tanner doesn't give a fuck about the people," Drake interrupted.

"He gives a fuck about the isles. He gives a fuck about himself, his family, and his freedom. I don't know where the captain of the Man of War got those charts, but he didn't get them from Tanner. And the cold hard truth of it, Drake, is that if you two don't hammer out some sort of agreement, and soon, none of this we're doing here will matter a damn. The bastards are trying to kill us, and you two are one step from handing them the knives to do it."

There was an insufferable clarity in what Stillwater was saying, and Drake knew it. He and Tanner had been circling each other for years, occasionally nipping at the other's toes, but never going in for the kill, and there was a reason for that. They needed each other if they were going to survive. Drake knew it, and he just hoped Tanner Black knew it too.

"What about the pickings?" Drake said.

Stillwater paused, looking around to make certain no one was within earshot. "They ain't good. Folk are having to venture further abroad and still coming back with little to nothing. The merchants are starting to avoid the isles, carving out new trade routes, and those are being patrolled by navy."

"Aye." Drake nodded. "Make us go further out to catch them while the navy ships come and slaughter our people back here. Can't keep on like this. We need food, water, ships, weapons, and more than any of that, Stillwater, we need people."

Starry Dawn

Fango never changed. For as long as Elaina had known the place it had been infested by semi-aggressive trees and run by her father, and it had used Quartermain as its legitimate front. Only the people changed, and Elaina wasn't certain that was for the better.

There were new ships in north port, and Elaina had already heard rumblings that there were some in south port too. The population of the town had swelled with the influx and was closing in on bursting point.

Fair View was gone now as well, and the list of pirate settlements was growing smaller. Survivors had managed to flee the massacre at Fair View, and they were telling stories of a ship like none they'd ever seen before, flying the Five Kingdoms flag and escorted by no fewer than three galleons. It was a terrifying prospect that the Five Kingdoms were able to field such a force. The surviving Pirate Isles refugees were fleeing to the place they considered safest: Fango. If only they knew just how dangerous the island was, they might flee elsewhere, but when the choice was between the Isle of Goats and the Isle of Many Deaths, it seemed an easy one.

It wasn't just refugees running to the safety of Tanner Black's island sanctuary. Pirate ships were appearing in greater numbers than ever before, claiming to need repairs and supplies. They were hiding from the Five Kingdoms ship, hoping that the bastards would either pass the island by or be scared away by the pirates' numbers.

Elaina stopped to listen to an argument some of the refugees were having with one of Fango's carpenters. From the sounds of things the refugees were less than enthusiastic about having their new home built above ground. The carpenter was, quite rightly, explaining that space on the ground came at a premium and only the rich could afford it. Elaina laughed and walked on. Tanner had long ago laid claim to the land, and he charged people a lot of money to live on the forest floor. Even funnier to Elaina, though, was that the floor was a much more dangerous place than the tree houses, but most folk wouldn't accept such a thing until they'd witnessed for themselves how a man could die from a simple shoe dropped from a great height.

"Captain Black?" Elaina turned to see a man in a faded Five Kingdoms navy uniform flanked by two bruisers with arms as thick as her legs. "You are Captain Black, yes?"

"One of 'em," Elaina said cautiously. "Reckon that uniform ain't earnin' you any friends, hmm?"

The man nodded. "Indeed not. Still, we must remember where we come from. Merridan Barklow, captain of *Hearth Fire*." Barklow extended his hand. Elaina ignored it.

"Good for you," she said, and made to walk past him.

"If you don't mind," the captain said, moving to block Elaina's flight. "I would like a private meeting with your father."

Elaina glanced at the two bruisers behind Barklow; they were unarmed, but looked like they could deal out some punishment even without a weapon. Barklow, on the other hand, carried a sabre attached to his belt and, judging by his uniform, had some experience poking folk with it.

"Best go see him then. He'll likely be up in the brothel." Elaina sidestepped the captain and started walking again.

"Now listen here." Barklow grabbed hold of her arm.

Elaina was in no mood for manhandling, and especially not from some ex-navy captain who clearly thought her just another waif. She turned her arm in a quick arc, removing Barklow's hand, and punched him as hard as she could in the nose. The captain stumbled away, collapsing onto the ground and clutching at his bleeding face. His two bruisers started forwards. Elaina drew her sword.

"Back down, lads," she hissed.

"Stop. Stop," Barklow sputtered from behind his bloody hands. He flailed about a moment longer before one of the bruisers helped him up.

"Ya bleeding, mate," Elaina said with a grin, still holding her sword.

"I meant no…" Barklow started, but was interrupted by a cough that brought up flecks of red. "I would like a private meeting with your father. I hoped you could arrange it. I have news for his ears only."

Elaina considered the request for a moment. Her father wouldn't be pleased if she turned the captain away only for his information to be valuable, but if it was shit then Elaina might well foot the blame. She put her sword away.

"How about you tell it ta me, and I relay it to Tanner, hmm?"

Merridan Barklow shook his bloody head.

Elaina felt like skewering the man. "Fine," she hissed. "Come up to the brothel with me and I'll have a word. Might want to leave your dogs behind though."

Barklow didn't look like he'd be willing, or able, to make the climb up to the brothel, so Elaina consented to using the lift even though she hated the idea of putting her life in the hands of the donkey winding the gears. In her experience donkeys ranged from placid in temperament to downright murderous, and it was nothing but luck as to which you got.

She stepped off the lift with Barklow just a pace behind, and once they were both inside, she told the captain to wait while she approached her father. Tanner was in his usual spot, presiding over his little court. Blu was there too, and Elaina wished the bastard would just pull up his anchor and actually play the pirate for once.

"Da," Elaina said, stopping in front of her father's gathering and giving each member a wary glare. Tanner was hosting a large number today, and Elaina counted fifteen men including his raping bastard of a first mate, Mace.

Tanner Black looked up at Elaina and smiled. He was a dangerous man when angry and even more dangerous when happy. "Come to weather the coming storm, daughter?"

Elaina needed to get her father alone; she had to talk to him about Keelin and Drake, and she didn't want to do it with Blu and the rest of the court around. Luckily for her, Captain Barklow had provided a useful opportunity.

"Captain of *Hearth Fire*," Elaina said, thumbing in Barklow's direction. "Reckons he's got some useful words to be said to you and you only."

Tanner Black leaned sideways to look past his daughter and stared towards the bleeding captain.

"Tell him to fuck off," Blu said with a sneer.

"Quiet, boy," Tanner snapped. "Never underestimate the usefulness of a pandering, rat-infested fop like Merridan Barklow."

"You know him?" Elaina said.

Tanner turned his dark gaze on Elaina, and she felt like shrinking from those eyes. "No. Perhaps we should meet."

Tanner drained his mug and stood. Blu got up with him, just as tall and just as broad but without the imposing air. Tanner Black didn't stop his son from following, so Elaina joined her brother, giving him a savage, three-fingered poke in his ribs. Blu swung an elbow in retaliation, but Elaina easily ducked it and hurried to catch up with their father, grinning over her little victory.

Merridan Barklow seemed to grow smaller as Tanner and his two children approached, and it would have been hard not to notice the intense fear on the man's face.

Tanner walked past the man into an unoccupied alcove, and Elaina followed him. Blu stopped by Captain Barklow and shoved him along to join them. Blu pushed Barklow down onto the bench that lined the alcove's walls and moved to join Elaina and their father, who were still not sitting. The poor captain looked ready to shit himself, and Elaina didn't blame him. It was frightening enough to be faced down by Tanner Black, but Merridan was also staring into the snarling face of Blu, who had inherited his father's imposing size, and Elaina, who had inherited her father's dark stare. She wagered that was more than enough to loosen most men's bowels.

For a long while the tension held, with Captain Barklow looking anywhere but at the three Captain Blacks facing him. Elaina fought to control a deep laugh that threatened to erupt, and managed to keep her face straight. Blu wasn't so composed, and a snigger escaped his lips, breaking the tension. Tanner turned a seething glare on his son, and behind his back Elaina pulled a stupid face at her brother.

"So," Tanner growled, putting both hands on the small table between him and Barklow and leaning forwards. "Captain Barklow. My daughter tells me ya got something to say?"

"Well…" Barklow coughed. "I would like to start by offering my allegiance to you, Tanner."

"Cap'n Black," Blu said quickly.

"Um…" Barklow coughed again. "Of course. Captain Black."

Tanner smiled, all teeth and flashing eyes, and Elaina watched him closely. "You'd give me command of that little ship o' yours, would ya?"

Barklow paled and his eyes bulged. "I mean to say I'll sail in your fleet," he corrected himself. "With *Hearth Fire* under my command, of course."

"Aye?"

"Yes," Barklow asserted.

"Good. I'll take thirty percent of your takes from now on then, mate."

"Thirty percent?" Barklow winced, his fingernails digging into the table.

"Of course. Standard cut for a captain in my fleet. In return ya get ta tell folk ya sail under my flag, and ya can call Fango ya home and *safe* harbour." Tanner Black was no fool; he was shrewder than most folk gave him credit for, and he knew exactly why Merridan Barklow was there. And he was more than willing to extort the fool. "Good?"

Barklow nodded, it was obvious he had no choice. With Sarth and the Five Kingdoms burning pirate towns all over, he needed to pick a side and sign his allegiance. Tanner and Fango would seem a safer bet than Drake and New Sev'relain.

"Good," Barklow said, tying himself to Tanner Black – and Tanner was not a man who let ties go easily.

"So what is it ya have to tell me?" Tanner sat down opposite Captain Barklow, and both Elaina and Blu quickly followed suit.

"There's a ship built by the Five Kingdoms, *Storm Herald*, and it's here in the isles."

Elaina couldn't tell whether Barklow was terrified because of the company or the thought of the ship.

"Was it the ship that destroyed Lillingburn?" she said.

Tanner shot his daughter a look then, and she realised that he didn't know about Lillingburn.

"I believe so, yes," Barklow said. "And Fair View. It's no normal ship. It's built to end our occupation of these isles. A warship with machines of war and as many soldiers as a Man of War. If that wasn't enough, it's also being escorted by three galleons. That's probably close to a thousand men. An army come to kill us all."

Even Tanner seemed speechless. He had maybe a thousand sailors under his command if he brought all of his ships into one fleet, but many of those were sailors only, not fighters. Not soldiers. If that number of troops decided to take Fango, Elaina didn't think even the dangers of the Isle of Goats would stop them.

"Do they know where Fango is?" Tanner said eventually.

Barklow shook his head. "I don't know. A source of mine from my old navy days got the information to me. He said the *Storm Herald* is being captained by Peter Verit."

"I don't know him," Tanner said sourly.

"I do, Captain Black," Barklow said with fear plain in his eyes. "A more experienced captain I have yet to meet. He is the type of man who will break before he bends."

"No dealing with him then?"

"Most certainly not. He's a royal bastard; the blood of the Five Kingdoms runs through his veins. I have also heard the soldiers have a number of knights among them, including the Sword of the North."

That gave them all a healthy amount of pause. If the Five Kingdoms were sending the Sword of the North, it meant they were no longer fucking around. There weren't many who hadn't heard of that bastard's deeds, and Elaina felt the sudden urge to sail as far away as she could.

"One man dies the same as any other in the sea's cold embrace," Tanner growled, but he'd waited too long, and Elaina could tell that even he was worried.

"They won't come to Fango," Blu said.

"What makes ya so sure, boy?" Tanner snapped.

"They just won't." Blu sounded worried as well, and he was right to be. "They can't. Not Fango."

Tanner waved away his son's foolishness. "Anything else, Captain Barklow?"

"Um, no. I don't think…"

"Then ya can go, mate. Enjoy Fango. I'll no doubt be calling on ya soon."

Tanner waited for Barklow to say his goodbyes and leave before he spoke again. Elaina shuffled around the bench in the silence to face her father and brother.

"Looks like we got ourselves a bit of a problem," Tanner said, making what Elaina could only assume was a purposeful understatement.

"I might have the solution," she said.

Both her father and brother turned unbelieving eyes on her, and Elaina felt her pride bristle.

"If we had Drake's ships as well as ours, we could fight these bastards off." Elaina searched her father's face for a reaction.

Blu laughed.

"I stopped off at New Sev'relain," Elaina said quickly, hoping her father wouldn't beat her bloody right there.

Blu stopped laughing, but his face was all a nasty smile.

"That why ya sail into my port without a drop of loot?" Tanner's voice was cold. "Trading with the enemy now?"

"Drake wasn't there," Elaina continued, despite the cold sensation creeping up from her guts. "Keelin was."

If anything, Tanner's expression grew darker, but he said nothing.

"They know they're fucked as well as we do," Elaina barrelled on. "And they know they need us. Keelin agreed to set up a meet between you and Morrass. On Ash, in thirty-two days' time." Elaina had been counting down the days in her head ever since their meeting on New Sev'relain.

"Turn up under the guise of friendship and kill both the bastards and take their ships and crew for my own," Tanner said, fingering his beard. "Certainly has a nice sound to it."

Elaina took a deep breath. All she had to do was keep quiet and let things run their course, and she would have revenge on Keelin for shunning her and the goodwill of her father for giving him Drake Morrass.

"Keelin is in on it," she said before her brain could decide it was a bad idea. Once the words were out she couldn't deny them.

"What's that now?" Tanner said.

"Keelin is Drake's second," Elaina continued, hoping it was true. "He'll bring Drake to Ash; we kill Drake, Keelin will bring the ships and their crews over to us."

"That's shit," Blu said. "Ya just don't want us to…"

"It's a good plan," Tanner interrupted. "Only you won't be there, daughter."

"What?" Elaina all but shouted. She needed to be there to make sure Keelin played his part and didn't try to protect Drake. Now she'd decided not to have him killed right along with Morrass, it dawned on her that she didn't want him killed. "I brought this to you, Da."

"Aye, ya did, and I'm thankful. But I've a need to send someone on an errand, and I reckon I'm choosing you. Ya don't think straight where Stillwater is concerned, daughter, and it might just be we need to deal with him and Morrass together."

"But, Da…"

"Quiet," Tanner roared, and the whole brothel silenced. "Decision's made." With that Tanner stood and walked away with a gesture towards his court that brought men scurrying after him. It was only then Elaina realised she hadn't even had a chance to ask after Corin.

"Don't worry, El," Blu said with a smile that almost bordered on genuine. "I'll make sure we bring back Stillwater's cock for ya. Reckon I'll nail it to his ship's figurehead along with his shrivelled up stones." He laughed and walked away, leaving Elaina to wonder if it was too late to warn Keelin about what was coming.

The Phoenix

Ten ships occupied the docks of Cinto Cena, a small fleet, and they all floated leisurely in the calm waters. Not all of them were properly manned – they simply didn't have enough pirates to fill them all – but five were fighting fit: *Fortune*, *The Phoenix*, *Mary's Virtue*, *North Gale*, and *Rheel Toa*.

Deun Burn, captain of *Rheel Toa*, had broken his rule of never bringing his ship into port, because the Riverlander had realised – as had they all – that the folk of the isles were in trouble, and a ship alone was asking for that trouble. It was a small fleet so far, but Drake insisted more ships were coming and more pirates with them.

Keelin didn't need to stay aboard his ship; he now had a small house in New Sev'relain. But the house was bare and unoccupied, and had been since its construction. Keelin preferred the ship. Preferred to feel the sea beneath him in its gentle sway and tilt. He also didn't trust Smithe to be left alone aboard *The Phoenix*. The treacherous quartermaster was ever looking to undermine Keelin's authority with constant threats and insults.

There was one other reason Keelin stayed aboard his ship, and that was Aimi. Even floating at leisure, there were still more jobs aboard ship than they had enough men for, which was made even worse by half of the crew being ashore. Some of the men were visiting taverns or the brothels, and some had even found a woman and a house to call their own. The jobs were mostly maintenance, from tending to rope to leaning the ship and scraping the hull. Aimi, as the lowest-ranked crew member aboard, tended to find herself on the business end of many of those jobs. Keelin could have used his authority to spare her from them, but she'd have seethed at the special treatment, and they were getting on so well he was loathe to do anything that might jeopardise the growing fondness.

Without fail, come the end of Aimi's shift she would knock at the door to Keelin's cabin and they would spend hours talking, sharing a drink, or even just enjoying each other's company. She'd listen, offer advice for his problems, and tell stories from her past. He'd do the same, though his stories never touched on his time before taking residence on *The Black Death*. After the incident with his father's old steward aboard the carrack, Keelin knew some of the crew had suspicions. He wouldn't risk his true past coming out even with Aimi. He knew he'd lose the crew's respect if they found out about his noble birth.

There was a soft knock at the door and Keelin felt his stomach flutter. "Come in," he said eagerly.

The door opened, and Feather stood at the threshold, looking in.

"Oh," Keelin said, feeling his spirits drop. "What do you want, lad?"

Feather looked uncomfortable. "Sorry, Cap'n," he said as he turned and walked away, exposing a giggling Aimi standing behind him.

"Damnit, woman, you're a menace," Keelin said with a grin. "Get in here."

Aimi stepped inside, closing the door behind her, and sauntered over to Keelin's chest. "I figured it's about time you treated me to the good stuff instead of that swill you like to drink." She smiled mischievously.

"What makes you think I keep any good booze in there?" Keelin asked innocently.

Aimi sighed, popped the latch on the chest, and opened the lid. It took her only a moment of rummaging to pull out the bottle of Bolera two-year brandy he'd taken from the captain's cabin on the carrack.

"How did you know?" he said, but Aimi only smiled by way of reply. She placed the bottle on Keelin's desk and collapsed into the chair behind it. It was his own chair she lounged in, and had it been anyone else he'd have given them a beating and launched them over the side of his ship, but with Aimi he could only smile and allow her the impropriety.

Keelin sat down in the chair in front of his desk, put his feet up, and pulled the cork from the bottle before taking a healthy swig and sliding the brandy towards Aimi. She put her own feet up on the desk, mimicking Keelin's position, and took an equally healthy swig. She winced.

"This is the good stuff?"

Keelin grinned. "It's the strong stuff."

"That makes it good?"

Keelin shrugged; he honestly couldn't tell the difference himself. "What has Morley had you doing today?"

Aimi grimaced. "I don't think your first mate likes me much." Keelin suspected it was her familiarity with the captain that Morley didn't like. "First I had to scrub down the poop deck, then he hung me over the side of the ship to wash the shit off. Have you ever had to clean shit off the side of a ship, Keelin?"

"More times than I care to remember, thanks, and I'm more than glad those days are over."

"I know we all have to shit over the side, but that doesn't make cleaning it any better." Aimi took another swig of brandy as if to wash away the thought. "I had to jump into the bay to wash the smell off afterwards. Morley caught me and decided I needed another job. So for the past..." She paused. "Well, I don't even know how long I was down there, but I've been below decks hunting the rat carcasses left by the mangy, flea-ridden hissing ball of death you call a ship's pet."

Keelin grinned at her. "All jobs that need doing, and there's not a man aboard this ship who hasn't done them a hundred times before. I bet Feather loves having you aboard. Those jobs always used to fall to him."

"Well, he can have them back." Aimi scowled, but it only made her more beautiful to Keelin. He'd never been interested in women who powdered themselves and doused themselves in strange scents. He liked women who smelled of the sea and weren't afraid to be smudged with dirt, and Aimi was both of those things and more.

He looked at her now and felt an almost overwhelming urge to leap across the desk. Her mousy brown hair had largely escaped its tie and was in complete disarray, her freckled face was dusty and sun beaten – though that only made her dark eyes seem even darker – and her breasts, though she strapped them, were large enough to be apparent through her shirt. Keelin longed to know them and every other curve, contour, and dimple of her body.

"Thanks for the attention there, Captain," Aimi said, and Keelin realised she'd caught him staring at her chest. "And yes, it is uncomfortable strapping them down. No, it's not more comfortable to not strap them down. And yes, it's hard work stopping your crew from catching an eyeful every morning while I do strap them down." Aimi paused. "Which is why I think you're the only member of the crew who hasn't already seen my tits. If you'd like to give me my own cabin to stop the puss-brained maggots from ogling me every morning, I would not say no."

Keelin wasn't sure how to deal with Aimi's outburst; he wasn't even sure if she was joking or not, so he just took the brandy bottle and drank while she laughed.

"So, when do we sail?" Aimi said.

"Soon. No more than a few days, I reckon. We should get there on time, but…" Keelin sighed. "Weather permitting, of course."

"You trust her?"

Keelin looked up to find Aimi staring intently at the brandy bottle, and he slid it her way; even once she had it she didn't look at him.

"No." Keelin stood and started pacing in front of the desk. "No, I don't trust Elaina. I don't trust Tanner. I'm not even sure I trust Drake."

"Why not?"

"I don't know. Because he's a pirate," Keelin growled. "Hells, I'm a pirate. We're all bloody pirates, and as a rule, pirates aren't exactly to be trusted." He turned to resume his pacing and found Aimi in front of him. He hadn't even noticed her move from behind the desk.

"What are you…" he started, but stopped as she slid her hands down his trousers and grabbed hold of his cock. "Oh."

It didn't take long for Keelin to forget what he was saying, about as long as it took his cock to get hard. Which, given Aimi's stroking, rubbing, and staring up into his eyes, wasn't long at all. Aimi dropped to her knees in front of him, pulling his trousers down as she did, and Keelin wondered how she'd undone his belt buckle without him noticing. Of course, that thought was soon purged from his head as well as she slid her lips down his cock and started sucking. Keelin gasped and gripped hold of the desk behind him, before relaxing into the pleasuring. He looked down to find Aimi staring up at him with dark, playful eyes as she moved back and forth.

Keelin didn't last long, and as she swallowed his seed and washed it down with brandy, he attempted to remember how to form words.

"So why don't you trust Drake?" Aimi asked again between sips.

Keelin said the first thing that came into his head. "Because everybody knows Drake Morrass is only out for himself."

"Figured that might clear your head. Aren't we all out for ourselves?" Aimi stepped close and placed the brandy bottle back on the desk.

Keelin looked down into her eyes. She was close, close enough to smell, and she smelled of the sea and brandy – but mostly of the sea, and Keelin felt himself going hard again.

"Do you believe the things we want," Aimi continued, her body leaning against his, "are always bad for others?"

Keelin scooped her up, struggled out of the trousers that were still caught around his ankles, and carried Aimi over to his cot.

Fortune

Drake was calling the little beasty Rag, and it was as vicious a little hunter as the giant spider, Rhi, had ever been. Already it was a foot long with razor-sharp scythe-like pincers and a venomous bite that caused intense pain and mild paralysis, as two of the crew could attest to. Rag wasn't just dealing with the rat population on board the ship, but had also proved to be an excellent fisher. The giant centipede would crawl onto the outside hull and dangle with its head just above the water's surface, its body bent like a reed under pressure. Then it would strike, darting its head into the water and, more often than not, pulling back with a fish skewered between its mandibles. It was an impressive sight to behold, and one member of the crew had already learned the hard way not to attempt to take the fish away from Rag. The poor bastard had spent the better part of three days unable to move his arms or legs.

The armour plating protecting Rag's body segments was already as hard as iron, and Drake had been assured that once the little monster reached its full maturity – and its full six feet in length – the armour would harden even further, and the beast's venom would become lethal. Thankfully, its voracious appetite would lessen. The creature had already explored the ship from top to bottom, giving Luter a shock up in the nest, and had decided, much to Drake's approval, to call the captain's cabin its home. The closer the beasty got to him the better. He wanted it as loyal as Rhi had been, and as dangerous too. Already Rag had taken to using Drake's body as a climbing frame. It wasn't entirely comfortable, having a foot-long monster wrapped around his body, but he appreciated the protection having a creature like that at striking distance of his enemies might provide.

For now, Rag was curled up in the corner of his cabin, wrapped around itself, and Drake couldn't be sure whether it was sleeping or watching the door with its pitch-black eyes. He wasn't even sure if the little monster did sleep.

A knock sounded on the door and Rag chittered, its legs tapping against its armour, but the creature didn't move. Drake rolled out of his bed, wondering how it had been so long since the sheets had smelled of a woman. He crossed to the door, still fully naked, and pulled it open, only to be reminded just why it had been so long. Arbiter Beck stood on the other side of the door with an apprehensive look on her face.

"Is it still in there?" she asked, her eyes fixed on his face. She didn't get on too well with Rag, though the centipede seemed to like Beck well enough.

"Aye," Drake said, purposefully scratching at his stones in an attempt to draw Beck's gaze downwards. "Seems to enjoy being near me."

Beck grimaced. "Captain Khan is here to see you." She turned away, never having reacted at all to Drake's lack of clothing.

Drake shut the door, disappointed, and started pulling some clothing together. He'd been chasing Beck for too long, and if she wasn't about to slip into his bed and let him slip into her, then he'd have to find some other release. He briefly considered a visit to the Dragon Empire. The Empress was always wet and willing for Drake, but he doubted Rei would let him leave without a few good months of service.

Captain Khan was standing at the bow of the ship, staring out at the town of New Sev'relain. Drake stepped up beside the giant pirate and cleared his throat.

"An impressive feat, building a town from nothing," Khan rumbled.

"Ain't from nothing," Drake said. "Towns are never built from nothing. They're built from people. Folk with a will and a need and…"

"Money."

"Aye, that too. Ain't much gets done without pay or promise."

"You are taking Poole and Stillwater to see Captain Black," Khan said, dispensing with the small talk. "Why not me?"

"Because I don't expect a fight, and I reckon that's where your strengths lie. Look, Captain, I'm taking those two because we all got history with Tanner, some of it good, some bad. But we all know each other. I also need someone trustworthy to stay and look after the town."

"I'm not much of a governor." The giant's statement came out almost as a growl.

"No. But you got a code of honour, and that makes me trust you. That, and I know where you come from. Folk north of the Five Kingdoms like you are raiders and devilish in a fight. You're also protective of what's yours. Well, New Sev'relain is yours. It's yours and mine and Stillwater's and even Tanner's. It's also all of theirs." Drake pointed out to the town. "It belongs to everyone that calls the isles their home, and those bastards from the Five Kingdoms want to burn it down."

Drake glanced at the other captain to see his jaw clenched and grating, and he knew he'd hit the right nerve. "I need you to protect it while I'm gone."

Khan grunted. "The bastards will not take another home from me."

After Khan had gone, Drake called Princess over. "How long 'til we can sail?"

"Loading supplies now, Cap'n. They ain't good though. We'll have just about enough to make it there and back, and we best hope the town gets resupplied whiles we gone."

Drake looked upwards; the sky was grey and dark and the season was turning. The Pirate Isles never experienced a true winter, but the temperature would soon start dropping, and with it would come the storms.

"First light," Drake said. "We sail tomorrow and hope we arrive at Ash before Tanner."

North Gale

T'ruck stretched his big shoulders back and squatted down on the railing. Then, holding onto the rigging with one hand and keeping his cock out the way with the other, he pushed, grunted, moaned, and finally relaxed into a contented sigh. Some men preferred to shit on land when they could, enjoying the privacy of a shed with a hole in the ground. T'ruck had no such qualms, and was more than happy to drop his turds over the side of his ship as he always did. He liked to think of it as giving back to the ocean the same way a farmer might spread manure on his field.

There was a ship sailing into the bay, one T'ruck didn't recognise, and no doubt the entire crew had a wonderful view of his arse. T'ruck didn't care; he'd often been complimented on the shape and musculature of his arse.

Berris Dey was written along the new ship's side, and it was written in red. T'ruck pulled up his trousers and waved for his crew to lower a boat into the water. Drake had charged him with looking after the town in his absence, and T'ruck took his duties seriously, especially when they involved protecting his home.

His crew rowed hard and T'ruck was soon standing on the beach, awaiting the arrival of the newest visitors to their little town. Little but growing. T'ruck would be proud once New Sev'relain could call itself the largest town in the isles. Until then he wouldn't be happy. He was a firm believer in the mantra of bigger being better, and he applied it to all aspects of his life. He liked his meals large, his ships huge, and his women big, although he'd made an exception for the daughter of Tanner Black, and she'd proved to be as wild and forceful as the biggest of women.

Indeed, T'ruck was of the firm opinion Elaina Black would have made an excellent third wife back home. Her hips were far too small for a first wife; she would never survive that many child births. He doubted she knew how to make a home, so she would never do as a second wife. But the third wives were for fucking and fighting, and Elaina Black could do both. The claw marks T'ruck had proudly worn for days were proof enough of that.

Not for the first time, T'ruck considered making New Sev'relain his home proper. It would be an easy thing to order a house built, and he would have little issue finding himself a new set of wives, breeding himself a new litter of pups. Ties were important, and family ties were the most important of all. If there was one thing he could say his life had been missing since leaving the mountains, it was family.

"Captain," Zole said with a tap on T'ruck's shoulder. "That dirty Riverlander is coming."

T'ruck glanced over his shoulder to see Deun Burn striding down the beach towards them, his skull tattoo a stark white against his sun-darkened face and his swagger setting his cloak swaying and the axe attached to his belt swinging. Many folk hated the Riverlanders, considering them vagrants and thieves even among the isles. Some even believed they carried diseases wherever they went and infected water supplies with their mere presence. T'ruck didn't entirely believe the stories, but it was plain as the sun in the sky and the water in the sea that Deun Burn didn't like T'ruck Khan.

"Admiring the ship?" Burn said as he closed in. T'ruck had hoped the man would simply walk on by, but hope, like happiness, often turned to ash.

"She is small," T'ruck rumbled. It wasn't entirely true, but *Berris Dey* was smaller than *North Gale*, and that was all that really mattered.

Burn made a sound between a click and a sigh. "Riverlanders believe it is not about size, but where you stick it."

T'ruck snorted. "Your sister thinks otherwise."

Burn snarled out some incomprehensible words that were likely an insult. T'ruck had no interest in learning the Riverland's guttural-sounding language and even less interest in knowing what the fool had said to him.

"Your mother too," he said with a smile.

Burn hissed out some more gibberish, followed by a tug of his earlobe. T'ruck yawned and burped at the smaller man.

"They were glad of a real man after all you" – T'ruck glanced at

Burn's crotch – "little Riverlanders."

Deun Burn looked set to pick his axe from his belt and make the last mistake of his life, so T'ruck decided to spare him the death. "Oh, it appears we have a boarding party, and… fuck!"

Burn's snarling hisses turned to smiles as T'ruck realised the new ship, *Berris Dey*, was filled with men and women whose faces were covered in tattoos.

"I should let me do the speaking, barbarian," Deun said with a sneer. "They won't care for your language, or your face."

T'ruck grumbled, but the man running from the *Berris Dey* towards them looked like he was in a right hurry, and the scales painted on his face did little to hide the fear there.

"Friend of yours?" T'ruck said.

"We Riverlanders are all family," Burn said, his voice cold.

As the newcomer drew near, T'ruck could see that the tattoo seemed to go all around his head, even under his hairline. The man almost looked like a snake, he was so scaly; not to mention his nose was so small it seemed to disappear amidst the inked lines.

The two Riverlanders started to hiss, screech, snap, and click at each other. T'ruck was sure it was actually some form of language, but the sounds the men made were so ugly they actually hurt his ears. To distract himself he wondered if the Riverland's women made similar noises while they fucked, and how off-putting that would have to be to the men fucking them. It was likely why there were so few of the people. Sex should rarely involve bloody ears. Although there was that one time with P'elpy, his first wife, which had involved bloody ears, nose, lips, and cock.

"Khan," Burn snapped.

"Huh?"

"Flen spotted a fleet just five days ago. He says four ships, including the largest he has ever seen."

"Did they chase him?" T'ruck was already intrigued by the mention of a giant ship.

Burn babbled some words at the scaled Riverlander, who prattled some nonsense back. "No. They ignored him."

Where Loyalties Lie

"Then why should we care? There are fleets all over the world these days."

Again Burn hissed and clicked, and the other Riverlander responded.

The skeleton of the Man of War, still sitting on the beach, caught T'ruck's eye. It was a giant, a behemoth. He wished he'd seen it before it had been stripped to build the town. He wished he'd been the one to take it.

He turned back to the two men. "How big was the ship?"

Burn and the other Riverlander ignored him.

"How big was the ship?" T'ruck shouted. "As big as that?" He pointed to the bones of the Man of War.

The scaled Riverlander waved his arms emphatically, and T'ruck didn't need Burn to translate. The new ship in pirate waters was even bigger.

T'ruck grinned. "Ask him where it was going."

Fortune

"Well, it's fair to say Tanner got here first," Drake mumbled as they approached the island of Ash. He was looking through his monoscope and giving what he saw the frowning of a lifetime. Three ships: *The Black Death*, Blu's monstrosity *Ocean Deep*, and *Hearth Fire*. "Looks like Barklow threw in with Tanner."

"Three ships apiece," Princess agreed. "Seems fair. If any shit does start we'll be evenly matched."

"If any shit does start it'll be the end of us all. Not to mention the isles." Drake shook his head. "We can't afford to be divided anymore."

Princess groaned.

"Out with it," Drake snapped.

"Ya really reckon Tanner's just gonna see sense and pull in behind our flag, Cap'n? He might see the need for unity right now, sure. But Tanner ain't exactly the type to take orders from anyone, least of all Drake Morrass."

Drake hated to admit it, but Princess made a good point, and it was a thing that had been on his mind for the entire journey to Ash. "I'll just have to be convincing," he said with false cheer.

"Or," Princess said cheerily, "we could just kill the fucker and see if that fleet of his falls in line. I'm just saying, Cap'n, options there."

Drake smiled. "Something tells me his fleet wouldn't just fall in line. Even if we killed Blu as well, I think his ships would rally around that damned daughter of his. We'd still be fighting a war against them, and Sarth and the Five Kingdoms would sail in and slaughter us all. No, mate, we do this the peaceful way. Tanner'll see sense." Drake wished he believed his own words.

"You're the cap'n, Cap'n. I've always wanted my own ship."

Drake shot Princess a glare, but the man was grinning. "Sail us in. Signal Stillwater and Poole to stay close. Just in case."

"Just in case," Princess echoed and walked away to carry out his captain's orders, just as Beck joined Drake at the railing.

The woman was looking less an Arbiter and more a pirate every

Where Loyalties Lie

day. Her skin had darkened from the constant exposure to the sun, her coat was a distant memory, and the shirt and britches she wore were stained and mended from heavy use. Beck kept her hair tied up tight beneath her new tricorn hat, and the brace of pistols she carried attached to her leather jerkin had seen a lot of use of late. Unfortunately, despite the burgeoning transition, the woman had still managed to keep herself out of Drake's bed, and that was as frustrating as her changes were welcome.

"I'll be coming with you," Beck said, her blue eyes staring out towards the island.

"Wouldn't have it any other way," Drake said. "I've got used to having you around. You make me feel all safe and cosy."

"Don't get used to it. I'll wager as soon as we've killed those Drurr who are after you, the Inquisitor will order me back to Sarth."

Drake almost laughed. He very much doubted Hironous would ever order Beck back to Sarth. She was as good as a pirate now, and Drake's brother would happily leave her as a bodyguard to the soon-to-be pirate king. He wondered if that was why Beck had been sent. Eventually Drake would need a strong queen to sit at his side. Sometimes he wished his brother would share more of what he saw in his visions of the future.

Ash was a small island alone in the surrounding water, little more than a rock covered in smaller rocks and even smaller trees. There was no wildlife to speak off – the island was too small to sustain any – and the trees were little more than wiry bushes clinging to what little life they had in such harsh conditions. The wind around Ash was relentless and merciless, gusting first one way then the other, and many a ship had accidentally got too close and gutted itself on the hidden rocks beneath the waters. The island was littered with the carcasses of ships and the bones of their sailors.

Drake's small fleet anchored just a short distance from Tanner's, far enough to be out of bow shot. Stillwater launched a boat, rowing it over from *The Phoenix* to the *Fortune* by himself. He tied it up and boarded Drake's ship with an anxious look that did little to lighten Drake's uneasy feeling.

"Elaina isn't here," Stillwater said in a hurry as soon as he saw

Drake.

"I had noticed a distinct lack of *Starry Dawn*. Should this be worrying me, Stillwater?"

"I don't know. It was her idea as much as it was mine to meet here. I just thought…"

Drake turned a stern gaze on his fellow captain. "You got a legitimate worry, or are you just pining for the Lady Black's cunt and trying to curdle my gut?"

"I just thought she'd be here," Stillwater said, his voice hard.

"Perhaps Tanner didn't want his daughter and you anywhere near each other. Find it hard to fault him, given your past relationship. Don't reckon either of you thinks clearly when near each other, and I bloody well hope your cock hasn't just clouded your judgement to bring us here. I see two men on Ash. One looks like Tanner, the other looks like Tanner, so I'm guessing his useless, mouldy, salt-licker of a son is with him."

"I have a history with Blu as well," Keelin muttered.

"There any member of that family you haven't fucked?" Drake grinned.

Keelin laughed. "We just don't get on so well."

"But you and Tanner are close as barnacles, aye?"

"Good point. Are we going ashore?"

"Mhm. Just you, me, and Beck."

"The Arbiter?"

"Can you think of anyone better to watch your back?" Beck said, strolling over to the railing and leaning against it, treating Stillwater to a cold stare. Drake was of the opinion those two needed to start getting along, but Keelin seemed to have some issues with the Inquisition.

"If we're taking a third person ashore I would rather it was Kebble," Keelin said, ignoring Beck. "I wouldn't trust her to watch my back if my life depended upon it."

"Well then, we'll be fine," Beck said. "I'll be there to watch Drake's, not yours."

"Both of you can fucking stop this shit, right now," Drake hissed. "We got enemies enough on that little shit of a rock without you two trying to screw each other over. Beck is coming along, Stillwater. The

Where Loyalties Lie

sooner you accept that, the sooner we can get in that little boat of yours and convince Tanner Black to join me rather than kill me. Good?"

Beck nodded. Keelin didn't.

"Don't make the mistake of thinking that was a question, Stillwater. Either you get on board now or you drown in my wake."

Drake could see the anger in Keelin's eyes as easily as the grinding of his teeth, but eventually he nodded. "Good."

"Right then," Drake said with a smile. "Now let's all have us a hug."

Both Beck and Keelin shot Drake an incredulous look.

"Of course I'm bloody joking, you damned idiots. Onto the boat with both of you."

There wasn't really a landing on Ash, so they followed Tanner's example and tied the little boat onto a rock, leaping overboard and splashing through the shallows to clamber up onto dry land. Green algae covered the rocks at sea level and made the footing slippery and treacherous, but all three of them managed without even a grazed hand among them. The climb up to the centre of the little island was steep and tough, and by the time they reached the top all three of them were short of breath. Drake was certain he would have been dripping with sweat if not for the gusting wind whipping at his face.

Tanner Black and his son were waiting for them in a small stony clearing surrounded by rocky outcroppings with a single bush clinging desperately to the ground. Tanner was wrapped up tight in a huge black cloak, and his hateful bird, bigger than most cats, perched on his shoulder, staring at Drake as he approached. Tanner was armed, the tip of a sword poking out of the bottom of his coat, but then they were all armed. If any trouble did start, it was unlikely any of them would make it off the little island alive.

"See anything off?" Drake whispered to Beck, and the Arbiter only shook her head by way of reply. He asked the same of Keelin, but the captain was locked in a vicious staring contest with Tanner and didn't answer. "Well, let's just hope fortune favours the fucked."

Drake stepped past the last few rocks into the little clearing on the top of Ash. Both Captain Blacks watched him, Blu with his arms crossed and his dark eyes full of hate, and Tanner with his hands in his coat pockets and a welcoming grin.

"Well, ya got me surprised, Drake," Tanner shouted over the whipping wind. "Can't say I thought you'd have the stones to turn up."

Drake stopped a good few paces from Tanner and his son. "Folk may say a lot of things about Drake Morrass," he shouted back, "but none of them call me a coward, mate."

Tanner laughed. "Reckon you're talking to the wrong folk then. And Stillwater." Upon hearing Keelin's name, the giant crow perched on Tanner's shoulder shifted its malevolent gaze and let out a piercing cry that ripped the air in two and seemed to silence the wind, if only for a moment. "Didn't reckon I'd ever see you again."

"Where's Elaina?" Stillwater said.

Tanner's grin disappeared, and for just a moment he looked angry enough to draw steel. "What do you care, boy? Girl was never anything to you but a hole to fill and a ship to steal."

Drake had the sinking feeling that if Tanner and Stillwater continued to air their differences the meeting would end in blood, so he cut in. "We here to piss into the wind? I thought we came to discuss terms. Forge an alliance."

Tanner's grin reappeared. "Ah, Drake, ya really should have known better, mate."

Out of the corner of his eye, Drake saw the rocks around them begin to move.

North Gale

"That's a lot of masts," Yu'truda said with a touch of awe.

"That's a lot of ship," Zole said with a touch of fear.

"I want her," T'ruck said with a touch of greed.

They were all watching the monster of a ship from a very safe distance through monoscopes. With the Riverlander's information, T'ruck had rightly guessed the invading fleet would stop at the island of Innikwell, an expansive isle with fresh water and trees and wildlife aplenty. It would normally make the perfect spot for a pirate settlement, only it was also widely known as a stopping point for navy ships from both Sarth and the Five Kingdoms. All ships needed regular supplies of fresh water, and the giant they were looking at now was no exception.

"That louse-ridden Riverlander said there was a fleet," Zole complained as he scratched at something behind his ear that was likely a louse. "I only see the one ship."

"And what a ship," T'ruck rumbled. The vessel before him was indeed the largest he'd ever seen, and that made it the only ship worthy of T'ruck Khan, last of his clan. He wasn't truly the last member of his clan, as Yu'truda and a dozen others had followed him into piracy, but he was the strongest of them all, and that made him the chief of what was left.

"We wouldn't get close, Captain," Zole protested. "I see weapons of war. Catapults, scorpions."

"A fine prize," T'ruck said, ignoring his first mate.

"Not to mention the crew," Yu'truda said, agreeing with her husband as she often did. They were a fine match, but neither had T'ruck's backbone. "We would be outnumbered three to one at least."

"I love the odds. We have faced worse," T'ruck said. "I would take any man or woman on this ship over a hundred Five Kingdoms cowards. They slither from their mothers' cunts mewling and bowing to their king. We from the northern clans are born with fire in our hearts and steel in our hands."

"Ain't that many of us left, T'ruck," Yu'truda said sadly. "Most of the crew are from the isles these days."

"And we ain't worth more than two or three of those Five Kingdoms soiled britches at the very most," Zole said, agreeing with his wife as he often did. "Taking *North Gale* was a miracle, Captain. No chance we're taking that fucker."

T'ruck hated to admit it, but they were both right. He wanted the beast before his eyes, but they couldn't take her. Not without a fleet, and even then the losses would likely be too high for it to matter. She was a machine of war from her size, from the metal ram on her bow to the scorpions and catapults on her deck, and it was more than likely she had trained soldiers on board, maybe even knights.

He made a decision. "Bring me the witch."

"Captain?" Zole said, a note of panic in his voice.

"Now," T'ruck rumbled in a tone that was not to be argued with, and Zole quickly scuttled away to carry out his captain's orders. Yu'truda kept quiet. Her cold stare was disapproval enough.

A few minutes later a woman emerged from below decks. She was small and beautiful with long dark hair, darker eyes, and curves T'ruck would have loved to explore but didn't dare to; he was far too scared of the woman. Three members of the crew escorted her onto the main deck, and all three were carrying sharpened steel pointed towards her. The witch walked with a casual grace, and the black dress she wore, though ripped in places and long past its prime, clung to her curves.

The woman wore a heavy iron collar much like the ones slaves wore, only she would never be slave to anyone. It was etched with ancient runes, and she wore it at T'ruck's insistence; he held the only key. Crew members, men and women alike, scattered out of the way as the witch approached, but she kept her eyes fixed on T'ruck. He wanted to shrink from that gaze, curl up in a corner and hide, but T'ruck Khan showed no fear. Not even to devilish witches.

"How can I help, Captain?" she said with a lazy smile and a voice like honeyed poison. "Am I to scrub the deck? Coil a rope? Choke a man to death with his own hands?"

T'ruck attempted to master himself, but the woman was an oppressive force. Even with her magic kept subdued by the collar, she made the sun seem darker and the sea rougher, and every man and woman on the ship stank with fear.

T'ruck pointed at the giant ship anchored in the bay of Innikwell. "What can you do about that?"

The witch glanced quickly at the ship, and T'ruck felt as though a weight had been lifted from his shoulders. Then her eyes were back on him, and her presence assaulted his senses again.

"If I were aboard it and free" – she tilted her head in such a way to show off the iron collar around her slender neck – "I could probably sink it. A sizeable hole in the hull is usually enough to sink even the biggest ship."

"I don't want to sink it." T'ruck shivered. He never felt the cold, even in his homeland where it snowed all but three days a year, but the witch was under his skin, picking at his nerves. He almost regretted ever bringing her on board.

"You want to take it like you did this boat." The witch nodded. She looked at Yu'truda, ignoring Zole as she always did. She had little to no respect for the *North Gale*'s first mate. "I assume you counselled against it?"

"I did, my lady," Yu'truda said, not meeting the witch's eyes.

"Then I suggest you listen to your counsel, Captain."

"I brought you on board," T'ruck growled. "Picked you clean from the Inquisition's hands and hid you, kept you moving so they wouldn't find you. Deal was you magic for me when I need it, woman."

"I have a name, *Captain*." The witch hissed the title.

"Sorry." T'ruck hated himself for the apology. "Lady Tsokei. But our deal…"

"Was one of necessity. I am not a member of your crew, and I will not be spoken down to even if I am required to wear the jewellery of a slave. Do not mistake my placid demeanour as one of subservience, Captain.

"As I have already said. If you were to get me aboard the ship I could sink it, but I do not believe we would be allowed to get so close. Do you?"

T'ruck shook his head.

"Then I can do nothing," she whispered.

As the woman turned and made her way back to her quarters, still escorted by the armed pirates, a shout went up from the nest. "Sail!"

T'ruck didn't need a bearing; he could already see it, and that it was heading their way. He pulled his monoscope from his pocket and looked through it.

"Is it one of ours?" Yu'truda said.

"Can't tell," T'ruck growled. Something didn't feel right in his gut.

"Captain," shouted another crew member. "That monster is turning, laying on sail."

T'ruck glanced up into the sky to check the position of the sun. With the big ship lying just south of them in the bay and the new ship heading their way from an easterly position, that left them the options of fleeing north or west, and fleeing was definitely the only choice. T'ruck couldn't be certain the new ship was unfriendly, but he had the feeling they'd wandered into a trap.

"Turn us north," he bellowed, "with every bit of speed we can muster."

Yu'truda raised her eyebrows. "Captain?"

"I reckon those filthy Riverlanders have just fucked us."

North Gale cut through the waves like a knife, speeding along as fast as her namesake, but the two ships giving chase were just as fast, even the behemoth. For half an hour they kept pace, matching both speed and course. The smaller ship moved a little further eastwards to stop T'ruck ordering a change in that direction. He almost ordered them further west, but he had a feeling that was where the bastards wanted him to go, and he wasn't about to make it easy for them. If they could survive until nightfall they could douse the lights on board and pray to any god that would listen to cloud the sky and dim the moon. Under cover of darkness, assuming they didn't hit any hidden rocks, escape would be easy. For now all they could do was run and hope they proved the fastest of the three ships.

When a third sail appeared to the north, T'ruck knew they were out of options. He wasn't sure how the Five Kingdoms ships had coordinated the trap, but they'd pulled him and his crew right into it, and now their only escape lay to the west.

T'ruck stormed over to the wheel, where Gurner was looking as nervous as a virgin. "Turn us east," the captain said, and the navigator stared at him with uncomprehending eyes. "I ain't about to be herded into their trap. They think they have us? We'll break free straight through their net. Turn us east."

In the face of his captain's fury, Gurner obeyed and set *North Gale* on a course for the smallest of their three pursuers.

The Phoenix

Keelin's swords were in his hands as soon as he saw the rocks begin to move, but even that was too late. They were too late from the moment they stepped into the little clearing on top of Ash and the moment they stepped into Tanner's trap. The boulders shifted and rolled aside to reveal Tanner's crew hidden beneath, and only then did Keelin see the rocks for what they truly were: wooden constructs excellently shaped and painted to mimic the island's stones. Tanner had clearly put a lot of effort into his trap, and it had paid off.

"Weapons down, if ya please," Tanner shouted over the wind as one of the fake wooden boulders caught a gust and began a tumble to the sea. Keelin counted ten pirates, and all appeared to be armed with pistols.

Drake looked calm, almost as though he'd expected the trap and had still walked into it willingly. He slowly drew his sword and threw it into the middle of the clearing.

"Now, luv," Tanner said to Beck, "I suggest ya follow Drake's example. I know just who and what ya are. If I see you so much as utter a word I'll have my boys test how hard it is ta kill an Arbiter. That said, I'd really rather not start a fight with ya Inquisition, so if ya put those lovely pistols down and keep ya pretty hole shut we'll be having no problems."

Beck didn't look convinced, but Drake nodded to her and she disarmed, throwing all seven of her pistols to the ground.

"You too, Stillwater," Tanner continued. "Just in case, ya see. Not that I expect any trouble from the likes of you."

Keelin dropped his cutlasses.

"Excellent." Tanner grinned and signalled to the pirates behind them.

Two men rushed forwards and grabbed hold of Drake, forcing him to his knees and twisting his arms behind his back. Another two men gave Beck similar treatment, pausing briefly to stuff a dirty gag into her mouth. The fury on the Arbiter's face was enough to give Keelin nightmares, but Tanner only smirked at the rough treatment.

"Don't want ya casting any of ya magic while we do this, now do we?"

"We should just kill her," Blu shouted, only to earn a hard stare from his father.

"Aye, because we currently don't have nearly enough enemies. Boy, ya foolish as that damned sister o' yours."

Keelin was left wondering why he was the only one not being restrained by Tanner's crew. Not that he was about to argue with Tanner if the man had decided to spare his life.

"I gotta say, Drake, I'm more than a little surprised ya turned up as ya did." Tanner stepped forward, putting himself close to Morrass. "Ya must 'ave seen this comin'. No?"

"I thought you'd be smarter, Tanner," Drake hissed. "Killing me won't save you or the isles. My ships will…"

"Your ships will turn and fight mine and we'll all go sinking down to Rin's watery abyss? Fair words, mate, but I doubt them very much. Without you to lead them, I reckon your boys will do the only sensible thing left. Join me. Especially with your little mate, Stillwater, beckoning them over to my side."

Drake turned his head to look at Keelin. Keelin in turn looked at Tanner. Tanner laughed.

"Aye. This was his plan. His and my daughter's, that is. Ya put ya trust in the wrong captain, Drake. Stillwater is as loyal as a shark and twice as treacherous."

Keelin thought about arguing, but he was still a little dumbfounded. He'd conspired to bring Tanner and Drake together on Ash; he just hadn't suspected Elaina's true intentions. He could only assume Elaina had told her father that he was in on it. Elaina had saved Keelin's life at the same time as condemning Drake to death.

"See how he doesn't even refute it, mate." Tanner looked down on Drake. "Don't feel bad. The little shit betrays everyone. First it was me, then my daughter, and now you."

Keelin wanted to defend himself, but he couldn't. Everything Tanner was saying was true.

Tanner waved to Blu, who stepped forward and handed him a small metal contraption. "First things first," he growled.

Tanner grabbed hold of Drake's head and forced his teeth apart, thrusting the little metal device between them and turning a screw on the side. It was a jack, and before long Drake's mouth was stretched wide open. Keelin could see real fear in his eyes. Morrass started to struggle then, but the pirates behind him held him tight.

"Tongs," Tanner said with a smile, and Blu handed his father a large, rusty implement. Tanner inserted it into Drake's mouth, gripping hold of his tongue.

"Knife," Tanner said, staring down into Drake's terrified eyes. Blu handed him a serrated blade. "Let's see just how silver this tongue of yours is, eh?"

"Stop." Keelin's voice came out as a whisper that even he couldn't hear over the violent roar of the wind, and he struggled to take his next breath.

"Stop!"

Tanner looked at Keelin just for a moment. "Nah."

Keelin didn't have time to think; he had to stop Tanner. "Kill Drake and you condemn us all to death."

Tanner was still holding Drake's tongue out in front of him, the knife just inches away. "I actually thought you'd be smarter than this, boy," he said. His crow, Pilf, shrieked at Keelin. "Elaina tried ta save ya. We all knew it ta be shit, but she tried. And here ya are, throwing away all her good nature by siding with this?" Tanner waved the knife in front of Drake's face, catching his nose and opening up a bloody gash. "Not very smart, boy."

"I won't follow you, Tanner," Keelin said.

"Well, no, probably not once yer dead."

"And neither will they." Keelin pointed towards Drake's three ships floating just off the coast of Ash. "Or any of the others. Your little fleet is as big as it will ever be, because everyone is too scared of you to join you."

Tanner narrowed his eyes and Pilf let out a scream.

"Don't listen to him, Da. Stillwater's a damned salt licker."

"Quiet, boy," Tanner hissed. "They'll fall in line once this one is dead."

"No," Keelin said. "They won't. They'll run as far from you and the isles as they can get. You'll find yourself facing Sarth and the Five Kingdoms alone."

Drake, thankfully, kept quiet; not that he could have spoken if he'd tried, with Tanner still holding his tongue ready for removing.

"You followed me before, lad," Tanner said.

"And never will again, Tanner. You rule by terror. I've seen you beat your children for just voicing an opinion, and I've seen you kill for no reason other than someone looked at you. No man or woman wants to live under that sort of fear, and we pirates have no need to live that way. We can sail wherever the winds and the ocean take us, so why would we suffer you? That's how the old Captain Black ruled, and look what happened to him. The other kingdoms came for him and his people deserted him, just like they will you."

"Yet you'll follow this lying sack of mouldy puss maggots?"

"Yes."

"Why?" Tanner roared.

Keelin hesitated for a moment, trying to decide if he truly believed in Drake. He didn't. But then, it didn't matter. Drake Morrass was the only one who could bring all the pirates together. He was the only one they would all follow.

"Because he doesn't just want to rule us, Tanner," Keelin said. "Drake wants to save us all, and he knows he can't do that unless we change. He knows he can't do it unless we stop fighting each other and band together.

"Drake came here suspecting a trap," Keelin continued, risking the lie, "but he walked right into it because he knows he can't kill you. Because he needs you. You need each other."

Tanner released Drake's tongue and threw both the knife and the tongs to the ground before stalking over to Keelin. Keelin wanted to back away, to run from the fury in Tanner's eyes, but he stood his ground and hoped he wasn't staring into the face of his own death.

"Why do you," Tanner shouted into Keelin's face, and punctuated the words by prodding him hard in the chest, "follow him?" He pointed at Drake, then lowered his voice so only Keelin could hear. "If not to betray him like ya did me? Like ya do everyone."

Keelin shook his head. "Because he's the only one who can bring us all together. He's the only one every captain and pirate and settler in the isles will line up behind. He's the only one with a plan to fight back and stop those bastards from Sarth and the Five Kingdoms from purging us ever again.

"Piracy the way we know it is all but dead, Tanner. There's too many of us, and the merchants know it as well as those navy fucks. Either we're wiped out, or they sail elsewhere. We're bleeding the bastards dry and they can't afford it. That's why this is happening. That's why they're coming for us, killing us. We can't just beat the bastards. We need to change as well."

Pilf screamed from Tanner's shoulder, but the man silenced the bird with a hiss. "My crews won't follow Drake," he said, staring down at Keelin.

"They will if you tell them to. That's why Drake needs you alive as an ally, not dead as a martyr. Help us, Tanner. Help us turn the isles into something other than a graveyard."

Tanner stared at Keelin for a few more moments before turning and fighting his way through the gusting wind to where Drake knelt, still restrained by two pirates.

"Terms?" Tanner shouted down at Drake.

Drake glanced quickly at Keelin before spitting out some of the blood that had run into his mouth from the gash on his nose.

"You keep command of your ships, but you follow my orders when I give 'em. You leave the ships I tell you to leave and attack any navy vessels you can take. You protect Fango and New Sev'relain and the people that live there."

Tanner growled but didn't argue. "The loot?"

"You keep half."

"That's a little steep, mate. Not many folk have the stones to impose such terms from their knees. I'll take seventy percent."

Drake shook his head. "You'll take half, and the other half will go to fortifying the towns, building new ships, and recruiting new crew."

"And I suppose I'll have ta kneel and call you king?" Tanner's lip curled as he said the title.

"Aye, you can call me king," Drake said. "But I don't give a fuck about your knees."

"Da..." Blu shouted, but he was quickly silenced with a hard stare from Tanner.

Tanner bent down close to Drake and said something Keelin couldn't hear. It didn't look much like Drake was pleased by it, but after Tanner had finished he nodded all the same.

Tanner Black stood back to his full height and stared down at Drake. He had a look on his face as though he was deciding whether or not to disregard their negotiations completely and gut the man there and then.

"I want ya to remember, Drake, when ya calling yourself king. Remember that I had you on ya knees and spared ya miserable life. Let him go. The pretty bitch too."

The two pirates behind Drake let go of his arms and he slumped, slowly pushing himself to his feet. He was a dishevelled mess, his hair slick and his face pale and streaked with blood from his nose. The pirates holding Beck were less gentle, shoving her forwards and dancing backwards lest her rage be directed upon them. She tore the rag from her mouth and surged to her feet, cold blue eyes flashing with all the calm of a violent storm.

Drake stumbled over to Beck and reached out to calm her, but she knocked his hand away and shoved him back.

"I should kill all of you," Beck screamed over the gusting wind, her voice breaking on her rage.

"I don't reckon that'd be too smart, luv. After I've just struck a deal with ya captain." Tanner smiled, all teeth and threat. Keelin remembered that smile well; it usually preceded violence.

"Beck!" Drake shouted, shaking his head as he did.

The Arbiter seemed to calm a little. She stalked over to her discarded pistols and began shoving them back into their holsters. Keelin let out a heavy sigh and picked up his cutlasses. He noticed for the first time that some of the ships had their sails up. It took a moment for him to realise that they were also much further away than they should be and were not any of the three ships that had accompanied Tanner or Drake.

"Tanner," he called over the wind. "Are they yours?" He pointed.

Tanner looked and cursed. "Not mine."

"I count five ships," Beck said, and Keelin could only wonder at how good her vision was. "At least two are as big as that Man of War we took."

The ships were moving fast and had the wind on their side. Whoever they were, they were coming straight for Ash.

"Are we good here?" Drake said to Tanner. He was trembling, shaking on his feet. "We have a deal?"

"Aye." Tanner nodded. "Deal'll stand, mate. Long as we get outta here alive."

"Then we should do just that."

Mary's Virtue

Daimen didn't like the situation one bit. Their three ships were still anchored facing Tanner's three, and these new boats were bearing down on them quickly with the island of Ash blocking their immediate escape. They'd have to first navigate around Ash before making a proper escape of it, and the wind was notoriously hard to rely upon around these parts, which made getting up to speed slow and laborious. If they did up and run now, they'd probably all make it, but they'd be leaving Drake and Stillwater and Tanner on the island to the dubious mercies of whoever was ambushing them. It was a situation Daimen usually referred to as "fucked", and one he tried to avoid at all costs.

Through his monoscope, Daimen could see Drake and the others scrambling down the side of Ash, jumping over rocks at a rate most would consider suicidal. Even then they would have to row out to their ships. There simply wasn't enough time. He was glad of one thing, at least: Tanner hadn't killed Drake.

Rin appeared to be smiling on Drake today, and hopefully that meant an alliance had been forged. If Daimen knew one thing, it was that only Drake could pull all the pirate captains together. He had the will, the charisma, the reputation, and the money. He also had a plan, and that was worth more than all the rest put together.

Of course, none of it would mean shit if Drake was hanged, and that was exactly what the Five Kingdoms folk would do if they got their hands on him. Daimen had never liked the idea of hanging; it seemed a really undignified way to go. He much preferred the tried and true method of dying in battle as a hero to a cause.

"How's the wind?" he said to his navigator.

"Chopping and changing like a dog with two masters, Cap'n. We don't leave now, we might not make it 'fore those ships catch up to us."

Daimen nodded. "Aye. Best get under way then. Give us some sail and bring us around."

"Course?"

"Do ya see those ships over there?" Daimen pointed at the five vessels heading towards Ash. "Point us directly at the fuckers."

"Cap'n?"

"'Fore ya say it, mate, it ain't suicide," Daimen said. "All we need ta do is slow the bastards down long enough for Drake and Tanner ta get back ta their boats. Then they'll turn the tide."

"How?"

"By givin' 'em something else ta chew on. Let's see how the bastards like a taste of good ol' pirate courage."

Daimen drew in a deep breath and yelled, "All hands on deck. Swords, bows, and axes, boys. We're gonna sail this bitch right down their throats and choke 'em. We'll buy Drake enough time ta get back to his ship an' come an' fucking repay the favour, eh?"

A few of the crew of *Mary's Virtue* cheered, but most who were close enough to hear looked uncertain and worried. Clearly Daimen's insistence that they would be pulled out of the fire by Drake was not as reassuring as he'd hoped.

"Tales will be told of how we helped build this kingdom, boys. We'll all be fuckin' heroes. Knee deep in whores an' booze for the rest of our fuckin' lives." That got a few more cheers. If Daimen had learned one thing in his life, it was that nothing motivated pirates quite like money and, more importantly, the pleasures that money could buy.

"So break out the weapons, step to ya jobs, and for the love of Rin, would someone start me a bloody shanty."

Maybe it was invoking the name of their goddess, or maybe it was Daimen's relentless optimism that they'd survive, but before long the sails were loose, the ship was turning, and every crewman with a pair of lungs and a tongue was singing along to 'Baring the Maiden Fair'. Daimen grinned into the wind, barked out a savage laugh, and joined in with the shanty.

North Gale

The fools weren't even changing course. No doubt they believed their soldiers were more than a match for a few poorly trained pirates. The Five Kingdoms bastards would soon realise just how wrong they were.

"Shields," T'ruck roared. Two dozen of his crew rushed forwards, circular shields in hand, and formed a wall on the port side of the ship. Another dozen pirates formed behind them with spears and grapples and little gourds full of black powder. T'ruck's people may be called savages by the citizens of the Five Kingdoms, but they were far from stupid, and T'ruck had long since learned the devastating uses of black powder.

The ship's boy stumbled forwards carrying T'ruck's own shield, a giant, curved rectangle of wood and metal, painted all in white and stained with blood and deep-rent scars. The shield was as tall as most men and most men struggled to lift it, but T'ruck was stronger than most men. With his right hand he drew his sword from over his back and paced along behind the shield wall.

There was some nervous shifting in the wall as those at the front tried to get themselves into comfortable positions. Soon comfort would be the least of their worries. They were mere moments from the Five Kingdoms ship and still on course to sail alongside her.

"Archers," T'ruck screamed, and men and women both in the rigging and some standing behind the shields drew their bows and waited. The Five Kingdoms ship was just a handful of yards ahead of them now, with a gap of maybe ten yards between them. A hopeful archer from the enemy ship loosed an arrow, and to be fair to the man, his aim was true. But T'ruck saw the attack coming, and caught the arrow on the top half of his shield, where it stuck. Still he waited to give the order.

A few more arrows crossed the gap, thudding into the hull, the deck, or the shields. None found their mark and none of T'ruck's crew went down.

Still T'ruck waited, knowing full well most of the crew on the other ship would be hiding until it came time to board. Some of T'ruck's crew were tall, but he was the tallest of them all and, even hidden behind his giant shield, he could easily look over their heads to see the enemy ship approaching. It slipped alongside *North Gale*, and the first wave of men stood to throw their grapples.

"Loose!" T'ruck roared, and the archers behind the shield wall stood, picked their targets, and let their arrows go. From above, the archers in the rigging did the same; they had orders to rain down death upon the enemy until they had no more arrows.

T'ruck heard the evidence of his archers' skill in the screams of those who didn't die straight away, but he wasn't watching.

"Now," he said to the three men just behind him, and they crowded around the lantern to light the fuses on the gourds, waited a few seconds, then launched them over the heads of the shield wall even as the first grapples gripped hold of *North Gale*.

"Tightly now," T'ruck shouted, and the shields held fast as the first gourd exploded, followed quickly by the second and third. The sound was deafening, and T'ruck grinned as the din faded into a cacophony of screams from the other ship.

He risked a glance over the shield wall to see a ship in disarray. Splintered wood, burning canvas, dismembered bodies. One sailor was stumbling around the deck, his right arm off at the elbow and dripping blood. The man looked lost, as though he couldn't tell where he was or why. An arrow thudded into the poor fool's chest and he collapsed.

T'ruck saw little resistance left on the ship and was about to order his own boat under way when soldiers began pouring out of the hatches. From below decks and from the captain's cabin, men in armour started swarming onto the deck. Some stopped and emptied their stomachs at the carnage before them, but most ignored it, charging over to the railing and forming up under the command of their superiors. T'ruck looked upwards, but it appeared his archers were running short of arrows.

"Captain?" Yu'truda called; she was one of the first ranks of the shield wall, and T'ruck could see her staring back at him.

"Prepare to repel boarders," T'ruck howled, and started banging his sword against the metal boss in the centre of his shield. Many of his crew took up the example, and in only moments the noise coming from *North*

Gale was so vociferous it could have scared a storm.

Some of the bravest or most foolish attempted to jump across before the ships had come together, and most of those were thrown back by the shield wall only to drown or be crushed as the ships collided. Some managed to scramble their way up the shields and were quickly killed by spear thrusts from the rank of T'ruck's crew behind the shields. Not one man from that first attempt at boarding survived the crossing.

North Gale and the Five Kingdoms ships slammed together with a jolt that rattled the shield wall and knocked some men from their footing. There was a scream from up above and a loud thud as one of T'ruck's crew dropped from the rigging to their death, but he had no time to look at who it was or mourn their passing. The next wave of soldiers from the Five Kingdoms vessel was attempting to board, and they were accompanied by others swinging across on ropes.

T'ruck cut his sword in a slash that near chopped one swinging soldier's leg off. The soldier fell to the deck screaming, and T'ruck finished him off with a stab to the face. He looked around for another fool thinking to come aboard.

Now the soldiers from the Five Kingdoms ship were attacking the shield wall, hacking at it with axes and stabbing with spears, trying to find gaps through which to kill or injure. In other places, where the wall was thinnest, soldiers had started to board *North Gale*, and T'ruck's crew were engaged in half a dozen small skirmishes. They were outnumbered, that much was clear, and the soldiers were only keeping his crew busy by attacking the wall while they swarmed over in other places and eventually surrounded his smaller crew. A glance over the shields gave T'ruck a better idea of numbers, and he could already see this was not a fight they were likely to win with a wall.

"Break and form up on me," he shouted.

As one the shieldbearers started moving backwards step by step. A couple of over-reaching soldiers fell into the gap left by the retreating pirates and were quickly dispatched by the spears behind. The soldiers from the Five Kingdoms ship didn't wait for orders; they saw their enemy retreating and surged forwards with a cheer.

T'ruck's crew closed around him, a new wall forming with him at the centre. Some of his crew were still fighting elsewhere on the decks, but they were quickly outnumbered and cut down. Before T'ruck could think of a way to save them, the first wave of soldiers hit the newly formed wall and men started dying.

Fortune

"What's he doing?" Stillwater said, pulling hard on the oar, his head craned around to stare across at *Mary's Virtue*.

"Saving us all," Drake growled. He could still taste cold iron on his tongue, and his pride burned with anger at the treatment Tanner had given him, but he swallowed down his rage for the sake of his plans. He could feign a little humility if the end result was a crown. "Stop looking and pay attention to your oar."

Beck was quiet, but her rage was a fire that Drake could feel even through the wind and the spray from the sea. He pulled on his oar hard, wishing there were some way to make the little boat move faster.

"*The Phoenix* is closer," Drake wheezed between breaths. "Soon as we're aboard, we sail. I'll signal the *Fortune* to follow."

"What's the plan?" Stillwater said.

Drake's arms ached. His back ached. His tongue was stinging and his nose hurt like a serrated knife had recently cut a gash across it that hadn't been patched up. And the salt water that kept splashing him in the face only made it hurt more.

"We run." Drake ground his jaw at the decision, glad that Stillwater couldn't see his face.

"We're just gonna leave Poole?" Stillwater said.

Spray whipped across Drake's face and he shut his eyes. When he opened them he saw Beck staring at him across the small boat; her face was a mixture of pity and understanding, and her cold blue eyes sparkled in the light.

"Can't save him or his ship," Drake wheezed.

With that there seemed little else left to say. Drake hated leaving Poole behind, but he wasn't about to sacrifice the rest of them as well. He sent a prayer to Rin, knowing it was pointless. The goddess didn't take requests.

North Gale

The dead and dying bodies at their feet were more than enough proof of their prowess and determination, but the dead and dying bodies behind them were more than enough proof of the Five Kingdoms' superior numbers. It felt like they'd been in the shield wall for hours, stabbing, blocking, grunting, swearing, screaming, stabbing, bleeding, stabbing.

Wave after wave of soldiers had fallen upon them at first, and at a heavy cost to themselves they'd succeeded in felling a good number of T'ruck's crew. After the Five Kingdoms commanders took control and formed a shield wall of their own things started to change. Most pirates weren't used to fighting with shields, but T'ruck had trained his own crew well. He'd been born a warrior first, and had taken his lessons from battle to the seas.

Now, with dwindling numbers and wounded men to tend to, the crew of *North Gale* looked on the verge of collapse. The very idea of surrendering to a Five Kingdoms cock-tickler made T'ruck angry beyond rage, and that rage lent him new strength. He was sure the enemy line would collapse if only they could get to the commander. With that plan in mind, T'ruck sucked in a deep breath and screamed out a battle cry to terrify the gods.

"Push!" T'ruck roared as he put both his strength and weight behind his mammoth shield.

Breaking free from his own wall and crashing into the enemy's, T'ruck slashed one way then the other. He charged through the ill-prepared Five Kingdoms line, hacking and slashing, and men fell around him like wheat to a scythe. He took wounds, but T'ruck was well used to wounds and none were severe enough to stop him, only fuel his battle rage.

The crew of *North Gale* surged through the gap their captain had opened, splitting the enemy wall and turning it, falling upon it from two sides and cutting down swathes of enemy soldiers.

T'ruck spotted the enemy commander, sabre in hand and shouting

Where Loyalties Lie

orders to his men, and wasted no time in cutting his way through to the man.

Pain blossomed in T'ruck's side, just below his ribs. A Five Kingdoms soldier, barely more than a boy, had stabbed him with a spear, but T'ruck was a big man with a lot of muscle and fat. The wound was deep, but not deep enough. He snapped the spearhead off with his sword and crushed the young soldier's face with the boss of his shield. T'ruck turned back to the enemy commander to find the man gone.

Again pain erupted in T'ruck's side, this time his right. He turned just as the Five Kingdoms commander, a greying fool with an inexcusably waxed moustache, slashed at T'ruck's belly with his sabre.

The commander drew back his sword for another strike and something large dropped on him from above, flattening him in an instant. T'ruck looked down upon the ship's boy, Fried, as he rolled away from the commander, his legs obviously broken. The commander looked stunned but otherwise uninjured; T'ruck remedied the situation by crushing the man's skull with his shield.

Looking up from the dead commander and dying boy, T'ruck could see his charge had worked. The shield walls were gone, replaced with bloody bodies and clusters of soldiers fighting with pirates. His crew were no longer outnumbered; they'd turned the tide and everywhere they were cutting down smaller groups of men who, without a commander to give them orders, seemed devoid of any organisation. The Five Kingdoms ship had no more soldiers to throw at them, and the captain and his crew were already cutting the lines and pushing the two ships apart. T'ruck would let them; he had no wish to linger.

A single soldier, still bloodcrazed from the battle, charged at T'ruck. It was a simple thing to knock away the man's sword with his shield, and then T'ruck skewered him, staring down into his uncomprehending eyes as the light left them. He would happily cut down every man in the Five Kingdoms for what they'd done to his family, and he would dance in their blood and drink from their skulls. But there was no time for revelling in the deaths today; they had to run away from the bastards.

"Finish them off and get us moving," T'ruck roared as loudly as he could.

"Captain!" The scream came from above, and it was raw, a guttural sound full of terror.

North Gale shifted. The world shifted. One moment T'ruck was on his feet and the next he was in the air, arse over head and falling, then rolling across the sloping deck of his ship.

T'ruck shook his head, attempting to still the world and figure out what had happened. Screams were drowned out by the sound of wood crunching and cracking, and T'ruck realised *North Gale* was splitting in half down its midsection, a rent opening up and travelling down the planks of wood as they bent and snapped. There, towering above his ship, blocking out the light and bringing with it the death of his crew, was the monstruous Five Kingdoms vessel, its ram splitting T'ruck's ship in half.

Dazed and too confused to be angry, T'ruck let go of both his shield and sword and pushed to his feet. He started straight into a run, charging up the sloping, snapping deck of his ship, towards the Five Kingdoms behemoth. He passed enemy soldiers and friendly pirates alike as they all struggled to understand what was happening.

The Five Kingdoms ship was crushing its way through his ship, and the beast wasn't stopping. T'ruck leapt for the monster even as he heard the mast of *North Gale* give way and snap. It was a terrible sound, the death of his ship, and it lent extra power and fury to T'ruck as he used all his strength to pull his way up the ram of the enemy ship. Hand by bloody hand he climbed, ignoring the screams of his crew dying below.

T'ruck couldn't tell if it took an hour or only a moment, but he reached the top of the ram and pulled himself up onto the railing of the Five Kingdoms ship before jumping down onto the fore deck and roaring his defiance at conquering this new monster.

Steel was drawn from scabbards, and T'ruck heard the tightening of bowstrings even over the sounds of his ship and crew dying. He looked up to see just how meaningless his struggle had been. The decks of this new ship seemed to stretch on forever, and they were crowded with hundreds of soldiers, more than he could count, and machines of war.

Soldiers rushed forwards to restrain T'ruck, and he let them, the need to fight squashed by the realisation of how futile it would be. A heavy kick forced him onto his knees, and he felt his arms pulled behind his back and ropes tied around his wrists.

An older man, impeccably dressed, with dark mahogany hair and an air of command, appeared from the press of soldiers. "Captain T'ruck Khan?" His voice was as cold as the northlands where T'ruck had been born.

T'ruck nodded, defeated and mourning the loss of his ship and his crew.

"Do you know who I am?"

T'ruck glared at the man and nodded again.

"Good," Captain Peter Verit said. "T'ruck Khan, you are under arrest for countless acts of kidnapping, murder, theft, and piracy. You and any surviving members of your crew will be transported back to Land's End and hanged for your crimes. Do you have anything to say?"

T'ruck grinned up at the man despite the pain from his wounds and the wave of despair that was threatening to choke him. "I like your ship."

The Phoenix

Keelin barked orders to his crew. A course change and a threat that, if the sails weren't properly secured, he'd use the unfortunate pirate's intestines to fasten new ropes. It was a hollow threat, they all knew it, but he felt the need to vent his rage.

They'd done it. Despite Elaina's betrayal, Keelin and Drake had convinced Tanner to join their cause and to follow Drake's lead. To accept the charismatic captain as king of the isles and their people, and to help fight the enemies at their door. They'd also paid a heavy price for their victory. *Mary's Virtue* and Poole were lost.

Under Drake's orders they left Captain Poole to his fate, turned their ships, and ran. Keelin watched the battle from afar and witnessed how Poole managed to turn his ship at the last moment, tying up two of the Five Kingdoms pursuers which, in turn, deterred the other three ships from chasing down a superior force.

Keelin had also watched *Mary's Virtue* go down.

The Five Kingdoms navy scuttled the pirate ship instead of capturing it, and they used black powder to do it, blowing a sizeable hole in the side of the ship. Keelin was starting to both respect and fear the destructive power of the powder like he never had before.

"Captain?" Aimi's voice soothed Keelin even in the face of his loss.

"Don't reckon I'll be good company right now, Aimi," Keelin said without turning to look at her. He knew that in his maudlin mood he should retreat to his cabin instead of haunting his ship like a spectre of doom, but he wanted to feel the wind and smell the sea.

"That's alright," Aimi said. "I'm excellent company and can easily take up your share of the conversation as well.

"I ran into Lumpy earlier. The mangy little beast looked at me with big eyes and meowed, so I knelt down to stroke her and she attacked me. I have claw marks and everything."

"She doesn't like being touched," Keelin said absently.

"Excellent advice, if only you'd been around two hours ago.

Anyway, it got me thinking. I reckon we need a new ship's boy. With Feather graduating to real duties... Did you know he's a weird? And me, well I just don't think it's right, me taking on the duties of *boy*, considering my obvious differences to your gender.

"I mean, I know I'm the newest member of the crew. Not the youngest though, but at least I take on real sailor duties as well. What about Kebble? He does nothing but sit up there in the nest all day, watching everything and everyone. Why can't he scrub the sides of the ship and chase down Lumpy's kills? Can you imagine giving that order? And even if he did agree, he'd probably be better at hunting down the rats than Lumpy. Perhaps you could get rid of the cat and give her job to Kebble."

Keelin had no idea what to say in the face of Aimi's torrent of chatter. He turned to stare at her and found her smiling at him.

"I just lost a friend," Keelin said, his voice sad even to his ears. "And not the first. Likely not the last." Keelin stopped there lest he find himself saying more. There was something that was eating away at him even more. He now knew he couldn't trust Elaina, and that was a friendship he'd never thought he'd truly lose.

Aimi nodded. She lowered her voice so none of the nearby crew members would hear. "Do you want to talk about it?" She nodded towards Keelin's cabin.

Keelin drew in a breath and sighed it out, turning back towards the sea and leaning on the railing. "I think I just want to be alone."

"Oh. Well, my shift just finished so I think I'll join you. We can be alone together." She leaned on the railing next to Keelin and stared out across the ocean.

Keelin smiled. Despite his gloomy attitude, Aimi had succeeded in cheering him up, if only a little. He looked away from the little woman and his spirits sank again. There, sailing along next to his ship, was *The Black Death*, and even in the dwindling light Keelin could see Tanner staring back at him.

Fortune

Drake sat in the mess of his ship, gnawing on a stale biscuit. He'd known from the very beginning that his plan, his rise, wouldn't come without sacrifice. Not even Hironous had been able to tell him what those sacrifices might be. They'd plotted and schemed for years. Hironous might have the sight, but Drake had something just as useful. He understood people. He could see how folk worked, and he knew how to manipulate them.

The first sacrifice had been Black Sands, and Drake had known it would happen. He'd planned it. He'd given its location to the Five Kingdoms. Black Sands was to be the catalyst to bring all the other pirates together under his rule. Sev'relain hadn't been part of the plan. Drake didn't know whether Hironous had seen Sev'relain's downfall, and that was part of the problem.

Lillingburn had fallen soon after. Then Drake had lost his fortune. Then Fair View had burned; and none of those losses had been part of the plan either. They'd all helped to bring the pirates together, but each sacrifice was a heavy burden for Drake to bear. Now he'd lost Poole, one of the very first captains to follow him, and he wondered if Hironous had seen that too.

For years Drake had lived with the certain knowledge of immortality. His brother had seen his death, and it wouldn't be for many, many years. And when it did happen, he'd be a king. Drake had been living his life accordingly, taking risks and knowing they wouldn't lead to his death. Now he wasn't so sure. Tanner had had Drake at his mercy. And for a while Drake had known fear again.

From the moment Tanner had taken hold of Drake's tongue and threatened to cut it out, he'd had been scared, and now he found he couldn't turn it off. What if Hironous was wrong? What if his death could happen at any moment? Had he been surviving on luck alone for all this time? It wouldn't be the first time his brother had failed to predict a death.

Drake wiped cold sweat from his forehead and tried to direct his thoughts elsewhere. He failed. He couldn't get rid of the image of Tanner standing there, holding Drake's life in his hands.

Rag uncoiled from a shadowed corner of the mess and began weaving its way across the deck towards Drake. The creature was near two feet long now, and Drake could already see it would be more than capable of killing a man. It was dangerous, and for the first time he found himself scared of the monster. He wished he'd relented and let Princess find a cat to hunt the ship's rats.

Rag reached Drake's foot and slowly began climbing up his leg, winding its way around and around, and Drake forced himself to sit still. He might be terrified, and he was certain the beast could sense that, but he'd be damned before he let anyone else see his fear. The giant centipede reached his waist and curled around it like a belt, and Drake let out a ragged sigh.

Silently he cursed his own weakness. He was Drake Morrass. He'd faced down dragons and demons. He'd made a pact with a goddess and escaped the Drurr slave pits. He sat at the table with some of the most powerful folk in the known world, and they considered him a peer. He fucked empresses, murdered kings, and drank toasts with death himself. He'd set plans in motion that changed the course of history. Ambition had always ruled his actions, not fear.

"Cap'n," said one of his crew as he sat down in the mess with a mug of rum.

Drake swept his gaze over the man, barely acknowledging him, and prayed to Rin that the pirate wouldn't notice how unmanned Drake felt. He needed to do something. Sitting still was serving no purpose but worsening his mood. He needed action and he needed to be in control, of himself and of others. Drake stood and tapped Rag on the head, hoping the beasty would respond as it always did and not simply attack. "Down. Go hunt," he said, and the centipede uncoiled itself, latched onto the bench, and scuttled away. With a shudder, Drake smoothed down his royal blue jacket and left the mess with a purposeful stride.

Drake hadn't known where he was going until he got there but, standing outside Beck's cabin, he knew why he was there. He wanted to fuck. He wanted to prove to himself he was still a man, and he wanted to do to Beck exactly what he'd wanted to do since the moment they'd met. Drake reached into a pocket and pulled out a set of keys. He had his own key to every lock on the ship, barring the crew's own chests. He paused. For a moment he wasn't sure if it was fear or common sense that stopped him from unlocking the door. In the end he decided he didn't care. He put the key back in his pocket and knocked. And waited.

Drake waited so long he almost thought Beck was elsewhere, or that perhaps she hadn't heard. Eventually he heard the key in the lock, and a moment later the door opened. Beck stood on the other side, her blue eyes cold and hard and her golden hair loose around her shoulders.

"What do you want, Drake?" she said, then looked up into his eyes. "Oh. I see."

Drake wasn't sure which of them made the first move. One moment they were standing either side of the doorway, and the next he was inside, lifting Beck up and pushing her against the wall as she grabbed hold of his hair and pulled his mouth down onto hers.

Beck tore open Drake's shirt while he fumbled at the leather jerkin that held her brace of pistols. The damned thing wouldn't budge, it was laced so tight. He pulled away from Beck, turned her around, and pushed her down face first onto the table.

"Hurry up," she hissed, grinding her arse against his groin. It did nothing to improve his concentration, and he fumbled at the laces.

"Fuck it," Drake growled as he pulled the knife from his boot and slit the laces, pulling Beck upright so her jerkin simply fell away. He spun her around and ripped open her shirt, sending buttons flying. She was staring at him with a feral hunger. Then she was pressed up against him, and Drake picked the Arbiter up and dumped her on the cot, sparing only a moment to whip his belt away.

Beck pulled off her own belt and dropped her britches, climbing onto her hands and knees. Drake took the hint and climbed onto the cot behind her. They made a night of it and no mistake, and Drake was as sore as all the Hells time they'd finished with each other. It turned out the Arbiter wasn't exactly the type to cuddle afterwards, and no sooner had they finished than she threw his clothes at him and locked the door behind him. Drake didn't care; he'd got what he'd come for. After months of watching and waiting, he finally knew how Beck felt and how she tasted, and it was just as good as he'd imagined.

Drake pulled on his trousers and buttoned them up, but his shirt was torn so he left it open. Climbing onto the deck of the *Fortune*, he welcomed the cool breeze on his skin and felt his spirits starting to lift again. He was Drake Morrass, and his accolades spoke for themselves. Now he could add seducing an Arbiter to the list.

He'd survived Tanner Black and even turned the old bastard to his side. He'd escaped Ash and the trap the Five Kingdoms had set, and with only one ship lost. It was no small loss, he knew that, but it could have been much worse. Still, someone had told the Five Kingdoms where and when Drake and Tanner were to meet, and that meant they had a traitor in their ranks.

Drake paced the deck of his ship and looked out at the lights floating nearby. *The Phoenix*, *Hearth Fire*, *Ocean Deep*, and *The Black Death*. Aboard one of those ships was a turncoat working against him and the isles, and he would need to find them sooner rather than later.

"Cap'n," Princess said, and Drake realised his first mate had dragged a stool onto the deck and was busy whittling away at a block of wood.

"What are you carving, Princess?"

"Not a clue," Princess said with a smile. "Just sort of work at it and see what comes out. Usually just tends to look like driftwood, but it calms me all the same. Were you worried, Cap'n? When Tanner had you. Couldn't see it all, but it looked a bit rough for a moment there."

Drake forced out a laugh. "Not at all, Princess," he said, the lie coming more easily. "Oracle told me when I'd die, and it's a fair way off yet. It was all part of the plan."

"Figured as much," Princess said happily, and went back to his whittling.

Drake had been helpless on Ash, completely at the mercy of Tanner, and so, even as he'd convinced the bastard to follow him, he'd had to concede to his demands. Drake spat over the side of his ship.

In order to keep Tanner's support, as soon as Drake crowned himself king he would marry Elaina Black.

Epilogue

The crew weren't happy, but then they didn't need to be. On board *Starry Dawn* Elaina's orders were law, and she'd ordered them here and she'd ordered them to leave every prize they spotted. The crew didn't need to know they were actually her father's orders. She still seethed at being sent away.

Elaina knew she should hate her father, that she had every reason to, but she didn't. Couldn't. He was her father, and she loved him fiercely no matter what atrocities he committed. Blu she could hate, and did so without remorse. Her brother was a devious, boot-licking coward of a bully, and it only made her hate him more that their father had chosen to take him along to Ash and leave Elaina behind. Not just leave her behind, but send her away.

A hundred other ships floated in the crystal blue waters of Rainbow Bay, their masts making the place look cluttered, like a watery pit full of wooden spikes. Elaina spotted merchant ships, fishing vessels, navy boats, and even the odd pirate ship, but there were more slavers than any of those.

Slavers were filthy vessels, with crews as filthy as the cargo and the conditions aboard. They were slow, ugly, disease-ridden, and completely unprofitable for piracy. Elaina hated them.

The city might boast a thousand different pleasures, and at least twice that many distractions, but Elaina wanted none of them. Chade was too clean these days. It had been more enticing back when it was a mess governed by criminals.

Today she was entertaining herself by running along the railings of the ship, keeping balance with feline grace and agility. Occasionally she would stop, leap up into the rigging, and scramble to the top before descending with reckless speed. She longed to go for a swim, but Rainbow Bay was renowned for its shark population, and though it wouldn't be the first time Elaina had battled a shark, it was not an experience worth reliving.

A vessel was approaching, a small rowboat moving lethargically through the water with the laboured actions of its two rowers, neither of whom looked happy about being out in the midday sun. Sitting in the front of the little boat was a single figure, a woman with shoulder-length, shit-coloured hair underneath a large blue cavalier hat.

Elaina watched the boat approach from her position in the rigging, hanging upside down by her legs. When it bumped against *Starry Dawn*'s hull, Elaina released her hold on the ropes, somersaulting in mid-air and landing easily on her feet. She strode over to the railing and stared down upon her visitors.

The woman was standing up in the boat and looking none too stable; it was obvious she didn't have any sort of sea legs. Elaina pitied those cursed to remain on the land. As the woman looked up, Elaina could see a criss-cross of scars on her face, and she was missing an ear. She sneered up at Elaina, who instinctively took a liking to her.

"Hello there, and welcome to my little kingdom," Elaina said with a grin, patting the railing of her ship.

"You Captain Black?" the woman shouted.

"Aye. How can I help you?"

The stranger sniffed loudly and spat into the water, an act which unbalanced her and almost sent her careening into the bay. Elaina struggled not to laugh.

"You can get down off that fuckin' boat an' come ashore," the woman said after righting herself. "Ya wanted an audience. Well, the Lord and Lady of Chade are jus' about ready ta grant one."

Books by Rob J. Hayes

<u>The Ties that Bind</u>
The Heresy Within
The Colour of Vengeance
The Price of Faith

<u>Best Laid Plans</u>
Where Loyalties Lie
The Fifth Empire of Man

<u>It Takes a Thief...</u>
It Takes a Thief to Catch a Sunrise
It Takes a Thief to Start a Fire

Printed in Great Britain
by Amazon